Praise for Nisi S____

Fi.. ...ouse

"This exquisitely rendered debut collection of 11 reprints and three originals ranges into the past and future to explore identity and belief in a dazzling variety of settings. [...] The threads of folklore, religious magic, family and the search for a cohesive self are woven with power and lucidity throughout this panorama of race, magic and the body."
— Starred Review, *Publishers Weekly*

"Sometimes enigmatic, often surprising, always marvelous. This lovely collection will take you, like a magic carpet, to some strange and wonderful places."
— Karen Joy Fowler

"From the exotic, baroque complexities of 'At the Huts of Ajala' to the stark, folktale purity of 'The Beads of Ku,' these fourteen superbly written stories will weave around you a ring of dark, dark magic."
— Ursula K. Le Guin

"Nisi Shawl uses the tools of future and fable, usually used to explore the other, the future, and the mysterious, to magically reveal what and who we all are here and today."
— Tobias Buckell

Our Fruiting Bodies

Our Fruiting Bodies

short fiction by

Nisi Shawl

Aqueduct Press
PO Box 95787
Seattle, Washington 98145-2787
www.aqueductpress.com

Copyright © 2022 Nisi Shawl
Library of Congress Control Number: 2022942135

ISBN: 978-1-61976-224-4
First Edition, First Printing, November 2022

Cover Illustration Cribraria sp. blue:
copyright © Barry Webb

Book design by Kathryn Wilham
Printed in the USA by McNaughton & Gunn

Prior Publication History

An Awfully Big Adventure, *An Alphabet of Embers*, July 2016; reprinted in *Talk Like a Man*

Women of the Doll, *GUD Magazine*, Fall 2007

The Tawny Bitch, *Mojo: Conjure Stories*, April 2003; reprinted in *The Mammoth Book of Gaslit Romance*

Luisah's Church, *Dark Discoveries Magazine*, Fall 2016

Cruel Sistah, *Asimov's SF Magazine*, October/November 2005

Big Mama Yaga's, *XPrize Future of Housing* as audio only, August 2017; first printed in *Antenna Works*, May 2020

Street Worm (first Brit Williams story), *Streets of Shadows*, September 2014; reprinted in *Street Magicks* and *Exploring Dark Short Fiction 3: A Primer to Nisi Shawl*

Queen of Dirt (second Brit Williams story), *Apex Magazine*, February 2017

Conversion Therapy (third Brit Williams story), *Exploring Dark Short Fiction 3: A Primer to Nisi Shawl*, December 2018

A Beautiful Stream, *Cranky Ladies of History*, March 2015

I Being Young and Foolish, *Sword Stone Table*, July 2021

Looking for Lilith, *Lenox Avenue Magazine*, July 2004

Vulcanization, *Nightmare Magazine*, January 2016

She Tore, *Hath No Fury*, August 2018

Salt on the Dance Floor, *Beasts Within 3: Oceans Unleashed*, December 2012; reprinted in *Not Your Average Monster*, February 2016

Beyond the Lighthouse, *River*, November 2011

To the Moment, *Reflection's Edge Magazine*, November 2007

Just Between Us, *Phantom Drift: A Journal of New Fabulism*, Fall 2011

Dedicated to the new ones.

Contents

Introduction
What Soft Power Creates/Destroys
by Linda D. Addison

I fell in love with Shawl's writing before meeting them in person. When I write fiction, I keep their work nearby for examples of characters that instantly connect and high energy stories that hold the reader's interest. When I had the honor of sharing a room with them at a conference, I was dazzled by their humor, compassion, and focus. I value the friendship that came out of the time we spent together. Getting to read this collection before anyone else is like winning an award I didn't know existed.

I like short stories in general, because they allow me to experience the beginning, middle, and end of a story in one sitting. I love Nisi Shawl's short stories in particular because they totally transport me to wherever they choose to take me and enjoy (or rightfully ache) every step of the journey.

As I expected, there was no reading just one story in a sitting. I was completely drawn into each one from the first line to the end and then carried through to the next story. Each opening took me into the soul of the characters and the intriguing stories by way of the powerful music of Shawl's language!

The opening story has a whimsical title, "An Awfully Big Adventure," but I quickly found that the adventure is not as playful as the title suggests. This is Shawl doing their masterful thing, carrying me through a story that is sad but so beautiful and chilling in the way they tell it that I simply went up and down with the character. At the end of the story, the poet in me took a moment to sit and marvel at the poetic prose.

The second story, "Women of the Doll," begins with a poetically beautiful opening to the sensuous magical journey of Josette, who is never alone and is now protected from a past that could have shattered her soul.

The rest of the stories continue to mesmerize, giving us realized and unrealized sorceresses discovering the power to protect their own and others or to avenge violence done in the name of greed, racism, or religious discrimination.

Some of the stories are written in different formats, or using familiar characters, but told from new, striking points of view. For example, "The Tawny Bitch," is a riveting tale told in the form of letters discovered in an old house, written by a young woman kidnapped from a comfortable academy and held captive in a sparse room for reasons involving greed and her being one quarter Black.

There are two pieces inspired by biblical references. "Cruel Sistah" tells of two Black sisters, Dory and Calliope, and how one sibling's jealousy (in the way of Cain and Abel) was more than cruel and made my heart fracture a little from the first line to the end. The meaning of the one sister's name, Calliope, as beautiful voice/instrument, became a haunting part of the story.

The second tale, "Looking for Lilith," is the quest of "a light-skinned girl," whose name isn't revealed and doesn't matter in this dangerous, magical expedition to find Lilith because in Shawl's powerful imagination we learn that the answer to a question isn't the final goal.

Merlin, a magician, and a king are in the story "I Being Young and Foolish," but more importantly, Nia, a remarkable sorceress arrives from another land to learn from Merlin. I fell in love with her as she ate some of the fungal lace in the woods to link into the flora's web. The magic and nature-filled rituals of Merlin and Nia filled me with joy.

"She Tore" puts us in the middle of an adventure with a machine-gun-carrying grown Wendy and a drowsy Tink on a rescue mission without Peter Pan. This exciting venture is not for children, but just as much fun for this adult, with life lessons to match.

Three stories, "Street Worm," "Queen of Dirt," and "Conversion Therapy," follow the evolution of a character, Brit, a teenager who uses Ebonics to piss off her professional-class parents and discovers she has a power that allows her to see things that no one else can, dangerous non-physical entities. When Brit uses her power to make the vicious invisible entities visible to others, Shawl expertly builds on the scientific definition of real worms, bees, carpenter ants, and Zombie Fungus to create the menacing organisms in these stories. It was thrilling to spend time with Brit as she acquires a mentor and learns how to use her power to save others as well as to teach talented kids. I could read more about this world and Brit. (Just saying.)

Shawl's characters struggle to embrace their strength and power, both soft and hard, to define a place in their world by destroying (and sometimes creating) barriers. Some tales take us back in time to the harsh days of slavery and some forward into strange, surrealistic futures. The nerd in me was completely psyched by science references to real life forms.

The stories that refer to known deities reminded me of how fascinated I am by the various ways cultures from around the world interpret feminine energy through different goddesses, as well as gods that embrace masculine and feminine identities. Each culture provides fables that represent these deities as both death and creation, and as being both protective and dangerous. It's an interesting counterpoint to the fact that women on this planet still struggle to be treated equally, to have their intelligence, strength, and power acknowledged.

Shawl's writing is mindful; every word has a purpose. So, after reading the collection, I Googled *fruiting bodies*. Reading about the fruiting bodies of fungi, I discovered that they are plant organs (aka mushrooms) created specifically for reproduction. Mushrooms are created from tiny threads that make up most of the fungi. A network of these threads, known as a mycelium, extends in all directions through the soil.

This fantastic collection unveils fruiting bodies and a network of feelings and images extending through the characters and stories. It will join Shawl's other books that I keep near me as lessons for my ongoing evolution as a writer.

My fruiting body, perfect and imperfect, no longer can reproduce, but I feel the connection to earth and living beings through the network of my life force. I was lifted and expanded by the poignant journey Shawl's stories took me on. What a gloriously big adventure!

An Awfully Big Adventure

I'm going first. I'm the last girl to be born, and what's left to pick by then? My oldest sister already gets to be the smart one, and the middle girl, everybody decides, must be the most imaginative. So I'm the brave one. Usually—except for being born—that means that I go first.

And this is why, if there has to be a reason. I go first. I don't have to know what I'm doing. Don't have to know how, why, where. I'm the first. I'm the brave one. This is an adventure. Like life. I'm going.

It all begins with a short stay in the hospital, barely overnight. Stress test in the morning, but all I can think about during that is where's my gold tennis charm necklace. My mom and my sister look everywhere, but it probably got stolen.

My tests don't prove nothin. The health care providers decide I've been experiencing anxiety attacks. Counseling is prescribed.

Couple years pass by. Turns out there's a growth on my left adrenal gland. The doctors plan on taking it out. My oldest sister talks about the friends she'll stay with in the town where they say they'll do the operation. Then something more urgent comes up: breast cancer.

It's early. Stage 0. Still, the providers decide they have to deal with that before anything else. They schedule my mastectomy.

Anesthesia. I tip into the dark. Like falling out of a canoe. The me I'm used to has been dry, always, crackers or toast; now everything I am is soaking wet. To the core. Melting apart.

I bob to the surface of the darkness. There's my sister. Nearby a woman sobs and cries about how she can't breathe. For an hour.

Finally I'm wheeled back to my room. There's dirt in the corners.

Blood keeps draining from my incision, fast and steady. We have to empty the plastic bag where it gathers every twenty minutes. The nurse lies to me and says my surgeon's not around. I get up to pee and drop through the surface again. Down under the light and air and feeling. Down. Then back up again to my mother, and back down, put there on purpose this time, to sew up the uncauterized capillary that has been pouring out blood to soak me and sink me.

Up. Light. Food. I'm home in time for Thanksgiving. I will even eat lima beans. Even beets. Coconut. Anything. Never going to turn away any blessings I'm given ever, ever again.

But I no longer trust the light the air the feeling. They went away before; I got no reason now to believe they're here to stay.

Another year passes. Time's trying to lull me. It does. I wear halter tops, tell lopsided jokes. But one day playing on the courts with my son I pull a muscle, I think. I lie down on the living room couch. Low to the water. Ripples of pain spread out from my back, lapping up against me. One hand hangs over the boat's side, trailing through the darkness, dipping in. I could sleep so long. I could sleep for always and still feel this tired.

I fight my way back to dry land. I go to the store. I talk on the phone with my oldest sister far away, ask her what remedy to take. Confess I'm out of strength. For the first time in my life. For the last.

Tell her I love her.

Don't wanna be in the hospital again, but my mother takes me anyways. The dirt in the corners is piling higher, thicker, crowding out the light. They send me home from the emergency room; they say there's nothing wrong. But there is.

A few hours later I return and the new shift realizes I have several different kinds of cancer now. One extremely rare. No good chance of a cure. They explain that, and then they carefully lay me out on the operating table, gently lowering me down.

Down. My heart has hardly been beating for weeks, they say. They want to make it beat even slower so they can work their way inside to fix things.

They can only fix them for a while. They're honest about that.

They put the sensing ends of machines on me to watch while I think. They put in drugs.

The water surges up to carry me away. To hold me under. Hold me tight. Hold me.

I'm usually the first among us three girls. Us sisters. I understand I'm the one going on ahead this time, too. Into what? Into what we don't know.

Slowly I sink down. Like before, it's way too cold. Numbing me. I don't feel. No longer. No light. Don't see. No direction. No up no down no in out forward back nothing but nothing but nothing. But.

But I remember being small and closing shut my eyes and shutting them so tight, squeezing them so hard, to make the colors come and here they are and are they real and is this real is anything and am I real and am I real—

And yes.

And yes. I am. And I am going.

Under. Down. Deep.

Going.

Gone.

Women of the Doll

The countertop was black marble, veined with green. Josette admired its sheen while she waited for the clerk. Like endless Niles etching dark and fertile deltas, she said silently to the stone. Like malachite feathers resting on a field of night. The reflection and the surface were interrupted by a white rectangle sliding toward her: the charge slip for her room. She signed dutifully. It would get paid; it always did.

The clerk had hair like black rayon. Her smooth, brown face was meticulously made up, copied exactly from some magazine. "1213," she said. "Elevators are across the lobby, to the left." Then she noticed. "Oooh, how cute! Does she have a name?"

Automatically, Josette tried to tuck her doll down further into her handbag. She wouldn't go.

"Viola," Josette told the clerk. She settled for pulling the bright blue scarf over Viola's long, woolen braids. The painted eyes stared enigmatically from a cloth face caught midway between sorrow and content. "I love her very much."

"I'll just bet you do. Can I hold her?"

Josette didn't want to be rude. She ignored the question. "What time does the gift shop close?"

"6 p.m."

Plenty of time to get rid of her luggage first. She wheeled it around and started toward the elevators, crossing alternating strips of that same wonderful marble and a whispery, willow-colored carpet. "Enjoy your stay," chirped the clerk.

Mirrors lined the walls of the elevator. Once that would have been a problem, but Josette had reached the point where she could make an effort and see what pretty much anyone would have seen: a woman with a soft, round, face; short, coiling hair; a slim, graceful neck. Breasts rather large; hips, waist, and legs like a long walk through the dunes. Blue cotton separates under a dove-grey woolen coat; knits, so they wouldn't wrinkle. Golden skin, like a lamp-lit window on a foggy autumn evening.

There was nothing wrong with how she looked.

Room 1213 faced east. Josette opened the drapes and gazed out over parking lots and shopping malls. Off in the distance, to her left, she saw a large unplowed area. A golf-course? A cemetery? The snow took on a bluish tinge as she watched. Dusk fell early here. Winter in Detroit.

There was a lamp on the table beside her. She pressed down the button on its base, and fluorescence flickered, then filled the room. A bed, with no way to get under it; less work for the maids, she supposed. An armchair, a desk, a dresser, a wardrobe, a TV, and a night stand. Nothing special, nothing she hadn't seen a thousand times before.

She sat on the bed and felt it give under her, a little more easily than she liked. Her large handbag, which doubled as a carry-on, held a few things she could unpack: a diary, a jewel case, handmade toiletries. Bunny was scrunched up at the bottom. She pulled him out and sat him next to Viola on the pillow. He toppled over and fell so his head was hidden by her doll's wide skirts.

"Feeling shy, Mr. Bun?" she asked, reaching to prop him up again. She knew better than to expect an answer, with or without the proper preparations. Bunny was a rabbit. Rabbits can't talk. Anyway, he wasn't really hers; he belonged to Viola.

The clock radio caught her eye. Three red fives glowed on the display. Oh no, she thought, and rushed out, leaving her doll behind. Probably Viola wouldn't care. She might not even notice. Certainly she'd be safe alone for just a short time.

Josette made it to the gift shop with a minute to spare, but it was already closed. Frustrated, she stamped her foot, and was rewarded with a stinging pain in her ankle and a lingering look of amusement from a passing white man. She ignored both and quick-stepped back to the elevators.

There was a wait. The lobby was suddenly filled with people, mostly men, mostly white, mostly wearing name tags. A convention of some sort. She let a couple of cars go up without her, but when the crowd showed no signs of thinning, Josette resigned herself to riding up in their company. The amused passerby joined her load just as the door began to close.

The elevator stopped at nearly every floor. The men all stared at her, surreptitiously, except for the latecomer, who smiled and was quite open about it.

There was nothing wrong with how she looked. She stared right back.

He was tall. And thin, not all slabby like over-bred beef. A runner's body, nervous and sensitive. He wore black sweats, actually sweaty sweats, she noticed. His unusually long brown hair hung in curls over one shoulder, held loosely in place by a rubber band.

His smile broadened. He thought he was getting somewhere. They were on the tenth floor. All the other passengers were getting out. "Join me for supper?" he asked.

"I'm sorry, I have so much work," she murmured politely as she edged through the closing doors. She located the stairwell and walked up two flights to her floor. He was attractive, though.

Everything was just the way she'd left it.

She opened up her tool-kit on the bed and added recently scavenged supplies: rum from the airplane, salt packets from various restaurants. From her handbag she took the small jar of urine she had collected that morning. She was ready.

Salt first. Between the bathroom and the bedroom, there were surprisingly many corners. Josette put a square of toilet paper in every one, and dumped a packet of salt into the center of each square.

Next, she swept down the walls above the squares with her rum-sprinkled whisk-broom. Little bits of dirt and straw and flakes of dislodged wallpaper fell into the salt. She picked up all the debris and flushed it down the toilet.

She turned on the tap at the washbasin, splashing her fingers through the water till it ran as hot as it was going to get. Which wasn't very. But she was used to that. She let the sink fill while she added her other ingredients: brown sugar, melting in the warm water like sand into glass, golden piss, and a swirling white cloud of perfume.

She soaked a hand-towel in the mixture, wrung it out to dampness.

"Oh, my young man, oh, he is so fine,
Sweet Rosemary did say"

Her voice was high and clear, and sweet as the scent of her wash-water. Getting down on her hands and knees, she began to sponge the room's royal blue carpet, continuing:

"She gathered flowers and she sang,
All about her wedding day..."

✳

She built her altar in the center of the room. It didn't take long. She used a round table from in front of the window, covering it with her shawl. Between the printed wreaths of lilies, roses, and forget-me-nots, she laid out the stones: a moss agate from Mexico; a white egg-shape covered with barnacles, from Whidbey Island. Polished, flat, black, red, rough, round, brown, the stones and their stories circled the cushion where

12

Viola sat, a new white votive candle at her feet. A bowl of water before it trembled with light as Josette struck a match. The candle spat and crackled, flaring up, dying down, then steadying as the wick pulled up the melting wax.

"Is it safe?" Viola's voice was dry and whispery, cloth rubbing against cloth.

"Yes, honey, I promise. It's as safe as I can make it," Josette answered her.

Viola had no neck, and her stitches were tight, but she managed to turn her head enough to survey most of the room. "Hi, Bunny." She waved to her toy where he waited on the bed.

The pearls dangling on the doll's flat chest gleamed as she twisted her stocking-stuffed body, still looking for something that wasn't there. "What about the flowers?

"I, uhh, I couldn't get any yet, Viola, honey. I'm sorry..."

"But you said we were gonna have flowers this time." The painted face showed bewilderment and betrayal. "Can't you just go out and pick some?"

Josette sighed. "No, darling. See, it's winter, and we're way up North, and—" She broke off. It was so hard, Viola was so *little*... If she'd gone to the gift shop first instead of dawdling in her room, she wouldn't have had to try and explain all this.

She checked the clock radio. It was 8:30, not terribly late. "You wait here, honey, and I'll go get some flowers for us." Somewhere. Somehow.

✳

Josette tried the bar first. From the moment she walked in, though, she knew it was not that kind of place. Grey plastic upholstery, murky purple neon. Artificial twilight trying to pass for atmosphere.

She glanced around at the tabletops. They were decorated with some sort of oversized Crazy Straws or something. No flowers.

She turned to leave. Someone was blocking her way. The man from the gift shop, from the elevator. He was smiling again. "Join me now?" he asked.

"I was just leaving." She stepped around him and out into the hall.

"Right. Me, too. Check out the restaurant together?"

She surrendered. "Sure." It was probably about time for another client, anyway, and he looked likely to come up with a valuable offering.

"I think it's quickest if we take the escalator," he said. "My name's Danny Woods, by the way."

"Josette," she told him, without waiting to be asked. She made sure he stood above her on the escalator and kept a couple of steps between them. Standard operating procedure. He was wearing black, again, slacks, with a dark, piney-looking green plaid shirt. As he turned to smile down from the top, she noticed with surprise how broad his shoulders were.

The restaurant's entrance, swathed in pink-and-gold lace, looked promising. But when the hostess had conducted them to their table, Josette saw that the flowers were false. Scrap silk and wire, sewn with sequins. She made a show of examining the menu. Dramatically swooping script filled the pink cardboard pages.

Her eyes met Danny Woods'. "See anything interesting?" he asked her.

"Yes," she admitted. "But nothing that I really want."

He grimaced, but his gaze stayed steady. He folded up the menu and laid it on the table. "You know, this—" he tapped the pink cardboard "is just a list of suggestions. You're not bound by it, not by any means. If you know what you want, you should just say—"

A young woman in a pink uniform and shimmery gold stockings came up. "Good evening, and welcome to Chez Chatte." Her voice squeaked and see-sawed, like a five-year-old in high-heels. "I'm Dee-Dee, and I'll be your server this evening. Have you made your selections?"

"I'll have your Caesar Salad and a bowl of the minestrone soup," said Danny Woods.

"And for the lady?"

"Flowers," said Josette calmly.

"Flowers?" repeated Dee-Dee. "To eat? I'm not sure I— Where do you see that on the menu?"

"I don't," said Josette. "But I would very much appreciate it if you could bring me some."

Dee-Dee backed away from the table. "I'll have to ask," she explained apologetically, then fled to the kitchen.

Danny Woods smiled a quick smile. "What's that make you, a floratarian?"

"No. I'm just not hungry is all. Jet-lag. I'll order out later."

"Where you from?"

"All over. And you?" she added quickly. It was a little harder than usual, but she managed to get the client talking about himself, his aims, pursuits, goals, methods of achieving them. Danny Woods was a building design engineer, which as far as she could tell was an architect, except that architects were to be despised. He was here for the conference on appropriate technology. He had a presentation to make, a red Camaro, at least three credit cards, and a secure position with a Boulder-based consulting firm.

He seemed genuinely interested in finding out what she did for a living. She told him fund-raising. Freelance.

His soup came. He ate it quietly, and she slowed the pace of her questions to let him. He offered her bread, buttered it for her, touched the inside of her wrist somehow as he handed it over. Warmly, deliberately. He wanted her.

She decided he would do.

Dee-Dee brought her flowers with his salad: three red roses in a crystal bud vase, placed with professional aplomb

15

upon a white dinner plate. Viola liked lilies better, but these would certainly serve to fulfill Josette's promise. "Thank-you," she said. "They're lovely."

Dee-Dee beamed. "From the breakfast trays for tomorrow," she explained. "Are you sure there's nothing else I can get you?"

Josette shook her head, but Danny Woods was nodding yes. "Actually," he said, "I think you ought to just wrap this salad up to go and bring me the check." He turned to Josette. "That all right?"

"If you pay for it? Sure, thanks."

The rest of the second floor was deserted. As they passed the empty function rooms Josette caught glimpses of the shallow arcs of gleaming chairbacks, scalloping the darkness, of ghostly white tablecloths beneath hollow urns.

He pressed the up button, and they waited silently. He touched her wrist again just as the elevator chimed.

Inside, there was no one, except for their reflections. She didn't look.

He was reaching for the controls. Josette put her hand over his, pulled it away from "10" and made it push "12" instead. "You can see me to my door," she told him. Probably that would be all right. But Viola wouldn't want him to come in.

"Yes," he said. He raised her hand to his mouth and lightly grazed her fingertips with the edges of his teeth. Then he continued down the side of her index, gently scraping against her skin, his warm breath a whispering echo of this caress. At the juncture between two fingers, he touched her with his tongue.

Josette was very still. Seconds passed, and she remembered how to inhale. She got in a couple of hurried breaths, and then he kissed her. His lips were soft, barely brushing her passive mouth, then inquiring into the corners, sweet and strong and sudden and sure, sure that she would accept his offerings and take him, take him away from himself. And she could, she could do that...

His hands stroked the wings of her shoulderblades as if they were covered with angel feathers, and she shuddered against him, and let go of the vase. It thumped down onto the elevator's carpeted floor and tumbled away, making soft, bumping sounds. The bell chimed, and the doors rolled open. Josette stepped back from Danny Woods. There was no resistance.

According to the indicator, they were on the eleventh. A short man in a beige suit got on. "Banquet level," he said, facing the front.

"But we're going up," said Danny Woods. Josette knelt to rescue the flowers. The short man watched her. She could tell, even with her back turned. The doors slid shut and they started back up without a word from him.

The vase was unharmed. The roses were still so tight, almost buds, that they were none the worse except for a little lint. If she got them in some more water soon, they would be fine. She stood. The beige suit man looked away.

The bell chimed for the twelfth. Josette got off, with Danny Woods following. "Oh," said the suit to the closing doors, "this is an up car, isn't it?"

They walked in silence through two turns and a long, straight stretch. At the door to 1213, Josette turned and spoke. Firmly, she hoped. "I'd better not invite you in."

"No?" The self-assured smile got backgrounded.

"No," agreed Josette. She wanted, for the first time, to tell a client the truth. "I have—" She hesitated, and he finished for her.

"—a lot of work to do. I understand. Me, too."

Josette nodded. It was easier than trying to explain.

"You still gonna be here tomorrow? Tomorrow night?" asked Danny Woods.

"Sure. We could get together then."

"There's a banquet—"

"Oh, no," said Josette. "I have other plans. But afterwards would be nice; say, nine o'clock?"

"Okay, I'll say nine o'clock." The grin was in the foreground again. "Where?"

"Your room."

He gave her the number. He was going to kiss her again, but she already had her key out, and she was inside closing the door before he could do more than decide to try.

The white votive burned steadily, putting forth an even globe of light. Viola leaned forward as Josette walked towards the altar with the roses. "Oooh," the doll said. "How gorgeous! Are they soft? Let me touch them." She reached out one stocking-stuffed hand, but Josette reached past it and rubbed the red roses against Viola's cheek. "Mmmm," she said. "Those are nice. Thank you, Aunt Josette."

Josette refilled the vase with warm water. She re-cut the stems, too, with the knife from her tool kit.

When the flowers were in place on the altar, it was time to think about food. Almost 10:30. She called room service and ordered "basketti" for Viola and a salad for Bunny and herself. As an afterthought she asked them to include a copy of Sunday's paper if any had come in yet.

She finished unpacking. Viola was in a talkative mood. She had made up a story about the house they were going to live in, and the garden they were going to grow, and all the toys and books she would have once they finally settled down.

"I have to work tomorrow night," Josette announced. Viola was suddenly silent. The votive candle crackled, the flame spurting high then dwindling to dimness. "I *have* to, Viola. It's been weeks since we turned in a new account number, and the last two didn't have anything worth putting in a flask. Besides, I think he's really nice."

"Ok-a-a-ay," the doll said slowly. "But you're not going to do it here, are you?"

"No." Josette winced to think of the one time she had tried that. It might be better for her own security, but it had scared her doll stiff.

"You like him?" asked Viola after a minute.

"Uh-hum. He's cute. His name is Danny Woods."

"What does he do?"

"Makes houses. Not builds them, but he makes the plans."

"He could make one for us, then. With secret passages!" Viola bounced a little with excitement at the thought. It was going to be all right.

The food came while she was standing in her flannel night gown, washing out her bras in the sink. The waiter was a slim man with a moustache. He looked Hispanic, so she didn't bother trying to hide her set-up. Odds were he'd figure it for some sort of Santeria, as long as Viola stayed still. Nothing that might necessitate calling a manager. Anyway, there wasn't going to be any trouble here, not of any sort. She'd spent the evening making sure of that.

She looked at the paper while they ate. The salad was good, romaine and spinach and buttercrunch, with a honey-dijon dressing. She had to remind Viola several times not to slurp her noodles.

"But it's fun," the doll protested. Her dry voice was querulous.

"But it's *messy* fun," Josette told her. "You'll get stained."

The want-ads contained a number of good-looking prospects. Josette circled them to check out tomorrow. She glanced at the clock-radio. Make that later today, she thought. It would be wonderful to be able to adjust to one time-zone.

"All right, squids. Bedtime." She sponged spaghetti sauce from Viola's mouth and dressed her in her flannel nightie, a diminutive twin of Josette's own. She tucked her doll into her half of the bed, with Bunny at her side.

"Leave the candle on, please, Aunt Josette?" asked Viola.

"It's the last one. I'll have to fix another tomorrow night, when I get back."

"Oh. Okay. Well then, goodnight."

"Goodnight, baby." She kissed her doll on her soft forehead and Bunny on his fuzzy nose, and then put out the light. After a while, she slept.

✳

Josette woke several times during the night. At last, at nine a.m., she decided it was late enough to get up.

On her way to the exercise room she found the maid, a woman barely taller than her service cart. Korean, Josette decided.

"Cheon-ibaegsibsamhoneun cheongsohaji maseyo. oneul-eun meideu seobiseu pil-yo eobs-seubnida."

"Ne eomma."

There were separate facilities for men and women, which was a relief. Mirrors again, of course, but she knew what she looked like. What other women saw. What men saw, too, even the ones who stared. They didn't do that because of her appearance. It was something they smelled, or sensed some other way. Something they wanted and sometimes got.

She took her time with her asanas and showered briefly. She wasn't even a tiny bit worried about Viola and Bunny, alone up in the room. It was clean and safe. If her instructions to the maid hadn't stuck, her guardians would certainly be able to prevent any intrusion. She even stopped at the Chez Chatte on her way back up. They had a Continental breakfast buffet. She helped herself to a plateful of boiled eggs and muffins, and carried it up to the room.

It took a while to get everyone ready. They didn't really have any winter clothes, so they had to dress in layers. Of course Bunny didn't have anything to wear. Josette decided to leave him there. "Rabbits aren't that interested in houses anyway," she explained to her silent doll.

Josette called a cab and they went down to wait in the lobby. The black and green marble floor had been newly buffed, and shimmered with resplendence. Josette lost herself exploring the branches of stone rivers, of jade-filled chasms, of sap-filled veins in forests of onyx.

A blaring horn brought her back. It was the taxi. The driver, for a wonder, was a woman. A bit butch, in denim and nose-rings. White and plump as a pony beneath her denim cap. "Hi, I'm Holly," she said, introducing herself. There was a plastic partition between the front seat and the back, but it was open. "And you two are—"

"Josette. Viola." She waited nervously for Holly to ask to hold her. Instead, the cabby sat without comment while Josette strapped her doll onto the seat next to her.

"Ready?" At Josette's nod, Holly put the cab in gear. "Where can I take you folks today?"

Josette handed her marked-up classified section through the partition. "We thought we'd take a look at some of these places. I've got a map, but maybe you know the best way to go to hit them all."

"Sure, Josette. This here's my turf."

Holly drove fast, braking smoothly when necessary, accelerating and turning as if dancing with herself. The deconstructed landscape of light poles and parking lots soon gave way to an actual neighborhood. Frame houses, mostly painted white, tried unsuccessfully to hide behind young, spindly trees.

"Used to be all elms," Holly explained. "Some places they try to keep em up, inject em with fungicide every spring. Down on campus they do that, feed the stuff in through these plastic hoses. Goddam trees look like giant junkies, noddin out."

There were three addresses in close proximity. Josette told Holly just to drive on by.

She got out of the cab for the next stop, a fieldstone bungalow with no yard to speak of, just so they could catch a breath of air. But most of what she'd circled in the paper they rolled right past: the wrought aluminum porch rails, the train-crossing frontage, the sandstone split-level shoved up against a fried fish stand.

Late in the afternoon they came to an area of red-brick houses. Josette's heart warmed itself in their glow. But there were no trees, not even immature ones, here. And one place was next to a convenience store, the other right across the street from a body shop with a chain link fence and a big, gaunt dog. The dog barked nonstop as Holly used the drive-way to turn the cab around. The angry sound followed them down the block.

They crossed a boulevard, and suddenly everything was quiet and rich. Maples laced their twiggy fingers overhead. The lawns were longer, the streets and sidewalks completely clear of snow.

Holly pulled up before a beautiful house: two stories, brick, with a one-story white frame addition and attached ga-rage. "Are you sure this is it?" asked Josette.

"Well, yeah, and there's the sign says they're havin an open house today, even."

"Wait here, then, please, while I check it out."

"No problem."

Josette tucked Viola inside her sweater-coat just to be sure she'd stay warm, then stepped out of the cab and walked up the winding brick pathway to the house.

Beside the door she found a round, black button, a crescent of light showing where it had not been painted over. She pushed it. Faintly, from within, came the sound of a silvery gong, two-toned. Then silence. She tried it again. More of the same.

She opened the storm door to knock, then realized how useless that would be. The bell was working; she'd heard it. As she shut the storm, though, the door itself swung slightly open. "Hello?" she called. No one answered. Hesitantly, she pulled the storm open again, and the door was sucked back into place. She touched the white-painted wood gently, and it opened with a soft swish, brushing over light-colored carpet. "Hello?" she called again into the dark, still house. No answer.

She stepped inside and heard the storm's latch click shut. Instantly its glass clouded with condensation. She stood in a small foyer. A wooden table shared the space with her, and an oval frame hung from the pale grey wall above it. Inside the frame was grey, too. A mirror. She would have to pass it to see the rest of the house.

Easy enough. It was a lot smaller than the ones in the weight room or the elevator. But the dimness... Dark mirrors, especially, sometimes showed her other things...

She closed her eyes. Maybe she could get by like that. But then, that would be cheating. She wasn't a cheater, and she didn't have anything to be afraid of, anymore.

She left the door and faced the mirror, which had become slightly fogged with the cold air. Through a faint mist she saw herself, looking no different than anyone else. Because what had been done to her didn't show. No one could see whether it had hurt or whether it had felt good. Or both. No one could see who he was, the one that did those things. She knew that now, she really did. She didn't have to see that when she saw herself, either, if she tried.

If she tried, what she saw in the reflected dimness was what came after that, the memories that she had made, the life she'd learned to live since, as an adult. With the help of the Women of the Doll.

She had heard about them in a magazine. She wrote the magazine, and no one there knew anything. The author was a pseudonym, a cancelled P.O. box. But that was all right. Everything was all right, would always be all right, as long as she just stayed still.

How did they find her, eventually? Not through any move she made. In a bookstore, in a coffee bar, the woman waiting on her said "You look like you could use a little extra help." At first the help was talk. Then music, dancing, pretty things to wear. Then baths, and baths, and bells, ringing and ringing, and more baths. In salt, in milk, in chalk, in honey.

In the oval mirror Josette saw a steaming tubful of gardenias, surrounded by women, arms reaching, hands dipping up fistfuls of soft, wet flowers. She saw herself, standing in the center of their circle, clothed in nothing but the heavy, heady scent, the heat, the sweat, the songs they sang as they scrubbed and scrubbed and scrubbed her skin with flowers, with white, with innocence. She saw a mirror in the mirror, the one they held so often to her face, asking her to tell them what did she see, what did she see.

Hers was the Whore's Story, and they'd shown her what to do with it, how she could sell her body and still keep her soul alive. Her soul was in Viola now, all the time. And Viola was safe, she knew how to make her doll safe and keep her from being touched.

Josette looked in the mirror and saw what she decided she would see. There was a wall behind her. She could feel it when she leaned back. She knew that it was grey. She followed the grey paint into the next room, which was carpeted in a dusty green, like lichen. Sudden sunlight fell in thick strips between venetian blinds. "Look, Viola," Josette said, pulling back her sweater so her doll could see. "Look, a piano!"

It was a baby grand; dark, maybe mahogany. Josette took Viola out and scooted her over the top to show how smooth it was. The doll left no trail; it was a well-dusted place.

Steps rose to the right, two carpeted flights with white railings and dark, silky banisters. But Josette turned left, through an archway, into the living room. Or maybe it was supposed to be a library; empty shelves stretched floor to ceiling. There was a fireplace, too. Flint, though. Viola preferred fieldstone.

There were prints on the walls representing something wan and ghostly. Josette couldn't quite make them out in the room's dimness. She searched for a switch to turn on the chandelier, then gave up and walked out through a different door, into another empty room with bare, bright windows. There were four buttons on the far wall: two ebony circles beneath two protruding cylinders of pearl. She pushed the pearl stubs into the wall and the two ebony buttons shot out. And brilliance swam overhead, a whole party's worth of sparkling lights. She could see the prints quite clearly now from where she stood, lighted by the library's smaller chandelier. They were intricately frilled orchids with wide, speckled mouths.

Cream carpet, cream silk curtains, cream ceiling, arched and florentine with cherubs. The room was saved from its single-mindedness, though, by the leather covering its walls to the height of Josette's chin. Darker cherubs flourished there, amid tobacco-colored curlicues and sober squares.

"What do you say, Viola?" Josette asked her doll. "Me, I'm just not sure…"

She had turned left into the library, right into this place, which she decided must be the dining room. A door with a push plate led off to the right again. The kitchen?

Yes. Yellow like a daffodil. A cookstove, white porcelained steel topped in gleaming stainless. A sleek, slumberous freezer and a stodgy, upright refrigerator, both once-white, currently-ecru. But the counters appeared to be composed of compressed eggs, lightly scrambled. In butter. And the walls glowed cheerfully, electric saffron. And the glass-fronted cupboards, and the drawers below, and the linoleum below that. The color of morning, the color of our sun. Josette smiled. "I think," she told Viola, "I think maybe—"

A keychain jingled loudly. From where the linoleum descended in narrow steps came other metallic noises: The springing slide of an aluminum door closer, the heavy, brassy tumble of an opening latch. A woman's voice started out muffled and grew suddenly clearer over the sound of an opening door: "—ay in the van, sweetie, I'll just be a second, all I have to do is turn off these lights I left burning…" Footsteps scuffed quickly up the stairs. Then a woman stood at the top, auburn head bent as she dug in her purse. She hadn't seen them yet. "Don't be scared," said Josette. "Hi."

The woman froze, then peered up through fine red hair. "Uhh," she said. "O.K., I'm not scared. Especially since I've got a 9 mm Sig Sauer in here, and it's loaded, and my boyfriend's right outside in the van. So I'm not scared, thanks. So let me ask you what the hell you're doing in here?"

"A gun?" Josette hugged Viola tighter. "I—I was just looking. The door was open, and I'm interested in buying—"

The woman flung her head back and smacked her forehead with one hand. "Baby-jesus-son-of-mary!! *That's* what I forgot. I thought it was just the lights. I left the goddam *door* unlocked." Josette backed away as the woman walked briskly through to the dining room. "Excuse me but I—" Her voice became too faint to hear as she moved towards the front of the house. Josette followed slowly. "—dinner with his folks, and we're already late. Get that switch for me, will you?" she said, coming back into the dining room.

Josette nodded and turned off the chandeliers. A snowy twilight replaced the glare, gently washing away all contrast.

Josette decided she liked it better this way. Although maybe candles would be best. "How much do you think they'll settle for?" she asked, trying to sound casual.

"Didn't you just hear me saying? It's sold. Closed yesterday morning. But the ad was in, so I left the signs up and had the open house anyhow. Good way to meet people."

Josette felt her flimsy hopes crumpling like foil. "They closed? On a Saturday?" Her voice sounded high and tight. "Don't you still have to get the mortgage approved and the title searched and—and stuff?"

"No mortgage. Cash." The woman rummaged through her bag again. "Here's my card. Julie Saunders." She handed it over. "Sure, there's a chance things will fall through, but I wouldn't waste my time holding your breath. Maybe I can help you find something else, though. Give me a call." She noticed Viola and eyed her suspiciously. "You got kids?"

"No."

"Good. Makes it easier. Well—" She paused meaningfully.

"O.K. Thanks." Josette turned and walked through the cheerful yellow kitchen, down the four steps to the side door landing, and out. This was not going to be their house. Her eyes hurt, and walking down the concrete drive made tears spill over and fall out, warming her face. She had a pack of kleenex in her bag. Back in the cab, she dug it out and scrubbed away at her cheeks, still weeping. "It's sold already. Let's go."

"Hey," said Holly. "Hey, listen. It wasn't the right one." The cab was in motion. The house was already behind them, out of sight. "I mean it. I mean, if it hadda been the right one, you guys woulda got it, right? But it wasn't. Really. Honestly, now, was that place, like *perfect* for you?" She waited long enough for Josette to realize she ought to answer.

"No."

"-Course it wasn't. Cause there's some place better, better for *you*, somewhere down the road."

"You don't—you can't even begin—" Josette cut herself off before she said something inconsiderate. Holly was just trying to help her, with that tacky taxicab philosophy.

"Oh, yes, I can." Holly pulled up at a stoplight and turned around to face her, dim and multi-colored in the sodium and traffic glare. "See, my ex is just about done with her doll. House-maid's Tale, that's what *she's* got. We're still friends, and she's been telling me stuff... I'm gonna miss her when she goes..."

Another initiate. Only the fifth she'd met since leaving the temple—well, heard of, anyway. "Oh, Holly, oh, that's wonderful. I'm sorry—"

"No, it's cool. But see—" The light changed and she swung around to drive. "—see, you gotta *know* it. You're gonna find your place, Josette, and it's gonna be kickass, just absolutely swollen... How long you been on the road?"

"Four years."

Holly absorbed that in silence for a short while. "Right. So you're closin in on it now, see?"

Josette tried to see. Then she gave up and just looked out the window.

✳

The candle guttered, burning low. Spurts of sooty smoke rose and disappeared. Josette's skirts swished silkily against her bare legs as she spun before the altar. "Ooh, pretty," Viola said. "Do it again."

"Not now, there's no time. We've got to get you tucked in before I go."

"Please?" The doll's sad, painted eyes were hard to resist. Josette twirled once more and her skirts swirled out: crimson, amber, viridian, waves of ocean blue. "All right, Miss Muffet," she said as she stopped, "off your tuffet." She swooped Viola up in her arms and waltzed her to the bed. Gold tissue floated from her head, caught and wrapped and tied around her arms and breasts in careful knots.

Her doll was unusually silent as she helped her into her night gown and tucked her in with the already somnolent Mr. Bun. Josette thought at first this was because of the candle. It was just about out.

But as she bent to kiss Viola's cheek, she saw a fold, a worried wrinkle in the spot between where her eyebrows ought to be. "What's wrong?" she asked.

Viola's soft red lips twisted. "Auntie Josette," she said, her dry voice filled with dread, "you're not going to let him *hurt* you, are you?"

"No, darling. I'll never let anyone hurt me. Never, ever again."

"That's good." The doll settled back on her pillow, and the flame went out.

Josette glanced at the radio. Eight minutes to. She liked to be reasonably prompt when dealing with clients. It made it easier to keep things on a professional footing. She picked up her tool-kit, slipped her sandals on, and headed out the door to work.

Danny Woods' room was on the sixteenth floor, three stories up. She took the stairs to avoid crowds. And so that she could stand on a landing and sing:

> "I wish I were a little bird,
> With wings, that I could fly;
> Then I would fly to my own true love,
> And when he'd speak, then I'd be by…"

The echo was surprisingly mellow, for all that concrete. Not to mention metal railings.

> "My heart would flutter like the wings,

To see my own dear one;
And pretty words I'd like to sing,
All beneath the morning sun..."

She opened the fire door and there he was, waiting, a silhouette that loomed against the dim hall light. His hair was loose and fanned out in long curls, past his waist. Josette smiled coolly and walked forward. It was like moving into the shadow of a fir tree on a moonlit country road. Keep going, she told herself. That's how you reach the light.

"I heard singing, and I thought it must be you." He turned so they were standing side by side and started down the hall. She could see his face, the grin.

"Am I late?" The door to his room was propped open, and they went in.

"No, I got back early. Didn't want you to have to stand around." He nudged a green cushioned stool out of the way, and his door slammed shut. "Want the heater on? Window open?"

"I'm fine, thanks." The room was a double. A brown hard-shell suitcase and a camera occupied the far bed. Josette sat down on the end of the near one, and set her toolkit near her feet. The spread and carpet almost matched. Rose and burgundy.

This was always the hardest part. Sometimes the client knew exactly what he wanted. Sometimes he even knew he would be paying for it, though usually not how much.

At least Danny Woods had heard of the Women of the Doll. Josette brought them up right away, while he poured her out a glass of pineapple juice from the vending machine. She sipped the sweet, tinny stuff politely and listened to him trying to explain.

"They're a secret organization—" he started out to say.

"No. Not secret. Hidden."

He sat on the footstool and cocked an eyebrow at her. "There's a difference?"

"A secret is something you can't tell. By definition. If you can tell it, it's not a secret. Never was."

"Whereas hidden just means hard to find. I can appreciate that. Okay, so they're hard to find, and they help women in some sort of trouble, different kinds, I guess. And the women they help—do things for other people. For a—um, consideration."

"Donation," Josette corrected him.

"And we're talking about this right now because you're—"

"It's tax deductible," she told him. "501(c)-3. Religious and charitable."

"But, Josette—" He reached for her, then stopped himself.

"Danny. In return I promise I'll give you *everything*. Whatever you want." Except her suffering. She would not be made to suffer, ever again.

"'Everything'—in return for what?"

She opened up the kit, got out the terminal. "I run your card through this, and you sign a blank authorization form. Just like they do here at the hotel."

"But Josette, that's—that's stupid, I can't do that!"

"Sure you can. Think how proud your accountant will be." She patted the bed beside her. "If you don't think it was worth it, when the bill comes, tell the bank it was a computer error. Give them a different figure. We won't protest it."

"Never happened before, hunh?" She shook her head. Her veil rustled. The sound seemed to draw him. He reached into his pocket and brought out a worn leather wallet. "I must be crazy," he said, handing her his Visa. His hazel eyes pleaded with her to tell him he wasn't. He had an awful lot of fight in him, to be thinking even semi-rationally after this long in proximity. Josette wondered where it came from. She took his card with a casual scrape of one short nail against his palm, and still he stared at her, unbelieving. "Am I really doing this?" he asked.

"You won't regret it," Josette promised.

While waiting for account to clear, she tried to get an idea of what he wanted. Often it worked best just to ask. He seemed reassured by her question, and answered it with another of his own. "Simple version or the complicated one?"

"Either. Both." She set out her work candle and lit it. Then the incense.

"O.K. The simple version is I want you, as much of yourself as you're willing to share with me at this time, in this place." Viola, she thought in sudden panic. He wanted to get at her doll. But he didn't, couldn't know. He went on. "If this is how it has to be for now, that's fine. It's a limited setting, but a definite improvement over the escalator at O'Hare, or the limo stand outside that place in Berkeley, the hotel with the Edwin Hopper hallways. Or that florist's in Madison, or—"

"You've run into me before." Had he built up some sort of resistance over time?

"Right." He held his hunger back, clasped it in with arms crossed below his knees. "The complicated version—I can't— can I touch you? Or do I have to use only words?" He held out one hand, kept it fairly steady in the air.

"All right." She wasn't going to figure him out any other way.

He stood closer and ran his palms lightly over the silver veil. "I want to, I want—" He tugged the veil back and bent to kiss her hair. His breath circled gently in, gently out, whispering among the tips, warming the roots. Hot on her crown, then spiraling down to her forehead, feathering the fringe. The slightest touches of his tongue drew points of light along her brow and outward, vanishing. Then his lips were firm, pressed full on the center.

"Ahh," she said. A sound like a snowdrop, blooming early.

"That, that," he murmured. "Yes. Josette..." He sank down beside her on the bed, and used his chin to brush aside the fabric where it drifted around her neck. A river of delight ran down to the hollow above her collarbone and collected there. He lowered his head and lapped it like a deer. She sighed and melted against him, soft as heated honeycomb. "And this, Josette—" he whispered in her ear. He swept his tongue out and around in a circle behind it, searching. He found the spot and washed it patiently, faithfully, through her hisses, cries, and trembling sobs. She came, her voice arching high, trying to describe to someone, anyone, the pitch of pleasure's peak.

"That," he said, lowering her gently to the bed. "That's what I want. In a moment, I'm going to want you to give me more."

Josette stirred weakly on the rosy coverlet. He'd received some of whatever he was looking for, yes, but unless she got him to make an offering the temple labs could accept, she'd have to bring about a really spectacular healing. No other way to justify charging more than her expenses. Usually she was able to cure her clients of some unintentionally inflicted childhood wound. That's why they never argued over her rates. Only how could she concentrate enough on him to sort out the source of his troubles, while serving up the kind of responsiveness that would keep him satisfied?

She watched him while he untied her bodice knots with patient hands. The fingers were surprisingly strong, the knuckles scarred white in the midst of his uneven tan. Her golden tissue unwound in satiny profusion around her on the bed. Her breasts, fully exposed to her client's gaze, waited stoically for his touch. Instead, his hands slipped around her waist, resting comfortably in its curves. "Ready?" he asked. She nodded, and his hands slid under all four waistbands, then spread to stretch the elastic. They cupped her buttocks as she lifted them, obedient, and let the filmy colors slide below.

Carefully he raised her sandaled feet and freed them of the fallen skirts. "I wish you could see yourself right now," he said as he knelt before her on the floor. She didn't tell him that she didn't need to. She knew what she looked like. Mirrors. There was one right now on his closet door.

Her sandals were coming off. That was it; nothing left. Now he could fuck her. But Danny Woods stayed where he was. He lifted her left foot and sucked the bone of her ankle, so hard, so vulnerable, her whole life so forlorn.

Like leaves his fingers brushed up against her calves. He spoke. "Can I get you to turn over? And you'll probably want to move a little higher on the bed." Those were the last words he uttered for an hour. She had an orgasm in the back of her left knee, another, longer, in the right. Another one six inches up from that. Mounting to heaven like a lark in the morning, each height feeding and leading to further exaltation. Of which she sang.

When he stopped, the spread beneath her was sodden, dark as the carpet. "Thank you," he said. "My dear."

Soon she was able to move again. She turned on her side, facing him. He was still half-dressed. Beyond him, the candle burned steadily at half its height. In its half-shadow, she saw his shy grin, dog-teeth gleaming.

What should she do? Asking hadn't worked, and she wasn't getting anywhere this way, either. She smiled back sleepily, let her eyes flutter shut and turned away, nestling her shoulders against his broad, bare chest. He hesitated hardly at all, then wrapped his arms around her, cradling her toward him.

Keyed up the way he was, feasted on her arousal, it took her quite a while to bring him down. Bit by bit, though, he relaxed around her. She timed her own breath, shifted the intervals slowly, lullingly, set her heart beat rocking both their bloods, stilly, stilly, stepping over seconds stretching longer, longer…till at last, her client slept.

Cautiously, she opened her eyes, then shut them back up tight. The mirror on the closet door; the lights were off, and her work candle burned low. But maybe the dark reflections could help—she'd never tried before, but maybe they could show her someone else's story, the story of Danny Woods.

She slid off the bed quickly, so as not to break the slumber. Slipping around to the far side, she peered over her sleeping client's shoulders, into the shadowy surface confronting her. In there he was young, very young. Only a little boy, with a look of stubborn, customary loneliness. Around him the room's dimness swirled in shapes like angry screams. Nothing more specific showed itself, and she gave up, resuming her place on the bed.

Rough childhood, Josette thought. But there's a fair chance he knows that much himself. She wasn't going to get away with more than a couple of hundred for tonight, and no offering. Not even enough to break even. Not unless she at least got her client's pants off for him.

She let loose of the slumber. Her client stirred, but didn't waken. Resistant, was he? Perhaps she'd been too sophisticated in her approach. She focused, made adjustments upward. Her sweat sharpened, breath hardened—not with delight, but with dirt-simple demand. A calculated grind brought her the contours of good news: through sleep's light draping, Danny Woods had responded.

Suddenly his hands held her shoulders, twisting her clumsily, face down. The too-soft mattress shifted as he came to his knees, bore left and right as he stripped the denim off one leg, then the other. Then he was on her, kneading and nipping, urging her haunches higher. The sheath, she had to check the sheath, make sure she still had it in place. She freed one hand, felt the rolled rim, numb among her sensitive wrinkles, and braced herself once more, barely in time.

Without a word he thrust inside and worked away. Fierce, not fancy. Without a word, but soon not silently. Strange, muffled grunts, snuffles, snorts, and growls came from him as he rose and fell, rose and fell. The pace increased, as did the noise, and Josette risked another look into the closet mirror. Her heart jumped shut as she found and met them there, those yellow, glowing eyes. Held them, poised for flight or fight, those wild eyes of the beast. And stayed still, gazing as her blood slammed back through, opening its accustomed gates. Pulse pounding, she considered pretending not to notice the eyes, with pupils slit, not round, and the fur roughening her client's silhouette, already pretty vague within the mirror's frame. And without, his skin still seemed smooth and relatively hairless to her touch. It—he—obviously didn't expect he would be seen this way. After a short, puzzled pause he went back to his business. He made his offering and collapsed with her in a fairly graceful heap. From there he fell into another sleep, this time his own.

She lay and rested on her back a while, feet up, knees held loosely to her chest so she wouldn't lose a drop. Throughout it all she'd felt no threat. Once she'd checked to find him unchanged outside the mirror, the fear, like dry ice, had evaporated, leaving no residue except an odd chill, and a lingering curiosity.

She glanced at the work candle. It still had a little more to burn. Should she tell her client about encountering the beast? She wasn't exactly sure of their relationship. Was the one the other's curse? Or animal emblem? Was Danny Woods possessed, or just lost in a story he had no idea how to tell? A sudden tide of liquid wax swamped the candle's wick and snuffed it out, deciding her. She had done enough for one night.

She rose, picked up her tool kit and felt her way into the bathroom, where she carefully removed the sheath. Singing softly. It had, after all, gone fairly well.

"Oh, when I was a lass at school,
I looked up at the sky;
And now among the woodlands cool
Gathering sweet primroses, I…"

She took her oversized tee and orange tights from her toolkit's bottom tray and sat down on the stool to pull them on. Leaving the door ajar for the light, she came back out to the bedroom. Her skirts were on the floor, still. She picked them up and smoothed them out, letting them hang over one arm.

"Josette—"

She turned. Danny Woods was awake. He had propped himself up on both his elbows. His hair swam over his bare shoulders, tangled currents running down the hollow of his back. "What?" she said.

"Nothing. Just—Josette."

She found the veil and rolled the skirts in it. Stuck the candle remains in a small brown paper bag, ready for disposal.

She paused at the door. What would it be like to stay with him, to hear his tale and tell him hers? A white man, but he hadn't committed any racist stupidities, at least not yet. The beast, though…and Viola. They might not like it, either one.

"Good-bye," he said, turning away.

"O.K." she said. She left.

The hallways were as murky as ever, night and day and night and day again. Outside some doors pairs of shoes stood, waiting to be polished, or stolen, or ignored. She called the elevator. It came quickly. They always did around four in the morning, convention or no.

Back in 1213 she drank a couple of glasses of tepid tapwater, loaded the sheath's contents into a cryoflask and checked out Danny Woods' credit info. The card he'd given her had thirty-three hundred available. Low. Must be the one that he'd been travelling on. She took a third, but left the line open, undecided. Maybe it ought to be more…danger pay. But had she really been in danger?

She didn't know. She was tired, and so she shut it down.

It had been a long, long night, but she got out the candle fixings anyway: lavender and lotus and mugwort oil. Baby powder. Clover seed. A pinch of earth from Milham Park, in the town where she was born. And a blue ceramic bowl to mix them in.

She thought again about the house that afternoon. The wrong one, obviously. Holly had been right. Only, it was so long now since they had started looking. And Viola needed a home of her own so desperately.

Josette's eyes blurred. She blinked and shed quick, hot tears into the blue bowl.

Mix wet and dry ingredients with rapid strokes. One more thing, she thought, and lowered her head to the bowl. In, out, in again, she breathed the sweet, musty aroma. There.

She was in the middle of anointing the votive when a knock came at the door. She glanced at the radio. 5:45 a.m. She hadn't ordered any breakfast. She ignored the knock and kept working. It came again, a short while later. This time a white sheet of paper followed, sliding under her door.

The water on the altar looked a little cloudy. She changed it, then lit the new candle.

Her doll slept peacefully. Her small chest rose and fell steadily now, in the light of the low flame. It seemed a pity to disturb her, so Josette packed as much as she could beforehand. Then it was almost seven. That would be a good nine hours.

She called a courier for the cryoflask, then picked up the phone again to order a cab for 8:30. The dispatcher put her on hold, to the tune of Sammy Davis, Jr.'s "The Candy Man." While she waited, she gave in and read the note. Several times.

It was short; all it said was "I love you." No signature. The handwriting belonged on a blueprint, even and precise.

The line clicked and the dispatcher was back. "To Metro," she told him. "My flight leaves at ten-thirty. AM." She gave him the hotel's address, then asked, "Is Holly driving this morning?"

"I don't know. I can take a message for her, if you like."

On the bed, Viola stirred and pushed sleepily at the covers. "That's all right. Thanks."

"Thank you for calling Rite-Ride."

Josette went and sat on the bed. "Hey, squids, you ready to motivate?"

Viola smiled and stretched her short, fat arms. Josette loved to watch her wake up this way, with the candle going. The doll's face shone with joy.

But when she saw the suitcases, she sobered up a bit.

"Do we *have* to go already, Aunt Josette?"

"I'm afraid so, darling. There's no place for us here." She paused in buttoning up Viola's pink cardigan. The buttons were white and yellow daisy shapes. She twirled them around in her fingers while she spoke. "I think, maybe, yesterday was a good lesson."

"I was sad we couldn't get the house," Viola said.

"Yes, but…it wasn't right, it belonged to someone else. If we're going to start another temple, it has to really be our own. I think we're going to have to just make it. From scratch. From the ground up."

"Is that going to be a lot of work?"

"Probably." Josette pulled her blond mohair sweater over her head. It was big; it came down to her knees. "So we better get going. We've got enough saved up to buy some land that's really *beautiful*, maybe on a lake, even."

"O.K."

"What's the matter? You don't seem too enthusiastic, Viola."

"Auntie Josette, are you ever sorry you made me?"

She picked her doll up, cradled her in her wooly arms. "Oh, darling. *No*. Never. Before I had you, everything was horrible, just awful. I never got to smile or play, or anything. It was like I was dead, Viola. But now I'm alive, honey. Cause you're alive. And why would I be sorry about a thing like that?" She kissed Viola's long, black braids. "I love you, you silly squid!"

"And Bunny too?"

"And Bunny too. Now we better get you in the purse or we'll miss our ride to the airport." She got her doll to sit down in her handbag, with Bunny on her lap.

The stones were packed away. Only the votive and water remained. She snuffed the candle, emptied the water in the sink, stuck the still warm votive in a wax bag in her coat pocket. Wheeled her bags out into the hall.

One last look around. Nothing left behind, she thought, and closed the door on 1213.

Down to the lobby. She was going to miss this floor.

The same clerk checked her out as in. Her eyes were red-rimmed now, from tears or smoke or lack of sleep, Josette couldn't tell. But her perky smile was identical. "Did you enjoy your stay?" she asked, trying to disguise her curiosity. The cryoflask gleamed cryptically on the beautiful, dark counter between them, waiting to be picked up.

"Oh, yes. Can you tell me, has the party in 1610 checked out yet?"

"Doesn't look like it. Want me to ring them?"

"Oh, no, it's too early. Just see that he gets this." The card was embossed, pearl on white. "Women Of The Doll," it read. "Tell us what you want." No address. Just a phone number, prefix 1-900. She was sure he would be using it. Any messages would be forwarded to her.

A car horn sounded outside. "Come again!" chirped the clerk as Josette hurried to the door. As she stooped to ease her luggage wheels over the threshold, she noticed a place where the marble floor was cracked. It looked loose. She pried up a small section and put it in her pocket. Bit by bit, she would build it, her own place. She and all the others. Piece by piece.

The Tawny Bitch

My Dearest Friend,

This letter may never reach you, for how or where to send it is beyond me. I write you for the solace of holding you in my thoughts as I would that I could hold you in my arms. So rudely as I was torn from the happy groves of Winnywood Academy, I can only conjecture that you also have been sent to some similarly uncongenial spot. Oh, my dear, how I hope it is a better one, even in some small measure, than the imprisonment forced upon me here. I inhabit a high garret: bare of wall, low of ceiling, dirty-windowed. Through the bleary panes creeps a grey light; round their fast-barred frames whistles a restless wind. Some former inmate has tried to stop up the draughts with folded sheets of paper, and these provide the material platform on which stands my fanciful correspondence with you.

My pen is that which you awarded me, my prize for mastering the geometric truths of Euclid. Sentiment made me carry it always with me, next my heart. How glad I am! It is now doubly dear to me, doubly significant of our deep bond. As for the ink, I must apologize for its uneven quality, due entirely to its composition. In fact, I have rescued it from my chamber pot. Yes, love, these words are set down, to put the matter quite plainly, in my own urine, a method imparted to me by my old African nurse, Yeyetunde. It has the advantage, in addition to its accessibility, of being illegible, almost invisible, till warmed above a flame. As I am allowed no fire of any sort, I may not see to edit my words to you. I hope my grammar and construction may not shame me, nor you, as my preceptress in their finer points.

But I believe I will soon cease to trouble myself about such things.

Whom do you suppose to have betrayed us? I am inclined to suspect Madame, as she was the only one, probably, who knew of our attachment. Certainly none of the other pupils was in a position to do so. Though Kitty was most definitely set against me on account of my race, and pretended not to understand the difference between mulattoes and quadroons such as myself, she had no real opportunity to do us harm.

It vexes me that I made no attempt to buy Madame's silence when I had plenty of gold at my disposal. She dropped the most enormous hints on the subject, which I see quite clearly now, in hindsight.

I must school myself not to fret about these matters, over which I have no control. There is enough with which to concern myself in my immediate surroundings. If I spend my days fussing and fidgeting, I will wear out my strength, both physical and mental. My first concern is to preserve all my faculties intact.

When I came to myself in this place, I did doubt my senses. I had lain down to rest on a bed of ease, confined, it is true, as a consequence of our discovery, but still with my own familiar toys and bibelots ranged round me. I awoke with dull eyes, a throbbing head, and a fluttering heart, in these utterly cheerless surroundings.

Well, some evil drug, perhaps, subdued me to my captor's power. He has yet to reveal himself to me, and my two gaolers say not a word in answer to my inquiries, but I have no doubt as to who it is: my Cousin John. When informed of our behaviour, he must have once more assented to be burdened with my maintenance. Certainly he could not have hoped to have kept me in school much longer, the backwardness ascribed to my race and colonial upbringing having by now vanished under your tender tutelage. I have thought much of these things during the two days I have spent here, there being little else to occupy my time, and I believe it must be so.

But now I have the comfort of writing. To hold intercourse with you, even through so attenuated a medium as this, will give me strength to endure whatever trials lie ahead.

I continue with the description of my prison. I believe I neglected to mention that the walls are washed a stark white; harsh, yet tainted, soiled with the careless print of unclean hands. The floor is a mere collection of loose boards. It is there that I shall hide this letter, and any other secrets my time in this place vouchsafes to me. Gloomy pillars rise at intervals to the rough rafters above, and a brick chimney from which proceeds all the warmth afforded me.

The windows, barred and begrimed, afford an ill view of the countryside. That I am in the country I deduce from the silence surrounding me, unbroken save for the moaning wind and the monotonous nightly barking of a solitary dog. The glass is so befouled as to disguise all distinguishing visual characteristics of the neighbourhood.

I have just formed the project of cleaning it, when left on my own as now, that I may perhaps ascertain my whereabouts. There, you see how good you are for me, what a salutary effect so slight a contact with you even as this can have upon me? Then do not chide yourself for the predicament in which I now find myself, love. The danger may yet be won through, and the rewards have been so richly sweet as to defy description. No need; you know them. Back, then, to the present.

One door only serves my prison, and it is a heavy barrier, much bolted. It opens twice a day to a brutish pair, whom for a while I thought to be deaf-mutes, so little did they respond to my pleadings for release. But just this morning—Stay! I hear

~

I have been honoured by such a visit, such attentions as would surely drive me to destroy myself, were adequate means within my reach! No, I remember my promise to you, and there shall be no more attempts of that

45

sort, whatever the goad, however easily the weapons were to come to my grasp. But oh, the insult of his touch! The vileness of the man, the ghastly glare as of his rotting soul, shining through the bloodshot eyes with which he raked me up and down, the moment he stepped in the room.

"Ho," said Cousin John (for it was he), "the little pickaninny loses what small comeliness she had. Martha, Orson, does she not receive good victuals? Remember, I pay all expenses, and shall have a thorough accounting made."

The shorter of my gaolers, a man (presumably Orson), replied that I consumed but a small portion of my meals. This is true, for who could be tempted by a nasty mess of cold beans and bloody sausages, or a bowl of lumpy gruel?

My cousin then turned back to me and said "So you would starve yourself, would you, my black beauty? Well, that's no good, for then your fortune will revert to that b_____ Royal Society. And though I am your guardian until you come of age, your father made no testamentary provision for me upon your death." These last words were almost murmured, and seemed to be addressed to himself. He sank into a silent reverie, which lasted a few moments, then roused himself to his surroundings.

"Now Martha! Orson! You must bring up some refreshment, and the means with which to partake of it. And a chair or two would not be amiss." (For the lack of any furniture in my description of this room is not owing to your correspondent's negligence.) "I dine with the young lady. What! Why stand you gawping there? Be off about your business!" Orson muttered something about the danger in which his master stood should I try to escape.

"Nonsense! This twig of a thing harm me?" And he laughed aloud at the idea, a heavy, bloated laugh. And indeed, he is much larger than I am, and stronger, too, as he had occasion to prove at the conclusion of our interview.

For the moment, however, my cousin was all affability. He surveyed the sparseness of my accommodations and shook his head, saying, "Well, 'tis a sad comedown from Winnywood. But you have been a very naughty puss, and must learn to repent your errors before you can be allowed anything like the liberality with which you have been used to be treated. I must not throw away money on the cosseting of a spoiled, sulky, ungrateful schoolgirl."

"Why should I be grateful?" I thought to myself. "The money is mine, though you seem inclined to forget this."

As though he had heard my unspoken words, my cousin showed himself somewhat abashed. He crimsoned, strode away, and hemmed and hawed for a moment before trying a new tack. The gist of this was, that by my shameless behavior with you, I had ruined for myself all hope of any respectable alliance with a man. He veered from this presently by way of allusions to the unacceptableness of my "mulatto" features, the ugliness of which also unfitted me as a bride.

He paused as if for breath, and I spoke the first words I had dared to utter in his presence: "Love, affection of any sort, then, is quite out of the question? My fortune forms my sole —"

"Love! Affection!" interrupted Cousin John. He seemed astonished that I should dare to feel their want, let alone speak of it. "After giving way to the unnatural perversions which have reported themselves to my ears, Belle, you ought to be grateful for common civility."

He went on in this vein for some time. I confess that after a while I paid his lecturing scant heed. It put me in mind of my father's scolds to me when, as a child, I showed myself too prone to adopt the quaint customs of Yeyetunde and the other blacks about our place. As Cousin John prated away I seemed almost to see my parent stand before me in his linen stock and shirtsleeves, urging rationalistic empiricism upon a child of ten. Of course I was eventually brought to Reason's worship. But well I remember the attraction to me of the island's cult of magic, with its grandiose claims to control the forces of nature which my father sought only to understand. The brightly coloured masks and fans and other ceremonial regalia, surrounded by highly scented flowers; the glitter of candles in dark, mysterious grottoes, hypnotic chants, and sweetly chiming bells, all clamoured at my senses and bade me admit in their train the fantastic beliefs with which they were associated. Then, too, I felt these practices to be connected somehow with my mother, of whom, as I told you, I have no true, clear, conscious recollection. Yet her presence seemed near when I was surrounded by these islanders, to whom the barrier between life and death was but a thin and permeable membrane.

Indeed, I can still dimly picture the altar that Yeyetunde instructed me to build in my mother's honor. It was a humble affair of undressed stone, with a wooden cup and a mossy hollow wherein I laid offerings of meat, fruit, and bread, and poured childishly innocent libations to her spirit.

My thoughts had wandered thus far afield when I was roused to my senses by the sudden seizure of my hand. Cousin John knelt, actually knelt on one knee at my feet, and held me in a grip firmer than was pleasant. Ere I had time to discover what he meant to be about, came a knock on the door, and the sound of its several bolts and chains being shifted about, in preparation for someone's entry.

My cousin with difficulty regained his feet, and the man Orson entered the room, bearing with him two chairs, followed by Martha, who carried a collapsed, brass-topped table.

I have not yet made you see these two, I think, fixtures though they are in my prison. Both are tall, stout, loose-fleshed, and grim of countenance. Did they for some reason of deviltry trade clothes, one would be hard pressed to note the change, for they are distinguishable otherwise only by the female's slightly greater height, Orson's face being smooth shaven.

In bringing in their burdens, this pair left open the door. I stepped 'round as noiselessly as I could to obtain a view through it, that I might determine what chance I had of making off. None, it appeared, for the door's whole frame was filled by a large, bony, yellow dog, a bitch. She eyed me suspiciously, and her hackles rose, and a low growl emanated from some deeper region, it seemed, than her throat. Martha heard it. "Come away from that!" she ordered harshly, whether speaking to me or the bitch, I could not tell. I backed away anyhow, and the bitch held her place.

I realized that in this apparition I had an explanation of the tiresome barking that plagues my dark hours here, and bids fair to keep me from ever obtaining a full night's sleep.

But my light and my ink both fail me, and I must postpone the telling of my thoughts and the rest of the day's events, till morning.

~

I cannot recall exactly where I left off in my account. The door was open, I believe, and I had discovered it defended by the tawny bitch... Yes, and I had just remarked how I believed her the source of the irksome barking that, together with the poorness of the pallet provided (Martha or Orson brings it in the evening, and it is removed on the arrival of my dish of gruel), and the uncomfortably chilly atmosphere conspires to ruin my nightly rest. The barking goes on literally for hours: low, monotonous as the drop of water from some unseen, uncontrollable source. It is tireless, hopeless almost in its lack of change in tone, pitch, or volume; in frequency just irregular enough that one cannot cease to remark its presence. With daylight, it ends, but so soon as I am able to fall into a broken slumber, my gaolers appear, remove the pallet, and the miserable day commences. No wonder, then, that this animal and I viewed each other in instant and seemingly mutual detestation.

"Come away from that," cried Martha (have I already said?), and not knowing to which of us she referred, I retreated anyway. The two servants dropped their burdens and took turns in bringing in the food and other necessities, then shut the door and proceeded to set before us our dinner. This was much nicer than I usually get, consisting of a baked chicken, boiled potatoes, a side dish of green peas and a steaming hot pie, fragrant of fruit and cinnamon. I could not but imagine that Martha and Orson had designed this for their meal, and my mouth fair watered at the sight and smell of such good things. But Cousin John would have none of it at first and raised a fit, asking for soup and fish, jellies, cakes and such, and demanding that all be taken away and replaced with something better. However, there was nothing else, Orson told him, be it better or worse, so he was forced to make do with what was before him. But he did demand wine to drink, and two bottles were brought, and the servants then dismissed.

I made quick enough work of the portions on my plate, and surprised and pleased my cousin by requesting more. He helped me to it, refreshing himself with great draughts of wine between his labors. "That's the dandy!" he said, spooning forth a quantity of gravy. "Mustn't have you wasting away, merely because you are under a punishment." Well fed, I felt an increase of courage. How long, I asked him, must my punishment continue? "Why, till you repent your sins, little Belle, and show that you are truly sorry for them." As he said this he gave a heavy wink. Then he bellowed for Martha and Orson, who cleared the dirty dishes and broken meats, close-watched once more by the bitch, which confined itself, nonetheless, to the passageway. Orson would have taken the wine with the other things, but his master bade him leave it.

Then we were alone, without hope of interruption. I had not drunk my wine, but lifted my glass now as cover for an inspection of my cousin's face. I hoped to reassure myself by tracing in his blurred, reddened outlines some coarse resemblance to the beloved features of my father. I saw puzzlement there, and thick, unaccustomed lines bent the brow in frowning thought. I lowered my eyes, and when I looked up again upon setting down my glass, his expression had shifted to a false grin.

"Come, Belle," said he, "you are not so unseemly to look at when you smile a little, and let down your guard. Black but comely, a regular Sheba, one would say. As for your schoolgirl episodes, I could bring myself to set all that aside. Many a man would not have you, but for myself I say you're as good as a virgin, and a blood relative besides. Thicker than water, eh? You want no more than a proper bedding, which your little adventure proves you anxious to receive. I'm not proud, I'll take you to wife, let the world say its worst."

"No more you will," I muttered through hard-clenched teeth. In the next instant the table top was swept aside with a crash, and my cousin on his feet, dragging me to mine.

He seized me in a horrid, suffocating embrace, mauled me about with two fat, hairy paws and breathed into my shrinking face a thick, wheezing lungful of tobacco-scented, wine-soaked breath.

Half-swooning, I yet fought with ineffectual fists for my release. The monster loosened his grip, but only to change the angle at which he held me, leaving more of my frame subject to his inspection. And not with his eyes alone did he examine me! But with eager hands he sought to undo my bodice and gain sight of what its strictures denied him. Busied thus, he failed to notice my slow recovery, until I <u>made</u> him know it! He stooped to bestow upon my bosom a noxious kiss and received a sharp bite on the nose! Alas, not sharp enough, for no blood flowed, but a torrent of curses and ugly expressions of wrath.

I took advantage of my attacker's pain and distraction to extricate myself from his hold and with trembling hands tried to restore somewhat of my customary appearance. When he saw this, he laughed. "Don't bother yourself with that business," he sneered. "I've not finished yet." In a most sinister manner he advanced, and I retreated to the utmost corner of my prison, protesting uselessly. A bully and a tyrant I called him, and other fine epithets, but it must have gone hardly with me if not for intervention of a most unexpected sort. A great noise arose at the door, a confusion of *banging, barking, scratching, scraping, howling, and I know not what else. Though loud enough to herald the arrival of a pack of hell-hounds, it proved, upon Orson's opening the door, to proceed solely from the tawny bitch. The beast rushed past him to a position that would have forced my cousin to engage with her in order to come at me. Though she is an ill-favoured brute, I admit an obligation to her for this timely interruption. A few blows quieted her and gave vent to most of my cousin's spleen. This was further relieved by his cursing Orson and demanding to know what he was about to keep such an unruly animal. And why had he not better control of it, and what meant he by unlocking the door to it and exposing my cousin to its attack?*

As he restrained the barely subdued dog, Orson seemed somewhat puzzled to defend himself and made out that the bitch was not his own, but his master's. Hadn't he seen it trotting up behind my cousin's carriage as he arrived that afternoon?

"Mine?" cried Cousin John. "Why should I saddle myself with such a wretched looking animal as that? Put it out, have it whipped from the grounds!" And that he might supervise the execution of these orders, he left me to soothe my disordered nerves and recover from his attack as best I could on my own. No apology or inquiry as to my well-being came either that day or the next, today. Only I cannot think he was successful in barring the tawny bitch from the property, for again last night I heard her constant, irritating bark.

But perhaps it is not the same dog. These disturbances have gone on ever since my arrival here, and according to Orson, the bitch came with my cousin.

~

now afternoon, I think. Cousin John has not approached me all the day. Perhaps he may be gone away again. If not, if he should once more assault me, what shall I do? How defend myself? Should I agree to marry him in order to gain some measure of freedom? I do not think that in a case of coercion, the contract would be valid. Yet I hesitate to take such a step, uninformed as I am of my rights here in England. Who could tell them to me? Who would deign to defend them? Escape is a better tack to try.

I contrived this morning to retain a damp cloth from amongst the meagre provision for my ablutions. With this I have been rubbing at the window panes, at least, as much as I could reach of them through the iron bars. Of course, a great deal of the dirt is on the outside, but I do think I have made an improvement. In one corner, I can see a bit of the landscape. From this I judge that the house in which I am confined is in a hollow, for a dingy lawn sweeps up almost to a level with this window, topped by a row of dreary firs. A road, very rough, little more than a cart track, falls gradually along this declivity, till it disappears from sight around the house's corner. All is grey and forbidding and altogether Northern in its aspect.

Forgive me, my friend, I know you love this land, even its rural solitudes. You, in your turn, are as sensitive to my longing for the smiling skies of St. Cecilia, for the loss of which you comforted me so sweetly. But now, separated alike from my home and my dear solacer, and ignorant as to how long this separation lasts—oh, my spirits are abominably low. I cannot go on writing in this vein. Besides, it grows too dark.

~

Very low. No plan as yet. My situation seems very bad, though still without sign of Cousin John. Left alone to brood on my wrongs. The food is as inedible as formerly. If it continues so, I shall not have to weigh my promise to you. Starvation will put a period to my troubles.

I try to think on happier times. It is now five days since I have been here. Allowing time for travel, and for the effects of the drugs I believe to have been administered upon me, it is perhaps not much more than a week ago that we were together.

Do you remember the delight with which you caressed my hair, likening it to rain clouds, and the weightless fluff of dandelions? How you loved to twist and smooth and braid the dark masses, remarking on their softness and compactability! And how I loved your touch there, so gentle yet so thrillingly luxurious . . . I had not known such tender attentions since the sale of my nurse, on my father's death and the breaking up of our household. It frightened me sometimes, your tenderness; it seemed but a fragile insulator for the energy of your passion. As if, the more delicate its outer expression, the deeper and more primordial its final essence. Exactly so did I find this essence, when at last it was unveiled to me. And in its echoing through the sad hollowness of my orphaned heart I heard, I felt, music, rapture, bliss! To hold with all my might this joy, and to enfold my own within it, to wrap myself around you and your fierce love, to feel you yield it to me with such voluptuous uncontrol, and in your pleasure afford me mine, oh my dearest, it was right, it was good and inevitable. My maiden hesitancies melted all away in these heated storms, as a summer downpour annihilates the hard pellets of hail strewn before it.

I know that you believe our separation to be a judgment upon us. So much I was able to divine from your hasty note, though I read it only a few times the night I received it and could not find it on waking here. I understand your assertion, but I <u>deny</u> it. We have harmed no one, have behaved only according to our natures. This time of trial is troublous, but hold fast, and it, too, shall pass. My cousin may confine, he may persecute me, but over the passage of time he can have no control. In a few short months I shall be twenty-one and mistress of my fortune. Better if I spent those months free from this confinement, but however slowly they may slip away, whatever horrors or privations I may have to endure, I will live to come of age. Nothing, then, can divide us. I will find you; I will

⁓

A carriage has come up along the road. A sound so unusual stood in need of investigation, so I ceased my writing for a moment, to see if I could catch a glimpse of the equipage. I just made out the closed top of a smart brougham, giving no hint of its occupant as it wheeled swiftly by.

I cannot contain my hope and curiosity. The sound of the carriage's movement ceased abruptly. Has it brought rescue? Another prisoner, perhaps? Perhaps — my love, could it be _you_? I am agitated; I think I hear signs of an approach —

~

So very wretched a turn things have taken, that I cannot bring myself to write for long. Dr. Martin Hesselius is the name of this new visitor; a proud, sparely fleshed man, with a Continental accent, and a cold eye, and an even colder heart. My entreaties for release engrossed him but as symptoms. He has been persuaded of my insanity, and sees in me a rare opportunity to exercise his theories on the causes of, and effective treatments for, mental disorders.

Upon examining me he was greatly surprised that I spoke the Queen's English and never seemed quite possessed of the idea that I could understand it. He made many offensive remarks on my physiognomy and physique, as of their primitive nature, and was deeply derogatory of my mother, hardly less so of my father, citing his "degenerate lust" and her "cunning animality." Any protest I uttered against his infuriating statements was made to stand at no account, except that of proving my madness.

And then, my friend, Cousin John brought in his report of our doings. It was sickening to witness the happiness with which he made sordid-seeming all that I hold in my memory as sacred. And much worse was the light in which Dr. Hesselius received these tidings. I take it now that for a woman to love a woman is more than just a crime, it is the very definition of insanity ... How shall I ever, ever win my way from here?

~

Distracted. Bitch barking throughout the entire night. Early in the morning, just at dawn, I detected the sound of a carriage leaving, but I take no heart from that. By something I overheard Martha to say to Orson, I believe Dr. Hesselius has left, but only temporarily, in order to procure some "medicines" and "instruments" for my torture — he would have it, for my cure.

~

Somewhat better now. I have had a meal, the menu of which was decided by the good Doctor: boiled lamb, finely minced, and asparagus. I had some difficulty in eating this, as I am no longer entrusted with cutlery, nor any implement more dangerous than a wooden spoon, even under the watchful eyes of my guards. The meal was not ill-prepared, though, and I did it some justice. The whole washed down with great lashings of green tea, of which, I am told, I am to have any quantity I like, this dietary regimen being a part of Dr. Hesselius' recommended course of treatment.

Three other changes are to be instituted as a result of his prescription. I learned of them through indirect means, as neither of the servants will answer my questions even now that I can call them by their names. But Orson complained to Martha of having to draw and haul the water for my baths, which I gather I am to be given daily from now on. Martha retorted that she was just as much put upon by the order to accompany me on my airings in the garden. Then there are "salts" to be administered, which I hope will prove harmless when they arrive. I believe there are other points in the Doctor's program, with which I must wait to acquaint myself till his return.

The idea of being able to walk out of doors fills me with an almost unhealthy excitement! At last, I shall be able to look about me and form some estimate of possible means of escape. To abide in my cousin's power any longer than necessary, even though he make no further advances upon me, is an uncountenanceable thought. I am not mad, to be so confined, nor a naughty, impetuous little girl. I have full and clear possession of all my faculties.

~

Just returned from my first, highly anticipated airing. It was not much in the way of what I had expected. Martha wrapped me round with a rough, woollen shawl and hurried me out to a dull little plot of grass divided by a gravel walk. Along this she proceeded to lead me back and forth, under skies in that irritating state of not-quite-rain, and between thick, tall hedges which retained just enough of last year's leaves as to make it impossible to spy out any significant features of the landscape barely glimpsed between their branches.

Still, I managed to obtain some intelligence from this outing. From the general air of dirt and neglect visible on my quick trip through the house, I am strengthened in my belief that it has probably no other inhabitants than myself, Martha, Orson, and (if he yet remains) my cousin. There is no one else, then, whose sympathies might be won to aid me in my plight. However, one may also say that there is no one else to hinder any efforts I am able to make on my own behalf.

~

My evening walk and meal differed slightly from those of earlier in the day. Celery stalks substituted for the asparagus, and a muffler made an addition to my walking _ensemble_.

As we stepped rapidly along the gravel, I noted a peculiar effect occasioned by the stems of the hedges which we passed. Lit now by the pale, watery yellow of the declining sun, they alternated with their shadows in such a manner as to produce the illusion of _something_, some animal, perhaps, keeping pace with us on the hedge's further side. It was most marked. My eyes were able to discern that the effect rose to a height somewhat equal to my waist, in a blurry, irregularly shifting mass. That it was an illusion, and not an actual animal, was proved by the precision with which it matched our speed and direction; pausing where we paused, hesitating, turning, and recommencing along with us with an exactitude not to be explained otherwise.

I amused myself by imagining to which natural laws my father would ascribe this curious phenomenon, from the wisdom accumulated through his naturalistic inquiries. He had studied thoroughly many occurrences that our islanders saw in a supernatural light, always assuring me, when I became frightened at one of old Yeyetunde's tales, that there was a rational explanation for everything to be encountered in

~

Such an uproar as there was last night! No one thought to inform me as to the cause of the hubbub, and I wracked my brains in sorting out its details, trying to see how they might be made to fit together to accompany a reasonable sequence of events.

First came the sound of an approaching carriage. Or was the noise sufficient for two? I got up and strained my eyes to look through the dark, dirty windows. There were lights, as of coach lanterns, but briefly glimpsed and not steady enough for me to count their number.

The horses halted. Muffled shouts, cries for assistance came in coarse, workmen's voices. Then a furious gabble of frightened screams, heavy crashes, and ferocious barks. Now canine, now human tongue predominated, till at length came a lull, followed by the sounds of a carriage in movement again. This soon ceased as well, so presumably the vehicle was just led round to the stables. Then came a long silence. Then the sharp report of a pistol.

Nothing further disturbed the night's calm, not even the customary plaint of the tawny bitch.

I am left to surmise that she attacked the arriving carriage, or its occupants, perhaps dislodging some heavy piece of luggage, and for her sins was shot. The sadness with which I greet this conclusion surprises me. Dogs are lowly animals, as my father taught me, unworthy of their fame as faithful, noble creatures. "A wolf," he would often say, "is somewhat noble. A dog is a debased wolf, an eater of human waste and carrion, fawning, half-civilized, wholly unreliable." The islanders, too, hold dogs in very slight esteem. Their use in the tracking of runaway slaves, perhaps, has led to their general abhorrence.

I am not sure whether any were sent after my mother. She was not a slave, because married to my father. Somehow she wandered away from the plantation and became lost. The exact circumstances leading to her death were never spoken of.

Yeyetunde, with that patient obstinance so typical of the African, said only that my mother had met her fate deep in the forest, after being missed at home for more than a day. What was she doing there? Who found her? And how came they to know where to look? I could not induce her to answer me, save with the stricture that such things were for my father to tell me, if he would.

He would not.

Oh, he spoke of my mother, and that frequently enough. Almost, I could believe his memories my own. Her beauty, her skin described in a multitude of hues such as amber, honey, and the pure light of dawn; her genius for discovering rogues and ill-wishers amongst his pretended friends; the portside hostelry where first they met; the speed and ease of her confinement and my delivery; with these I am more than familiar. They only serve to make the blankness following them less bearable.

In time I grew so used to my father's evasions and silences on the subject of my mother's death, I began to conclude that the occurrence had been excruciatingly painful, and that he omitted to recount it, not from any conscious design, but from his positive inability to do so.

Still, I learned to note one peculiarity in his responses, which, however, I am yet uncertain as to how I might interpret it. For hard upon his silences, or at the heart of any irrelevancies with which my father might choose to distract me, came the subject of dogs: their viciousness, their unruliness, and their unpredictability, especially when dealt with as a pack.

—

I grow weary of lamb. Asked of Martha if there were no other provision to be had. She answered me with stony and insolent silence.

The tea is good, and very warming after my cold immersion baths.

If last night's arrival was the doctor, or my cousin, I have neither heard from them nor received any word of their coming. How annoying to be dependent on the doings of servants for my augury of what goes on around me! Orson has been absent, all my needs being met this morning by Martha, even the toilsome task of hauling up and filling the tub for my bath. Was he injured in last night's fracas? Or perhaps another was hurt, and requires his attendance. That would make of the present an opportune moment for my escape. I wish I knew.

Gathered no further intelligence from my morning's excursion, save that the odd phenomenon of the shadow beyond the hedge seems not to confine itself to evening hours. Mentioned this to Martha, who took it just as she takes all I say: with no further notice than an evil, impertinent look. But I noted her eyes trained nervously on the blur as it accompanied us, and I believe our exercise was curtailed as a result of its effect upon her. I shall not mention it aloud again, for I grudge every step denied me. I must keep up my strength. It would not do to come upon a chance to flee and be physically incapable of taking advantage.

—

Languid all the day. This must be the consequence of my perpetually disturbed rest. The bitch is back. That expressionless bark, as of a monotonous lesson learned by rote — I cannot sleep, but I begin to think that nonetheless I dream, for words fit themselves to its untiring, evenly accented rhythms. Admonishments, warnings, injunctions to take up unclear duties, the neglect of which foreshadows danger, yet the accomplishment of which is impossible because ineluctable. The whole effect is one of unbearable tension. I rise and pace, barely able to keep myself from rattling *the barred windows, the bolted door—I <u>dare</u> not give way as I should like to do. I must remain in possession of my faculties, that I may engage the belief and sympathies of whomever I first come across on breaking free of my captivity. It may be the keeper of a nearby inn, or some pious and upright local divine; for their sakes, I must retain a rational appearance.*

I must escape while I have the wit to do so.

~

Violation! Oh, foul and unwarrantable assault! To live and endure such a burden of shame, oh, my friend, how? How can I?

My hand shakes, I have not the strength to write. But if I do not, I may be moved to relieve my outraged feeling on myself, and I have sworn to you—

I have a further thought that these words, so poorly penned, will yet stand witness to my sobriety. In order that I might give the lie to my cousin's claims as guardian of an unhinged mind, I will recount here all I recall. The sickening details—

The bed—I cannot bring myself to rest there. It is a symbol of my humiliation, with its awkward headboard and thick, stiff straps. When it arrived in my prison this afternoon, I thought I might perhaps be able to recoup some of my lost sleep, and so fight off the half-dreaming state that recently has plagued me. The straps repelled, but the thick mattress was more welcoming than my poor, vanished pallet. I had just lain down to test its softness when my gaolers made an unexpected return, wheeling with them a strange apparatus. A large, inverted glass bottle hung suspended from a tall rack. At its neck dangled a long, flexible tube, and on the end of this—oh, it is of no use, I cannot—yet, I will go on—a hard, slick nozzle, fashioned of some substance such as porcelain: white, cold; horribly cold … I fought, but Martha and Orson together managed to restrain me to the bed, strapped in so that I lay stretched out on my side. Beneath me they tucked a piece of thick, yellow oilcloth. As they did this they lifted and disarranged my skirts, and draped sheets over my head and shoulders, and also about my knees. Thus I lay with my fundament exposed, while I had no way to see anything further of what passed.

Imagine my sense of shame, then, when I heard voices approaching and recognized the tones of Dr. Hesselius and Cousin John! They entered the room discussing my case as though I had not been there. Far from protesting this rudeness, I maintained a foolish, cowardly silence. A child with her head hidden beneath the counterpane, avoiding nightmares; that is how you must picture me.

Dr. Hesselius spoke of how a host of substances he termed "mortificacious" had deposited themselves throughout my inner workings. "I deduce that they have chiefly attached themselves to the lower end of the patient's digestive system."

My cousin cleared his throat. "Mmm. Er—how did you arrive at this conclusion, sir?" He sounded a great deal embarrassed.

"You intimated that the patient's studies progressed well, exceedingly well, in fact, for one of her primitive origins. This indicates that the head's involvement is only a partial one. As the mortificacious material tends to gravitate to its victim's polar extremities—" So much I am sure he said, and a quantity of other quackish nonsense besides. My attention was distracted by a clatter nearby, as of glass and metal rattling together. Then came a liquid sound, like water running into a narrow container. I cannot convey to you the sense of unreasoning dread these noises aroused in me.

Suddenly, gloved hands seized me upon—No—seized me, I say, and I was forced—forced to accept the nozzle. My shame and confusion were such that not for several moments did I realize another's howls of pain and outrage were mingled with my own. As this was borne in upon my suffering consciousness, I subsided into sobs, listening. The other sounds quickly died down as well, though a low, near-constant menacing growl made evident their author's continued presence.

The good doctor had ceased his ministrations at the clamour's height. He now ventured to ask my cousin why he had not done as requested, and shot the d_____ bitch?

Cousin John replied that he had done so, "and at pretty near point-blank range. But the revolver must have misfired, for the beast got up and ran away, and I suppose it was only wounded."

"A wounded animal is all the more dangerous," Dr. Hesselius informed him. "I have already paid to your hell-hound my tithe of flesh. Better take care of the problem at once."

Only my cousin did not chance to have any weapon handy, so that these two brave, bold gentlemen were required to cringe in my prison with me while Orson was sent forth into the now silent passage armed with a board torn from the floor. Meanwhile, I lay in my sodden clothes, half-naked, half-suffocating in a cooling puddle of noxious liquids. After some moments, the quiet continuing, Martha was ordered to unbolt the door again and go in search of the other servant. From her hallooing and remarks subsequent upon her return, I deduced that the house appeared empty.

~

that this filthy, <u>soi-disant</u> treatment is to be inflicted weekly. I do not intend to remain a captive here for so long.

~

The hedge-haunter is no spectre, but live, flesh-and-blood. It is the tawny bitch who has followed me on my daily walks. I saw her outline quite clearly through the hedge this morning, despite the rain. Orson accompanied me; I fancy Martha has taken a dislike to her duties, or to my other escort. I know not why, for the poor beast cannot help her looks. As for temper, the only signs she has shown of that have come upon threats to my well-being. I could almost love her.

~

Walked again with Orson this evening. I made sure he noticed how marvellously close the tawny bitch was able to follow our various paces. He liked it not.

Barking commenced earlier, at sunset, long before dark. Text: How sharper than a serpent's tooth it is, to have an ungrateful child, etc., etc. Well laid arguments, but I cannot see anything apposite in the quotation. Does it contain some hint as to how I may make my escape? I must reflect on this.

~

Oh, my friend, my best and most beloved friend, soon now I shall be able to confide my heart unto your very bosom! I have quite a clear presentiment that it will be so.

This evening I was let out to accomplish my walk on my own. Martha's eyes were ever on me, it is true, as she stood in the entrance to the kitchen garden, with all the long gravel walk in her plain sight. But she could do nothing to prevent my plan.

It came to me because they would give me so much lamb. And the poor thing looked so thin, gliding along outside the hedge. And indeed she must have been quite wasted away, to have slipped through those tight-packed branches and come to me. I coaxed her to take the meat straight from my hand. Such a pet! I called her my honey, and kissed her cool, wet nose, and collared my arms about her soft, smooth-furred neck. Goat's meat would have been preferable. I remember that from Yeyetunde's teachings. It was goat's meat I placed upon her altar as a child. But the lamb was quite acceptable.

Twice more shall I make my offerings. I can hardly contain my great joy, but soon the barking will begin, so steadying to my nerves. So reassuring, to know that she is there.

~

Afternoon. This morning I have given unto her the portion brought to me to break my fast, and she has shown me the passage preparing for my escape. Thin as I am, the hole will yet need widening. My feeble hands have not been of much help. I am to leave this evening. She says she can dig all the day, and that it will be ready. Of course I shall have to crawl, and become fearfully dirty. So much the better if my light clothes are thereby darkened; they will not so easily betray me to my pursuers.

Pursuers I shall have, but she says she can distract them. I do know that she can set up an awful cacophony at will. But would she actually turn back to attack them? If so, she shall no longer fight alone. Together we will tear, we will savage

~

Editor's note: The preceding text has been assembled from a collection of fragmentary writings discovered during the demolition of an old country house. Their presentation is as complete and chronologically correct as my efforts could make it, and I have directed my publisher to use a typeface meant to evoke their author's charmingly schoolgirlish hand. The veracity of these fragments' contents, however, has proven somewhat difficult to determine.

Penmanship and internal references (Dr. Hesselius drives a brougham; oilcloth rather than a sheet of India rubber is used during the enema's application) lead to the conclusion that the events narrated took place between 1830 and 1850. This very rough estimate I narrowed a bit further by deeds and entitlements pertaining to the purchase of the property, in 1833, by a Mr. John Forrest Welkin, presumably the narrator's "Cousin John." Parish records show his death as occurring in 1844. He would, at this time, have attained forty-eight years; he was not young, but certainly he fell far short of the age at which one dies suddenly and without apparent cause, as seems to have been the case. He was single, and had no heirs of the body.

Of the locations described by the author, only this house's "high garret" is of unquestionable provenance. The papers were found secreted beneath the loose flooring of just such a bare, comfortless room. The house itself had been uninhabited for half a century, commencing early in the reign of our Queen. The place has a bad reputation in the district, as being haunted, and reports of various canine apparitions are easily obtainable at the hearths of all the neighbouring alehouses. Of course such superstitious folklore can scarcely be credited. No two "witnesses" can agree as to the size or number of the pack, though as to coloring there seems a fair consistency. To the rational mind, however, the house's situation down in Exmoor, half-way between South Molton and Lynmouth, and its less than luxurious appointments, ought to be enough to account for its long state of tenantlessness.

Turning to those proper names revealed by the text, often so fruitful of information for the careful investigator, my researches became more and more problematic. Winnywood Academy may possibly have been located in Witney, near Oxford. A relevant document, a six-year lease, apparently one in a series of such contracts, has been uncovered. It stipulates an agreement between one Madame Ardhuis and the fifth Viscount Bevercorne for the use of Winny Hall. Contemporary records also indicate a pattern of purchases by this Madame Ardhuis at stationers, chandlers, coal merchants and the like. Quantities and frequency are sufficient for the type of establishment sought.

Though the narrator writes of the "smiling skies of St. Cecilia," there is no trace of such an island in any atlas. Santa Cecilia is a small village in the mountains of Brazil (26 .56' S, 50 .27' W). Also, there is a Mount Cecilia in Northwest Australia (20 .45'S, 120 .55'E). Neither of these satisfactorily answers the description. We are left to make do with the uncomfortable knowledge that place-names do change with time, and local usage varies.

In reference to most of the persons depicted above, none but Christian names are used: Belle; John; Martha; Kitty; Belle's old nurse, Yeyetunde. Four others are referred to only by title: Father, Mother, Madame, and the document's intended reader, "my friend." The research involved in matching all these references with actual historical personages is beyond the scope of a lone amateur. Belle may have sprung from the loins of the irresponsible Hugh Farchurch, a connection of Welkin's on the distaff side. In postulating this, equating "Madame" with Madame Ardhuis, as seems reasonable, and achieving the identification of "Cousin John" with Welkin, I have done that of which I am capable.

In the case of Dr. Martin Hesselius we have a surname, and corresponding historical linkages. The doctor was well known during his professional career (1835-1871), and his presence would seem to vouch for the text's authenticity. But Hesselius' character as represented here is quite at odds with his reputation. He was known as a layer of mental disturbances, not as one who raised them into existence. Moreover, the few details of his personal appearance given us do not tally. We are left with the distinct impression that in this matter someone has been imposed upon.

Luisah's Church

Jerena hung up after listening to the on-hold loop six whole minutes. She knew those needle-sharp mini-shrieks ending each repetition were supposed to annoy her. "Well guess what? They worked," she told her mousy-grey cat. Human Services had won another round. Not hard when they made the rules.

She sat up on her futon and stretched. Lie down too long, and her pain shifted from feet to back. Shrink—well worth his food and vet bills—waited patiently as Jerena shut the case of her access point and shoved it to the side. Then he climbed onto her lap and nuzzled against the warm spot left behind. With claws mostly retracted, he kneaded her pill-strewn sweater for milk she'd never had and hoped she never would.

Not that HS clients weren't allowed pregnancies. But her lousy physical condition aside, Jerena couldn't imagine sharing this precarious existence with a dependent. A new life at the mercy of the arbitrary application of some "objective" measurement of disability. Shaped by Human Service's dictates. Warped.

Music thudded behind her head, highs dulled by the wall between her and F, the two-level apartment on that side. Hers, H, was larger than the corresponding apartment below because on Jerena's floor no hall went to F's upper half. And usually her neighbors were nice and peaceful, too, since the upper level was where they slept. But evenings, they pumped up the tunes in the mistaken belief, apparently, that this drowned out the sounds of their sex.

She looked out the drafty window at the old bank clock on the corner. Right. 5:30. The enforcers at HS had wasted her whole day making her prove her needs. Shrugging on her good green coat, stuffing a bag of breadcrumbs into one pocket, and grabbing a pair of ski poles on the way, she went carefully down the three floors—six steep flights—to sidewalk level. Holding the rail the whole time, except where she had to trade hands where the landing became the hall to F. Shoving open the nonfunctioning automatic door at the bottom and slipping through. Breathing deep the damp autumn air.

Which way?

Left, west, lay the sculpture garden. Yeah, sure. Ten blocks. Twenty, round trip. Jerena *used* to be able to walk that far; when she'd finally gotten the apartment that had been one of its main attractions, but these days, even with the afternoon's meds kicking in… Pressing her lips thin as a white woman's, she turned right.

At least the poles looked cooler than a cane. Maybe not a lot cooler, but some.

Now watch HS disallow them next time she had to buy replacements.

A patch of blue sky opened up as she entered the vacant lot one street past the drycleaner. Crows swirled off the sagging wires strung across the intersection. She saw that first. Then understood what she'd absently heard was an explosion. Then turned to see a huge cloud of smoke rising from somewhere back near her building.

Jerena had given up running a few months after her doctors told her to. Grimly she plodded back the way she'd come, sirens speeding past. By the time she reached home, they'd cordoned off the walk. She had to get to the very front of the crowd before she could see that the bomb or whatever had gone off just past her building, at the site of a long-shut-down lighting shop. So her hard-won studio apartment was safe. And Shrink would be crazy with fear, but alive.

She let relief relax her, let the Brownian motion of the people surrounding her carry her to their rear. "You all right?" The voice came from above and behind her—from a tall, East Asian-looking man with a Clark Gable haircut.

She said nothing in response, but he talked on. "You seem pretty okay, but kind of—" He hesitated. "—wooden? Shocky, maybe? I don't know you—"

"Right. You don't know me. I don't know you." She kept the words short so they wouldn't wobble with emotion.

"But we're neighbors. At least—" The man grinned and cut his eyes at the burning duplex. "—at least we *were* neighbors. That was my place they got."

He stuck out a hand and smiled. "My name's Gordon. Pleased to meet you."

Anger wiped out the treacherous residue of fear. "Are you *serious?*" Jerena clenched her poles tight, dug at the concrete. "Look at that place! It's destroyed! How can you stand here so calm and talk about nice to meet me?" She waved a fist at the ruined storefront's stinking, smoldering walls, at the fire's eerie red-orange glow like a second sunset. "Look at it! Just look!"

Gordon dropped the hand she'd igged. "Yeah. But I didn't live there. We're staying with friends up in Willow Grove."

"Oh. Sorry. Of course." Of course his "place" hadn't been his home. The glimpse she'd gotten of vévés freshly painted on the one remaining crack-webbed plate glass window should have made that plain. Now she recalled the rumors that there was going to be a branch of Luisah's Church here…but she had ignored the notices of NIMBY protest meetings those rumors sparked, since she knew she'd never have the energy to attend them. Apparently she'd also acquired the habit of ignoring the slowly accumulating signs of the church's readiness.

Belatedly Jerena realized how rude she was acting, scolding this man who'd just lost his house of worship to another of those awful bombings. Voodoo might be scary, but violence wasn't the proper response. "Sorry. I'm sorry." She transferred the right pole to her left hand and held her right out like he'd held his. He touched her palm lightly with his own.

"No problem. The elders sort of expected it. Twelve attempted attacks this year this makes, and three successful. The Church hasn't let anybody stay in the sanctuary since Christmas of '25."

Almost two years. "But—"

"Excuse me." A slender, dark-skinned woman with a satin-smooth head of hair jabbed the man's exposed ribcage. His shoulders went up, but relaxed again when he saw who'd interrupted them. "Gordon—excuse me, baby, but the officers over there need to talk to you. No, here they come—"

"Thanks, Bet." Gordon turned to meet two police shouldering their way toward him. Then paused. "This is Jerena. She lives on the third floor of 1616. Jerena, Bet is the Church's Director of Ritual." He seemed to want to say more, but he must have changed his mind.

He left. Jerena watched him greet the police like lost brothers. When had she told him her name?

"Gordon is our Outreach," Bet said, as if answering a question Jerena hadn't asked. "He's good. He'll have ideas who bombed us."

Jerena stared at her. "Isn't it obvious? The Saviors!" Everyone called the Defenders of Aryan Christianity "the Saviors" because of the motto on their logo: "Jesus Saves his Saviors."

"Can't charge a whole organization. Not without proof. Not such a big one, national. We need witnesses, collaborators, somebody been manipulated into carrying out orders against their will." Sarcasm dripped off the last phrase like compost tea.

A short but awkward silence followed.

"Look—"

"Listen—"

Both women started and stopped at the same time. Bet laughed without turning up the corners of her mouth or crinkling the edges of her long eyes. As if only she knew what was funny about the situation. Jerena met and tried to hold her glance. The woman's pupils glittered like rare brown gems. She shifted her attention away from their shine.

That just made Bet's voice stand out more. Soft, but ridged with highs and lows. "Look, any kind of clue you have about any individual—" slight stress there "—who you think would hate on Luisah's Church hard enough to plant explosives, you'd say, wouldn't you?"

A corduroy voice. Jerena wished she could run her fingers along the grooves. "Sure." She forced her thoughts back to what she'd noticed. Nothing? Her rear window had a good view of the alley, and she sat there a lot in fall and winter, soaking up the southern rays. But today she'd mostly been in the front, and she'd focused on protesting Human Services' rejection of her latest claim.

She didn't have much. HS wanted it to be less. She was going to beat them at their own game. Somehow. The prospect of the contest ahead drained the last of the adrenaline-driven strength out of her and let the familiar pain and exhaustion flood in. Up from her aching ankles it climbed. She needed a nap.

Cuddled up with Bet, she'd feel no pain.

"Listen," she began again. "You can use my apartment to, um, coordinate? My access point's not the most super powerful, but it'll help." While she still had one she might as well share it.

"Yeah, but no. We've got mobiles." Bet lifted the lanyard on which hers hung.

"Which we can keep for incoming calls if we take you up on your kind offer. Nice and close to the scene, too—the police will like that." Gordon leaned over Bet's shoulder, plucked the acid yellow lanyard from her hand to hang it back on her lovely neck, and thrust the mobile back inside the vee of her sweater. "It'll be perfect."

Jerena hadn't invited Gordon, but he was the one who'd introduced Bet. As long as she was being stupid and trusting… "Anyone else?"

"Nope. Janitor's gone for the day. Kitchen Director was supposed to start Friday. Haven't hired the rest of the staff yet."

"Yet. Friday." Bet's thick lashes swept down, her darkened lids shrouding the lamps of her soul. "Guess we'll need to cancel tomorrow's interviews."

"Reschedule them, you mean. This is a great neighborhood; we'll find somewhere even better nearby. Come on." Stopping to check in with the hovering police, Gordon steered his colleague by one shoulder to the front door of Jerena's building. She stood still where they'd left her for a moment, then caught up quickly.

Was this really a good idea? And whose was it? Had one of these surprise guests taken control of her mind with magic as some whispered was possible? She wondered about that even as she swiped her key and recited the entry code. She wondered why the thought didn't bother her more.

❧

The middle of next morning found Jerena beneath the itchy folds of a multicolored afghan, looking out over the alley. Alone. She'd given up the futon to Bet and Gordon and slept here in the kitchen, in her recliner. If they'd fucked they'd done so silently, in the middle of the night—and not during one of her frequent visits to the bathroom. When it got light enough for her to see them as she walked past, they lay sprawled on opposite sides of her bed but held hands across its black expanse.

She'd banged around in the narrow space between cupboards on one side and counter, sink, cooker, and fridge on the other then, feeding her cat, taking her morning meds, making tea, which her guests roused up and shared.

No sinister, unexplained impulses on her part. No more wondering why she'd invited them. She'd made her peace with that. It was the right thing to do whether it got her in Bet's drawers or not.

On waking they'd set up a simple altar: a bowl of water and a stick of incense on a white scarf thrown over the radiator shelf, which didn't seem at all threatening. Their prayers there were in English and actually sounded more like pop-psych affirmations than heathen hoogedy-boogedy. They'd made more calls, mostly follow-ups on yesterday's, then left—separately. Gordon was gone to take possession of a new location for the church—more expensive but bigger, and right on the sculpture garden. Bet had to run a grief circle on the old site—though the bomb had left no dead, no wounded. No casualties except dreams.

Not *her* dreams, Jerena reminded herself. Those were intact, untampered with, safely wrapped up with her in this warm nest where she'd slept. Where she rested now till she was ready to make them real.

Her reminder rang nine o'clock. Time to try calling HS again. Time to risk everything on the premise that she'd be treated like a human being instead of a set of program requirements.

She leaned the side of her head against the window and sighed. Condensing breath formed a cloud on the glass, fanning out from her lips, spreading to merge with the foggy patch above her mug. Automatically she wiped it away with her fingertips—then stopped mid-smear. Movement—a white man in overalls, shivering and rubbing his arms as he ran up the alleyway. Everything about that was suspicious. Did she know who he was? She pressed against the pane, but he'd passed from sight. Last spring she'd gotten the window open—she banged at the latch, lifted it, wrestled with the rusted-shut crank, hurting her wrist without doing any—

BANG! "Sorry!" Like the noise, Gordon's voice came from the entry. He walked in behind it and stood next to where she sat. "I had my hands full and I didn't realize—I kicked the door too hard, I guess, and it hit the—You all right?"

Jerena looked up from her poor wrist. "Sure. Maybe a sprain but nothing broken. What's in there?" She pointed an elbow at the blue net bags he carried.

"Donations. Canned stuff. The gym one block over is starting a drive. You wouldn't believe how popular we are; most Christians—"

The mysterious runner was back! "Shh!" Jerena renewed her attack on the window crank one-handed.

"What?" Gordon knelt on the seat cushion beside her. She hadn't even asked him to help but, infuriatingly, he succeeded where she'd failed. Though the crank glitched and barked like a hyena as it opened. And the running man paused and looked right up at them.

"Hey, Nesto!" Gordon shouted.

The man in the alley smiled and waved both arms, then ran off.

"You know him." Jerena collapsed backwards.

"Yeah. He's our janitor. Was. Wait! He can clean the new place—" Gordon leaned out the window again, his bangs flopping. "Nesto, we got a new home! When you want the key?"

A fading shout answered him. Jerena couldn't understand the words. Gordon's frown when he pulled his head back in looked more puzzled than angry. "He found another job."

"Overnight?" How likely was that these days? None likely.

When she returned, Bet sounded as skeptical as Jerena felt. "Not to disrespect the power of prayer alone, but we hadn't even thrown odu, let alone made appropriate offerings." Odu were divinatory verses the priests of Luisah's Church used to help choose which rituals needed performing and other decisions. Jerena knew that from listening to Bet and Gordon talk about their protection—what they had, what they could rely on, what they needed besides that.

Bet had brought back a carry-out of stewed chicken wings, fried plantains, and slaw for lunch. Jerena was relieved she didn't need to serve oatmeal again. She gave Bet a cereal-jar lid for an offering dish and willed herself to look the other way while the priest filled it with slivers of meat and vegetables and set it on the altar. None of her business. Even if this was her home.

Since there wasn't a table big enough for everyone to eat at, Jerena set the food out on the pair of boxes holding her old costumes and hand drums. Which she should have sold long ago, because she was through dancing for good. She had a hard enough time scooting the boxes out of the little closet where she kept them to in front of the futon.

"Heavy?" Gordon flipped the futon frame up into couch mode like he was closing a point shell.

"No." Realistically, they wouldn't be. For most people.

The three of them ate perched in a row on the futon's edge, Jerena in the middle.

"Yum! This is so great!" Gordon's enthusiasm plucked at her nerves like the wailing of a wet-diapered baby—someone else's. Bet's velvet-covered thigh pressed against hers in a way that could be accidental. But then it stayed there. That couldn't.

Bet's point chimed. Licking the wings' spicy brown gravy off her fingers, she tapped the pendant on her chest to answer it. No holo appeared. Like most mobiles most of the time, it was set to audio-only. "Yes?" Bet's eyes blanked. She twisted away, their thighs parting. "Sure. I understand."

Straining to hear the conversation's other end wouldn't work; Bet had a mastoid implant. Not so expensive. If Jerena's increase was approved, she might be able to afford one, too.

Bet got up and strode around the room, talking to her point. "Of course. Of course. No, waiting till Friday won't be a big deal. And it's going to stick?" Facing the futon, she rolled her eyes and grimaced. "You really think the cops or whoever will catch the bomber in time to claim the bounty? I know, but even Gordon has his limits, and he hasn't said anything about who he suspects. Don't you think involving the government before he—Well, but—Yeah, if you're so sure it's that favorable I guess we—"

Returning to her seat, Bet seemed to give up. "No, I wouldn't presume to question what she divined. No. No. Yes. I'll tell him. Odabbo." She tapped twice to disconnect and slumped against the futon's arm.

"Hartford's talking about canceling," she announced.

Gordon reached across Jerena's lap to cover Bet's hand with his own. "So the elders have invoked the policy's anti-terrorism clause."

"Yeah. There's a reward for an arrest leading to conviction of anyone attacking the Church," she explained to Jerena. "Has to be applied for within seventy-two hours of when we invoke the clause, though."

"And the government's liable for anything the insurer pays if we can prove this was a hate crime," Gordon added.

Which, of course, it was. "But what was that about 'presuming'?"

"Iyanifa herself threw the odu. She's making the right offerings, too. All we have to do is nothing till the arrest is made." Bet glared at Gordon and shook her head. "Literally, *nothing*. No trying to handle this ourselves. No work on the new facilities. We're supposed to sit tight till the bomber's caught and the bounty's collected. Even *you*, Gordon."

"Or until it's not." Gordon's expression was uncharacteristically serious.

"You want to go against odu? You want to tell our godmother she don't know how to suck eggs?"

Gordon's hand withdrew. "I suppose not."

More calls, postponing interviews till after the moratorium on action. Jerena let them use her point again. Shrink woke from his post-feed nap under the recliner. He sidled up to the nearest box, stretching to plant his forepaws on top and sniff hesitantly at Gordon's dirty plate. Jerena snatched it away and stacked it with the rest. She was dumping them in the kitchen compost bin when Gordon yelled from the other room: "Jerena—callus interruptus for yoo-ou!"

HS. Had to be—who else would try to reach her since Big Mama disowned her? And yes, the picture ID was blocked, an anonymous "public" icon filling most of her visuals, an obvious pseudonym displayed below: Terry Smith. And a number: HS1667223.

"Client designation?" asked the filtered voice.

"Jerena Crawford." She spelled both names. "Hi. I wanted to check on the status of my counterclaim—"

"Case designation?"

She hunted for the right thread. "Five-zero-three-em-why-five-sea-eight-gee-ex—no, make that ex-gee. All caps." Then she had to repeat what she'd said. Twice.

But "Terry Smith's" response the third time made it all worthwhile: "Approved."

Approved! She didn't have to pack her stuff and move—she could keep the apartment even though the rent was going up! She could buy shoes, get her teeth x-rayed, pay down the bill for her labs!

The forms she'd need to fill out verifying her acceptance of the increased stipend were available now. She smiled as she typed. An hour later, as she sent them off, she was still smiling.

She went into the front room. Gordon was looking through the window. He'd shoved the futon ninety degrees so it faced out toward the bank. The sound of the shower came from the bathroom.

"I think it was Nesto." He turned around and fixed her with an intense gaze.

"That bombed the church?"

"Yeah. Don't you?"

Maybe. "Have you told the police?"

"What if they're involved somehow? A couple of Savior sites claim cops are members."

The bathroom door popped open. Only a few inches. Steamy air billowed out into the cool dryness—and a scent Jerena couldn't quite name. It seemed out of context: sweet, hot, exciting in a way that evaded immediate identification.

Christmas morning? "What's that I smell?" she asked Gordon.

Bet pushed the door wider and walked through. "*Zingiber officinale,*" she answered. A clean sheet swaddled her in pink spots and yellow flowers. "AKA, ginger. I rinsed with a decoction. Part of my daily spiritual regime."

"You had ginger with you?"

"Keep it in my purse."

A plain pillowcase wrapped Bet's head. On her it looked stylish. She bent over the neat stack of her clothing. "My stuff gettin in your way?"

As long as Jerena had a way, she wanted Bet in it. "Not much."

"We probably need to be headin back up to where we been stayin. When I talked to Alma earlier, they expected us home tonight."

"I told the police that if they wanted to ask me anything, they'd find me here," said Gordon.

"You think we should split up?" Jerena sure did. But by the half she heard of Bet's next call, it would be the wrong one going back to their friends' house. The wrong one staying.

Gordon took his turn in the shower. Bet donned her pants—commando—and bra underneath the sheet, then tossed that aside and picked up her fuzzy scarlet sweater. She held it against her rich, brown skin but didn't move to put it on. "When we allowed to start prepping the new space Friday, you could help."

Friday would be the thirteenth. Jerena wasn't the least bit superstitious. "You want me to?" She wished she'd had the courage to leave off that last word. To compensate, she let her voice grow low and husky.

Bet's nearly straight eyebrows arched. She lowered the sweater. "You want me to want you?"

The downstairs doorbell buzzed. In the front room, Jerena's point chimed. Great timing.

She went to answer the call, glancing on her way at the tiny monochrome feed off the building's security camera. The feed never showed much, even when it worked. Enough so she could tell when there was more than one person was about all.

"Expecting anybody? The cops?" she asked.

"No. But who ever does? I'll get Gordon."

Jerena stabbed at the door's antiquated physical interface. For a wonder, its two-way speaker clicked on. "Hello? Who's there?"

"Police. A few more questions for your guests, Ms. Crawford?"

If she didn't let them in, the manager would, or another tenant. And non-cooperation would look bad to HS. She stabbed again at the interface to release the lock. "Come on up."

Her point quit chiming. She'd check for a message later. She slid off the door's chain and undid the deadbolt. Fast steps on the stairway—were they running up? Sounded like more than the two the camera'd caught.

Bet had come to hover at her shoulder.

"Gordon getting dressed?"

"No. He's not in there."

"What?" That made no sense. She'd have to have more of an explanation. Maybe go see for herself. The cops knocked. A cane rested against the bank of cupboards walling off the kitchen. She grabbed it as a prop.

She put her free hand on the knob but the door was already opening. Two men, two women. Two white…ish, two black. Two in uniform, two plainclothes. She recognized the uniforms as having been at the blast site.

Lady Plainclothes identified herself and her colleagues as they crowded in. Jerena wasn't sure she got all their names exactly. And especially the spelling: Sweeny and Kline from yesterday wore their badges. But the pair of detectives she'd never seen before were Gratton and Prucher? Grafton and Plutchak?

Not enough room on the futon, not enough chairs for everyone to sit. Jerena knew she couldn't drag the recliner to the front room by herself, knew she wouldn't ask anyone to help her. Then it didn't matter. Kline and Grassfed moved her into the kitchen to "take her statement." Which meant listening to her stammer through the same non-events twice, then twice more, correcting her natural omissions and errors, cross-examining her like she'd actually seen something.

An hour must have passed. More. Where was Gordon? It shouldn't have taken him this long to emerge from the bathroom. Had what Bet said been right?

She levered herself out of the recliner. "I have to pee."

"Whoa!" Kline lurched away from the counter where she'd been lounging.

"No, it's all right." Prunetang and Bet appeared in the apartment's entryway, his doughy hand resting too casually on her collarbone. "Sweeny and I are taking Ms. Ortiz to the station for a line-up." He didn't say whether she'd be looking at the line-up or in it. "When her boyfriend—"

"*Friend,*" Bet interjected.

Prunetang's hand squeezed down hard. "Friend, sure. When Mr. Lim returns, let him know we'd like to see him there, too."

So then Gordon must actually and truly be gone.

"What about our reports?" Kline asked.

"Give em to me. I'll file em."

Jerena's two cops popped a media bead each out of their bulky pocket points and handed them over. Grassfed loaded them into a holder. He hesitated before transferring his own and looked at her expectantly. "You got anything you suddenly feel like telling us?"

She did, but she wasn't going to blow her hard-won approval slinging insults. She shook her head no.

By the time she'd shut the door on them and watched them walk out of the security camera's range, she really did have to pee. And the bathroom really was empty.

Above the splash of water as she washed her hands, she heard her point chiming. Again—she'd forgotten about the call before the cops came. She tottered over to answer it, stiffness a delayed reaction to the stillness she'd forced on herself under their eyes, dried her wet fingers on the futon cover, and answered despite the "Undisclosed" locater tag.

"Is Bet there?" Gordon.

"Where are you?"

"I don't have time! Just put her on. Is she there?"

"No—she went with the cops to—"

"Did they arrest her?"

"Not yet, far as I know. Was that you earlier?"

"What? When?" The point squealed, over-amplifying him. Or else he was yelling. "Answer me! Where's her point? She wouldn't answer—did they take it?"

"I mean was that you calling me. Did you call me? Before this?"

"I shouldn't be calling you now." The point went dead. She tilted it and twisted it around and tried to re-establish the connection. No cigar.

Evidently, with the cops gone Shrink judged it safe to come out. He batted fiercely at the loose tape dangling from her widest costume box, shredding it and the cardboard it held together. "Hey, man," she warned him. He stalked away as if in obedience, then whirled to execute a spectacular two-meter pounce, landing on the box's lid. Which immediately gave way.

He only dropped half a handbreadth, since the box was mostly full. That was enough to send him spitting and snarling and running around like a starved games contestant. Her saffron silk trailed after him, snagged on his claws. Worse, he'd knocked her jewelry-making basket onto the carpet, spilling charms and loose gems and tiny clasps to disappear into its pile.

With a moan Jerena lowered herself to the floor. Sometimes doing this sort of thing was fine. Sometimes, like now, it was not.

Her point sang its "message waiting" song, all the way up on the futon. It must be from that call she kept forgetting. Since she was already down there, she finished taking care of Shrink's mayhem first, then hauled herself high enough to reach her point.

The call had been HS. They'd left both text and audio. She read and played them simultaneously. Her approval was revoked. There would be no increase in her monthly stipend.

Why? She checked and checked again for attachments that would give reasons, links to rules she'd unintentionally broken. Only the usual appeals form had been sent. She began to fill it out but had to stop when she couldn't see through her tears.

Her rent was going up. Where were she and Shrink supposed to live? She tried so hard. What else was she going to have to do without?

She made herself get up and go to the bathroom for toilet paper to blow her nose. Which reminded her that Gordon had vanished. Figuring out how and where would be a helpful distraction from self-pity.

She tugged a curtain away from the window over the laundry hamper. Sure enough, the paint that used to seal it shut was cracked. This was the building's third story, though. Had he jumped? Without getting hurt? Jerena raised the window—still tough—and leaned out to look for—what? A ladder? A trampoline? Nothing but the gravel and patched asphalt of the alley lay directly below her. But down and to the right she saw the gentle slope of the awning covering the balcony of the two-level apartment beside hers. She judged the leap possible for someone fit as Gordon, fit as she had been, and yes, a suggestive smudge in the dirt just *there* supported her theory. Another three or four meters from the balcony to the ground; no spookiness required.

Okay. He'd booked out the window, and just about the same time the police arrived. Why?

Jerena pulled her head back inside. Familiar thumping filtered through the bathroom wall; the open window let in her neighbors' music's higher, wheedling overtone. And their stupid pre-coital laughter. She shuddered. If she had to leave, she wouldn't miss that. Time for a walk.

Today she headed left out of the front door. No poles, she realized as it snapped shut behind her—but no way she was going back up to get them. She wouldn't make it to the garden, but so what? Four blocks west and south was an open-air market. She could sit on a stoop and watch the last of the fall's stall-keepers pack up for the night till it was safe to go home.

But a drizzle started as she crossed Pearl. Before she reached Maxwell, it settled into a steady, miserable rain. The few merchants left this late into autumn were cutting their losses and closing early. As Jerena peered out from a partially roofed dumpster shelter, a final van drove off in a spray of dingy puddle water.

Maybe she'd better get used to being wet. Get used to freezing, actually, unless she could stretch her income, somehow put off eviction till March or April. Or ask Big Mama or her old friends for help—the friends she'd deliberately lost track of when the diagnoses commenced to rolling in.

She'd appeal, of course. She'd also have to plan for losing.

The rain came down harder. At least she had a hat on. Cold drops formed along its brim and fell, soaking into her jacket. The smell of decaying Brussels sprouts made itself all too evident. And something else—

"Don't look at me." Gordon's voice. Nearby. She felt his breath on her neck—its odor was what she'd detected beneath the overwhelming vegetable rot.

"I'm not. Not looking. Where are you? So I can be careful to avoid it." She kept her eyes focused straight ahead.

"You're doing fine. Probably no one's watching, but in case they are, I don't want you to even nod your head."

"Sure." Outreach my flat ass, she thought. Some kind of spy, that's what this creep was. Crawling out the window. She remembered that he'd known her name and address.

"In a few more minutes, after a sufficient wait for me to get a head start, you're going to the church. I've got the keys. I'll let you in. If you notice anybody following, you go home instead."

"But it's a burnt down—wait, you mean the new one?" No answer. She chanced a look around to where she thought he was. Had been. No one there. A gap between the shed's loose boards and the brick wall behind them could have held him, but it didn't.

Should Jerena do what he'd said to? Maybe she could connect with Bet through him—or maybe the police would set Bet free to return to the apartment. Or charge her—and who would hear about that? Gordon.

The rain let up as she stepped out of the shelter. She turned toward the side street Gordon had mentioned when telling Bet about the advantages of the new place. Apparently Jerena was off to meet him.

⌐

Lights shrouded in mist shone in at the high, blind windows. Between bars of washed-out brightness, darkness marked the room's floor in large, indistinct rectangles. Gordon's hand, glowing seashell pink with contained fire, floated slowly away from the shut door. He spoke over his shoulder to her as he carried his candle toward the building's back. "This is really a much more suitable space. Plenty of room to drum and dance. We'll put paper on the walls so we can draw the veves there instead of on ground-level windows. And no one can see in."

Or see out, Jerena thought.

"Careful on the stairs." Gordon stood at the top of a short flight leading up to a low stage. "Here's where they had readings, slams, acoustic groups, entertainment stuff like that for people who wanted more than books." She followed him to the rear of the stage. "And here's where they did their invoice processing and bookkeeping and so on." He slid aside an accordion-pleated wall of beige plastic. "Perfect for private consultations. One step down."

Setting the glassed candle on an empty desk, Gordon grinned. "I'm guessing you're full of questions."

"Yes."

"Well…where to start? You've figured out my work involves a little more than getting along with the community."

"Like stalking me to find out where I live and—"

"I wouldn't exactly call it 'stalking'—"

"—and my name and who knows what else."

"Research."

"Research," she repeated. "And avoiding the cops by escaping out of my bathroom window. And—and luring me here." A nervous twitch of her head back toward the door. The path was clear. But he would beat her to it in a race. Anyone would.

"I got a call from Bet. Coded."

"When? Is she okay?" Suddenly the cold room seemed colder.

"Coded, like I said. They're arresting her. Accusing her of planting the bomb."

"But she wouldn't! She didn't…" Jerena trailed off. How could she know that?

"I'm thinking this is just a ploy to get me there, grab me, put me in custody. What they were asking me the day it went off… They know about my background in Special Forces."

Jerena hadn't. "So turn yourself in and get her out." Silence. "If you're innocent—" The look of exasperation Gordon threw her over the flickering candle shut her up. She tried again. "If you're—"

"Of course I'm innocent! I *told* you it was Nesto."

"Then—"

"There's no guarantee they'd let one of us loose because they caught the other. Come on."

She nodded. "But if you gave them Nesto, they'd be satisfied."

"Not if *I* did. You."

"Me?" Jason Bourne she was not. Lord Peter Wimsey even.

"You have no ulterior motives. Not a church member, not in a relationship with Bet. Nothing tempting you except maybe the bounty. Which, if my information's right, you could use?"

Goddammit. "How much?"

"Twenty thousand."

Almost a year's rent at the new rate. "Hells yeah. Anybody could use that." She unclenched her hands. A tell for her desire. "What do you need?"

⌖

He needed her to do his dirty work. He had a plan. She went along with it till it was time to improvise.

For two more days Gordon continued elusive, but he managed to call Jerena from "undisclosed" points several times, reassuring her over and over that she was doing what needed to be done and updating her on Bet.

No one posted her bail. That was forbidden by the odu as the church's elders interpreted it, according to Gordon. No one was allowed to visit her in jail. Not even Jerena, who after all wasn't a member.

"It wouldn't look right for you to go," he told her. "Why? They'd want to understand the connection. They'd tighten up their surveillance—"

"Wait—they're watching me already?"

"So? You're not committing any crimes, are you?"

In fact, Jerena spent her days shopping for curtains and supervising paint crews. Haunting sculpture galleries. Completely innocuous activities. Wednesday afternoon the bomber showed up of his own volition, as Gordon had promised he would.

A beanied head peeked around the doorway to the back room where she'd rendezvoused with Gordon. "Ma'am?"

She hated being "ma'amed." Not even HS called her that. She suppressed the feeling. "Yes?"

"They told me I'd find you here, and you were the one in charge. But actually I was looking for Gordon to tell him my other job didn't—well, I had to quit. So if there's gonna be a custodian position here like I had at the church before, I wanna ask if I could be considered. You know? Any idea if he's hired anyone else yet?"

"He hasn't." True enough.

She got Ernesto Penderson to fill out some employment forms for show's sake, and then took him to her apartment. Ostensibly this was so he'd carry back her costume boxes full of fabrics and gems for decorating the newly built altars. The main purpose, as Gordon had explained, was to convince him he'd won her trust.

She received acknowledgment of her appeal from HS. "Let's hold our breath," she said to Shrink, picking him up and stroking him, crown to tail. "You first." He purred and nipped her forearm instead.

Thursday Jerena found what might be a genuine Nevelson in a formerly trendy Pine Street auction warehouse. The doll arms and carved letters seemed right, but the heavy chain wrapping its waspish midsection seemed wrong. Her ex would have known. All Jerena was able to do was buy it cheap, bargain for delivery, and tell Nesto to haul the heavy wooden assemblage off the truck and into the church. She had him set it against the stage's back wall, and was pleased to notice he took plenty of time doing it. She borrowed some white from the painters to cover a couple of unfortunate black strips like skid marks left by bicycle tires. It took more than one coat.

She had Nesto push the piece a little further right, toward the stage's northern edge. It looked good there. The whole place looked good. Strings of tiny bells intertwined with twinkling lights and slowly twirling leaf-shapes gave the ceiling a sky-like depth, and the leaves' stirring caused the bells to ring randomly. Pews, and benches salvaged from train stations formed a square around a central dance floor. And on the stage's shallow proscenium stood seven altars, each decked with fabric in what she hoped the congregants to come would deem appropriate colors: deepest blue, green and black, white and crimson, red and black, gold and green, white on cream, and magenta covered in a scattering of mirrored rainbows.

It looked beyond good. It looked great.

Jerena had studied more than color schemes, and she'd come to admire the tenets of Luisah's Church as she learned them. She liked how everyone was responsible for their own spiritual growth, setting their own pace, tracking their own progress. It seemed so practical. And not one word about only being given burdens she was fit to bear. Which Big Mama had always said when claiming Jerena's illness came from Jesus. Perhaps, after Jerena kept the church from getting blown up, she'd join it.

She'd ask Bet how.

Thursday evening, Nesto asked if she'd let him stay overnight on a cot in the de facto office she'd established. "Just till I can move into my new room. The guy I'm subletting from is spozed to take off by noon Friday." Five hours before the bounty expired. He'd be counting on any investigation to begin there, on a cold, dead trail.

She gave Nesto permission to put up his cot, walked home, fed Shrink, took her evening meds. Waited for Gordon's call.

It came close to midnight. She told him about Nesto's request.

"Sounds like this is it." The cheap, anonymous image in her visual field didn't even pretend to open its mouth in sync with Gordon's speech. "You should get back there right away."

She knew it had to be her because of the church elders' temporary taboo against action, besides the reasons Gordon had given. Anyway, the plan now was for him to turn himself in. She'd protested—weakly, but she had—when he got to that part of the proceedings. "How else can I prove it isn't me?" he'd asked, and that silenced her.

Jerena had nothing against winning a twenty-thousand-dollar reward, either. But as she returned to the church through the dark streets she wished she'd brought someone else with her. Bet, of course. Small but fierce, she'd be. Or even her ex. Big Mama. Anyone.

An alley like the one behind her apartment. Darker darkness. The coal cellar no one had used for maybe a century was ostensibly a secret, the rusty steel door that led from there to the rest of the interior clumsily sheetrocked over. Jerena had dropped a few hints as to its existence in Nesto's hearing. Those had been taken, judging by the faint light coming through the cellar door's loose planks. Jerena peeked between them. Shadows shifted around meaninglessly. She shrugged to herself. Somebody was in there—probably Nesto. If not him, another attacker. She found the greased bar she'd hidden among the tall weeds and slid it into staples fastened to the exterior's double doors on either side.

Then she went in at the front. Quietly, cloth tied to the ski poles' tips, she crossed the main room and opened the office door. An empty cot greeted her. Well then.

Back out to the stage. Yes, upon examination it seemed the Nevelson had been shoved forward and aside to gain access to the coal cellar's badly disguised door. Before her illness she could have simply shoved the sculpture into place again and trapped Nesto in the cellar, surrounded by bomb-planting supplies and obviously guilty. That had more or less been Gordon's idea—using a heavy sculpture of some sort—and she hadn't told him why it wouldn't work. Because she was such a proud fucking idiot.

She laid down her poles and inched into the gap sideways. The naked door yawned open before her like the way down to a crypt. No rubble to trip on—he would have hidden that below. Was any of the debris piled high enough to block the door? Jerena pulled the door to test it. No. It moved toward her easily. But noisily.

A moment's hush was quickly followed by a startled "Hey!" Work fast. Jerena undid a length of the sculpture's painted chain and threaded it in and out of the holes where the door's knob and deadbolt used to be. Slammed it shut. Scrambling steps climbed the stairs behind it. On the end of the chain she held was a giant hook. She drove that through one of the chain's links with blows from her bare fist. Blood seeped from ragged cuts.

"Let me out! That you? Cunt!" The door jerked. The chain tightened. The Nevelson scraped doorward an inch, knocking her against the wall. "Bitch!" Rhythmic jerks matched an obscene chant beat for beat. "Cunt! Bitch! Slut! Whore! Chinga! Culo! Fucker! Bruja!" Dragging the Nevelson tighter to the wall, ramming her, smashing her, crushing her with every curse. She sucked in dust-filled air and grunted it out before she could scream. The pain—she had to fight free of it. Had to squeeze herself between the swear words and not care how much it hurt or she would never hurt again.

She lost all feeling in her feet and fell. More room! The sculpture was warped, its bottom slightly further from the back wall than its top. Like a snake, Jerena wriggled from behind the Nevelson. For seconds she lay gasping as if dying of asthma, sweat stinging her eyes, tears and snot pooling under her head.

The muffled yells ceased.

Worry hovered over her, landed. What was Nesto doing? He wasn't going to get out by himself unless he had a—could he trigger the bomb? The first one had had a crude timer, Gordon said. This one would be pretty similar— Would he cut the fuse or whatever if it meant killing himself too?

She couldn't walk. Her feet were numb—her entire legs, knee down.

She hadn't brought her point, but there was an emergency unit in the office. She crawled. She got there. She reached the police. They came. Nothing more that was bad happened that night.

～∽～

Luisah's Church opened at its new location in time for Samhain. Which as Jerena pointed out was hardly a traditional Vodun holiday.

"Convert," Bet accused her. But she smiled and clasped Jerena's hands in her lap.

Sitting on the same bench on Bet's other side, Gordon expounded on Vodun's innate syncretism. But soon the drums drowned him out. And soon after that, the three of them were swaying and singing, snapping and clapping, dancing reverently in place, right where they wanted to be.

Cruel Sistah

"You and Neville goin out again?"

"I think so. He asked could he call me Thursday after class."

Calliope looked down at her sister's long, straight, silky hair. It fanned out over Calliope's knees and fell almost to the floor, a black river drying up just short of its destined end. "Why don't you let me wash this for you?"

"It takes too long to dry. Just braid it up like you said, okay?"

"Your head all fulla dandruff," Calliope lied. "And ain't you ever heard of a hair dryer? Mary Lockett lent me her portable."

"Mama says those things bad for your hair." Dory shifted uncomfortably on the sofa cushion laid on the hardwood floor where she sat. Dory (short for Dorcas) was the darker-skinned of the two girls, darker by far than their mama or their daddy. "Some kinda throwback," the aunts called her.

Mama doted on Dory's hair, though, acting sometimes as if it was her own. Not too surprising, seeing how good it was. Also, a nervous breakdown eight years back had made Mama completely bald. Alopecia was the doctor's word for it, and there was no cure. So Mama made sure both her daughters took care of their crowning glories. But especially Dory.

"All right, no dryer," Calliope conceded. "We can go out in the back garden and let the sun help dry it. Cause in fact, I was gonna rinse it with rainwater. Save us haulin it inside."

Daddy had installed a flexible hose on the kitchen sink. Calliope wet her sister's hair down with warm jets of water, then massaged in sweet-smelling shampoo. White suds covered the gleaming black masses, gathering out of nowhere like clouds.

Dory stretched her neck and sighed. "That feels nice."

"Nice as when Neville kisses you back there?"

"Ow!"

"Or over here?"

"OW! Callie, what you doin?"

"Sorry. My fingers slipped. Need to trim my nails, hunh? Let's go rinse off."

Blood from the cuts on her neck and ear streaked the shampoo clouds with pink stains. Unaware of this, Dory let her sister lead her across the red and white linoleum to the back porch and the creaky wooden steps down to the garden. She sat on the curved cement bench by the cistern, gingerly at first. It was surprisingly warm for spring. The sun shone, standing well clear of the box elders crowding against the retaining wall at the back of the lot. A silver jet flew high overhead, bound for SeaTac. The low grumble of its engines lagged behind it, obscuring Calliope's words.

"What?"

"I said, 'Quit sittin pretty and help me move this lid.'"

The cistern's cover came off with a hollow, grating sound. A slice of water, a crescent like the waning moon, reflected the sun's brightness. Ripples of light ran up the damp stone walls. Most of the water lay in darkness, though. Cold smells seeped up from it: mud, moss. Mystery.

As children, Dory, Calliope, and their cousins had been fascinated by the cistern. Daddy and Mama had forbidden them to play there, of course, which only increased their interest. When their parents opened it to haul up water for the garden, the girls hovered close by, snatching glimpses inside.

"Goddam if that no-good Byron ain't lost the bucket!" Calliope cursed the empty end of the rope she'd retrieved from her side of the cistern. It was still curled where it had been tied to the handle of the beige plastic bucket.

Byron, their fourteen-year-old cousin, liked to soak sticks and strips of wood in water to use in his craft projects. He only lived a block away, so he was always in and out of the basement workshop. "You think he took it home again?" Dory asked.

"No, I remember now I saw it downstairs, fulla some trash a his, tree branches or somethin."

"Yeah? Well, that's all right, we don't wanna—"

"I'll go get it and wipe it out good. Wait for me behind the garage."

"Oh, but he's always so upset when you mess with his stuff!"

"It ain't his anyhow, is it?" Calliope took the porch steps two at a time. She was a heavy girl, but light on her feet. Never grew out of her baby fat. Still, she could hold her own in a fight.

The basement stairs, narrow and uneven, slowed her down a bit. Daddy had run a string from the bare-bulb fixture at their bottom, looping it along the wooden wall of the stairwell. She pulled, and the chain at its other end slithered obediently against porcelain, clicked and snapped back. Brightness flooded the lowering floor joists.

Calliope ignored the beige bucket full of soaking willow wands. Daddy's tool bench, that's where she'd find what she wanted. Nothing too heavy, though. She had to be able to lift it. And not too sharp. She didn't want to have to clean up a whole lot of blood.

Hammer? Pipe wrench? What if Mama got home early and found Calliope carrying one of those out of the house? What would she think?

It came to her with the same sort of slide and snap that had turned the light on. Daddy was about to tear out the railroad ties in the retaining wall. They were rotten; they needed replacing. It was this week's project. The new ones were piled up at the end of the driveway.

Smiling, Calliope selected a medium-sized mallet, its handle as long as her forearm. And added a crowbar for show.

Outside, Dory wondered what was taking her sister so long. A clump of shampoo slipped down her forehead and along one eyebrow. She wiped it off, annoyed. She stood up from the weeds where she'd been waiting, then quickly knelt down again at the sound of footsteps on the paving bricks.

"Bend forward." Calliope's voice cracked. Dory began twisting her head to see why. The mallet came down hard on her right temple. It left a black dent in the suds, a hollow. She made a mewing sound, fell forward. Eyes open, but blind. Another blow, well-centered, this time, drove her face into the soft soil. One more. Then Calliope took control of herself.

"You dead," she murmured, satisfied.

A towel over her sister's head disguised the damage. Hoisting her up into a sitting position and leaning her against the garage, Calliope hunkered back to look at her and think. No one was due home within the next couple of hours. For that long, her secret would be safe. Even then she'd be all right as long as they didn't look out the kitchen windows. The retaining wall was visible from there, but if she had one of the new ties tamped in place, and the dirt filled back in…

A moment more she pondered. Fast-moving clouds flickered across the sun, and her skin bumped up. There was no real reason to hang back. Waiting wouldn't change what she'd done.

The first tie came down easily. Giant splinters sprung off as Calliope kicked it to one side. The second one, she had to dig the ends out, and the third was cemented in place its full length by dried clay. Ants boiled out of the hundreds of holes that had been hidden behind it, and the phone rang.

She wasn't going to answer it. But it stopped and started again, and she knew she'd better.

Sweat had made mud of the dirt on her hands. She cradled the pale blue princess phone against one shoulder, trying to rub the mess clean on her shirt as she listened to Mama asking what was in the refrigerator. The cord barely stretched that far. Were they out of eggs? Butter? Lunch meat? Did Calliope think there was enough cornmeal to make hush puppies? Even with Byron coming over? And what were she and Dory up to that it took them so long to answer the phone?

"Dory ain't come home yet. No, I don't know why; she ain't tole me. I was out in back, tearin down the retaining wall."

Her mother's disapproving silence lasted two full seconds. "Why you always wanna act so mannish, Calliope?"

There wasn't any answer to that. She promised to change her clothes for supper.

Outside again, ants crawled on her dead sister's skin.

Dory didn't feel them. She saw them, though, from far off. Far up? What was going on didn't make regular sense. Why couldn't she hear the shovel digging? Whoever was lying there on the ground in Dory's culottes with a towel over her head, it was someone else. Not her.

She headed for the house. She should be hungry. It must be supper time by now. The kitchen windows were suddenly shining through the dusk. And sure enough, Calliope was inside already, cooking.

In the downstairs bathroom, Daddy washed his hands with his sleeves rolled up. She kissed him. She did; on his cheek, she couldn't have missed it.

The food look good, good enough to eat. Fried chicken, the crisp ridges and golden valleys of its skin glowing under the ceiling light. Why didn't she want it? Her plate was empty.

Nobody talked much. Nobody talked to her at all. There were a lot of leftovers. Cousin Byron helped Calliope clear the table. Daddy made phone calls, with Mama listening in on the extension. She could see them both at the same time, in the kitchen and in their bedroom upstairs. She couldn't hear anything.

Then the moon came out. It was bedtime, a school night. Everyone stayed up, though, and the police sat in the living room and moved their mouths till she got tired of watching them. She went in the backyard again, where all this weird stuff had started happening.

The lid was still off the cistern. She looked down inside. The moon's reflection shone up at her, a full circle, uninterrupted by shadow. Not smooth, though. Waves ran through it, long, like swirls actually. Closer, she saw them clearly: hairs. Her hairs, supple and fine.

Suddenly, the world was in daylight again. Instead of the moon's circle, a face covered the water's surface. Her sister's face. Calliope's. Different, and at first Dory couldn't understand why. Then she realized it was her hair, *her* hair, Dory's own. A thin fringe of it hung around her big sister's face as if it belonged there. But it didn't. Several loose strands fell drifting towards Dory. And again, it was night.

And day. And night. Time didn't stay still. Mostly, it seemed to move in one direction. Mama kept crying; Daddy too. Dory decided she must be dead. But what about heaven? What about the funeral?

Byron moved into Dory's old room. It wasn't spooky; it was better than his mom's house. There, he could never tell who was going to show up for drinks. Or breakfast. He never knew who was going to start yelling and throwing things in the middle of the night: his mom, or some man she had invited over, or someone else she hadn't.

Even before he brought his clothes, Byron had kept his instruments and other projects here. Uncle Marv's workshop was wonderful, and he let him use all his tools.

His thing now was gimbris, elegant North African ancestors of the cigar-box banjos he'd built two years ago when he was just beginning, just a kid. He sat on the retaining wall in the last, lingering light of the autumn afternoon, considering the face, neck, and frame of his latest effort, a variant like a violin, meant to be bowed. He'd pieced it together from the thin trunk of an elder tree blown down in an August storm, sister to the leafless ones still upright behind him.

The basic structure looked good, but it was kind of plain. It needed some sort of decoration. An inlay, ivory or mother of pearl or something. The hide backing was important, obviously, but that could wait; it'd be easier to take care of the inlay first.

Of course, real ivory would be too expensive. Herb David, who let him work in his guitar shop, said people used bone as a substitute. And he knew where some was. Small bits, probably from some dead dog or rabbit. They'd been entangled in the tree roots. He planned to make tuning pegs out of them. There'd be plenty, though.

He stood up, and the world whited out. It had been doing that a lot since he moved here. The school nurse said he had low blood pressure. He just had to stand still a minute and he'd be okay. The singing in his ears, that would stop, too. But it was still going when he got to the stairs.

Stubbornly, he climbed, hanging onto the handrail. Dory's—his—bedroom was at the back of the house, overlooking the garden. His mom kept her dope in an orange juice can hung under the heat vent. He used the same system for his bones. No one knew he had them; so why was he afraid they'd take them away?

He held them in his cupped palms. They were warm, and light. The shimmering whiteness had condensed down to one corner of his vision. Sometimes that meant he was going to get a headache. He hoped not. He wanted to work on this now, while he was alone.

When he left his room, though, he crossed the hall into Calliope's instead of heading downstairs to Uncle Marv's workshop. Without knowing why, he gazed around him. The walls were turquoise, the throw rugs and bedspread pale pink. Nothing in here interested him, except—that poster of Wilt Chamberlain her new boyfriend, Neville, had given her...

It was signed, worth maybe one hundred dollars. He stepped closer. He could never get Calliope to let him anywhere near the thing when she was around, but she took terrible care of it. It was taped to the wall all crooked, sort of sagging in the middle.

He touched the slick surface—slick, but not smooth—something soft and lumpy lay between the poster and the wall. What? White light pulsed up around the edges of his vision as he lifted one creased corner.

Something black slithered to the floor. He knelt. With the whiteness, his vision had narrowed, but he could still see it was nothing alive. He picked it up.

A wig! Or at least part of one. Byron tried to laugh. It was funny, wasn't it? Calliope wearing a wig like some old bald lady? Only...only it was so weird. The bones. This—hair. The way Dory had disappeared.

He had to think. This was not the place. He smoothed down the poster's tape, taking the wig with him to the basement.

He put the smallest bone in a clamp. It was about as big around as his middle finger. He sawed it into oblong disks.

The wig hair was long and straight. Like Dory's. It was held together by shriveled-up skin, the way he imagined an Indian's scalp would be.

What if Calliope had killed her little sister? It was crazy, but what if she had? Did that mean she'd kill him if he told on her? Or if she thought he knew?

And if he was wrong, he'd be causing trouble for her, and Uncle Marv, and Aunt Cookie, and he might have to go live at home again.

Gradually, his work absorbed him, as it always did. When Calliope came in, he had a pile of bone disks on the bench, ready for polishing. Beside them, in a sultry heap, lay the wig, which he'd forgotten to put back.

Byron looked up at his cousin, unable to say anything. The musty basement was suddenly too small. She was three years older than him, and at least 30 pounds heavier. And she saw it, she had to see it. After a moment, he managed a sickly smirk, but his mouth stayed shut.

"Whatchoodoon?" She didn't smile back. "You been in my room?"

"I—I didn't—"

She picked it up. "Pretty, ain't it?" She stroked the straight hair, smoothing it out. "You want it?"

No clue in Calliope's bland expression as to what she meant. He tried to formulate an answer just to her words, to what she'd actually said. Did he want the wig. "For the bow I'm makin, yeah, sure, thanks."

"Awright then."

He wished she'd go away. "Neville be here tonight?"

She beamed. It was the right question to ask. "I guess. Don't know what he sees in me, but the boy can't keep away."

Byron didn't know what Neville saw in her either. "Neville's smart," he said diplomatically. It was true.

So was he.

There was more hair than he needed, even if he saved a bunch for restringing. He coiled it up and left it in his juice can. There was no way he could prove it was Dory's. If he dug up the backyard where the tree fell, where he found the bones, would the rest of the skeleton be there?

The police. He should call the police, but he'd seen Dragnet, and Perry Mason. When he accepted the wig, the hair, he'd become an accessory after the fact. Maybe he was one even before that, because of the bones.

It was odd, but really the only time he wasn't worried about all this was when he worked on the gimbri. By Thanksgiving, it was ready to play.

He brought it out to show to Neville after dinner. "That is a seriously fine piece of work," said Neville, cradling the gimbri's round leather back. "Smaller than the other one, isn't it?" His big hands could practically cover a basketball. With one long thumb he caressed the strings. They whispered dryly.

"You play it with this." Byron handed him the bow.

He held it awkwardly. Keyboards, reeds, guitar, drums, flute, even accordion: he'd fooled around with plenty of instruments, but nothing resembling a violin. "You sure you want me to?"

It was half-time on the TV, and dark outside already. Through the living room window, yellow light from a street lamp coated the grainy, grey sidewalk, dissolving at its edges like a pointillist's reverie. A night just like this, he'd first seen how pretty Dory was: the little drops of rain in her hair shining, and it stayed nice as a white girl's.

Not like Calliope's. Hers was as naturally nappy as his, worse between her legs. He sneaked a look at her while Byron was showing him how to position the gimbri upright. She was looking straight back at him, her eyes hot and still. Not as pretty as Dory, no, but she let him do things he would never have dreamed of asking of her little sister.

Mr. Moore stood up from the sofa and called to his wife. "Mama, you wanna come see our resident genius's latest invention in action?"

The gimbri screamed, choked, and sighed. "What on earth?" said Mrs. Moore from the kitchen doorway. She shut her eyes and clamped her lips together as if the awful noise was trying to get in through other ways besides her ears.

Neville hung his head and bit his lower lip. He wasn't sure whether he was trying to keep from laughing or crying.

"It spozed to sound like that, Byron?" asked Calliope.

"No," Neville told her. "My fault." He picked up the bow from his lap, frowning. His older brother had taken him to a Charles Mingus concert once. He searched his memory for an image of the man embracing his big bass and mimicked it the best he could.

A sweeter sound emerged. Sweeter, and so much sadder. One singing note, which he raised and lowered slowly. High and yearning. Soft and questioning. With its voice.

With its words.

"I know you mama, miss me since I'm gone;
I know you mama, miss me since I'm gone;
One more thing before I journey on."

Neville turned his head to see if anyone else heard what he was hearing. His hand slipped, and the gimbri sobbed. He turned back to it.

"Lover man, why won't you be true?
Lover man, why won't you ever be true?
She murdered me, and she just might murder you."

He wanted to stop now, but his hands kept moving. He recognized that voice, that tricky hesitance, the tone smooth as smoke. He'd never expected to hear it again.

"I know you daddy, miss me since I'm gone;
I know you daddy, miss me since I'm gone;
One more thing before I journey on.

"I know you cousin, miss me since I'm gone;
I know you cousin, miss me since I'm gone;
It's cause of you I come to sing this song.

105

"Cruel, cruel sistah, black and white and red;
Cruel, cruel sistah, black and white and red;
You hated me, you had to see me dead.

"Cruel, cruel sistah, red and white and black;
Cruel, cruel sistah, red and white and black;
You killed me and you buried me out back.

"Cruel, cruel sistah, red and black and white;
Cruel, cruel sistah, red and black and white;
You'll be dead yourself before tomorrow night."

Finally, the song was finished. The bow slithered off the gimbri's strings with a sound like a snake leaving. They all looked at one another warily.

Calliope was the first to speak. "It ain't true," she said. Which meant admitting that something had actually happened.

But they didn't have to believe what the song had said.

Calliope's suicide early the next morning, that they had to believe: her body floating front down in the cistern, her short, rough hair soft as a wet burlap bag. That, and the skeleton the police found behind the retaining wall, with its smashed skull.

It was a double funeral. There was no music.

Big Mama Yaga's

Joke was, we relocated to Texas cause Katrina flooded us outta New Orleans. Then, of course, Harvey took possession over half the state, losin me my husband Vernon. One side of the Gulf to the opposite; I wonder why we thought movin would make a difference.

I mean, Harvey was spozed to be a "500 year event." More like 500 days. I can laugh now, but back then it wasn't funny.

The house I got when I first come here with my sister Tini was one a them build-it-yourself deals like Ikea coulda made. Real basic. No floor but a plastic sheet. Plain white walls; one door. Four windows and two vents, though. The land we put it on was what we could get for our little savins. We wanted a nice spread: places the rest of our family could put somewhere to live, and for when we could spend more on a bigger and better building. What this amounted to in the end was a plot on an extension of Fidelity Street, right up against Buffalo Bayou. I don't need to tell you what kinda mess *that* wound up bein.

We come back soon as we could, not to lose our claim on the land we'd bought. While stayin up north we'd connected up with Uncle Spree via NextDoor, and he put together our GoFundMe, forwarded us a lotta money from his friends and audience members. So ever year since I been expandin— bought that old tofu factory and the steel warehouses beside it, and more ruined industrial properties than even Google Earth showed. Prudent? Nope. Tini figured I was pure-dee insane.

"Why come you didn't at least buy us a trailer, Tami?" she ask me one cool, cloudy night in April '26. "We could use the extra room, and Lafcadio wouldn't mind towin us to Uncle Spree's when the water rise again this August." By now my Malia was twelve-goin-on-ninety-three and needed her own room for sure. Especially with Tini and Lafcadio's eighteen-month-old twins crawlin around the shelter when they wasn't messin up my workshop.

Lafcadio knocked to come in. Like he didn't practically live there. Same charade every evenin, soon as my phone struck eight: tap-tap-tap. So polite. "Hold up!" I yelled, gatherin my tool belt. When I let him in I stepped out to the yard—that's how tight our little refuge was. Didn't help that he such a big bull of a man, or that he always brung sample bags from stock Kralovec Growth Supplies was considerin. That night, in addition to a sack a some hybrid grain it was all these squares and bars a plastic and metal clatterin around a cardboard box. "What's this?"

"They was throwin em out. Said since they merged with Squire Brothers—that construction outfit?—they'd be gettin sensors already integrated in they new plantbed frames."

"Thank you." I tucked the box under my arm and went across the lot to my workshop, which was modified from a flat pack deal like we lived in. Tini had no call to give me a hard time for what I used it for; she hadn't barely begun to show when I bought it.

Up the steps. They was my first project on my own once me and Lafcadio shoveled a high enough mound and assembled the shop on top. I would say my second project, but we hollowed out the mound together, though Lafcadio didn't know then it was for me to build the chicken leg inside.

Behind the workshop door we kept a similar Elegba statue to what Uncle Spree had us put behind the door into our house. African juju, that's what *that* was; Elegba in charge a making the impossible not just possible but true. I'd say it worked.

I slung the box of sensors in the far corner to inventory later. Fast as I could I hauled up the lid in the shop's floor, lookin through the scaffold around the leg and foot.

Between steel wool and mother wit, I had cleaned my scavenged warehouse servos and repurposed em in there: lifts, rotators, stabilizers, brakes. Heavy duty shocks was a problem: had to steal em from the truck garage I worked in twice a week, and even still you'd feel when I set my shop to spin and bop. Whatever wasn't locked away went flyin, the twins rollin around gigglin like this was their favorite game—Tini didn't know or I doubt she woulda ever sent em here for me to sit, no matter how horny she got. No matter whether Lafcadio do it good or not.

Like she was sendin em right that minute. Didn't take long for her and Lafcadio to rouse each other up. "Mama!" shouted Malia from the staircase. "Open up! These babies fat!"

I slammed down the cover on the access. What mattered I'd check out tomorrow: that five claw foot, which would do the actual walkin.

"Quitcher bitchin. At your age I took care a babies all day." Rain was startin. I let them in.

"Got paid for it too I bet."

Smart mouth. But she did keep them boys outta my things—Malia headed em off from the box a sensors by ticklin em so hard they couldn't get up on they hands and knees. Thank Jesus, because some a them sensors turned out to be crucial—motion, light, height, all kinda feedback I added. Had to made a difference in my business plan's reception. Had to be why when it come time that microloan was mine.

Ten years later to the day I won it, now, and ain't nobody no different. Except maybe me gettin rich from my patent on these Yagahuts—just had to make sure them manufacturers a the shelters I modified got their cut. And Malia married now—she and her wife Spike and they bitty son Grigio comin here from campin down by Corpus Christi. Tini and Lafcadio and they boys—big as Malia was—be here in the mornin, and Uncle Spree and his new boyfriends—everybody comin to celebrate at Big Mama Yaga's. Bringin they houses—or you could say they houses bringin them.

Homes of a feather flocks together.

Street Worm

Down, down, down: dust and mud and mortar and steel plunged story upon story into the earth. Brit Williams clung to the chain-link fence surrounding the construction site as if only the desperate strength of her thin, brown fingers kept her from falling in.

She could see the pit's bottom—barely. Late afternoon in Seattle during the first week of February meant darkness owned the corners, shadows filled in all the low places and rose like dirty water to hide everything, eventually, even…

Dragging her eyes up along the building's still-exposed girders and beams, Brit spotted the giant nest, shining grey and silver in the last of the twilight. She hunched smaller in her good leather coat. But as far as she knew, the worm-like things that lived between those web walls couldn't see her.

"You all right, kid?"

The cops sure could, though. "Yeah," she lied, meeting the policewoman's eyes. White people liked that. "Just wanted a look before I got on the bus home." Did that sound suspicious? Had she said too much?

No. The cop let her walk downhill and cross the intersection without interference. She strode briskly into the cold drizzle as if she really did have somewhere to go.

Well, she did. If she'd only admit to her parents she was crazy, she could go home. She could fit herself right back into their careful, bougie lives.

Except she was sane. Brit was pretty sure of that.

No one else seemed to see the nests, though. Whereas for her they were everywhere. Heading north on First Ave she walked by three, all stuck to the sides of skyscrapers in the throes of renovation. People going the other way faced her and passed on, oblivious office workers and ignorant drunks. The traffic light ahead changed, and Brit hurried out into the street to get away from a close one hanging only a few floors above the sidewalk. Behind the nest's pale sides, paler shapes writhed disgustingly, knotting together and sliding apart—she stopped to watch in fascination till a rough jolt to her shoulder and a muttered curse got her moving again. On the street's other side she checked her pants' front pocket. Her cash was still there.

But the clerk at the Green Tortoise Hostel wouldn't take it.

Brit tried. She showed him she really had enough money, laying a wrinkled twenty on the greasy counter and smoothing it out flat. The man shook his shaggy head like a refugee from a Scooby-Doo cartoon. "Nope. Not without proper ID."

Brit glared at him. She'd shown him that, too. "What ain't proper about—" She slapped her hand down on her fake driver's license fast, grabbing it back before he could confiscate it. His large hand rested awkwardly between them.

"Look, do you need help? Somewhere to stay the night?"

Wasn't that what she'd wanted to pay him for? If she hadn't been so damn short, he might not have asked how old she was. Lots of people told Brit she acted four, even five years older than her age. She could have passed for eighteen, easily—if she stood a little taller. But no.

"Problems at home? Let me call somebody—" He turned for the phone behind him and Brit bolted back outside.

Getting dark. The rain had slacked off, but the cold felt worse. At least she couldn't smell Shaggy's stale cigarette butts anymore.

She took in a deep breath, convincing herself she was better off. So much for Plan A. Plan B was more flexible. Okay, less well-formed. The basics were the same: stay away from her parents till they gave up labeling her "disturbed." Skip the appointment they'd made for her tomorrow afternoon with a psychiatrist.

She plodded stoically uphill. East. And south, away from the Green Tortoise. The library would probably still be open, but Brit wasn't in the mood to read. Too hungry. She pushed open the door of the Hotel Monaco's restaurant and went in.

Warm air caressed her, carrying in its soft swirls the aromas of fresh bread, baked herbs and onions, roasting meat—

"May I help you?" The way the woman walking towards her spoke made it clear she didn't think helping Brit was in her power or anyone else's. Brit had eaten here before. Only lunch, though. Everybody on that shift was used to her, but obviously she was just another black kid to this high-heeled blonde. And obviously she was too young to be eating dinner alone. "Meeting another party?"

Brit's gaze swept around the room. The only other customers were a couple of old ladies in red and purple suits and bizarrely flowered hats. "Yeah. Spozed to be. Look like I'm early."

Mostly Brit talked the way she did to make Mom and Dad angry. Ebonics didn't fit in with their image as "professionals." Of course it pissed off her friend Iyata's mother Sylvie, too, but that only meant they had to meet at school half the time. Not such a hardship. And maybe the use of Ebonics reminded the blonde it was National Brotherhood Week or something: she showed Brit to a nice table and gave her a menu without any more questions.

She ordered a cup of tea to drink while she was "waiting." She sipped it slowly, trying to figure out what story she'd tell to explain why the imaginary adults didn't show up for their ostensible rendezvous with her. She'd need to fake a phone call...

The outside door opened again, and she glanced up exactly as if she really was expecting to meet someone here. In came a round-bellied white man in a navy blue coat, his long grey hair in a ponytail. Probably friends with the two old ladies. "There she is!" he said, brushing past the hostess and heading straight for Brit. Not the old ladies. Brit.

"How's my little half-pint of cider half drunk up?" The strange man smiled and plopped down in her table's other chair. "Play along!" he whispered. "Pretend you know me till I get a chance to—"

"Ready to order?" The waiter had appeared from nowhere to stand by the table at attention. He had a green notepad in his hands and a mildly worried expression on his face.

Brit could get up and scream for him to call the cops. That'd be great—they'd take her right back home. Besides, this table-crasher guy suddenly looked familiar. She narrowed her eyes. An actor? It was coming back to her: the race-flipped production that The Conciliation Project had brought to her school—"Uncle Tom?"

One of the man's bushy eyebrows lifted. "Don't look so surprised! Didn't you get our message? Aunt Eliza came down with the flu and sent me by myself." He turned to the waiter as if just noticing him. "I'd like a Jungle Bird, if the bar's open."

"Yes, sir!" The waiter left, looking reassured.

When they were alone again, "Uncle Tom" hunched forward and laid his arms on the table. "Thanks," he said. "That was pretty brave of you."

"Yeah, well, get any nearer and I'm leavin."

"Fair enough." He leaned back. "I guess I ought to be grateful you recognized me—from that play version of *Uncle Tom's Cabin*, I take it?"

Brit nodded. "But that don't mean I trust you no further than I can throw the chair you sittin in."

"Fair enough," he said again. The waiter returned carrying a glass round as the man's belly, full of ice and an orangey liquid. A section of a pineapple ring gripped its rim. He left again after taking their orders: lasagna for Brit, which was what she usually had at lunch, and quail for her supposed uncle.

"All right, before we're interrupted anymore, let me try to tell you what I'm doing talking to you. Did you ever read—or see—'The Shining'?"

Brit was tired of white people assuming she was stupid simply because she was dark-skinned. Another reason she'd started talking hood; before, they always said how she was so "articulate." "I can read!"

"Never said you couldn't. Lots of kids don't bother with books, though; young people nowadays seem to prefer movies. Anyway, the book and the movie *are* different: the Scatman Crothers character doesn't die at the end of the novel. But what both versions of the story got right was how some of us, some of us who can do special things, have this glow to us, this 'shining,' if you will…like you."

Like her. "You sayin I'm magic."

"For lack of a better word, yes. Yes I am."

"How bout 'insane'? How bout 'hallucinatin'?" She was standing—her legs shook. She hoped it didn't show. She kept her voice low. "How bout 'depressed an delusional'? All kinda things people be sayin I am, an ain't none of em good—" On the edge of her field of vision she saw the waiter approaching with a basket of bread.

"Ima go the bathroom. When I come out you be gone." She picked up her backpack from where she'd dropped it and fled.

"Wait, let me finish—"

She slammed the restroom door behind her and turned on the water so she wouldn't have to hear what he was saying.

Peed, wiped, flushed, washed her hands. Eyes on the mirror, she pulled out her pick and went to work on her short little fro. Then a touch-up to her liner and mascara—Mom and Dad didn't allow her to wear make-up, but Brit kept a supply for use away from home.

She took a long time, but when she emerged, the man—she didn't even know his real name!—was sitting where she'd left him. Between her and the exit. He stood up as she walked by—he didn't attempt to stop her, though. All he did was say, "Sorry. I don't blame you for being scared."

That made her turn around. "I ain't scared!"

"No? Then maybe you'll sit down and eat quietly with me?"

Brit suddenly noticed that the hostess, the waiter, the old ladies—everyone in the whole restaurant was staring at her. She didn't need that kind of attention. With an angry look at "Uncle Tom," she sat back in her abandoned chair.

"Maybe put on a slightly less murderous expression?"

Brit closed her eyes and took three deep breaths like her dad was always counseling his clients to do. When she opened them there was a white card on the table in front of her. "Elias Crofutt" read the first line, in a flowing, cursive-like script. Below it, in much plainer letters: "Theater, Language, Hierophance"—whatever *that* was. Below those words was a phone number. All printed in dark purple ink.

"Ken Rodriguez—at the hostel—called my pager after you left so—precipitously."

Shaggy. "He had one a these?" she asked. "Why come?"

"Often there's trouble at home when a talent such as yours emerges. I keep an eye out for kids at risk, and I have my contacts in likely spots watching for—"

"You got spies? You a nasty fuckin creeper!" Brit scraped her seat away from the table.

"Wait! Don't you want to know how I found you?"

Yes she did. The Green Tortoise was eight blocks away, too far for mere coincidence. And she'd never heard of this sort of operation in Seattle. Both her parents worked with teens—Dad as a psychiatrist, Mom as a social worker. It was why they were so sure they knew what was wrong with her. They were always warning her about things she'd never be enough of an idiot to get mixed up in; surely they would have mentioned running across a scheme like this? What if she could tell them about something they'd missed? That would make her look on top of everything—completely sane. She nodded cautiously.

"I was trying to tell you: you *shine*. I followed your light—" He stopped midsentence. The waiter brought salads and set them on the table in the abrupt, awkward silence.

Brit smothered her lettuce and carrot chips in ranch and picked up her fork, determined to get some food in her stomach. She'd been too busy arguing with her mom to eat this afternoon at home. "You was sayin." She crammed a loaded fork in her mouth.

"I keep an office at the Y."

So cross off staying there. That put a big dent in Plan B.

"When I called Kenny back, he described you—not only what you were wearing, but—well, it's like invisible fireworks coming out of the top of your head—"

"Riiight." Let the man spew out his newage sewage. She would concentrate on getting some nourishment under her belt. One forkful at a time.

"I know how this sounds. Believe me. Or maybe it's more like sparklers than fireworks, because you leave a trail in the air for a minute or two...well. Anyway. *I* can see it, though most can't."

Grimly, Brit swallowed and began chewing a third mouthful of crunchy, oil-coated salad. Plan C was even hazier in her mind than B. And this dude was seriously woo-woo.

Or maybe not. If she was sane, he could be, too. Maybe? Would he back her up? Would her parents believe him? Or would they call him nuts—politely—to his face?

The waiter came back with their entrees before she could decide. Steam wafted off her lasagna when she cut apart the crusty cheesy top layer. Too hot to eat yet. "What my fireworks look like?" she asked.

"White and gold with flecks of ruby-red," Crofutt replied promptly. Not hesitating as if he was making stuff up. "I've never seen anything quite like it."

"That mean you don't know what kinda magic I do?"

"Correct. But I can help you figure it out. If you need me to." He sliced meat off the quail's breast and ate a couple of bites before he spoke again. "Anything else you need, just ask. Money, weapons, somewhere to stay the night…"

There was being scared and then there was being smart. She flagged the waiter down. "Put this in a go box," she said, gesturing at her food. She dug out the same bill she'd offered Shaggy. Kenny. It ought to cover her share. Plus tip.

"Through already?"

Brit stood up and the man didn't try to stop her. "So through." She kept her voice low so no one else would notice her anger. "Here some cash to pay for my food. You can see I don't need your stinkin money. Don't need you runnin crystals up an down my body, neither, or whatever freaky thing get you off before you stranglin me—"

"No! You're wrong!" Crofutt protested. "Sit down—*please!*"

"I ain't!" She tilted her head to one side and grinned ferociously for the benefit of the waiter coming back with her boxed up lasagna. "Tell Aunt Eliza I hope she be better for church Sunday," she said, too sweetly. "Thanks for the offer, but I gotta go." She swung her pack onto her left shoulder, took the box from the waiter, and headed for the door.

Behind her Brit heard the white man getting up and following her. She made it almost to the door before she felt his touch on her coat sleeve. She whirled fast and he dropped the offending hand. But he held the other out to give her the card from the table. "You almost forgot this."

Rather than attract more attention she took it and shoved it in her coat pocket. "Good *night*."

"Be careful!" he shouted as she stepped outside. "It's—"

The door banged shut and cut the last words off. Full night had fallen and a freezing wind blew off the bay.

There was one spot Brit knew would be probably a little warmer. And empty. Not somewhere safe, exactly, but she was out of other options. She walked downhill again and turned north on Third to avoid the Green Tortoise. She wasn't paranoid; she didn't really think Shaggy would even know she was going by the building. It was just better not to take any chances.

She wasn't paranoid. Something told her to look back up the street at Third, though, and here came Crofutt, striding after her as fast as his fat self could go. Which was surprisingly fast.

The second door past the corner had an "Open" sign hanging behind its glass. Brit yanked it out of the way and hurried inside. She put a couple of rows of shelves between her and the window before she came to a halt.

This was a cigar store. A pretty swanky one, too. Shelves and shelves of boxes full of brown cylinders: fat, thin, dark, light, short, long, banded in gold, wrapped in cellophane, as various as people.

"May I help you?" The man asking that question this time sounded as if he might really want to. He looked nice, too. He had curly, medium long hair, black mixed with silver; smooth skin the color of one of his cigars; a nose curved like a bird's beak; a mustache lifted up at its ends by his smile.

"My dad birthday comin up," she improvised. Actually, that wouldn't be till June. "I wanna get him somethin extra cool."

"Of course. He is already a smoker? A connoisseur? I may know him. What's his name?"

"He only started round Christmas." What a tangled web. Would she have to make up a reason why he'd started then?

With a few more lies, Brit stretched the visit out to half an hour. She bought a gold-plated cigar trimmer, a bead-covered lighter shaped like a butterfly, and six of the hugest cigars she could find. That took two of her hundreds.

It was worth it, though. When she left the shop there was no sign of Crofutt the Creeper. She continued north toward the Denny Triangle neighborhood, then walked east again on Stewart to Westlake, keeping out of the Belltown bar scene.

The crowds dwindled and disappeared. Someday, Mom said, this part of town was going to get bought up and gentrified. Meanwhile it was home mostly to what the planning commissions her parents monitored called "light industry": newspaper offices, award plaque engravers, embroidery factories, etc. Low brick buildings, their walls dull with old paint, all dark and empty now. Including the one where Brit was going to have to spend the night.

Kind of ironic, she thought, keeping her eyes on the ground as she walked the final yards to the building's back entrance. Her fight with Mom and Dad had been all about not coming anywhere near this place they bought for a teen center. No way. But here she was.

She would probably be okay. As long as she didn't look up.

The realtor's lockbox still dangled from the dead fluorescent lamp beside the door. Her parents didn't know she knew the combination. The key was still inside it.

The key undid the lock easily. The door creaked. Only a little, though. Could the giant wriggly things on the rooftop even hear anything?

Brit peered inside. Greyblue squares glowed dimly on the floor where the city's faint light had funneled in via the high, dirty windows. The pale patches wavered like reflections. A real hallucination? No.

The floor was under water.

Brit stepped cautiously in. The linoleum beneath the rubber soles of her Converse shoes squelched as if it was wet, but at least she didn't hear her feet full-on splashing. Not deep enough, maybe? She shut the door and felt in her pack for her flashlight.

Crouching, she aimed the light low, hoping no one would see it. Nearby, the beige tiles she remembered from her first reluctant visit glittered only faintly, as if covered in sweat. But in the wide room's middle, the row of poles supporting its ceiling rose from a shallow pool.

As she walked around the room's edge, Brit's mood sank lower and lower. Tops, there was maybe half an inch of water anywhere, but it went almost from wall to wall. Not real comfortable to sleep in. Her bag would be soaked in no time, wherever she put it down.

Four doors led off the main room on its far side. The first opened on a closet. She felt its floor to be sure. Dripping wet. The second and third doors were locked. The outside key didn't work on them.

The fourth door was locked, too—but with the deadbolt's knob on *this* side. Behind it a stair climbed up to a dark landing.

Brit frowned. From what she remembered, this place had just one story. Arriving on the landing, she looked up from there and saw that the stairs stopped at a metal fire door with a push bar for its handle.

A door onto the roof. Where an enormous tent full of worms waited.

She couldn't go there. Anyway, outside she'd be cold and, if the rain came back, just as wet as lying on the flooded floor below. With a sigh, she scuffed back down to the landing. Tiny, but so was she. She unrolled her bag and fluffed it out, slipped inside. Her coat folded up into a big pillow. She tucked it under her head and waited.

The landing was concrete. Dry. Hard. Dad said it took the average person fourteen minutes to fall asleep. She waited some more. And some more. And some more.

She checked her watch, and sure enough she'd stayed awake a lot longer than fourteen minutes. Maybe she needed more padding. She opened her coat up and put it under the bag. Now she didn't have a pillow—her pack was too lumpy, filled with pretend birthday presents. She shouldn't crush the cigars. That left—her lasagna! She must have dropped it somewhere—no use trying to figure out the exact spot now. But with nothing else to do, she backtracked mentally anyway and decided she'd left the box balanced on the rim of a trash-can when she re-tied her shoelaces. Maybe she was too hungry to sleep.

Maybe it was too early: only 8, and she usually went to bed around 9 on a school night.

She switched from cradling her head on her left arm to her right.

No use going back over the fight with Mom, either, think-ing of what she should have said. Like, "Why don't you trust me? Why don't you believe me?" Like, "Just because all the other teenagers you deal with are on drugs doesn't mean I have the same problem." Like, "I am *not* insane!"

Instead, after a while, she'd given up saying anything. Talking wasn't going to do any good. Brit decided she was simply going to have to disappear. Actions spoke louder than words. She would take off; that way she'd miss school, miss the "counseling" appointment scheduled right afterwards, miss her parents picking her up from there to drag her along to the infested building they'd bought.

So how ridiculous was it that she'd wound up spending the night in the same building, practically right next to a worm nest after all, on her own? Alone? In the dark?

Well, coming here hadn't been her first idea. Or even her second.

The problem was, everyone in Seattle who was supposed to help kids knew her mom and dad. Now she had a chance to think, a bus or a train ride seemed like her best option. To Yakima or Spokane, or somewhere no one would look. Soon as it got light she'd walk to the station. Before school started, so she'd be less suspicious.

But if she was going to leave town early tomorrow morning, she'd better get to sleep soon. She checked her watch again. 10:00. Past time. Her alarm would start beeping at 6. She put the watch back away in her pencil bag and zipped that in a pocket she never used so it would be harder to find and hit snooze. Shoved her pack a couple of stairs up so she'd have further to reach for it. But she could still hear it ticking.

Except her watch was digital.

It didn't tick.

Had someone followed her in? How? She *knew* she'd locked the door. And there hadn't been any other way—she'd gone all around everywhere. Except for those two locked doors.

She pulled the pack back down to the landing and held it to her ear to be sure. Nothing. Let go of it and listened again. Louder, now, and faster. And coming from above—the opposite direction of whatever was behind the doors. And faster. And louder. Like a shower of rocks. Like a storm of hail—was that it? A storm? Maybe she should retreat to the ground floor for safety. A hurricane could rip an old building like this apart—there hadn't been any predictions of a storm that bad, though. Had there?

She needed to see. But the worms were up there. Did the noise come from them? What were they doing?

She could find out looking from the street. She put her shoes on and grabbed the key and her flashlight. She turned that off at the bottom of the stairs for a moment and immediately stepped in a stray puddle. Great.

Sticking near the wall, she reached the front door without further mishap. And of course it was locked like she'd left it.

But the ticking noise was loud, even down here. She went out on the sidewalk and it was worse.

At first Brit couldn't see anything weird. The sky glowed a silvery grey with the city's ambient light; it was filled with low, slow-moving clouds—no! Those were the worms! She'd never seen them outside their tents before. What were they crawling on? Like ghosts in a movie they looked sort of see-through, rippling along what she could gradually make out as branch-like structures—and filmy-looking—leaves? Fainter than the worms themselves, the "leaves" shimmered in a way that made Brit's heart ache oddly, as if she was reading a sad love story.

What about that ticking noise, though, which she could hear all around now? It sounded tinier than the tiniest hail, and—she put her hands out to be certain—nothing was hitting her. Straining her eyes, Brit could finally see hundreds of miniscule white specks dropping from the worms. They bounced noiselessly off her skin and coat—and presumably her head—and clicked against the ground.

Experimentally she tried to crush some of them beneath her right Converse. Silence. Not even the soft scrape of a rubber sole on the cement. But when she lifted her foot she'd smashed the white specks beneath it to a powder, and an acrid smell wafted up to her from the pavement, like mildew. What—

On the street's other side a parked van lit up for a second as its door opened and shut. The brief light showed a navy coat; a long, pale ponytail; a round, pink face—Crofutt! He'd followed her somehow. Via those fireworks and sparklers he'd babbled about?

"Hey! This isn't a good place," he shouted across the road. "You really ought to come with me—"

Who cared how he'd found her? Brit ran back inside the building and slammed the door shut and locked it.

Crofutt kept shouting. "Dreams are dying back these days, and I think the reason for that's somewhere around here."

Her shoes were wetter than ever. And her socks. First chance she got—

"They're dying back. Something's killing them, something dangerous."

Dry socks and shoes. Clean underwear. She'd forgotten to—

"Are you listening? If you don't come out, I'm going to call the cops."

"Go head!" Brit yelled back. What had he been raving about? Dreams dying back, like some kind of occult crop? "I've got a right to be here!" Well, she did, sort of—her parents had signed the mortgage papers yesterday. "What they gonna say bout you stalkin a underage girl?"

That shut him up. Only for a moment.

"I'll call anonymously," Crofutt amended. "You shouldn't stay here. Not here."

An anonymous tip? How quickly would the cops respond? She might get away before they came.

And go where?

"At least tell me what you saw?" the man asked.

"What I—" She ought to stop answering him. It only encouraged him to keep talking.

"You were looking up. What did you see?"

Well, this was one person who would probably believe what she said.

Brit described the tents, the worms, the leaves and branches. The rain of specks. When she was done it was quiet again. Except for the ticking.

"That explains a lot." Crofutt wasn't shouting anymore. His voice felt close, like he was leaning on the door.

"Explain what?"

Crofutt had it all figured out. He called Brit a "Visioner," and said her power was translating the ways of "non-physical entities" into "concrete, manipulable analogies." It boiled down to her boiling down demons, angels—and other things, things without names, all the things most people couldn't see or understand—to simpler forms. The worms ate dreams—that was what the leaves were. The specks were their—excrement.

And so on. It was the nearest anyone had come to making sense, assuming she truly wasn't crazy. Brit felt completely willing to listen to Crofutt—through the door.

"Say you right," she finally half-admitted. "These worms eatin up everybody's hopes an dreams till ain't none left?"

"Pretty much. Then *they'll* vanish—leave, starve, however you lay out the concept. I've seen the effects of the cycle over and over—the '60s, the '80s—a lot of innocent people got hurt."

"I can look after myself okay," Brit assured him. Maybe he wasn't a creeper after all.

She still wasn't about to let him in, though. He could prove that another time, in the daylight, around other people.

And part of what he said didn't quite compute— "I can make these what you callin 'entities' do like I want by how I see em?"

"Sort of; what they do also influences how they appear to you—"

"Awright. So what these worms turn into after they eat up everyone dreams? Some kinda gigantic moth?"

"Hmmmm. Could be."

Images of Japanese monster movies flitted in and out of Brit's head. She let them come and go. What she really needed to figure out was how to keep the worms from stripping all the silver dream leaves from people's thought vines—that was what she had decided to name the translucent branches curling through the night: thought vines. Which could belong to anybody. They were tangled up but there must be a way to trace them to their roots, to their sources, which could be anyone. Even her parents. Even her.

Wet and hungry and tired—that didn't matter. She had left home to find a way to convince Mom and Dad that she wasn't a whack job. That she knew what she was doing. Which meant she had to know it.

She stopped answering Mr. Crofutt's questions, and after a while he stopped asking them. She walked straight across the puddle to the stairway where her stuff was, not caring anymore how soaked she got. Because of the idea forming in her achy mind.

If the "entities" had to act like worms once she'd made them take that shape, they had to die like them. Die like worms.

She remembered from her sixth-grade science report how to kill tent caterpillars. You could cut down their nests and grind them to a pulp with heavy boots.

Brit didn't have boots that big. Nobody did.

You could burn them out.

Could the nests only she saw catch fire? And if they did, would the flames spread and burn down her parents' building? Would the fire she set burn her to death?

She rolled up her sleeping bag and stuffed it in the pack. She pulled out her watch. Midnight. A long, long time till morning. Maybe she'd go home. Slog over to the Westin and find a cab. That'd be a laugh. She wouldn't have accomplished anything except to piss off Mom and Dad.

She wasn't scared. She climbed the rest of the way up and opened the door.

The roof was flat and covered in gravel. Brit scrunched over to the edge where the tent stuck up, betting it would be empty. Sure enough, the webbed walls were blank. No writhing. All the worms were out devouring dreams.

She took her box knife from her pants pocket and slashed at the nest's nearest side, but the knife sank in past its hilt and left no trace, while her hand wouldn't penetrate the webbing at all, not even a fraction of an inch. She remembered one of the rules for magic in the torn-up book of a runaway staying at their house: you should never use the same tools for mundane and spiritual tasks.

Brit cut things open with her box knife all the time. Mundane things. That left the cigar trimmer.

She hadn't really been going to give it to Dad. She got it out of the pack and the shop's bag: a pair of scissors with short, round blades. They made a nice, neat hole in the tent's side.

She pushed her head into the hole before she could think too much about what she was doing. It was awful anyway. She cut and cut and cut, past layers and layers of webs. Like squirming deeper and deeper inside a haunted house. Arms, shoulders, chest, stomach—she wanted to throw up. Here came that salty taste and the extra spit squirting into her mouth.

She wiggled back out again and breathed through her mouth, hard. And heard a siren in the street below. That was the goad she needed. She grabbed up her pack and went back in the tent. Completely.

The siren died away in the distance. So Crofutt hadn't turned her in after all. When she was sure they really weren't coming to get her, she wiggled back out again. Drizzle had begun to fall while she shuddered and gagged inside; she actually thought about staying inside the nest all night.

But she had no guarantee the worms would stay out eating till sunrise.

Instead she sat cross-legged on the cold, damp gravel. She took out and unrolled the bag and half unzipped it so it lay like a puffy, down mantilla on her head and neck and shoulders, and formed a little shelter on either side of her. She laid out her tools underneath it: the butterfly lighter, the six fat cigars, ends ritually trimmed, ready to burn.

Then she waited for the worms' return. It wouldn't do any good to destroy an empty nest.

She tried not to sleep but dozed off despite the cold and discomfort. Obviously that meant she wasn't one bit scared of the morning. The red dawn. The horrible vibrations shaking the nest as its denizens poured back inside, ignoring—as she'd hoped they would—the slits and slices she'd made in their home.

Drawing on it as deeply as she could, Brit lit the first cigar. When it was going strong she reversed it and put the glowing end inside her mouth, bending to blow a stream of fragrant smoke into the nest's heart.

At first the worms stirred at the intrusion, blind heads seeking nonexistent fresh air, but by the fourth cigar they settled down where they were. To rest. The fifth. To sleep. The sixth. To loosen the grips of their hooked legs, fall to the tent's floor, and die.

She tossed the mantilla over the hole she'd used, changing it to a shroud.

Dizzy and nauseated, Brit struggled to her numb feet. Up, up, up: light and air and hope towered height upon height into heaven. The sun rose clear of a band of clouds. Too bright to the south and east to tell how many more nests awaited destruction.

She stumbled to the roof's other end. Her shadow stretched north across the city. Beyond it lay her parents and her home. Warmth. Blessed dryness. Anger, undoubtedly. But she would apologize. Even go to the psychiatrist a few times if that was what they wanted. She'd tell them that she'd been wrong, that they were right. That she wasn't scared anymore, because there had never been anything to be scared of.

She would tell them where she'd spent the night. And let them think they understood.

Queen of Dirt

Brit lowered her wooden sword and sighed. She loved her students. But the girls kept hesitating, getting hung up on the moves, lagging behind. The three boys in the class of nine had stayed with her through the form, but when they thought she wasn't looking they whaled at the ground with their weapons like taiko drummers. Could they be any more clichéd?

Bees buzzed over flowers blossoming in scattered patches of sunlight. That was all right; none of the kids were allergic. And not all bees stung. From the pond beyond the trees a cool breeze blew, drying the light sweat coating her arms. "Everybody siddown." The rustle of the blue plastic tarp rose and fell as they obeyed. It stilled as they looked up at her, their faces so *earnest*. "You learnin fast," Brit told them. Not a lie. Little kids *did* learn fast. Way faster than adults, or even teenagers like herself. "But not countin Sunday we got five more days before the show. That all. An we ain't even come up with our routine." Sunday was unscheduled. A lot of kids and teachers went to church.

Tanzi raised her hand, though Brit hadn't asked the class a question. "Yeah?"

"Can we figure that part out in our wing meeting at the dorm tonight?"

Grey barely waited to be called on to object. "But we're sleepin in different wings."

"Okay, in the cafeteria at dinner. If we all sit at the same table—"

"Other teams could hear us!" Grey's cousin Jazman was the most competitive kid in camp. "They'll steal our ideas!"

"The cafeteria's big," Tanzi scoffed. "Let's all sit by the window farthest from the serving line. You could hold it for us, right, Mizz Brit? Make the other teams stay away?"

"Sure." Brit slid her blade into its beaded scabbard and pulled her watch out of her front pants pocket. "We got enough time to meditate. Anything you wanna ask me before we start?" On the first day of camp she'd told the kids she would answer anything.

The smallest girl peered up from underneath a rolled and knotted turquoise bandana. "Did you ever, you know, ever hurt somebody really bad? I mean like—"

"You mean have I ever kill anyone?" Brit had promised herself she would learn all her students' names in the eleven days of Experience Outreach, even the ones in the big morning classes. She had most of them, and just about every kid on her afternoon concentration team. Was this Denighta? Denesta?

"I never kill no one." At least, she'd never killed another human being.

"Now shut your eyes. Let your breath come an go slow— slower—slower—like shadows movin with the sun, like the turnin of the world...." The smell of peace, of green grass and water, calmed her mind. She liked it out here with the kids. Quiet, compared to the city. Calm after her work clearing out nests of entities.

So far she'd been able to stay away from the abandoned bunkers up the hill, site of the park's mysterious string of suicides. So far she'd ignored the feelings they gave her.

The hour before mealtime was unassigned. Brit led her team along the overgrown walkway to the dorm entrance where their chaperones waited. She assured the kids firmly that exploring the bunkers would take too long even if they left immediately. She barely had enough time herself to get back to her cabin, shower, and read a few pages of *Return to Nevèrÿon*. But she did manage to beat them to the kitchen building, joining Mr. Crofutt and the other six instructors on the porch outside five minutes before the line opened.

"How's my little half-pint of cider half drunk up?"

When they first met, Brit had thought he was creepy: an old white guy, ponytail and flamboyant purple shirt marking him as a liberal like her mom and dad, trying no doubt to "relate to the youth"…but he'd helped her figure out some important stuff. He'd never hit on her or done anything else inappropriate, either.

"I got them students eatin outta my hand. Specially my concentration team."

"They think you're cool because you're just about their size." Mr. Crofutt peered back to where the students were gathering along the porch's fieldstone wall, more or less by dorm wing. "Have you worked out your routine yet?"

"Tonight." The line began to move. Brit took a plate of spaghetti and meatballs from behind a sneeze guard, and a bowl for the salad bar. "I'm spozed to make sure we have a table by ourself. You mind?"

Mr. Crofutt dropped behind as they entered the high-ceilinged dining room. "Not in the least. Want me to run interference with Lisa?"

"That be great, yeah." Experience Outreach's Language Arts teacher Lisa Plowden was fascinated with Brit's assumed dialect. Her attention had started to feel like stalking.

Brit could talk Standard English whenever she wanted. She'd proved that in her job interview. First day she told her classes not to copy her; they promised, and her Ebonics ceased being an issue for everyone except Mrs. Plowden.

Mr. Crofutt headed off on his mission as Brit speed-walked to the room's far corner on hers. She picked a window table with a close view of a row of fluttering, silver-leaved poplars.

Boys and girls came to the table separately and sat far apart. Sixth graders.

"You were right, Mizz Brit," admitted Jazman. "The drummers only went to Battery Vicars, and they still aren't back! We never woulda made it in time."

After dinner, though, Brit's excuses for avoiding the bunkers ran out. Predictably, the boys wanted to base their team's presentation on a war story. Tai Chi was a martial art, after all. Less predictably the girls did, too—if at least one of the two sides fighting were zombies. Much enthusiasm for Tanzi's plan of blocking out their routine on the site of one of the abandoned gun emplacements. Brit would have looked weird vetoing it. Other instructors didn't have the heebie-jeebies over visiting the bunkers, and Experience Outreach was supposed to be about connecting art with the environment.

Curfew wasn't for another two-and-a-half hours, and the sky was plenty light at 6:30 on an end-of-June night. So as the sun drifted down toward the hazy horizon, touching with pale gilt the white clapboard sides of Fort Worden State Park's museums, halls, and dormitories, Brit climbed the hill, surrounded by her charges. It was another idyllic moment. Kids were great. If only you didn't have to have sex to get pregnant with them.

Over the gentle slope of the daisy-sprinkled lawn. Up the crumbling asphalt road where no vehicles were allowed. Brit's heart jumped as a dark, humping shape scuttled behind an empty cabin—but it was only an otter. Onto the sunken timber steps, then the gravel drive circling the hill's crown. Sweeping around to every obsolete battery the stupid soldiers had built.

That wasn't fair. Brit knew it. Experience Outreach's staff orientation had included a brief history of the Fort. Most of it was constructed so long ago air war was no more than a wild-eyed sci-fi concept involving zeppelins and ornithopters. 1897. Nearly a century had passed.

They came to an open field and stopped a moment. Clouds had gathered overhead with typical Quimper Peninsula swiftness. Between them sunrays shot out to backlight a line of firs. Grey and Jazman argued about which way to go. Grey won. They followed the road's bend to the right. Toward Battery Tolles and the bad feelings.

Mr. Crofutt called Brit a "Visioner." He had found her a couple of years ago, running away from home, and helped her understand the weirdness of her life. Said she translated "non-physical entities" into "concrete, manipulable analogies." When Mr. Crofutt offered to recommend Brit for this gig teaching with him at the Experience Outreach camp, he had mentioned there was some sort of problem with entities on one area of the grounds. People kept killing themselves: soldiers, then a couple of local "troubled teens," then an annual average of one camper—usually retired RVers. Not an epidemic, but over the years it had added up to about twenty.

Brit ignored that and accepted the job because it was with kids, young black kids, kids like she used to be and wished she could someday have. Also, it made a nice excuse to spend less time with the rents and their impossible, "realistic" expectations. Like how they wanted her to talk "proper" English the way she did in elementary and middle school. How they kept on expecting her to go on dates.

Besides, one little problem spot in the entire park hadn't seemed too much of a challenge. Hadn't she rid a whole city of an infestation of spiritual tent worms?

Under the firs' shadows it felt an hour later. And colder. Brit clasped her hands around her upper arms and zipped her hoodie. None of the kids acted like they noticed. They laughed and hit each other playfully with springy, green-needled branches they picked up from the side of the road. "Hey!" she warned them. "None a that!"

"But Mi-izz Bri-i-i-it," Tanzi pretend-whined. "You let us hit each other with the practice sticks. What's so diff—"

Brit halted. "Stop right there." A ragged wave of obedience. "Turn aroun an look at me while I talk to you." All nine students turned to face her.

"They ain't sticks. They swords. Ack like it. *Believe* it. You believe, your audience gonna believe too." She and Mr. Crofutt had talked a local supplier into lending the wooden practice swords in exchange for a free ad in the performance night program.

"Also." She stared as fiercely as she could. "How you movin in the form? Whatever routine we put together for Thursday? It gonna be slow, and *directed*. *Purposeful*. That's what so different. Unnerstan?"

Every head nodded. "Go on then." She started walking again and the kids, subdued, bunched up, went with her.

Soon the low bowl of Battery Tolles spread to the road's right. A trail spun down its sides. Blank darkness filled the doorless entrances to the concrete shelters at its bottom. They reminded her of giant skulls. Dead eyes and open mouths gaping like the heads of half-buried trolls. Brit shook her head to empty it of that idea. If she thought too hard about trolls, there might be trolls for real. She wasn't sure exactly how Visioning worked.

Grey and the other two boys headed up the stairway to the decommissioned gun carriage on the bunker's roof. "What about if we attack from up here?" That was Byron according to the attendance sheet, but his friends called him Skinny.

"You can't be a zombie, Skinny—only girls!" Tanzi yelled from the bowl's floor. "And we have to hide down *here*. Right, Mizz Brit?"

"Let's vote." Her favorite way to delegate. It was a land-slide victory, six to three. The boys grumbled, but quickly got into the rehearsal, looking relaxed and innocent as they de-scended the battery's steps, assuming exaggerated poses of horror and surprise as the girls staggered out of their dank lairs. Brit forgot her foreboding in the work of choreography. The feints and disarms and deliberate stumbles she helped them choose drew closely on the forms she'd taught, but there was a nod to MJ's "Thriller," too: "Stomp, stomp, stomp, *rear*! Stomp, stomp, stomp, *rear*!"

When Brit thought to check her watch, it was fifteen minutes to the 9 o'clock curfew.

Delighta—one of the boys had settled that question by yelling at her when she accidentally flipped his precious ball cap into the blackberries—had been at Fort Worden last sum-mer. She knew a shortcut.

From the trail's head they walked a few feet back along the way they'd come, then took a narrow path that looked like it was going to bisect the main road's circle. As the class discussed how to transfer their routine's blocking to the the-ater—warrior boys on the stage, zombie girls rising from seats in the audience—Brit did her best to ignore her growing un-ease. Why did she have to notice this sort of feeling? Why couldn't she be like everybody else? According to Mr. Crofutt, making entities visible and palpable was something she did to fight them. To *win*.

But why did she have to know evil entities even existed, let alone sense where they gathered? Why couldn't she be like everybody else?

So dark, so early. Maybe the gathering storm was the cause. Looked like it would rain hard. Could even be some of the Northwest's rare thunder and lightning. Ahead of her in the gloom little Delighta paused. "This part's spooky!" she announced. "It'll get so you can't see." Delighta glanced at the student right behind her. "Maybe we should hold hands." She grabbed Jazman's. Both girls giggled.

And why not? They were only eleven, twelve years old, but kids had crushes all the time. Everyone did.

Everyone but Brit. Unless you counted Iyata, who was really just a friend. Really. Despite her mother and father's delicate questions and their reassurances that it was all right to be gay.

Brit didn't know what she was. Not gay, though.

Delighta and Jazman took a sharp turn, and she lost sight of them. For a moment only, she thought, but then she made the turn too, and they stayed invisible. She heard their footsteps continue, but they echoed oddly. Following the sound, Brit found out why: the two had entered a low tunnel. Short as Brit was, she could touch the ceiling when she reached up with one hand. She let her arm fall to her side. "Hold on!"

"It doesn't go far, Mizz Brit," Delighta said. "We're already out."

"I'm tellin you stop! Now!" Her voice reverberated hollowly off the tunnel's walls.

Then the reverberations ceased.

She pulled her sword. Wanted to. Tried to.

Nothing happened. She was frozen in place. Couldn't move. Paralyzed.

No! Could she breathe? Yes—but when she gasped in a big gulp of air, she felt something crinkle and tighten against her skin, a film of thick plastic like the tarp. Panic prickled over her and she puffed out hard and fast. The tightness eased. Brit experimented. Slow, shallow breaths kept the plasticky film from snugging in on her. She had to control her fear.

What else? She could roll her eyes, blink. "Can I talk?" she asked herself. The words sounded flat and dead, but she heard them.

She flexed her toes, the muscles of her calves, thighs, butt, stomach. She already knew her hands wouldn't obey her, but her fingertips twitched. Her mouth opened wide though her head wouldn't nod. Nostrils flared. Eyebrows raised, forehead wrinkled.

So partially paralyzed only.

Why? How?

How long?

Best guess, this had to do with whatever entities hung around here. Was this how they drove the suicides to take their lives? Or was it something else? Maybe if she could figure out what they'd done, she'd be able to free herself.

By when?

She was hungry. She had to pee. The air suddenly smelled stale—was she breathing the same stuff over and over? She'd suffocate! She'd—Slow down. Slow. Down.

She should meditate, the way she'd shown the kids—the kids! What were they doing? What had happened to them? Complete darkness filled Brit's eyes, even when she opened them wide. That was magic of some kind, the work of this new crop of entities, but evening had been settling in fast, and it must be night by now. How would her students find their way? Were they wasting time looking for Brit? They'd gotten out of the tunnel ahead of her. Eventually they'd get back and tell the chaperones, who would organize a fruitless search—What was going *on*?

Again she took deliberate control of herself. In. Slow. Out. Slow. Gradually she wiped from her mind the useless chafing about her students. Nothing she could do to help them except get out of here. They'd shown no signs earlier of being disturbed by the entities. They'd show up at the dorms without her, and things would proceed according to established policies. Pointlessly. Though maybe Mr. Crofutt would have *some* idea what kind of trouble Brit was in. He knew about entities and how to fight them.

Meanwhile, what could she do? Without access to the sword at her side or any other weapons—except her mind. Her memory.

Minus the usual immediate sensory distractions, Brit's mental movie of what had gone on before her paralysis reeled past in lucid detail: the giggles of the girls holding hands ahead of her, the gritty sweep of the tunnel's wet cement ceiling against her upheld hand, the slight mound of dirt beneath her feet… Wait. That was new. She'd felt the low mound at the time, but till now it hadn't registered.

Brit reviewed the sequence over and over in her head. Nothing else stood out, and she finally got tired of thinking about it.

And no one had found her yet. Hours must have gone by.

A textbook on the sociology of interrogation she snuck out of her mom and dad's library had a chapter about sensory deprivation as a torture technique. Supposedly it worked pretty well. Supposedly it produced horrible hallucinations. Over the course of days, she reminded herself.

So what was that crawling sensation on the top of her head?

Not real! Not not not! It felt heavy, wet, warm, runny, dripping down to her eyes so she had to shut them as it poured faster and faster over her nose and cheeks and if she opened her mouth to scream she'd taste it but she couldn't help it couldn't—" Help! Help me! Hel—"

Sweetness?

She choked, spat reflexively only to get the spit right back in her face, saliva dribbling off her chin mixed with the—

She told herself it was not blood. Not vomit. Forced herself to lick out her tongue and try another taste, try to analyze it.

Like nectar. Spicier, though. Perfume.

It was good. She sampled it again. Yes. A bit of an acid edge, which only made it easier to eat more.

The feeling of having to pee went away.

Realizing that brought her crashing back down to scaredness. She had swallowed some random emission of an entity. She didn't know what the stuff represented, what it did. She didn't even know what the entities themselves were like — they'd be something she was familiar with, but what? What had she shaped them into — Visioned?

Another cascade of liquid flowed over her, sticky and smooth as when her grandmother filled jars with her homemade —

Jelly. *Royal* jelly. She'd read a description of its flavor that matched. And her prison fit.

The entities were manifesting as bees. And trying to make Brit into their queen.

She couldn't wipe the jelly off. She let it dry on her skin, blinking hard so her eyelids wouldn't stick shut. Lips pressed firmly together; no way was she consuming more, no matter how hungry and thirsty she got.

Why bees? Because she actually knew a lot about them, that was why. She'd researched them last quarter for a Poetry of Biology paper. She understood the differences between solitary and eusocial species, and between primitive and evolved eusocial swarms. Not all bees stung. Not all produced honey. Some lived in hives provided by humans, some in dead trees.

Some nested in holes in the ground marked by low entrance mounds, lining them with secretions that hardened into natural polyesters.

Apparently facts about various kinds of bees had mushed together in Brit's unconscious mind to create these entities' manifestation. The way she'd made the ones in town into giant invisible tent worms. These were giant invisible bees.

Very nice. Now how did that get her out of here?

Maybe she could just be rescued? Left to his own devices Mr. Crofutt should be able to track her down—Locating was *his* superpower, the way shaping entities by Visioning them was hers. As long as she didn't breathe too deep or fast the air would probably last. Probably. The entities seemed to want her to live. Plus if they could pour royal jelly into her cell, it probably wasn't completely sealed up. Probably.

Her face began tingling. Softly at first, then harder, like the vibrating of a million tiny alarm clocks. Her neck and shoulders got in on the act too. Her upper arms and chest. Everywhere the jelly had touched her.

Hadn't her mom said something about how women used to rub bee jelly on themselves for beauty? How they absorbed its activating proteins directly into their tissues—

"Hnnnngg! Mmmmmvvvv!" Brit shrieked with her mouth shut. Did she still have a mouth? "Hmmmmnng!" Panting through her nose, she felt the cell's plastic lining shrink tight like a too-small rubber glove. "MmmmmMMMMMMMM!" Thrashing around only made it worse. Made it impossible to move. Soon all she could do was shiver and shudder and sob. Without daring to open her lips. Tears ran from her closed eyes; mucus threatened to stop up her nose.

She would choke on it and die, choke on her own snot. She would die here, buried underground. Nobody would ever see her again.

Unless she got it together. Unless she immediately quit freaking. Unless she surrendered and opened up her mouth. Of course she had one. The substance might trickle in. But how else to get air? She breathed in. Out. In. Out. Slower. Slower.

She felt the plastic wrapping her relax. For the second time. The buzzing tingle kept going, though, got worse—

Screw the tingle. She might lose her shit again unless she igged it. She'd think straight while she could. Until her brain turned into a bee's—No. That was not an all right idea to have in her head.

The entities wanted to change her. Maybe because she had changed the entities? She never knew what she was doing—or she hadn't anyway with the tent worms, the only entities she'd dealt with so far. What happened had only made sense afterwards, when Mr. Crofutt explained it.

So. If worms ate leaves and the worm entities ate the leaves of people's dreams, what did bee entities eat? Some nectar analog. Something harmless, most likely, since bees didn't hurt flowers.

They hurt people they stung. If they stung.

Did these entities hurt people? Yes. Or made them hurt themselves. Especially people who were allergic.

Most bees died after stinging once. Not queens. If the entities transformed her as she suspected they were trying to do, she would be capable of triggering mass waves of suicides.

Though the main function of a queen bee was to breed.

That started her struggling again. She yelled and tensed her muscles and *pushed* at whatever kept her pinned in place. Got nowhere, but she didn't *care,* she would rather *die* than lay six million eggs, six million fertilized—

A glob of royal jelly covered her face. She sneezed and coughed her nose and throat clear. And gulped some down. Had to. More kept coming. It puddled around her ankles and crept up her calves, climbed over her knees, drenched the bottoms of her shorts, making her legs buzz madly. Halted just below her crotch.

For the moment.

Based on her research Brit expected that soon the cell would be filled completely. Then…then she would drown. Or worse.

But she was supposed to *win.* That was what Visioning, her superpower, was *for.* Entities real enough to touch were real enough to kill.

How did you kill bees? Tent worms you crushed or smoked to death, and she'd figured out how to poison the worm entities using cigars.

Beekeepers used smoke to soothe their swarms to sleep. If she had her cigars with her here…they'd probably be useless. She couldn't light them if she couldn't move.

Anyway, she didn't want the bee entities to fall asleep. Maybe she didn't even want them dead. Not right now. Right now all she wanted was to get herself *out*.

But how?

The quiet of Brit's underground cell had slowly shredded apart. Whispers, squeals, and bursts of piping cries built up in the velvety silence, from ones and twos to a steady thrum of sound. The music of the hive. Almost she could make out individual voices. They felt like they came from very close. Almost she could see the members' individual dance steps, see them bow and shake their tail ends, neon gold on black. Almost she could understand their instructions.

Any queen had to go on at least one flight, to mate. Eventually they would let her out for it.

She didn't want to wait that long.

Another torrent of jelly. Viscous and faintly fragrant, the growing pool lapped up to her navel, her nipples, her armpits. Everywhere it touched came painfully awake, like circulation returning to crushed arteries. Then there was another break in the deluge. It had to be the last.

What did Brit have to fight with? Her memories had helped some, helped her identify what shape she'd given the entities. What else was she made of? According to an old hippy album song of her mom's she used to play when she was little:

> "Earth, water, fire, and air,
> Met together in a garden fair…"

Earth was all around her, holding her in. Earth was part of what was wrong. Water she'd never had much use for. Air was scanty, most of it far away—but fire—fire! Fire could burn her out of any jail. If she could strike a flame—didn't sparks fly up from flint and steel? But all she smelled outside her cell was plain old dirt.

Except the dirt was not exactly plain. It was charged with energy—lines of fire! Like lightning—which leapt to heaven from the earth. Could she call the fire to come through her?

Brit searched for the energy's pathways. She heard them? Felt them? Knowledge of the fire's routes came in by her ears, but not as sounds. More like pressure. As if someone were reeling in a bunch of knotted scarves, squeezing them in through holes in her head. Scarves stretching out around her miles and miles and miles and miles.

The feed rate of the bumping knots sped up to match the buzzing pain. The buzzing pain got brighter, brighter!

Power! Glory! Blazing up, onto her feet, into her veins, her nerves, her brain, along her hair, the fire, the flame was burning hotter! Higher! Whiter! Channeling itself into her, burning faster! Hotter! Higher! Burning higher! Bursting through her skull up to the sky!

KRRRAAAKKKKK! BABOOOMMM! Thunder tumbled out of the clouds. Rain fell with it. The jelly thinned, washing away as Brit clambered out of her lidless cell and stood laughing and free in the wild night. She could move! Wind whipped the brief storm away. She could spin in and out of it and twirl around and she could run all she wanted— beneath her flying Spiras the road's gravel glittered wetly in the light of the emerging crescent moon.

Mr. Crofutt and the two East Wing chaperones met her on the stairs leading to the road behind the dorms. They'd been looking for her for an hour, finally deciding she must have hit her head and been knocked out in an inexplicable collapse no one had yet found any trace of. She let them take her to Mr. Crofutt's van. He drove her to Urgent Care and didn't ask any questions she couldn't answer. He didn't ask any questions at all.

The drugs they gave her at the clinic slowed the buzzing way down but didn't stop it. Brit told Mr. Crofutt as much as she knew about what she'd been through. He said he'd sleep on what she said, figure out what it meant in the morning.

◊

Brit tuned out the ever-present humming in her bones and focused on how things looked: pastel green walls, polished wooden floors, dim hanging lamps, and padded stacking chairs laid out in sixteen rows of eight each. No curtains hung before JFK's primitive stage—or anywhere else in the theater building. How things sounded: the babble of eighty-five Experience Outreach students echoed off hardness on every side, bounced back and forth and became so confused she couldn't make sense of what anyone was saying. Not even her parents shouting politely inches from her face. Something about how difficult it was to come all this way on a weeknight ordinarily, but the holiday tomorrow helped. Brit nodded, her eyes darting side-to-side, seeking escape.

Oh no. Here came Mrs. Plowden. Grinning insincerely, Brit introduced her to Mr. and Ms. Williams, aka her dad and mom. Kids began taking their seats, which cut the noise enough that even with her head turned away she could hear her parents being complimented on their extremely articulate speech.

Please. Half the reason she talked the way she did was so she didn't have to hear this sort of "compliment."

The other half was to piss off the rents, which usually worked well enough. Though they'd surprised her by showing up tonight. Okay, she'd surprise them, too.

Someone flipped the lights on and off a few times fast. In front of the stage Mr. Crofutt cupped his hands to his mouth and called "Out!"

"Reach!" responded the crowd of students. A couple more calls and responses and pretty much all the ambient chatter died away. Except Brit's mother's. "—her whole life! We're proud of how different our daughter has been—" In the sudden silence Ms. Williams stopped midsentence.

Proud? Of Brit? First time she'd heard of that. She hurried to the seat in the staff section where she'd left her sword.

That afternoon the staff had met and decided on the order of show. The opening number was an all-camp rendition of a modified Balinese monkey chant led by the Movement Arts team, who remained onstage afterward and segued into what they called their Tidepool Dance. Then the Visual Art Team's slides played while the Percussion Team (the drummers' official name) set up; after Percussion came Martial Arts to end the first half.

The artillery-mimicking boom of the taikos nearly drowned out that buzzing hum. Not quite so painful anymore, now Brit was getting used to it.

The Martial Arts team's girls had spaced themselves strategically among the unsuspecting audience members. Yesterday—far too late—Tanzi had asked her to help their "side" of the mock battle, but Brit declined. She stuck to her teacher role.

She mounted three of the stairs to the stage and looked back at Mr. Crofutt, who'd gone to stand by the light switch. The building's shades, lowered for the slides, had been left that way, as she'd specified. So when she raised her sword and swept it down in the signal they'd agreed on, total darkness descended.

And then not quite total. The braided strand of roses and stargazer lilies she wore around her neck began to glow. At first softly. The vases of iris placed where footlights would normally sit filled with shimmering color and overflowed. The shadowy forms of Grey and Skinny and Slaydell shuffled hesitantly into that spectral light. No dialogue, but the boys *moved* scared, weapons at the ready.

From their chosen spots the girls stole forward, glitter-dusted faces beautifully ghastly in the shine of the white gardenias Brit had pinned into their hair. They stumbled through the steps she'd lifted from "drunken" Zui quan forms. She called translations of the steps' names in cadence: "Swaying Hips! Pour the Wine! Spill the Soup! Tripping on the Trailing Hem!" The zombie girls crept and leapt and crawled around and above her, wooden swords carried in deceptively slack hands. They surrounded the hapless warriors and attacked! The boys yelled the names of their defenses as they fought. Though valiant, they were outnumbered two-to-one. Of course the zombies defeated them.

Good guys didn't always win. Something every kind of artist had to learn.

The boys stopped writhing around and the girls sat back on their haunches, showing their faces. Their mouths and chins were covered in a paste of mashed red petals: dahlias, peonies, glads—whatever Brit had been able to buy at the Port Townsend farmers' market. Blazing smears of blood red streaked their cheeks. They lifted crimson hands to gleam like torches in the hushed dimness.

The audience began applauding prematurely.

Grey sat up jerkily, as if he was strobing. Brit hadn't been able to convince any of the boys to paint their faces with crushed flowers, but she got them to carry bags of bee pollen from the food co-op—expensive, but when they'd rubbed it on their sweaty faces under cover of the girls' feeding frenzy, it became possible for her to provide their skin with a nice yellow-green luminosity.

The freshly undead got unsteadily up, and now all nine Martial Arts team members did the MJ moves in unison, complete with crotch grabs. And it was over, and the audience was on their feet, hooting, cheering, and whistling while they clapped, loud and hard and long.

A show-stopper, exactly as Brit had expected. She slipped out of the handicap access door stage right as the house lights turned up for intermission. Milky clouds covered the sky, reflecting back the town's and the park's streetlights, but Brit no longer needed them to see the lay of the land. It swelled and dipped before her, curving fire lapped by the wine of the sea.

The volume of the audience's murmuring increased for a few seconds as the door behind her opened and quickly shut. She turned to face her ally Mr. Crofutt. "So anointing them with flowers and nectar and pollen like that made them yours?" he asked. "Your kids?"

"As much mine as the women's they was born to." New queen, new hive. New rules. New reproductive techniques, not involving sex.

"And they won't die? Won't kill themselves?"

"Prolly not." Brit frowned. "You say them suicides was like allergic reactions to the entities. Rare."

"Better keep an eye on them anyway."

"Yeah." Or a sensory organ of some sort. She closed her eyes and checked just to make sure. Everyone was fine.

Conversion Therapy

These people won't let me do anything! Delighta's artistic scrawl complained. *Including sleep—they keep waking me up all night to check I'm not dreamin about sex with other girls. They feed me rotten bananas and nasty peanut butter crackers for breakfast lunch and if I don't answer their questions right for dinner too.* The rest of the lined and dirty page was torn away, leaving behind only random letters for Brit to guess into whole words.

She pulled the paper straighter, flatter, as if stretching it further would make the missing parts reappear. Of course not. She looked up at her friend and mentor, Mr. Crofutt, seated in her dorm room's sole chair. He nodded and frowned. "Looks like the trouble you picked up on is real," he said. She'd met him in Seattle two years ago, as a fourteen-year-old runaway. He was a counselor, freelance, and got her last summer's job at the arts camp he sometimes worked. The one where Brit gave in to the "bee" entities she was supposed to fight. The one where she'd used magic to lay occult claim to the nine kids she taught.

But arts camp had closed for the year, and they'd scattered to their parents' homes. The one compensation Brit had received for letting go of her adopted charges was sensitivity to their whereabouts. Kids had to leave the nest, and Brit's nest wasn't even official—she'd only been the camp's martial arts instructor. Their parents came for them on the last day, but Brit had felt them near, had kept in touch all the following year via dreams and emails. And now—

"Where you find this?" Brit stood and went to the window. Nothing but trees outside.

"In the canoe, like I thought I would, from what you said. Easy enough to insist on a tour of the facilities; the camp director swallowed my 'concerned parent' cover story, and Grey and Tanzi are good actors."

And their parents trusted Mr. Crofutt, an established counselor in the community.

The window Brit looked out of faced east and north, away from Puget Sound. Toward Scrolls of Glory Purification and Rededication Camp, where Delighta Johnson was apparently being held against her thirteen-year-old will. Brit's worry over Delighta had soured her early matriculation into Evergreen College. The Ebonics she espoused to spite her bougie Mom and Dad hadn't fazed admissions. They knew brilliance when they saw it.

But Delighta—something was wrong with her. Brit could tell. Not only were they spiritual mother-and-child, they were both short and cursed with voices like Betty Boop. Both the fiercer because of that.

Soon as she moved in, Brit hung the folding fan Delighta had colored for her above her dorm room's doorway. She loved its rich colors—like a Summer of Love butterfly. But it only made her happy a few days. After trying a solid week to ignore the grinding unease she felt in her room and the extra jolt of queasiness she felt whenever she touched it walking in, Brit began trying to reach her favorite unofficial adoptee. When that didn't work she went on to contact all the other eight. It was Grey's cousin Jazman, Delighta's former crush, who tipped her the clue as to why Delighta hadn't answered Brit's calls and messages: she'd been sent away in disgrace. Incommunicado.

Brit broke out alternative methods then and finally got through. "Okay. I can communicate—a lil bit." Precision was not the strength of the bee-entity channels she'd employed. She'd persuaded the girl to write a letter about her abuse and leave it for Mr. Crofutt to collect. But the three fluttering scraps he and his supposed children had retrieved—only one of which bore anything like a coherent sentence—were not much help in terms of planning a rescue. And they'd be none at all in executing it.

Frustrated, Brit slapped the double-paned glass, flat-palmed. She could have broken it with an edge-strike, she was pretty sure. But what good would martial arts do? "We need us a map!"

"I could draw you a fair one from memory," Mr. Crofutt claimed. His supernatural power was Finding, and making maps was as easy for him as breathing in and out. Brit's power was called Visioning. She could make the invisible visible, make any non-physical magical entities she encountered physical so that they were vulnerable to physical attack. Like she'd done to create the giant tent worms the first time she met Mr. Crofutt. Like she'd done with the entities she turned into mystical bees last summer, when she took responsibility for Delighta and the rest of her class.

Problem was, doing anything about entities required a face-to-face confrontation. Besides, were entities even involved in this?

Grey and Tanzi swooped into the room, jangling the bells dangling from Brit's doorknob, fluttering the fan, laughing and drinking juice they'd bought from the hall's vending machine. They stopped after only a couple of steps. "What? Didn't we bring what you wanted?" Tanzi asked.

"You need us to go back?" Grey didn't wait for a response. "Cool. That place had a serious stench." At least that answered the entity question. If Grey smelled entities, they were around the camp somewhere. Like Mr. Crofutt, the teen was shaping up to be another ace Finder.

"Yeah. Overnight if you can."

Mr. Crofutt grabbed his silver ponytail and put the fist holding it under his double chin. "I suppose I could make a sizeable donation to the church in exchange for a trial stay for my 'kids.' And there's a motel near the road into the camp for you and me, Brit."

"The donation gonna be funny money, I hope?"

"Oh, I'm canceling that check soon as I issue it."

⤚

Brit kicked her heels in the Scrolls of Glory waiting room. Literally: her feet barely touched the carpet tiles beneath the padded stool where she sat. Scoot back far enough, and her tai chi-slippered feet swung free. She hoped the ragged beat she drummed against its metal legs annoyed the woman keeping her waiting.

To be fair, on the phone the woman had clearly stated that they weren't actually looking for staff. Which made sense; the summer was practically over.

But the neck-pricking sensation of entities hovering over the adjacent property wouldn't allow Brit to wait calmly in the hotel for darkness and a chance to sneak onto the camp's grounds with Grey and Mr. Crofutt. She needed to be here *now*. Applying for a nonexistent job was the best excuse she could come up with for walking in here openly.

"Thanks for your patience. The Director is ready to see you," said the woman. No detectable signal had passed to her—no buzz of intercom or flash of light—but the woman sounded sure, and the door behind her opened. Sliding off the stool, Brit went in.

Peculiarly yellow dust motes filled the midafternoon sunlight slanting in at the office's windows. They gilded the spines of the books standing upright on the edge of his desk and smeared the frames of cross-stitched samplers lining the wall to Brit's left. She itched to wipe them clean. To her right ran a shelf holding more books—these stuffed with tasseled bookmarks and tattered, browning papers.

A slumping silhouette settled into the dark, high-backed chair behind the desk. From it came an entity vibe and a creaky voice. "Be seated, please." Brit perched on the edge of another stool. "An interesting application, Miss Williams."

"Ms."

Impossible to see the Director's expression with a row of wide, bright windows behind him, but he sounded more amused than angry. "As you wish. I suppose you refer to homosexuals as 'gays' as well. Or 'queers.'" He laughed, a sound like crumpling a grocery bag. "What I wonder is how you expected to gain anything by filling out our form at the end of the season and then insisting on an interview. Invoking the Equal Employment Opportunity Commission is hardly going to…endear you to any prospective employer. So—" The door behind Brit opened—silently, but she felt the slight breeze of its movement dry the sudden sweat on her scalp. "—we suspected a trick."

Brit dropped to the musty carpet. Arms closed shut above her, where she'd just been—the receptionist—another entity. Rolling away and jumping upright she grabbed a book in each hand and ran toward the windows. *Smash!* Glass and wood scattered everywhere. Brit leapt through the jagged opening and landed on her feet, hardly stumbling. No one around to see. A quick glance and she oriented her bee-entity sense of the land with Mr. Crofutt's intel. Downhill lay the lake and boathouse and storage racks for a dozen canoes—full. Uphill lay the cabins. Dead ahead, the commons: cafeteria probably empty, but classrooms likely full of kids. Next to that the showers.

No time to launch a boat—and they'd only launch another after her. Brit ran for the nearest shelter—the showers—

shoved the pine board door open on the cool darkness, the dampness—a scent of mildew rising like the echoing scuffs of her footsteps and a sniffling breath—No. No one should be in here but her.

But there again—a tiny, choking sob—

"Hello?"

"Mizz—Mizz Williams?" Spoken in mucous-clogged tones of disbelief.

"Delighta! What you doon alone and cryin in the dark? Where the light switch?"

"By the door where you are."

Brit reached and found it. "Why you ain't—" She stopped talking. The light flooding the cement walls and floor showed Delighta bound hand and foot, lying face down by the shower drain. Her short twists were mashed against the sides of her head, a sure sign she'd been fighting. White fuzz grew on the drain's grating and in a narrow circle around it, nearly touching the girl's tear-tracked cheek.

"Baby! What happen?" Brit made out extension cords hanging from towel hooks, clamps, gallon jugs, and a funnel on a wooden bench. She dragged the bench over to block the door; strange nobody had chased her here yet. Where was everyone? She went back to Delighta, sat her up, kissed her forehead, and began working on her knots.

"They—the counselors—they been tryin—"

Brit bit back the impulse to correct her charge's diction. If there was ever a time to relax her prohibition on her kids using AAVE the way she did, this was it.

"When other stuff didn't work, they said maybe spendin time in here on my own would open my heart to the Glory."

The "Glory"? The rope was wet, the knots stubborn. Brit pulled a six-pointed shuriken from a secret pocket and began sawing. "What 'other stuff'?" She had an idea.

"Torture." Delighta's voice attempted matter-of-factness; a hurt quaver betrayed her. "Tellin me it's for my own good so I'll grow up straight; they give me shocks for lookin at naked girl pictures and enemas if they catch me play—*Ow!*"

"Sorry." Brit dropped the knife from her traitorously trembling hand. She pulled loose the wet clothesline and exposed Delighta's wrists. "Only a scratch." She rubbed the girl's shallow cut; already the bleeding had basically stopped. Big exhale. Out with the shakes. In with the patience. She moved on to Delighta's ankles. The clothesline there glimmered in the grey light coming through the building's louvered vents. Not clothesline, but something thicker: clear plastic over a metallic core—the cable of a bike lock. Brit slashed at it in sudden frustration, blunting her blade, and Delighta jerked her legs back. Brit sighed and slouched forward, defeated. She would have to carry the girl to safety. She was strong enough. They'd be slow, though…

A scraping noise came from the wall standing at right angles to the door with the bench in front. From outside. Low. But the bench-stopped door didn't budge or even rattle. More scraping—higher? Climbing up the wall? Sliding over another bench, Brit used it to step onto a sink back and peer out of the vent at the wall's apex. She could barely see the ground; it teemed with ants—huge ants, big as throwing stars, though not absolutely-nuts sci-fi movie giants.

Visioning at work—Brit's secret power. She'd transformed the entities infesting Scrolls into ants, so now they'd be vulnerable. Though ants and bees were deadly enemies, anything that could kill ants could get rid of the entities.

She had come prepared. The other two times she'd Visioned entities, they came out insects also.

From a pocket—not a secret one, since nobody would think the contents mattered—she took a stick of ordinary-seeming chalk. Broke it in half. "Here." She handed part to

Delighta. "Draw a line where the wall meets the floor, all aroun us."

"This is magic?" Delighta crawled to the far wall and began tracing a wide line at its base.

"Naw. You gonna find it in almost any hardware store. Boric acid." Not a pesticide but a repellent. Quickly, Brit finished laying down her sections of the chalk line and ran to reinforce the barrier at a few crucial spots with the last of her stub: the vents, the narrow space underneath the door, the white-circled drain. She checked for chinks in the cement where water pipes came in, and sealed off five.

"There." The ant entities would stay away. For now. For long enough, Brit hoped, that Grey and Tanzi and Mr. Crofutt could find them and get them out of there. She examined the bike lock. With the help of icy water to reduce the swelling in the girl's feet and a few pumps of liquid soap for lubricant, they worked it off.

After that it was a mere matter of waiting. She cradled Delighta in her arms, leaned the girl against her legs, her knees up like mountains. All around them, all the rest of that soon-clouded afternoon, every wall scratched and scrabbled with the flood of questing entities.

Then, toward sunset, the flood receded. Ants were diurnal animals, Brit knew.

They had water. They had a place to pee and toilet paper. They had the power bar Brit brought to eat, but hunger persisted, and boredom combined with it almost irresistibly once Delighta finished her inflectionless recital of the tactics used to "purify" her of her emergent sexuality. So after only forty minutes of silence and a score of swift peeps out through the vents, Brit scooted the bench aside and opened the showers' door.

The surroundings were completely deserted. No sign of huge ants or humans. The commons a few feet away looked dark and empty, though this must be suppertime.

The original plan called for sneaking in to rescue Delighta tonight. Mr. Crofutt's final recon should be happening now. Where was he? Where were her kids Tanzi and Grey? Where was *anyone?*

Brit almost headed south, back to the offices she'd escaped earlier, to see who might be holed up there. But good sense prevailed, and she shepherded her charge northward, to where a trailhead entered the forest's spreading shadows. The main road curved around the property's boundary to eventually hug the lakeshore, so they'd come to it if she could keep them on track, dead ahead. Over unfamiliar terrain. In the falling dusk.

Under the first of the alders Brit explained this strategy to Delighta, sounding confident. She reminded herself she had reason to: since last summer, when the bee entities transformed her, Brit no longer got lost.

The main path was broad. Distracting smaller branches coming off of it led nowhere important, so Brit hurried Delighta past them. Which was why they didn't find the first corpse till they'd been walking three quarters of a mile.

"I hafta pee," Delighta announced.

What could Brit say? They'd left the showers' toilets behind just minutes ago, but so what. She nodded toward the nearest side trail. "Go on. I be here."

Discreet rustling marked the girl's progress. Then: "*Ah! Aaah! Aaaa—*" Screams yanked Brit through tall weeds and brambles to where Delighta clutched her panties and pointed.

From the underside of a poplar's springy-looking limb hung one of the camp's five-inch ants, coated in what seemed like sunlit dust. Except there was no sun. A long spike protruded from its head, a sparkling ball stuck onto it like a weird Christmas ornament.

Brit knew what this was. *Ophiocordyceps unilateralis.* "Quiet," she said, and Delighta obeyed. For a wonder. She lectured into the silence. "That thing cain't hurt you. It dead."

At least part of it was. The part that threatened her and her swarm.

"Look." Brit picked a stick off the ground and knocked the ant's body down. The head stayed locked to the poplar limb by lifeless jaws. Delighta gave a tiny shriek followed by a nervous giggle.

"See? Dead." She kicked the crumbling chitin apart. "Now come on." They resumed their journey. Brit wished she could sing to stave off her worries, but someone searching might hear them.

But who? Who was chasing them? Who—or what—were the entities in control of Scrolls? The oversized enemy ants she'd first seen, or the fungus that appeared to be taking over the ants? Or both?

The next corpse settled that.

As twilight's dimness rose between bushes and tree trunks, smoke without fire, Brit found she guided Delighta more and more closely. She held Delighta's hand tight in her own, then wrapped an arm around the girl's tee-shirted shoulders. She told herself their mute caution would help them spot Mr. Crofutt and the others if the Finder came looking for them. That she was not really afraid.

She saw the man's dangling body ahead and covered Delighta's eyes. She clenched her teeth. She did not scream, or even grunt. Made no noise at all.

The bulging eyes and gaping mouth recalled the strange fruit of lynch mobs. But the gold powder dusting the dead man's skin was identical to the "sunlit" dust on the ant's corpse, and it tied their deaths together. The same danger had caused them: *Ophiocordyceps unilateralis*, aka Zombie Fungus. While studying the bees who were the template of the entities taking her over, Brit had delved into the biology of their natural rivals and frequent combatants, carpenter ants. And that of the *ants'* natural enemy, *O. unilateralis*, which apparently was in the process of enslaving and killing the camp's original entities. Her Visioning power had physicalized the first entities as ants, and the invaders as this fungus.

Zombie fungus. Which could attack both ants and other organisms. Such as human beings. Converting them to monsters. As it had apparently already done before Brit arrived. And now—probably this very afternoon—

"You known the Director? Mr. Scribner?"

"Ye-e-e-es...Mizz Brit, what's wrong?"

"Hope you didn't like him much. He dead too. Hangin up ahead in a tree we gotta go by."

"Dead? You mean like—"

"You be all right?"

"I guess."

They began to shuffle forward. In short glimpses as they passed, Brit saw how the Director's hands locked together around the branch he hung from. How the fingertips of his left dug too deeply into the wrist of his right. How the toes of his shoeless feet strained skyward, flexed hard in the same pain or ecstasy that threw back his head and opened his silent mouth. And though the true spore-bearing body would take days to develop, she thought she saw a soft, incipient bulge at the crown of his head....

So. Two entities. One the other's prey.

More indistinct shapes crowded the darkening treetops. Brit ignored them as well as she could and urged Delighta on. Finally, finally, they stumbled down into and back up out of a mucky ditch, and there they were. The road. Impossibly civilized.

Which way to the motel? She checked the glowing geomagnetic grid underlying the world. South. They'd have to pass the camp's entrance. Maybe go off the shoulder on the opposite side.

A few feet beyond Scrolls' dirt-and-gravel turnoff, Mr. Crofutt's van sat, lights doused, motor running. "Stay here," Brit ordered Delighta, and ventured out of the horsetails and fireweed on her own.

Tanzi sat shotgun. Brit couldn't see anyone else.

Tanzi rolled down the window. "Hey! Grey and Mr. Crofutt found you?"

"Nope." She waved Delighta in. "We took the long way round."

Tanzi opened her door, smiling. "Lighta! I'm so glad you—but don't—don't cry!" She thumped Delighta awkwardly on her back as the girl climbed in over her.

"I'm not!" Wiping furiously at her lying eyes, Delighta shrugged off Tanzi's attempts at comforting her and flopped sideways on the back seat. "Let's blow."

"We gotta wait," Tanzi objected. "They'll be back soon—" Her voice thinned uncertainly.

"When?" Brit demanded. "They say?" She sat behind the wheel. "I got my learner's license. How about I drop you two at the motel an come back?"

Tanzi didn't know whether there'd be time. Brit decided not to push it. Fish-smelling mud caked her Spiras; she dug at the clumps on her left shoe with the toe of the right. Then cleaned the right with the left. Should she return to face the entities on her own? But the girls needed her protection. And she might miss the others.

Minutes passed. Full night reigned by the time Mr. Crofutt's white-and-purple clad paunch jounced into view. An old-fashioned flashlight illuminated it, pointed at the ground. Brit thought Grey must be invisible because he walked outside the bright circle. Then Mr. Crofutt switched the light off and got in alone. He shut the door. "Move over. I'm driving." He sounded gruff: sad or angry. He let out the brake and backed into the camp's entrance, but only to turn around and head the other way down the main road, toward the motel.

"Stop!" Brit lurched off the back bench and crouched between driver and passenger seats. "You gonna just leave? Where Grey?"

Mr. Crofutt kept going. "Time for the police. Grey's captured by the ants you Visioned up. They caught us outside a cabin." He leaned forward as if checking the left rearview mirror, then looked briefly over his shoulder at the empty road behind them. His enhanced eyesight—part of his Finder skill set—must have shown nothing to alarm him. He flipped on the van's headlights and sped up.

"You know for a fact the po-po wanna listen to you? Bout some little black kid foun trespassin on private property?"

"Well, you have a point, but yes. Since I'm white."

"Awright." Brit settled back into her seat. "We try it your way." She had to think what was best for her kids.

⤝

According to the motel rooms' "Welcome to Aberdeen County!" booklets, the closest police station was fifteen miles away. Too far. Mr. Crofutt agreed that neighboring Copalis Crossing's Volunteer Fire Department was a better gamble. That was only three.

Filling the shallow tub for Tanzi and Delighta, Brit laid out the shirts she'd brought for them to sleep in. A tiny bottle of free shampoo dumped in under the faucet turned the water into a bubble bath. The girls squealed with pampered glee.

She loaded her jacket pockets with the rest of her power bars and hesitated, then turned on the TV. *Star Trek* reruns. "I'ma lock yall in, an you don't let nobody through that door cep me. Awright?"

Only one voice answered her. "Yes, Mizz Williams." That was Tanzi.

"Delighta?"

"She's holding her breath, Mizz—"

Brit rushed back in the bathroom. Half-obscured by hills of white suds, Delighta lay flat on her back, six inches underwater. Eyes open, staring at nothing. Suiciding? "Out! Git out the tub!" Her fright startled Tanzi into jumping over the tub's rim.

"Delighta!" Arms plunged in to her elbows, she hauled her adopted daughter free of the steaming bathwater. "Delighta!"

The girl blinked. Twice.

Brit turned to Tanzi, shivering and dripping on the bathroom floor. "Gimme a towel. Git one for yourself too." She pulled the plug to let the tub drain.

Dried off, Delighta seemed content to continue to stand naked and blank-faced. "You hear me?" Brit asked her. A slow nod. "You okay?" Another. "Why you so weird then?" No response. A hasty examination revealed nothing out of the ordinary except the cut on her wrist from Brit's shuriken, which was oddly pale. White, almost. Dead skin rendered transparent by soaking?

A knock on the motel room's front door roused Brit from her contemplation. Mr. Crofutt was ready for their return trip. "Comin!" she yelled. But what about Delighta—could Brit leave her here? Was that fair to Tanzi? She'd been unsure before, and now... With sudden decision she tugged a too-large glitter-printed tee over her damaged daughter's head.

"Put your clothes back on again, Tanzi." She yanked the covers from the nearest bed. "An carry this. You gonna spend the night in the back a Mr. Crofutt's van."

He led them down to the parking lot without one remark. Which was a good thing. Mr. Crofutt was the one who'd left Grey, who'd made this whole second trip necessary.

What a lie. It was all her fault.

She'd had no business adopting nine kids like that last summer. Barely not a kid herself anymore.

Copalis Crossing Fire Association shared building space with Aberdeen County Emergency Medical Services. Mr. Crofutt cut the van's engine and opened his door but then sat there.

"What we waitin for?" Brit asked.

"I called ahead. The dispatcher said somebody'd meet us." He gestured at the empty asphalt, the lightless windows. "Looks like we beat them."

Brit would have cursed if not for Tanzi and Delighta. "What kinda Deliverance—" Before she could finish, a blue-and-white squad car pulled in. Its human-looking driver and passenger glowed golden with dusty fungus spores. "Go! Gogogogo!"

Mr. Crofutt peeled out, door hanging open till he veered sharply enough to slam it shut. Zooming up Ocean Beach Road he shouted over the engine roar, "Entities?"

"Bad ones! Fungus infections—same as at Scrolls of Glory!"

The cop car was following them. Tanzi was visibly trying not to cry and having no luck. Delighta—Delighta craned over her seatback like she was ready for dessert and the cop car was made of ice cream. In its headlights, a hungry gleam shone from her eyes.

"No siren," Mr. Crofutt observed. "You think they really are cops with no entities infecting them and—"

Whoop! Whoop! Whoopwhoop!

"Don't pull over! We almost to the camp!"

The siren began undulating nonstop. Mr. Crofutt shook his head and slowed down, edging off the pavement.

"A little farther!" Brit begged.

"My reputation!" Mr. Crofutt objected—but he turned at the right intersection. The cop car gave up following them and sped ahead to park across the road.

"Stay in here!" Brit ordered the girls. The van was still—barely—rolling, but she got her door open and for the second time that day scrambled into and out of a weedy, mud-filled ditch. Running through the blinding white cones thrown by their car's headlights, she escaped the cop's roadblock. Headed for ants and more fungus. Shadowy trees surrounded her on three sides. On the fourth, the openness of the camp's entrance drive beckoned. But the cop car would come that way if Mr. Crofutt couldn't defeat either group of entities on his own. But the trees' shadows probably contained the same horrors she'd seen as she was leaving—

A loudspeaker squawked, then blared recognizable words: "Come out with your hands up!" The squad car cruised into view. The driver steered with one hand and held a bullhorn in the other. He stopped and offered it to someone—some-*thing*—riding beside him. "*Chik-lik-tikki-kik-kik-kichh!*" it shouted. From cabins and other buildings came the ominous sound of opening doors. Brit imagined giant ants and fungus-ridden kids and counselors pouring forth, spilling down the hillside to fight each other.

Before she saw them, she saw Delighta. Barreling toward the cop car—with Mr. Crofutt and Tanzi right behind her. Delighta reached the car and opened its door and dragged out the driver. Brit couldn't see exactly what happened then—the back of the car blocked most of it. Both fungus cop and girl landed on the ground, and only Delighta got up from it.

The near door—the one on the passenger side—burst open. The other entity tumbled out and scrabbled at the dirt. It began crawling away. Delighta fell on it from above.

Tanzi and Mr. Crofutt caught up. "Wait! Stop!" They grabbed Delighta by the shirt and tried to pull her off her victim. Brit ran to help, but they succeeded before she arrived. In the backwash of the car's headlights, Delighta's mouth shone gold and silver, as if smeared with metallic lip gloss.

The misshapen uniform lying on the shadowed earth seemed to move. It *was* moving: twisting and teeming like hot syrup in cold water. And the cop's face: ripples ran over it from opposite directions, crashed, receded…

"Get back!" Grey came down the hill surrounded by a crowd of ant entities. "You're not inoculated like me!" He flapped his arms. "Back!"

"What?" Brit and Tanzi edged away from the fallen cop. Delighta stood, turning her head in a slow, even arc as if scanning the cool night air. For something.

"The zombie fungus—the bad mind control entity?" Grey stopped just outside the headlights and gestured at the dozens of oversized ants. "The originals, the ants, started farming a—guess you'd call it an enemy? A different fungus that fights it."

Mr. Crofutt peered up from where he crouched over the shivering entity body. "So *that's* what I smell!" He straightened and pointed. "Strongest over that way, right?"

"Yeah. It needs a ton of water, so they picked the showers to incubate it in." Brit recalled the white ring around the floor drain by Delighta's face—her cut wrist—was that why she'd submerged herself in the bathtub? To irrigate her infection?

"So they your friends?" She caught Delighta in her arms, trapped the girl's head in her hands and forced it still. "Ants ain't want nothin from us bees but our honey. They kill us—"

"'Us bees'?" Grey's voice came now from the blackness where the other fungus cop had fallen. "I thought we were humans. With powers, sure, but look, ants—big ones like these even—they can sting us, eat our picnics I guess. That's all. It's the zombie fungus we've gotta be careful of, and once you've been inoculated with the one against it that the ants made—" He stood and stepped fully into the headlight beams, holding out arms glinting white to the elbows. "—and gave me? You're safe."

Brit looked at Mr. Crofutt. The enemy of my enemy is my friend? Was he buying that? "Listen. We come here to rescue my—my child." If Brit was a bee so was Delighta. So was Grey. So were all nine of the kids she'd claimed. "An that's what we gonna do! Tanzi! Come on! You too, Grey!" Shooing Tanzi ahead and dragging Delighta behind her, she walked fast as she could up the driveway—till she saw the swarm of ants following them. Then she ran.

Easier this way than through the undergrowth.

She heard human feet behind her. But others too, and when she finally reached the van and she got her kids in and climbed in herself, she saw out of the windshield not only Grey and Mr. Crofutt in the middle of the shadow horde of ant entities gobbling up the ground. She saw the reception-ist and another couple of vague, golden, adult-shaped outlines walking in their wake. Almost, it seemed, herding them.

Brit slammed the passenger side door shut, then lunged to lock the one on the driver's side. Delighta had the handle, trying to open it! "Git in the back," she yelled at Tanzi. "The way back." She fought Delighta and of course won—but why did the girl want out? The influence of the anti-zombie-fun-gus? "Delighta!"

Grey and Mr. Crofutt came up and pounded on the win-dow. Didn't Mr. Crofutt have a key?

"I'll let them in my end," Tanzi announced from the rear, and before Brit could object, she had opened half the double door past the last benches and covers and storage and Deligh-ta, slick as tung oil, slipped out. And was running toward the attackers.

"Stop!" Brit shouted, pushing the door wider, shoving at Grey who was in the way! "Stop her!" she told Mr. Crofutt, but instead he stopped Brit! Caught and held her arms and *forced* her back into the van's interior. *Made* her sit. And saw her start to cry.

"Listen," he said. "Listen. Listen. *Listen. Listen!*"

"De-Delighta! Delighta's gone!" She forgot to use her "bad" English. "G-g-gone!"

"She'll be back! She'll be fine!" Mr. Crofutt eased up on the downward pressure and actually helped her stand. "Look at—oh, wait—I forgot you can't see as well as me in the dark. Let me—" Leading her around to the van's front end, he fished out his keys and stuck one of them in the ignition. "There." He snapped on the van's headlights.

Straining, Brit made out struggling figures where the camp's entrance drive met the road. The shorter ones—the kids were winning! Grey and Delighta rode the receptionist and the only other visible adult like they were playing piggyback. "Closer!" Brit commanded, throwing herself in the seat. She popped the parking brake off, cranked the key, and was reaching for the shift stick when Mr. Crofutt got in the other side.

"You ever drive a standard transmission before tonight?" he asked, swinging himself into place.

"My cousin Blaise's Beetle," she explained. "It a Volkswagen too." Though she drove as fast as she could change gears, by the time she got the car to the camp entrance the brief battle was as good as done. The ants swarmed over low, gradually deflating mounds. Whoever—whatever—their teeming shininess covered, it wasn't Grey or Delighta. Those two remained erect. Ignored, they straddled the rivers of insects streaming between their legs. White-coated arms on her hips, Delighta looked like a titanium oxide Colossus.

She looked nothing like a bee.

The ant entities made no move to attack her or Grey. Maybe when they "caught" him it hadn't been a hostile move, merely necessary for his inoculation?

Did Delighta still need to be rescued? Not if the zombie fungus was the entity to blame. Still—

Brit rolled down her window. "Let's go!" she shouted. Grey nudged Delighta, and they came and got in. She turned around using the driveway, carefully avoiding crushing any ants.

The motel parking lot was mercifully empty and she had no trouble pulling in.

They weren't supposed to spend the night here, according to the original plan. Too easy for the entities to find them.

But dealing with Delighta's parents? Brit wanted to put that off as long as possible. She was muddy. Sweaty. Prickers in her hair. And so, so tired.

She gave her room key to Tanzi. Grey took one from Mr. Crofutt. She heard yelling and laughter as they went up the building's outdoors stairs. Three kids. Just kids.

And yet much more.

But what? What were they?

She asked Mr. Crofutt.

"I've been thinking about that," he said. "There used to be quite an array of skills. Besides me and my wife as Finders, and her brothers forming a pair of Visioners, my crew in Spokane had someone like Delighta could turn out to be—we called her a Pen. Like an EpiPen, though, not what you write with. She delivered...doses. She told us that in New York she'd worked with someone whose power was Charming—a man who lured the entities in. And there could be additional functions. Probably are. We only had five members."

"Counting me, now you got eleven."

Eleven. A family of eleven entity fighters. Though on good terms with certain entities themselves.

Tanzi's power hadn't even emerged yet.

Wearily, Brit opened the van's door, descended to the parking lot and set off for the stairs, wondering what wonders awaited her when she reached their top. And tomorrow.

A Beautiful Stream

Her daughter's hatred would be seen as Gabrielle's fault. What of it? Such an outcome was not to be lamented or evaded, but accepted. Better for little Gazouette to believe her mama indifferent than for her to be used as leverage. Or worse, to be trapped in identical coils.

Gabrielle-Sidonie Goncourt looked down at her sleeping daughter, taking in the rucked sheets, the petal-colored cheeks, with deliberate coldness, then walked from the room into the lampless passageway. She had never wanted to bear a child, anyway, she reminded herself. One would think that at forty the chance of doing so had passed.

She shut the bedroom's door and leaned against its dark panels, their wood creaking slightly.

Strength. She willed herself forward. There were appearances to keep up. No one must know of her escape. Tonight.

Gabrielle's skirts rustled as she walked along the corridor, sweeping the tops of her shoes, rubbing against the silk sleeves covering her arms as they moved forward and back, forward and back. Turning a corner, she heard with sudden clarity the sounds of the diners below: her lover, faithful Missy, and the ballet backers she'd brought with her—the loud, rather coarse ice magnate M'sieur Hanse; the abstemious M'sieur Falco Tessiter and his equally sober son Robert. And of course Gabrielle's husband. Who did not ask of her more than she could give.

The ballet was to be dedicated to Gazouette: a show, literally, of her mother's affection. Probably she would want more. Too bad.

Gabrielle knew how to walk downstairs; her mother, Sido, had shown her how not to lower her head, how to keep the line of her neck taut and appealing. Hand on the bannister, eyes on the chandelier, she glided along in a smooth descent. Wasted; not one of her guests had peered through the doorway of the dining room to see her coming.

The maids had cleared the plates with their unsightly burdens, brushed crumbs and fallen titbits from the damask cloth. In a proper household the ladies would have now withdrawn, but Missy remained in the chair where she'd been seated during the meal, and Gabrielle found a glass waiting for her as expected at her own place, filled with a tawny vintage.

Goncourt and the Tessiters rose quickly; Hanse lagged somewhat behind them, one hand on the back of his chair. "Madame," her husband began, "we have been wondering if, perhaps, there might be some discussion of business?"

Gabrielle nodded. Goncourt eased the padded chair beneath her as she resumed her spot. "We are on good enough terms now, are we not?"

She turned to Tessiter Pére on her left. "It is in my mind that you would like best to give us support in the matter of costumery, maquillage, scenery—the materials bought once. As soon as the war ends, of course. While you—" She faced the other way, towards Hanse. "—would be the one to supply ongoing expenses such as rents, advertisements, and dancers' and musicians' salaries."

"Yes, but how are the proceeds to be disbursed?" asked this worthy. "Proportionally to our costs? Our risks?"

Missy intervened. "There is no risk. In a few months, when the war ends, we proceed. Our composer is Ravel; our choreographer Nijinsky. Our shining star is Gabrielle."

The older Tessiter demurred. "It is 1915. Nearly ten years now since they rioted in the streets over your kiss, Mesdames." He looked long and meaningfully at Missy's handsome but aging countenance. "The sensation has died down. Forgive me if I seek some other surety for our investment."

"I am good for it," Missy replied. Her voice was heavy with disappointment, as if she scolded a cat of whom she anticipated nothing better than a certain level of misbehavior. "Goncourt also may be relied upon."

The evening went convincingly, she thought. At last the Tessiters' carriage rattled away in the dull moonlight. From her seat on the chaise longue before her boudoir's velvet-draped window, Gabrielle watched their departure with tempered relief. Now the die must be cast.

Goncourt would be expecting her in their shared bedroom, a long walk and two turns along the passageway. Well, let him wait. She had a private farewell to make.

She arrested the hand of her lover, captured it firmly in her own so Missy could no longer toy with the tendrils escaping from Gabrielle's carefully inexact coiffure. Still plump and smooth, the mound under Missy's thumb yielded softly to Gabrielle's teasing bite. A heavy sigh—a sound too soft to be called a moan—escaped her lover's lips. Gabrielle drew her down to kiss not her mouth but her neck.

Soon the chaise held them both, a pliant twist of flesh and pleasure. No fire filled the room's grate, so they didn't remove their clothing, merely rearranged it. Nor did they linger long in the chill that followed passion.

Missy sighed again as she sat beside her, pulling up her stockings and fastening them in place.

A third sigh. Gabrielle rose to put enough distance between them that she could ask what was wrong without the danger of a collapse into her arms.

"I wish I could go with you," Missy replied. The shadows thrown by the candle on the mantel showed only half her lover's face. That half held a stoically sad expression Gabrielle knew from earlier separations.

"But it is to Goncourt's estate we go," Gabrielle objected. "Inviting you would not be fair to him. Here, in the house you let to us, it is different."

"Yes." Missy stood also, shaking out the skirts of her gown, smiling ruefully. "Here, it *is* different."

Kissing her lover goodbye, Gabrielle prayed silently that she and Missy would meet once more in safety. That someday she'd be free of the shadowy militarists who sought to bind Gabrielle to their service by threatening those she loved.

But not soon. Her ostensible masters would learn where she had fled to, eventually, though they wouldn't be able to manipulate her so easily at Rozven. Her husband's family was well-established, his retainers loyal.

In their bedroom, Goncourt, fully dressed, paced in front of the glowing hearth. "All is in readiness?" she asked, to give him a chance to reprove her.

"This past hour. Where have you been?"

"With the child," Gabrielle lied.

Goncourt laughed. "A likely story! Haven't I always known—"

Though she had instigated it, she found herself suddenly bored by the prospect of the coming lecture. So she simply stopped listening. As her husband thundered on, she glanced around, noting the table newly emptied of his cosmetics: wax for his moustache, cream for the shining skin atop his head. Cologne and manicure set were also gone. A carafe and drinking glass occupied the bedside table, but overall the room's air was of a location soon to be abandoned.

That was the doing of this so-called "great" war, which was to have been over by Christmas. Dragging on and on, it had brought "requests" from her government she found she couldn't afford to refuse outright: to travel, to spy, to report on their enemies. And to monitor even their ostensible friends.

Now her view of the room was obscured by memories: the awkward approach of her would-be "recruiter" during a lull in business at the dim café down the street; his laughable attempt to force her capitulation by publicizing her African heritage — as if that weren't a point of which to be proud! As if it weren't already widely known—and when that failed, his semi-obscure promises to do violence to Missy, which Gabrielle tried to face with equanimity, hoping that her lover's wealth would shield her from harm. And then his hints about visiting pain upon Gazouette. Which Gabrielle was not able to treat with the same disdain.

Hence her preparations for this evening.

"Do you suppose we fooled them?" Gabrielle asked, and knew from Goncourt's face she had interrupted what he was saying.

After being forced to vent his anger he usually became a penitent lamb. As was now the case: he gathered her gently in his arms. "Can you forgive me? In the morning it will be all over town—I have allowed a reporter to write about our little project for the *Journal.*"

Gabrielle grimaced, but answered cheerfully, "Then we had best be on our way, hadn't we?" By the time their departure was known, she and her child would be safe.

Her husband held the bedroom door open for her with a small bow and repeated the gesture at the entrances to the kitchen and the courtyard. Inside the cramped stables the loaded automobile throbbed loudly, the purring of an immense, watchful cat. Their driver got out and let Goncourt take his seat, then helped Gabrielle take hers. He arranged the fur collar of her favorite coat so it protected her ears without tickling her chin. He opened the cat's eyes, or rather, uncovered its headlamps.

"Where is Gazouette?" her husband asked.

"Gone ahead, with her nanny."

"They are to meet us in Chartres?"

"No. Tomorrow night, in Le Mans." That was when she would tell him that their child had embarked for Canada. By then she would be gone.

"Fine. As long as you are satisfied." He waved at the driver to open the courtyard gates, and they set off.

⧽⧼

But Gabrielle's ruse didn't work. A miscommunication of some sort. Less than a week after she and Goncourt arrived at Rozven, Taylor and Gazouette arrived also. Taylor sat challengingly upright on the uncomfortable chair in Gabrielle's office, her timid charge curled at her feet. "There were no suitable lodgings on the island," the Englishwoman explained. "I would have continued on, but then I heard the news of the fire on the Mauretania." Gabrielle had not heard herself till this morning. The ship on which she'd booked Gazouette's passage to Quebec was out of commission. For how long she didn't know. Nor did she comprehend why the woman hadn't journeyed on to her homeland and stayed there till repairs were effected.

Nonetheless, she nodded. "Of course. The nursery is being readied for you."

That change would lessen the space available to board nurses, for the house would soon be filled with wounded soldiers. Eventually there'd be no room to spare. The nurses would have to be made to fit somewhere—perhaps an outbuilding? Later she would reexamine their disposition; at the moment what mattered was that her plans for Gazouette's safety were ruined. Though no spymaster was in evidence, Gabrielle was sure one would appear soon enough.

She brought the interview to a quick close and went to the library. It had been her site of solace for three years now, during every visit since her marriage: the narrow windows admitting sunlight, stormlight, moonlight, mistlight; the polished stones of the floor, reddish black, stubbornly refusing to reflect more than smudges of those who stood upon them; and, of course, the books.

Not many remained on the rapidly emptying shelves. A quarter of the room's former inhabitants. Reaching almost at random, Gabrielle caught the top of one tall volume with a crooked finger and pulled it down toward her. An old favorite, this one, rescued from the sale of her girlhood home's contents. It was clad in blue twill, crammed full of colored plates depicting classical myths. She sat on a footstool and idly turned its pages till she came to Rubens's portrait of Thetis bathing Achilles. Here was an idea.

Though the hero had died.

But perhaps his death was owing to an error on the part of his mother? Or, perhaps the River Styx's hellish nature had precluded a happy ending?

Marking her place with one finger, Gabrielle carried the book of myths with her to her bedroom in the turret. The afternoon's long shadows stretched themselves out upon the naked staircase, concealing and revealing its scars, the result of removing the runner that had covered it so many years. That worn strip of carpet had been rolled up and stored temporarily in the entrance hall. It was to be laid down the middle of the transformed ballroom, between ranks of the hospital beds still stacked in the front drive, awaiting their installation.

She had written yesterday to affirm that they'd be ready to receive their first consignment of the "great" war's wounded by March 1. A fortnight.

Outside her door she paused. On the other side of the circular landing lay the nursery. From beneath the bottom of its door came murmurs, contented-sounding voices: low and womanly, high and prattlingly childish. She wouldn't interrupt; she could picture the scene clearly enough. Taylor would be unpacking, Gazouette staggering like a drunken doll as she struggled to follow in her nanny's bustling steps. The jumpers and heavy knitted stockings, the bonnets and leggings and jackets so carefully selected in anticipation of Britain's cool climate would be stowed away in chests of drawers.

Couldn't Gazouette and her clothing stay here? Wouldn't she be safe enough at Rozven, safe as her father and mother? Who could say if Gabrielle's best strivings to make it so would be enough?

Entering her half-moon-shaped bedchamber, Gabrielle rang for her fire to be lit. The sun would soon set, and she'd need the warmth and light. When the housemaid had come and gone she pulled a white-painted, flower-cushioned armchair to the hearth and reopened her book to the Rubens.

Bats. They besieged the painting, framed the subjects, surrounded them. In the distance, ghosts clamored to Charon for release from their dull afterlives—understandably. The river's waters, green and poisonous-looking, showed nothing of the miracle they were supposed to instill in those brought by supplicants to its shores. Brought to be bathed in the chill and cold, to freeze the body but soothe the soul…

And Thetis, that foolish nymph, had subjected her child to this treatment—to preserve his life, of course—but had failed to do it thoroughly enough. Why had she not submerged her own hand in the Styx, if that would keep her son from harm?

Gabrielle studied the painting's reproduction till the dinner bell. Would she need a dog? Or a friend such as the spinner Clotho to hold up an illuminating flame?

No—no flames, no bats. She'd try what she could accomplish without them.

After dinner she fended off Goncourt's attentions. It took very little trouble. She looked in on Gazouette, spoke a brief word with Taylor about the program for the following day, and went to bed betimes.

※

Gabrielle woke, as always, without recourse to an alarm clock. Only the faintest clues announced the coming of the day: a sky like milk from a dark blue cow, a western breeze laden with the merest hint of brine.

There was a bit of fuss in the nursery. To save time and lessen the noise, Gabrielle accepted Taylor's accompaniment out of the house and across lawns crackling with frost, to the path she had discovered during her first explorations. She insisted on carrying the child herself, though.

Even leafless with winter, the beech trees cut off much of the dawn's growing light. Taylor stopped at the woods' edge to adjust her lantern to a wider aperture, but Gabrielle, impatient, darted ahead, trusting to the bark's silvery glimmering to show her the way. "Leave that thing there!" she called back over her shoulder. "It's mostly unnecessary and will only become more so!" No flames. As soon as the nanny caught up, Gabrielle compelled her to abandon the undesirable hindrance.

Gradually, the land fell. The path, like a young girl, ran straight down precipitous slopes, then dallied flirtatiously with the stream at their bottom, climbing in opposition to its flow to the low granite bluffs occupying Rozven's eastern boundaries. At last, as glowing pink and yellow tints had just touched the clouds far above, they came to the sacred spring.

The source.

A curved wall had been built into the earth. From a crack between its grey stones poured a cascade of singing water. Caught momentarily in a round pool, it laughed and splashed itself out by way of a channel bridged with slabs of that same stone. Above the wall and to one side stood a gracefully bowed beech, its lower branches festooned with ribbons: gay and bright or tattered, faded, old. Each ribbon represented a prayer. So the old women seated before nearby cottages had intimated.

Gabrielle knelt on the ground, Gazouette in her lap. Taylor spread the rug she had stubbornly brought. Gabrielle was glad of it; the dead leaves were damp. She lay the drowsy little child down on the rug and went to work on removing her clothes.

Despite the harsh temperature, Gazouette seemed to enjoy her nudity. No sooner had her mother divested her of the last of her garments than she hoisted herself to her feet, fully awake now, running and stumbling in spirals and zigzags as the two women chased her. To Gabrielle's pride, it was she who gathered the giggling girl into her arms, not Taylor. But she had to relinquish her to the nanny anyway in order to remove her own boots, coat, and skirt, and to roll and tuck up her crinoline and her blouse's long sleeves.

For a ribbon she had brought the band off an old gardening hat of Sido's. That old straw hat was the only remnant Gabrielle had of her mother's practical wardrobe, which had been sparse at the height of its glory and was now all but vanished with time. The band's pale blue spoke of the dusty, sunny days she'd spent under Sido's watchful maternal eye, guarded, as she well knew, with the best of care.

So many others had petitioned the spring before her. Rumors among the women of the village said every single one had gotten her wish. But as Gabrielle chose her twig and tied her prayer to it, she wondered if some other sacrifice would be required.

Taylor parted with Gazouette reluctantly. Gabrielle carried the squirming, wriggling little child to the bridge and lay on her stomach on the big flat stone. Using both hands—she was not afraid, not she—she gently lowered her daughter into the babbling brook. Cold stole into Gabrielle's bones, but she held the girl firmly, swishing her back and forth, twice changing her grip to ensure every inch of skin received its blessing. Then she pulled the dripping and now hopefully invulnerable child back out of the water and wrapped her in the driest part of her under-chemise.

A weird, skirling cry split the air—getting louder and louder, sharper and sharper, hurting her ears. She threw herself prone again, sheltered Gazouette beneath her breasts and shoulders, peered up and saw a swelling black *thing* falling toward her. Its wide wings unfurled—an eagle?—osprey?—she could see its grasping claws, its dark, hooked beak—

It swerved aside! With a crash it hit the pool. Only a few feet away... And now she perceived Taylor squealing with fright, running forward with arms stretched out—What good would that do?

Gabrielle rolled to lessen her weight on the baby and saw the bird surface from the pool's depths and fly to the tree of prayers, a flash of silver held struggling in its feet. This it transferred to its mouth. It hopped higher, out of sight, but Gabrielle had no doubt the silver signified a fish, which the osprey—only ospreys dived so—would now eat in peaceful retirement.

Fending off Taylor's stupid attempts to take Gazouette from her, Gabrielle raised herself onto her hips, legs and crinolines swept to the right. She'd received an omen—but what did it mean? She couldn't decide.

Her hands, as she resumed her dress, felt oddly nimble. Shouldn't they be numb? Yet she barely required Taylor's assistance with her ties and buttons. Gazouette's were more trouble, but only because the girl ran about like a zany, and even once caught refused naughtily to submit to being clothed.

The way back seemed to take a shorter time than had the trek to the stream's source. They reached the house at the hour when she was accustomed to take breakfast. Early for visitors, and yet an unfamiliar car stood parked next to the piles of unassembled bedframes. It was empty. But Goncourt's man met her at the door and informed her of Missy's presence in the library.

Without any hesitation Gabrielle gave Gazouette into the nanny's care and hurried to greet her unexpectedly arrived lover—almost running along the gallery in her haste, plunging down the three steps to the Low Wing, thrusting open the library's door—and halting on the room's threshold.

Missy was not alone. She'd brought someone with her. A man.

A moment passed. Hardly any time. Gabrielle recognized her other guest: the younger Tessiter. M'sieur Robert. What could the fellow possibly want? The ballet's premiere was far in the future.

She walked forward at a seemly pace, hands open. "My dear! How good to see you!" Missy joined her in a swift embrace. The awkward pause went unnoticed.

"Will you have tea? Chocolate?" She faced M'sieur Tessiter politely. "I am afraid I can't offer you a place to spend the night. You see, we are in an uproar—"

Missy's throaty chuckle interrupted her attempt at an excuse. "But that's the news I've come to share! Robert will stay with me. I've bought a new home not five leagues from here!"

She wouldn't need to pressure Goncourt into hosting his rival, then. Yet Missy would be near enough to see, to touch, though her lover's safety became again an issue. What measures, if any, could be taken? Gabrielle cast about in her mind for the names of available neighboring estates. "Not—Broceliande?"

"But yes! Broceliande, certainly! Is that—is there something wrong with it? The house? The lands? The—"

"No." Gabrielle forced herself to think rationally. "Only Goncourt's people have an old feud with the former owners. And there is an idiotic tradition involving a curse—"

"A curse!" Missy collapsed onto the footstool. "Don't say such a thing!"

"Mere silliness, I assure you. Nothing at all to worry about if it *were* true." Nothing more than eternal enmity between their households.

<hr />

Goncourt drove. Rozven was low on male servants. Of course a woman could manage an automobile as well as any man, usually, barring a breakdown. Gabrielle herself, for example. Her newly sensitive hands were also strong. They longed to hold and turn the car's steering wheel.

By boat Broceliande was no doubt no more than five leagues away. If small enough, she and her husband could have sailed down the beautiful stream and over the dark pond into which it fed, then out again, past the farmers' fields and so on, and so at last to the sea. Gabrielle pictured their vessel as a dried brown leaf, sides deeply curling, a sail of white samite attached to its stem. An idle fancy.

In reality there were no good, solid, direct roads such as they needed; it took them the better part of the afternoon to reach the prim-looking house of Gabrielle's lover. Its walls were a delicate, biscuity yellow, the color of an aging beauty's complexion.

Missy served English tea: lavish cakes, plentiful sandwiches, hothouse fruits: pineapples and grapes. The grapes aroused in Gabrielle a startling greed.

The problematic M'sieur Robert Tessiter was still in attendance, a week after he'd come here. Goncourt could be managed: a hint that the house's previous inhabitants had left so hastily for South America that their cellars remained largely intact was sufficient to clear him from the stage. But M'sieur Robert was not so easily got rid of.

Tiring of his disavowals of boredom, Gabrielle had him open a window so she could more easily admire the room's view of the sea. It was admittedly magnificent. She blamed this quality for dazzling her into a clumsy-handedness she never experienced these days and causing her to drop her diamond bracelet onto the beach below. Then she stared at the man half a minute, until he volunteered to go and hunt for it.

He left. Gabrielle wasted not one second. She sped to the divan. Missy half-rose and drew her down. She tasted sweet juices dried to a slight stickiness on her lover's lips, a last trace of their shared meal.

Shouting floated in the open window. Impossible to distinguish any words in it, though the tone was querulous.

The women investigated only themselves. Each breathed the other's breath. The shouting outside continued, muffled by distance and the noise of the waves. Missy spoke over it, her voice close and low: "You will stay here tonight? And come to me?"

Gabrielle gave no answer.

"You hesitate—why?"

Gazouette would be safe. She must have faith in that. She must show her faith and stay.

Had she not seen proof? The day after her immersion the child had tumbled down the entire length of the grand staircase unhurt—just a bit frightened.

Then the head groom's mastiff had gone mad and dug up his stake, rushing chain and all at Gazouette, whom Taylor had lain to bathe in the unseasonably warm sun. With her own horror-filled eyes Gabrielle had watched from the terrace as the ravening dog ran toward her daughter, and as the stake caught on something not there—on nothing—on air—on the bare soil of the empty flower beds. Halting the beast till he could be shot.

"I will." A change in Gabrielle's attitude toward her daughter would be marked, were anyone watching.

As well she agreed. Her husband's hard-soled shoes sounded in the corridor. Automatically the two women moved a few inches apart. Nothing could have been more decorous, more placatory, than their attitudes as Goncourt entered.

Her husband's expedition to the cellar had been fruitful, and he was happy to accept Missy's offer of hospitality. That evening, with their supper, the four of them enjoyed several bottles of wines he deemed "satisfactory." More formally inclined than Gabrielle, Missy signaled her when it was the hour to withdraw from the gentlemen's company. But scarcely had they exchanged preliminary embraces than Tessiter and Goncourt followed them, to swallow more tea and converse ignorantly about the war—although M'sieur Robert's observations seemed oddly better than those of the older and more worldly man. They scanned, somehow, matching a rhythm of international affairs Gabrielle hadn't realized she'd internalized.

Not until she and Goncourt retired did Gabrielle find the note. Missy had apparently secreted it in Gabrielle's pocket without her remarking it. "Turn right, then left, then straight on till six," it read, a touch cryptically. Below that line it unambiguously added, "Midnight."

"What have you got?" her husband asked.

"A puzzle. Not a very interesting one." She threw it on the dying fire and set about to soothe him to sleep.

Gabrielle herself stayed awake, and when she judged it time—her mental clock was quite disciplined—slipped from the bed and made her way across the invisible floor on bare feet. She had memorized the furniture's location; she made it to the door without incident and exited quickly so that the candle left burning in the passage wouldn't disturb Goncourt with its light.

A right turn took her to where a narrow corridor branched off to the left. The crack beneath the corridor's sixth door glowed yellow. Inside, a curl of smoke rose above a high-backed armchair drawn up to face the bright hearth. As Gabrielle closed the door an arm clad in the tailored sleeve of a man's jacket appeared to one side of the chair, cigarette in hand.

"Is it not a little dangerous to dress so, even here in your home, my love?" she asked.

"I rather hope you are mistaken." Not Missy, but M'sieur Robert stood to welcome her in.

Gabrielle kept calm. "It would appear so. My apologies." She turned to leave.

"Oh, you have come to the right place," said Tessiter. He moved with surprising speed to block the door. "Congratulations. You executed my directions flawlessly."

"Your directions." Her voice lacked all intonation. She knew suddenly what was toward. The men who believed themselves her masters were again attempting to control her.

"The first set of them, at any rate." He gestured to the armchair. "If you'll be so kind as to seat yourself, I'll convey the rest."

She could scream. The room wasn't that isolated; someone would hear and come. But how to explain her presence in this unlocked room with a man to whom she wasn't married? Goncourt's smoldering jealousy would blaze up at the discovery, and servants, deplorably, talked.

She sat. With half her mind, she listened. An important spy had been gravely wounded. He was to be sent to her hospital. Via Tessiter the government instructed Gabrielle to tend to his needs herself. She was to ensure that whatever he said of his mission in Flanders fell on her ears alone: fevered ravings, lucid reports, or deathbed confessions. She should record his pronouncements and pass them on to Tessiter, using Missy as their go-between. Simple enough, did she not think?

She thought. As before, the government's requests seemed reasonable. The war itself, though, was not. Bluntly, it was a flaunting display of cretinism, a contest between heads of nations desperate to determine who possessed the longest metaphoric stick between their legs.

The half of her attention not claimed by Tessiter Gabrielle devoted to calculation. If Missy was to play the role of a messenger in this scheme, she was perhaps more deeply involved than first indicated. The threats against her must have been mere charades. Or perhaps her lover's status had changed between this approach to her and the earlier one. In either circumstance, Gabrielle had no need to protect her.

Goncourt she disregarded, as always. He could look after himself. His connections were more current, more powerful than Missy's—though if her lover was now an agent, their respective ambits might be evenly matched.

Which left her with perhaps one regrettable vulnerability. Gazouette.

Would Gabrielle's compliance guarantee her daughter's freedom? Probably not. Leverage once gained would never be abandoned.

As for the stairs, the mastiff: they could have been coincidence as easily as evidence of an answered prayer.

Did she believe her daughter safe? Or not?

Abruptly, there was silence. No sound but the hissing of the flames. Reviewing her memory of the past few seconds she realized Tessiter had asked a question: Would she do the job?

She shifted uncomfortably on the too-soft velveteen cushion and answered him.

"Yes."

※

At least the spy was handsome. Blond, almost silver-haired, with eyes an unusually deep green and a face like a young David—though Gabrielle couldn't help seeing him as a gape-mouthed fish caught in her talons. The wound to his thigh stank and seeped an ugly mixture of blood and pus when he arrived. She washed it thoroughly with lavender water and packed it with a special healing clay like one Sido had used. This was perhaps why the gaping hole in his flesh closed so quickly. Or it could be due to some supernatural quality in her touch, as many claimed she had these days.

Alas, the spy's mind recovered slowly. When she knew she wasn't going to be free to sit by his side, Gabrielle gave him drops of a tincture she'd brewed from valerian and poppy to still his broken ramblings.

The nurses and servants believed she tended Lieutenant Tranché because she desired him. Little matter that. Any story would do but the truth, and she took care to give their rumors no grounds. Nothing that could be laid before Goncourt as definitive.

Despite the house's pressing lack of living space, Gabrielle had maintained her private room. Here she wrote her tales of an irretrievable past. It made sense to use the same pen, paper, desk drawer, lock, and key for her secret work for the government. Scrupulously she inscribed every wandering sentence the lieutenant uttered, not venturing to decide its relevance. She sealed the results in scented envelopes and delivered them personally into the hands of her former lover at their too-frequent meetings.

She took care that they two were never again alone together. Nonetheless, Missy's eyes often spilled over with questions and unacknowledged tears. Gabrielle avoided noticing them.

For weeks there was no coherence to Tranché's speech. At last his green eyes focused on her, unmistakably seeing her and not some phantom of his illness. She introduced herself, said the password Tessiter had revealed to her, received his countersign. From that moment commenced Gabrielle's real labors in the fields of intelligence. She always remembered the exact date. It was one month from the day she had sent Gazouette away a second time. For good.

⋙

Gabrielle died at the age of eighty-one. Her estranged but dutiful daughter returned to attend her sickbed, traveling alone all the way to France from Greece, her most recent in a series of loveless homes.

Rozven had been sold years earlier, upon Goncourt succumbing to a malady of the heart; Gabrielle inhabited a flat in Paris, alone except for her beloved bulldog Beau and a paid nurse. The medal bestowed in exchange for her wartime activities hung framed above her headboard, in a spot where she didn't have to see it.

Propped up with massive quantities of pillows, as she insisted, she watched out her windows while the chestnuts blossomed, watched their leaves unfurl, darken, become brown. But she didn't see them fall.

When, at last, after two seasons of grudging patience, the inevitable moment came, Gazouette (who had never shaken her childish nickname) was where she knew she should be, holding her mother's always strangely youthful hands. She bent forward to catch Gabrielle's last words—for posterity, she told herself, because they could never be meant for anyone else.

"It was best that you not know," the old woman murmured. "I made my mind up never to tell you, and I never did. Even long after the danger."

Gazouette couldn't help questioning that. "Never to tell me what?"

Gabrielle seemed not to hear her, or at least not to make the effort to respond. "You never felt the smallest threat."

She shut her eyes a final time. "And even without you, I have had a beautiful life."

I Being Young and Foolish

Nia rose from her boat's bench smoothly, a skyward pour of milk. Her cat had made up their mind. Steady though she stood, her boat bobbed slightly in the rippling water. The boatman hunched uneasily against the bright wind, which fluttered Nia's sleeves and the ends of her headcloth, and pushed her robe of undyed wool against her chilled body. Nia reminded herself that this lake was reputed shallow, no more than a couple of fathoms at its deepest, in its center. And here among the reeds at the island's edge, even with the wetness of winter's onset, she ought surely to be able to wade to shore, as Odeh could leap the little distance—if only they *would* leap it—

On the beak of the boat's painted prow Odeh wriggled their grey-striped hindquarters, teetered their triangular head down, up, down, up, down—and jumped! King Bear's command that she come to study here was in accord with her chosen destiny, the knitting together of the world's webs. A sigh released breath Nia had not known she held. Then the rustling of dried grass told where Odeh walked ahead. Carefully, using an oar to provide balance, Nia stepped from the boat into the water's freezing cold. Only two paces and she reached the rock where her cat had landed, splashing the stone's lichened sides as she climbed to its low, flat top. She looked back.

She'd need her boots. Her slippers were wet, and the bottom of her gown, despite her having kirtled it. "My bundle. Pitch it here." The boatman frowned, then did as bidden. She caught his toss and ignored his face. In these strange northern lands, Nia had come to see such expressions as her common due, and they were certainly less frightening than some smiles she'd had to face on her journey. Or, for that matter, back in Nakasongola.

The boatman turned away obediently enough and worked his oars, gradually diminishing from sight.

Once he'd gone, the music of the land welled up to fill her. Wind rushing. Waves lapping. Birds crying. Stilling, she listened more widely. Clouds blowing above, so reliable, so welcome. And there: the soft brush of Odeh's tail against plants growing along the path they took. A narrow path, made by the shy Cymry deer coming down to drink. Nia followed it upward to a hazel copse where golden leaves and the empty fragments of split shells littered the ground. A good burial site. Odeh stretched contentedly along a low, flexible limb waving from the grove's queen tree, grooming a dainty forepaw.

Nia approached them, hand held out to caress. But stopped. Percussion interrupted the landmusic's flow: wood on wood. A door banging open. Banging shut. She dropped her hand and faced the sound's source. Nothing further came from its direction. She walked toward what she'd heard, hesitantly.

A new path. Human broad, the smell of a smoky fire hanging over it. This must be the way to the hut King Bear had described.

So it was. Soon a clearing appeared before her, and a small building, stone but constructed in the Cymru style, on one side, a brushwood wall on the other. A beautiful man of middle years standing in its center. Nia met his pale eyes and felt her current intensify.

He spoke. "Well that you come." He wore a dark, belted mantle, its hood pushed back to show straight brown hair cut to the blunted knife of his jawline. His voice was odd—louder than a whisper, softer than should have been audible sixteen paces off.

Nia gathered herself in. "You expected me?"

The beautiful man came closer, nodding and curling his slender fingers. "Say rather that I hoped for you. King Bear's messenger arrived the day before last Sabbath with word you had been advised to visit, but that you had received this advice without committing to heed it."

He spread his arms to show himself weaponless. "I'm right? You're the foreign sorceress?"

"So they call me." If she had stayed in Nakasongola she would by now be revered as a muganda. Unless, of course, she had been rejected, as had begun to seem more and more likely. Which likelihood had led to her present course of wandering the world to learn its many magics—and the misnaming that went with that course.

"And who is this?" The man's grey eyes were aimed over her shoulder. She whirled, but it was only Odeh.

"My cat."

"He came with you all the way from Ethiope?"

"No. Odeh didn't join me until I left Egypt." Ethiopia had not been the actual country of Nia's origin, but she let the error pass, as she had learned to let pass so many. "And you are Merlin, King Bear's magician?" He did not have a tame air about him, did not seem any sort of courtier, but she supposed he must be the one she had been recommended to seek.

"Yes, to be sure." His disturbingly light eyes met hers again and this time held them. Was that how her eyes appeared? "You'll want to see where you will stay. And to take refreshment—or perhaps you fast?"

"No."

Neither of them moved. Once again it was Odeh who tipped the moment's balance. Ignoring the magician, they dashed to the stone hut's threshold and abruptly halted.

Wards? No—well, perhaps; door wards would make sense, but the sudden scent of fish blood was most likely what had stopped Odeh here. Inquiringly, they raised their nose. A straw sack hung wet and glistening from a peg in the white-washed wood of the door's jamb. Merlin, ahead of her, grinned and shrugged. "You'll share them with me? Fresh-caught trout make for a fine dinner."

Entering the twilight of the hut's interior, Nia felt only the weakest resistance, like a bubble waiting to pop. Wards, but apparently she had been classified a friend and allowed to pass. A raised platform near the hearth bore a heap of heather. "Yours," said the magician.

Not "ours." She would be warm enough, but... "Where will you sleep?"

"The woods. Or the yard. Or the loft."

Nia noted the order of listing. Presumably it indicated preference. No, Merlin was not tame.

However, he was extremely civilized for a man of these parts.

Christianity had been rife since her voyage over the Tyr-rhenian Sea, but he didn't appear to practice it: the hut's walls bore no crosses, no bones or hair stolen from the bodies of dead ancestors. The fish were quickly baked in a mud made fragrant with sweet herbs and served on a board lined with rare greens: fresh, tender sorrel leaves, which tasted wonderful. Both mead and beer accompanied the meal.

Hospitality had ceased to be much of a problem for Nia once she left behind the dark-skinned peoples who viewed her albinism askance. As she had been told, the further north she traveled, the more acceptable her pallor, the more welcome her assistance with herbal formulae and other simple spells. She'd only had to share the most childish of enchantments to pay her wandering way.

They ate in the open air, seated on a felled oak a few feet uphill. Nia noted that a wind blowing from the direction of the lake afforded better hearing than could have been expected. No surprise visitors. Good planning. Odeh sat quiet as a hunting dog and watched every bite of the fish into her mouth. "You have a pet also?" she asked the magician.

"A serpent. Macha. The cool weather of the year's ending makes her sluggish and lessens her appetite. She'll still be digesting the rat she caught yestermorn."

Nia bent and lay her baked mud shell on the ground for Odeh, and they began to pick cautiously at the slivers of flesh she'd left clinging to its inside.

The magician laid his shell beside hers. "Come. I'll show you my workings while the light's good."

They returned to the hut. Was it larger now? Yes. Definitely. Outside and in. That stair in the corner was new. She climbed it behind him to another floor. A wooden floor, and on it a narrow table running the room's length. Windows at the room's far end showed a flowering hedge dividing a green hillside pasture, sheep grazing under blue heavens. But this hut stood in the midst of a forest.

"Where—"

"My mother's land. Brecheliant. And you should ask when, as well."

Hadn't she heard that Brecheliant was forested too? "When?"

"In times to come."

Without realizing, she had crossed the room, drawn to the unlikely scene outside. Now she turned her back on it to stare at him, to deny what he had said. "The future does not exist."

"Everything exists."

Gazing at Merlin over a table laden, she saw now, with shining metal boxes and thick glass bowls and colorful waxen effigies and all manner of curious items, Nia knew with utter certainty that Odeh had been guided aright. She needed to stay here and exchange teachings—powerful ones—with this impossible, beautiful man. She needed to know the world as he knew it. And so she formally asked him to instruct her, and he formally took her on.

~⌇~

She went to her bed of heather alone that first night and got up from it the same way. Odeh roused her when it was early morning. Outside the hut's walls, the still-sunken sun's light whispered the air awake.

A moment's wait in the clearing and the trail down to the hazels formed itself out of thinning shadows. She and Odeh followed it, and under the queen's branches she sought its roots with softly thrusting fingers, excavated the finest of their tendrilings, and ate them. She knew from previous repasts that these northern webs became less active as the year's cold came on. Nonetheless, it was Nia's practice to consume as soon as she could some sample of the fungal lace linking together the flora of whichever woods she lived in.

Another quarter, and it would be time for sowing.

A lingering redstart called her deeper into the forest, to where oak ruled the hillsides. Like her, surely, this little bird was a far-traveler. Unlike her, it had returned to where it began. Though soon it would leave again. She'd met one once on the shore of Lake Nalubaale; redstarts did not love the North's cold winters.

"Remain here," she instructed Odeh. They didn't, but neither did they accompany her as she sought for the singing, slipping off instead on a mission of their own. She was able to approach the bird alone.

Singing serenely despite her presence, the redstart balanced on a high, near-leafless sprig jutting up from a young attendant tree. Nia coaxed him to her hand. "Tell my auntie I am well," she crooned. "Find her where the shorebirds flock, casting her net from my uncles' boat, or resting in the shade of the iroko trees that our ancestors seeded there, the place we call Nakasongola. You will know you've reached her because she shines like me." She released the bird. He perched a moment more on her thumb and flew off southward.

Higher up and higher in she found the queen of these oaks, and again ate from among the roots. The taste was fine. But the hazels would be better for her burying. Circling wide, she came last to the silver trunks of the beech trees, performed the same actions there, and came to the same conclusion.

As Nia returned to the hut, mist closed around her like a memory. Out of the enveloping whiteness Odeh appeared, joining her as if they'd never left her side.

The trail weakened. Nia relied on her burgeoning sense of the countryside to guide her back to the hut. Merlin greeted her at its door. "You touch the land," he pronounced.

"The land touches me." Breathes me, drinks me, draws me in, lets me out, she thought. All the land and air and ocean she'd passed between here and Lake Nalubaale did so now. The strength of her magic depended on this intermingling. Her magic's strength and growth: she wandered in its service.

"Come."

The magician fed her a cup of dried and toasted grains mixed with hazel nuts and goat's milk. They must have been procured from an off-island farm, because she'd seen signs of none nearby this morning. With his food, Merlin brought forth the question she'd been expecting since they met. "Aren't the people of Ethiope black of visage?"

"Most of us," she answered. Like devils, she'd heard her race described. "But I've been as you see me from my birth."

"What of your parents?"

Odeh turned away from the pinch of grains Nia offered them, uninterested. "Both are dead. I never knew them."

"I'm sorry."

"I never knew them," she repeated. "My aunt and my uncles, who cared for me, tell me my mother and father were quite normal in how they looked." She licked off the grains Odeh had spurned and reached for the napkin to wipe her hand.

The magician held it. She tried to tug it away. He kept his hold tight, his gaze on her hand. On her skin. "Those in your village thought you a witch because you were not as they."

Indeed they had. But rather than respond so, to answer what had been stated, not asked, Nia reached with her other hand to lift that tucked chin and raise Merlin's eyes to meet her own. He stared without blinking. A Seeing was on him.

For five long beats of her blood Nia cradled the magician's jaw in her steady left palm. Then he jerked and drew back. He staggered to his feet, kicking a table leg. Bowls skittered to the table's edge.

What had frightened him? Something Seen? Her experience with other tutors had taught Nia not to pry early on in a relationship. She would wait for whatever explanation was offered.

"I'm sorry," said the magician, again. And that was all she got from him for the moment.

～～

The quarter passed. Seven days. A pattern emerged: While the sun hung above the horizon, she went about fishing, foraging (for berries, nuts, mushrooms, and other provender), and harvesting herbs it would be helpful to have over the winter. As evening dimmed and sank the sun, Merlin called her to him to teach her: in the ephemeral room above the ground floor or in a cave opening in the slope behind his hut. He showed her trays crawling with people as small and purposeful as ants, opened books filled with images that moved while she watched them, then returned to their starting places when she looked away. He blinked slow as Odeh in approval of her ability to sit motionless as a heron through a lesson on creating new homes for the future to live in. That brought a troubling bout of smugness. Stillness was the first skill the trees had taught Nia.

Tools for digging rested against the hut on the side opposite its entrance. On the seventh day, after gathering a pan of rosehips off a wild hedge the oak trees showed her, Nia began her grave. She left the full pan on the table for Merlin to prepare as he would, shouldered shovel and pick, and went to work. The hazels' roots parted easily for her. By midday the hole was deep enough. She set about widening it. Odeh watched her from atop the little hill of dirt she'd cast up. Only watched. Their part would come soon. Tonight.

She finished well ahead of time, even allowing herself a trip to the brook to bathe before returning to the hut to eat.

The rosehips steeped in warm water—a tea or syrup, then. To be consumed later. The meal itself consisted mainly of roots. But these had come in trade, from farmers' crops, and gave Nia no knowledge—what little they once possessed Merlin had peeled off with a knife and boiled away. There was much for him to learn. He had yet to ask her to teach it. Or to grant him any other favor.

The evening's study session commenced as usual, though in a new venue: a blooming bower, a summerish arch of flowers with two seats of living wood. The method of the bower's conjuration was Merlin's chosen topic; he ignored her attempts to lure him onto others until the lesson's end. For a moment, both of them sat in darkening silence.

The magician plucked a spray of sweet-scented briony and plaited it with another of honeysuckle. "You'll wear these during your burial this night."

He knew. "Who told you?"

"We have a similar…ritual in these lands, but for men. In the Spring."

As near to an answer as the magician ever gave. He twisted the ends of his plait together to form a wreath and presented it to her. "Here. Shall I accompany you, or is this working solitary?"

"I won't be alone. Odeh attends me. They'll finish my burial for me, and in the morning they'll begin my excavation. But I'm sure they'd welcome your help."

She donned the wreath over her head cloth and proceeded with him to the hazel grove. Her grave looked bottomless in the gloaming. She half-reclined in it as if in an oversized Italian bath. With Merlin's aid, the earth covering Nia rose quickly. Her white-draped arms submerged themselves in the soil for a final time.

"You'll come to no harm."

"Not the least," she assured him. Already the fungal threads of her comrades twined around her feet, tickling open the pores of her naked ankles. "You may safely cover my head cloth in no more than the chanting of a pair of recipes. Odeh will know exactly when."

"The flowers—"

"They too."

The magician recited the instructions he had given her for midnight travel between distant mountain tops while filling the grave high as Nia's chin. Odeh patted her cheeks with velvet gentleness and pawed rich loam from behind her line of sight to lie against her ears. Merlin's recitation became too muffled to distinguish. And her attention became diffuse, opening out into the wood's underground system, the slow routes of the trees' shared awareness. Spreading the light, the hum, the liquid proclamation of life. Shutting it down, retracting it, drawing off the precious power to store it within the earth. Within her bones. The quiescent essence.

Night was a dance without steps, without movement of any kind. Morning came: a smear of sunlight, a reddening of her eyes' lids. She lifted them and focused on Odeh's furry face, their pink and silver tongue licking the scum of dirt from her newly exposed skin. Merlin's long hands scooped up the loose soil imprisoning her neck and shoulders, but by the time she'd freed herself enough to look for more of him, he'd gone. Patiently she stirred herself, setting the dirt within her grave aseethe. She emerged unscathed though not unchanged, brushing away the broken tips of tendrils that had formed to nourish her. These would be repurposed in the spring.

Nia had thought perhaps Merlin would return to her at the burial site with a drink of water, or a blanket. Of course with questions. No. He came not at all. She shivered a moment in the sudden loneliness, unable to decide if it was his absence that caused it, or her loss of direct contact with the roots of the hazels. Then she went back to the hut on her own. And on her own she stayed, despite her desire.

❧

Snow fell the first night of Christmas. Three and twenty years had passed since Nia left Nakasongola, heading whiteward. This would be her sixteenth such snowfall, but she never tired of them. Bluer than her complexion, shadow versions of the stars, the soft flakes swirled to the low, black Earth from high, cold Heaven.

"Shut the door, won't you?" The length of Merlin's wool-wrapped body radiated warmth bare inches from her back. "It's not so marvelous to me as to you, this bleak winter."

She nodded and moved forward to take and pull the door's knotted latch cord, feeling the distance between them increase. "Will we still go to the castle in the morning?"

"Will the king still send a boat to carry us? I say so."

Despite practicing her own beliefs as well as she could in alien lands, Nia knew and publicly performed the rites of her hosts' religions, too. It made her passage easier, her sojourns less troubled. Merlin seemed to have come to a similar accommodation with the Christians' Church. In the lessons given her over the months past there had been no mention of Jesus, saints, or apostles, save perfunctory reference to who should be called on to bless which workings, aloud, before witnesses. However, as predicted, King Bear had invited his magician to return to court for the winter's holy days. And as promised he had agreed to go. She with him.

"But Macha—"

"She slumbers. She won't miss us."

"Will she not freeze? The frost—"

Merlin glanced down at the flat stones set around the hut's circular hearth. One short day a short while ago, Nia had watched the snake glide under the largest of them. "I'll bank the fire with utmost care. We are to be gone no more than a fortnight. Perhaps less. She'll be fine. I say so."

Time was Merlin's realm, and the principle Nia had discerned behind most of his spells was the deployment of it in surprising spots. The blossoming of the bower, the delving of the cave. Also he dealt in the comprehension of time: of the past's mysteries, and of the future, the present's oft-unexpected outcome.

The dry rustle of twigs disturbed Nia's thoughts. Odeh's head pushed through the heather bunched and tied to the hut door's bottom, golden eyes blinking open as they cleared the brush. Next came the white-gloved forepaws, the limber elegance of their front legs, the liquid torso, muscular back legs, and waving tail.

"Will they come with us?" Merlin had finally learned from Nia how to talk of her pet. This language had but one option for those neither male nor female.

Nia had not been apart from Odeh for more than a night since they'd adopted her. "Most likely."

"Shall I carry them? The horses won't bother them?"

"They weren't fretted on the way here." Neither the king's horses nor the asses of Dijon, nor any of the other beasts encountered on their way had daunted brave Odeh. Nonetheless, the magician stooped to gather them up and lift them. Odeh tolerated that, as they always did this man's touch. As they had never before tolerated others' handling.

It was this, her pet's acceptance of him, that encouraged Nia to ignore his avoidance of her, to step over the boundary of his determined deafness to her queries and invitations. To make her meaning plain, she sank onto her bed and pulled Merlin down by his mantle beside her.

"Ah." His face in the firelight lent depth to the simplicity of that sound: the depth of the knowledge and the wanting of what was yet to come. Her fingers traced the beardlessness of his cheeks, the strange straightness of his nose, stroked his stern brows, wings of a predator, a protector—

He reached for her wrist to stop her. "You understand this is not the price of my teaching? Nor of your lodging here—you take me to you freely, of your own will?"

She laughed and rose and shook off her robe. "And if I didn't understand by now that there's no barter involved? After these three moons you've held yourself aloof from me? I would be too stupid to understand anything. Too—" She sprang like Odeh in the hope of catching the magician off guard. But he was ready with a half-serious defense of his clothing. She settled for removing his gown to reveal the shirt worn beneath. Then she pressed him down to lie again on the red-dyed linen with which he'd covered her bed.

Soothing the shirt's hem gradually upward, she began to expose him. In the firelight his thighs glowed like candlewax, rippling when he rolled away. "Stay."

He obeyed her.

"You want me. Why do you deny—"

The first rage she'd seen on him fell over his face. "Deny you? Never! But what begins also ends."

Tentatively, Nia leaned over his shoulder to take his hands in hers. She met no resistance. "Does it so? Does it truly?" She turned him back toward her. "Have you not taught me otherwise?"

He laughed a creaking laugh. "Tomorrow we go to the king, to stay under his roof through the year's return. The young and lusty king."

"King Bear and I have met." Yellow hair, she remembered. Eyes resolved on cheerfulness. Thick whiskers covered his face, and below that his center burned, a belly full of determination. "Do you forget? He sent me here."

"I do not forget what has happened. Nor what will." He lifted himself on his elbows. The shadow of his hair cast itself between them. "I say you'll lie with him. I have Seen it. And I, damn me for an envious fool, will lie now with you." He leaned toward her and they kissed. Nia closed her eyes and Saw anyway: her phantasms or his? The visions ran so swift they blended into one another: fields reaped empty of their corn; harbors crowded with the masts of golden ships and the busy oars of tiny, bright boats; chests of gold coins spilling onto wooden tables where sat fine-wigged ducks and haughty swans… Each sight was more nonsensical than the last, and all the while she and Merlin kissed and touched these imaginary worlds whirled her merrily away. So to thrust her tongue into the magician's ear was to shoot above the roof of a byre and bathe in the silver tails of comets; to shudder at his breath as he suckled on the intricacies of her hair was to rain candied rose petals on a herd of apple-colored oxen. And to hold his heart to hers was to melt into dreams.

And to wake was to find him staring at her calmly. Objectively. Separately.

She sat up, holding his regard, such as it was. Then broke it to look around her. The hut had shrunk, once more comprising but one story. On top of a tall reed basket Odeh curled like a cake, unperturbed by the change.

"What's that?" Nia asked. She'd never seen the basket before, though she'd been everywhere inside the magician's home, and was as well acquainted with its surroundings. Better acquainted.

"That is your gift to the king. It will convince him to put you in my place."

"I don't want to take your place."

"No matter. He wants you there, or he will. As do I. Now more than ever. You will take him, be the making of him, mold him to be a leader of the land. All will be well."

Quickly Nia dressed. Last night she had packed a bundle to bring with her to the castle, after supper, before the snow. Before lying with Merlin. Stepping out into the yard she saw the far-off heat rising from men climbing the path from the lake, and flocks of chattering sparrows flying up ahead of their disturbance. These must be the king's men. They were going to arrive soon.

Behind her the sounds of the hut's door opening and of shoes crushing snow announced the magician's advent. Nia turned—but who was this stranger? An elder with white hair streaming out below a dun hood—Merlin's hood—and Merlin's pale eyes caught in a web of creases ending in the silver beard covering his suddenly ancient face—

"Why have you put on this seeming?" Nia asked.

"Is that what I have done?"

She nodded slowly. Odeh slunk past him to nose a shallow drift.

"How old do you think me really?"

"I—old. But—" But she had thought the years stayed their distance from him, as they did from her and many magicians. Though he'd not shared his method for accomplishing that yet.

"I was old when King Bear was born. It's in this guise he'll expect to see me."

Odeh sneezed and backed away from whatever had attracted their interest. They assumed a dignified pose on the train of Merlin's mantle. Obviously they perceived no difference in him. This reassured Nia, as did the matter-of-fact manner in which the two spear bearers approached moments later.

"Hail," they saluted the magician. Another two men entered the clearing, appearing no more surprised than the first two. "Lord Merlin. Lady Nia." Back at Nakasongola her name meant "intention." Here they used the same word for "brightness." Close enough.

The four had brought a pair of boats to carry the magician, the "sorceress," and their trappings to the lake's western shore. This part of the trip was restful. Water eased Nia's heart. Melting frost slid musically from the tips of the lakeside alders' branches. All was connected, and the drops of moisture rising almost visibly toward the mist-crowded sun would surely rain upon the land where she'd been born. Taking with them her apologies for leaving.

Transferring their effects from boats to wagon got complicated. The driver disliked cats. When it was finally settled that Odeh and Nia would walk together behind the others (she being a young maiden to the evidence of most men's limited senses), but a few handspans of light remained of the brief winter day. So Nia traveled the last of the road to the castle in starlight, and was greeted at the gates of Dinas Dinlle by the unsteady fires of braziers.

Trumpets shouted as the eight of them came into the castle's courtyard, which was known as its bailey. Surreptitiously, Nia removed one shoe, but the stones beneath her bare foot stayed silent of tales. As they had previously. As had those of the thick walls guarding the bailey also.

Felled oaks formed the sides of the buildings surrounding her here, and surrounding also the stairs climbing to the dark doorway leading into the largest building, the keep. Then the door's darkness receded, and out of that dawn stepped the king. Servants following behind him lifted high the torches they bore.

Under the torches' flames King Bear gleamed more ruddily than in Nia's memory. A golden circlet ran between his golden curls, the metal's color the wanner of the two.

"My lord! My lady! We wanted your company at supper!" Beckoning them forward, he came to stand at the stairs' top. "What kept you?"

Nia gave the king the curtsy these lands' rulers expected. Merlin bowed. Not low. "We apologize. We came as speedily as possible," the magician explained, "but it has taken all the day."

"Well don't hang back now!" The king pulled both Merlin and Nia into his embrace. "The other guests have finished eating, but they still await you in the Great Hall. The bard won't sing till I order it."

Past the torch flickers lay a short, narrow space, with a tapestry hung on its far side. The hanging's tasseled edges lifted as a youth swept it aside, spilling sudden sounds and momentarily dazzling firelight into her ears and eyes. At first the greenery which had been hung off railings and garlanded around the hall's high beams deceived her, with its color and scent and the sighing rustle of leaf against leaf. Had the room become a forest glade? No. Too warm for a wood in a northern winter: currents of air wafted toward her from the burning logs stacked in the wide cavern built at the hall's far end. This would be a seasonal decoration, a means of marking the birth of their god, as she'd observed happening in other Christian realms.

Sight adjusting, Nia surveyed those seated at the hall's tables for familiar faces. King Bear's retinue had changed in her absence, losing many former members, which was only sensible: they came to him to learn to fight, and this was a time of peace. Of the men gathered round him now she recognized none but the king's uncle, High Praise, and his foster brother, River. Newer warriors, numbering five by her count, laughed at their ease, swallowing gulps of what must be wine from brass cups.

These seven men, and the four women with them, stood at their entrance. King Bear introduced the men as customary, by the names of their home villages, which Nia took care to note. The women, also newcomers, were wife of this one, sister of that. The tall fellow known as Hollybush made room for Nia on the bench where he and the others sat, but the king beckoned her nearer, towards his place.

Merlin was already there. From somewhere he'd acquired a staff, and he leaned on it, ignoring the chair the king had summoned with a wave. So Nia sat in it.

The king smiled. The woman whose chair had been commandeered frowned. Nia knew her: an artist in clay and fine metals. Beloved was her name. Single and beyond the age of marrying, she had likely striven hard to catch the king's regard and win the spot next to him that she had just lost. Beloved looked annoyance Nia's way, but before Nia could relinquish the perilous seat, the harper struck his first song's first chords. They rang with surprising crispness over the hall's smoky mutterings, hushing them. Louder men heard the resulting silence and stilled themselves also. Even the whispering of the amputated leaves ceased.

The maid carrying the wine pitcher vanished momentarily and reappeared emptyhanded to crouch by the kitchen's door. Nia settled herself in Beloved's chair to listen to the drumless music, a song praising the beauty of local scenery. She would try not to thirst too obviously for the land that had once been her home.

Nantlle was so much smaller than Lake Nalubaale. Though it *was* a lake. And Merlin's solitary hut had many commonalities with Mukasa's shrine on Bubembe Island. Or more precisely, with the house before the shrine, where Nia had lived and studied prior to accusations of witchcraft.

Nor, Nia told herself, was Dinas Dinlle identical with Mbaale, the site of the temple of the war spirit Kibuuka, where she had often visited. The walls here walked straight lines rather than curved ones; the roofs here kept away the wet and the cold rather than the sun whose heat had helped to drive her to these cooler, cloudier climes — along with her escape from trial and execution, and her search for exotic wisdom.

But some traits the two sites shared, as she had come to accept previously. The men's fierce faces. The banners lining the walls — though those here were woven of animal hair, not pounded from fig bark. The bard sang of battles like a jali, and of spiritual traditions. The harp he played as he sang sounded like an endongo plucked by someone gradually falling to sleep.

Measure followed measure, each slower than the last. In addition to fighting the music's lull, Nia struggled to stay rooted in this domain, a task made doubly difficult by the absence of significant plant life. The artificial hill on which the castle had been raised bore only short-grazed grasses and a tiny garden. Even in winter there would have been comfort in the presence of a slumbering copse of rowan, or even of birch, that least outgoing of trees. With no anchor but the dying boughs of firs and vines of mistletoe, she drifted back to the shores of her childhood...

...to the fish jumping free of the boundary between breathing and drinking, so fat and slippery in her hands she laughed it loose and down it plunged while Maama shrieked at the waste, but the rippling silver glittered so prettily —

No. Marigold yellow the candle's glow before her. She must stay awake or offend King Bear's court and the king himself. In the ruler's shadow Merlin continued standing, wavering but a little, his sturdiness belying his apparent old age. One glinting eye pierced her like a sentient blade. She pried her gaze away, picked up her cup, took another draft of royal wine. A mistake. It was too strong. Drowning on dry land, she sank…

…low to the lapping waves, but the boat beneath bore her up and carried her on her way to Bubembe, where Maama had prayed her whiteness would be regarded as a sign of Mukasa's favor and her visions secure apprenticeship under the hand of the muganda, whose clasp on Nia's wrist cut sharp—

No. The clasp was Merlin's, so tight as to hurt and bring her back here. Nia turned her palm up and slid it to touch his. A thrill of coolness shot up her arm.

"I am glad you agree," the magician said. She agreed? Agreed to what? She had nodded, maybe, had possibly let her head droop, dozing off as the hall's soothing warmth and sedative airs overcame her. Treating that accidental nod as deliberate provided one way out. She inclined her head—again? The stress of Merlin's regard, the grip he established on Nia's hand, seized and lifted her the way a talon lifts a prize.

"By your leave." The magician assumed the king's assent and left. What twinkled in the air behind them? No chance to check. With a quickness Merlin brought her to the foot of the stairs leading to the divided chambers above the hall's annex.

Was it privacy the magician sought? She could have told him it would not be found here. Children, maidens, and a round-hipped woman Nia remembered from her earlier stay occupied the two largest rooms. A smaller third was piled high with bales of cloth and stacks of dead lumber, leaving no room for entry. The smallest, the fourth, contained nothing but another staircase. One which Nia was sure had not been there previously.

They climbed to where these stairs stopped: underneath a hatch reminding Nia of the ships on which she'd voyaged from

Tunis and Corsica. The hatch swung upward at the magician's touch, revealing a sky full of stars like goblets running over with light. Stepping out, Nia at last retrieved her hand from Merlin's grasp. She stood on the roof of a tall tower. Baring her feet, she felt flat tiles slippery with friendly moss beneath her soles. The keep, the hill on which it stood, and the wall around it were nowhere in sight.

Nia dug her toes deeper into the moss and it responded, sparkling in circles spreading outward from her feet. "When are we?" she asked.

"A time when I built what King Bear really needs. Not the future, not the past. A time of choice."

He seemed to be in a mood to answer questions. She asked another. "What's in the basket? What is my gift to the king?"

Green, yellow, pink, and white, the moss lights shifted and winked, showing by their abrupt absence the roof's edge.

"His sword." The magician looked upward, throwing his face into shadow.

"He has a sword."

"Not this one. This is a sword of destiny. He who wields it rules all Cymru."

"You give it to me so I may give it to him and thus usurp you as his counselor." Two steps and she touched his mantle, felt through its weave the warm muscles of his upper arm. "I tell you twice that's no wish of mine. I came to these lands to learn; I'm not here to conquer anything or anyone."

"Yet you have." His face remained averted. And they'd spent the day apart, he riding, she walking. How could Nia know what sense his words held? She did, though she didn't want to play this game she'd won.

Where was her pet? Odeh, who ought to have been helping her now, had approached the bailey by Nia's side but fled at the noise of the trumpets. Still, they should be able to reach her here as easily as within any other of Merlin's constructions.

She called to them using the blossom pressed flat beneath the cloth covering her head.

Abruptly the tower's roof caved beneath her. Or did it disappear completely? Disoriented, Nia staggered. Again Merlin had her wrist. Yes, her surroundings had simply vanished. No debris. Only the littlest scintillation of dust—mist?—that swiftly cleared from the air. At tables around them sat the same women and men she had left in the magician's company, in almost the same positions. And before King Bear stood the basket containing her gift to him. The sword. Softness assailed her calves—Odeh rubbing between her legs.

Again Merlin bowed. He stayed bent as he spoke. "Inspired by foretellings of your greatness, the sorceress Nia has procured for you that weapon of which I could only prophesize.

"Lady? You will perform the honor of untying the basket's lid?"

Simple knots in strands of supple ivy parted easily at Nia's touch. She removed the basket's lid and smelled more than saw its contents: damp, rich, earth, fully awake and clinging to the blade piercing its heart.

"Lord?" Merlin had straightened. He beckoned to the king.

The king rose. His golden beard did little to conceal the tension of his half-pursed lips. He swung his arms to match the rhythm of his stride. Reaching the basket, he stopped and faced his warriors and their women. "Witness as I fulfill the requirement. Father Peace? You will record what happens?" A shaven-headed, hook-nosed man seated at the hall's entrance nodded.

With a dramatic flourish King Bear lifted both hands high, turning them palms in, palms out, palms towards one another. He lowered both together, clasped with interlaced fingers something buried in the basket's earth, and pulled forth by its leather-bound hilt a shimmering blade of finest steel.

"Cleft-Cutter!" cried Merlin. "Bane of Cymru's enemies!" The king spun in place, showing the sword to everyone in the hall. "Drawn by our rightful ruler from this adamant rock!"

But the basket contained only soft soil. Nia thought to plunge her hands in it to prove this. The magician warned her back with a glance. The king paraded his prize from one fighter to the next, basking in their admiration. Cleft-Cutter seemed to reflect more light than it received, shining radiance upon the faces bent over it turn on turn. Magic, yes. But her magic? Not originally.

Now the king returned to kneel in front of her. "Lady Nia," he said, in a voice meant for all to hear. "Consider me beholden. A boon is yours in payment for securing me the chance to claim this gift."

Again the veil of glittering dust descended. And now she heard nothing. Saw nothing around her save a soft blur of colors hurrying past her eyes fast, faster. Felt nothing till the magician's touch calmed this weird storm. His thumb on her chin, the tips of his fingers a crescent of coolth about her cheek. The fire out and the hall empty but for Odeh waiting patiently at her tired feet.

Nia opened her mouth to ascertain what was happening. Two of Merlin's fingertips glided across her lips. "Shush you," he whispered. "All will be made clear in time."

"In *this* time," she insisted.

"Very well. At least, in an approximation of it."

More mist, more magic; then they lay together on Nia's red bed, in their future. Knowledge sat heavy on her uncovered head: it was to be their last night in one another's arms. They'd had their time. The winter months had gone, and the rains of spring wetted the hut's thatch. Thrice four quarters had passed since Yule, in this conjuration. Soon the seeds sown last autumn would wake from the sodden earth. By then Merlin too must be planted, in order that he grow.

The fire in the hut's center roared, painting their nakedness with changing jewels of light, light flowing over them like pleasure. "Did you hate me," he asked, "when I craved the king grant you my position?"

"As it was in your Seeing? Well, I did think you presumptuous."

"And I was. Being young and foolish." They both laughed, sadly at first. "Yet old enough at over a hundred years to understand that secrets can never be told. Only shown."

"Yes. That's their nature." Her white fingers flexed in his hair, which at this moment was brown as the wing of his namesake. "You have never expected me to teach you my secrets—only to share with you the joy of learning them."

The magician's fingers caressed her hair also, tugging gently at the sensitive roots, tracing the paths between them. "You'll not fight me, then? You'll help?"

"Haven't I promised? I'll dig your grave myself."

"And you'll care for the king in my absence? Fill all his needs? Love him as I do, for the sake of the union it's his destiny to form?"

"I'll care for him as you would, till the time of your return."

"But what then if I don't return?"

Nia rolled apart from him onto her belly. "Why shouldn't you? Is this your plan, to abandon King Bear's realm for the web beneath the woods?"

"Nothing is ever my plan. I only go where my life takes me."

The magic ceased. The drizzling shower of light marked its end. She stood again in the shadow-clotted Great Hall at Dinas Dinlle. Of course she hadn't actually left it. She snorted, unimpressed. "How was that time an approximation of this one?" she asked.

"It wasn't. Just a favorite of mine to visit." His hair was once more white, but his touch on her face felt smooth, and soft as morning dew. "I trust your curiosity is now entirely satisfied."

It wasn't, ever. She tried to distinguish the elements of her puzzlement and voice them. "Not on two points. What of your pet, your snake? What becomes of Macha?"

"And your other question?"

"Before our second—visit, if you will, the expedition to the time coming. The excursion after I gave the king your gift—how did you hasten the passage of the night? What did others see while the world flashed by me so quickly?"

The magician's beard hitched upward, result of an invisible smile. "They saw nothing out of the ordinary, nothing but what they expected. And in their unseeing they missed both moments when I isolated you from the stream of our present. I have taught you my methods of doing that. Look to your notes.

"As for Macha…I believe she will wake with the change of season, as is her custom, and seek for me. If I'm already interred and I've failed to respond to your rousing, show her my ground. She'll know what to do." He bent to pull Odeh's ears. "As will you."

‹›

The brooch glowed in the North's soft sun. Garnets and gold, amber and brass—these weren't colors Nia favored for herself, but she appreciated their beauty. She raised her head to display the gratitude in her eyes. "My king, this is magnificent."

King Bear nodded. "It is the work of Beloved; I've heard you praise her skill. As she praises your powers of healing.

"Allow me." The king lifted the brooch from the folded silk held by one of the servants he'd brought to fill Merlin's house and yard. "You use it to hold shut your cloak or overdress. Your woman will—"

"I own no one."

The king appeared suddenly flustered. "Of—of course not. Of course not." He dropped the hand holding the precious trinket to his side. "I only mean the one who helps you dress."

Who would that be, Nia wondered. And why would their help be necessary. But she relented for Merlin's sake and allowed the king to pin the brooch on a shawl she spread over her shoulders and bosom. Also for love of the magician, she let him remove it, and her shawl and robe and shift, and lay her down on the bed where the two of them had very lately loved. Merlin had shown her at Dinas Dinlle how he asked this of her on the night before his burial. And she had discovered on living through the scene that she was unwilling to refuse him. She had sworn to care completely for Merlin's charge. To bind him to her however she might.

Coupling with the king was a simple affair, face-to-face, his manner tender enough that Nia felt no worries. She could shoulder this extra duty. It added but a little to the trouble of maintaining herself in the position Merlin expected her to fill. Aided by him, she'd begun to counsel King Bear during that Yuletide visit, and in the four months since. She would keep at it on her own till Merlin emerged with the newborn moon. Soon.

He had asked that she adapt to the methods she'd evolved a few customs of his own people, and with these in mind had chosen to be interred among oaks. The glade of the oaks' nearest queen tree covered a hillock to the hut's north.

After their coupling and the king's reluctant departure, she applied salve to hands still aching from digging Merlin's resting place in the stiff, cold soil, twelve nights past. It had been a difficult burial. Not because of the work involved or any fear shown by the magician, but because she had no wish to watch him dissolve into the earth, though sometimes this was what he seemed to want.

Odeh sniffed her fingers cautiously. They approved of the salve's honey, though its pepper oil made them sneeze. They backed away as she knelt to the hearth—but not only to afford her room: the stone above Macha's resting place lifted just slightly, and out slid the snake. She coiled herself at Nia's feet,

resting her flat head where lately the king had lain his possessive cheek. Odeh assumed a pose of aloof inquiry at the edge
of the fire's warm circle.

"Greetings, Dame Macha; you are well come for your tidings of the new season's first steps." Nia put down a slow hand
to stroke the serpent's dry-leaf skin. "Your magician's away, but
will return."

The snake regarded her with placid skepticism. "Of course
he insisted on a fourteen-night immersion," she complained.
A month of pillow talk had not dissuaded him. "Quite sure
of himself. Thinks his training sufficient; says he'll never learn
any more without experience." Which was no doubt true, but
why should he try to pack a decade of experience into a single
lesson? What reason but pride spurred him to catch up to her
so quickly?

Secrets must be shown, not told, yes. And because of this
their learning required patience.

The serpent uncoiled herself and flowed away to a crevice
near the smoldering peats. Nia got up and got into her lonesome
bed. Odeh napped with her a while, but then left to go about
their obscure business. Three more nights she slept thus. Then,
finally, the time came. She donned Macha like a living collar
and covered them both with her cloak. Odeh stayed curled
abed, stubbornly refusing to waken. She went without them

Dawn broke slowly in these lands. Light like thin milk
soaked into the air from the east, the direction in which she
first traveled. The cloud of her breath preceded her, carried on
the softest of breezes.

Now north. Imperceptibly her walk changed to a climb,
steepness shortening her steps. The quiet, riddled with bird-
song and branchcreak, embraced and released and embraced
her again, without and within.

She reached the hill's crown, the shallow grave, its loose-
topped hummock already sprouting a few brave seedlings.

Crouching, she transferred these to one of the fired clay bowls she'd brought, saving the other to dig with. As she worked, Macha slithered free of her clothes.

Aside from the plants, the grave looked undisturbed. The straws she had put in for air stood angled as she'd placed them, away from unkind rains. But Macha knew, and so did she.

She uncovered him anyway. Though only his face. That was all she needed to see.

Merlin's skin was unmarked, smooth save where bearded. Examining it closely, Nia proved to herself this beard was not composed of hair. Strands of white rootlets pulsing with messages grew into the magician—or out of him? His eyes opened, shining with a pure and holy light. Inhumanly holy. Inhumanly pure.

His lips opened. Nia bent and pressed her lips against them ever so lightly. They moved, but produced no sound. No air escaped between them.

She withdrew. He had gone far—further into the web than she could follow. If he was going to emerge it must be on his own.

A wordless whisper came to her over the damp soil at her back. She turned to see Macha ascending the oak tree's trunk, a green stream running skyward. From there the serpent twined herself along a high brown branch and stopped. Watching. Waiting.

The magician made no sign he saw his pet. Or her. If she should chide him for his pride, he'd likely never hear. All she could do was as he'd asked. As she had promised.

Pressing the earth down softly, delicately, discarding the useless straws, she refilled Merlin's grave and headed home.

Looking for Lilith

Not a word. Looks, gestures, grimaces, or blank stares; that was all she got. Everyone was making baskets or printing "James Brown—Superbad" tee-shirts, or coming up with new recipes for hot sauce or wrinkle cream. Some of them didn't look busy, wearing out raffia chair-bottoms or tumbling pebbles in a heap of gravel. Still, one could never be sure. Not all work is visible.

But either they were preoccupied, or rude, or they didn't want to admit that they couldn't help. It was clear that if they had ever known the answers to her inquiries, they didn't remember them. She was pretty sure that once, they had known. She stayed in the hotel several weeks, and finally everyone got used to the crazy light-skinned girl and her persistent questions. And she was persistent. Down at the station at dawn, out at the clubs till two in the morning. She was tired, but she dared not sleep her fill. She might miss a whim, an evanescent urge to help.

It was George at the Sous Venir Boutique who gave her her first real clue. She was standing inside, watching the dust collect on new and old curios in his front window: useless things for useless people. A weathered, walnut-bark-skinned man walked past, balancing an ancient rattan suitcase on his head. It appeared to be held together by clothesline. His eyes stared fixedly forward, his jaw was locked tight, stubbornly holding onto his many secrets.

George nodded. "He knows."

At once she flew out of the shop. But the burdened old man was nearly out of sight. The battered case bobbed over the heads of the crowd, bouncing down the hill, deeper into the decaying core of the tourist sector. Sidewalk gave way to crumbling concrete, then to brick. The suitcase disappeared into the courtyard of a deserted hospital. Racing through the colorful throngs of foreigners and natives, she ran under the grey arch.

The old man was resting on the edge of a dried-up fountain. She came to his side and sat, waiting. When they had both caught their breath she asked.

"Where is Lilith?"

He met her piercing eyes with his dull ones. "I know. I show you the way. Come in here." He rose and led her under palms that had found the moisture lost by the fountain. They entered the bathhouse. "Here. Look. I made it."

She stared, beneath her feet, over her head, all around her, absorbed in the mosaic and the story that it told. Every part of every part mattered, and if you looked at a piece it made sense, and if you looked at the whole it made more sense.

She saw a tree before a mountain lake, high above a plain, flowering whitely. From below its stem a river tumbled and twisted, feeding the tree's far-reaching roots. Hollows darkened the cliff behind the falls. Water and wood intertwined harmoniously, following their common path. The tree's flowers burned brilliantly, casting shadows of the lower branches upon the flatlands. There were shadows, too, behind the tree, in the waters of the lake. The shapes of these shades were larger, bulkier, yet streamlined. All was lapped about by green darkness.

She walked forward and looked more closely, her steps hollow and gritty in the ruined bathhouse. Light fell through gaps in the roof and showed her tiny specks of black in the green border, specks swarming for a mass of mottled red. Ghostly, skeleton-like shapes were woven with snakes. There were spaces between the snakes. She slipped off a shoe and placed her foot in one of these spaces. A perfect fit.

She changed positions. Some of the tiles representing the savannah were glazed differently, though the glazes covered identical colors. Some tiles were shinier, or duller, or rougher than others. Depending upon her point of view, she saw the differences as spirals, ripples like heat waves rising from the grasses, or tall mounds pierced with fatal-looking blackness. Crouching, she seemed to see the blades of brown and green fashion themselves into other shapes: slings, sandals, baskets, nets, and lassoes.

The empty pools were tiled in black, veined with silver and gold.

Over all was a likeness of the sky, broken by the sky itself. Between expanses of blue, changeless clouds were interrupted by changing ones, leaving her to wonder at what might be missing from the picture.

On the walls and floor, too, pieces were missing. But these seemed almost to have been removed on purpose; this was not vandalism, nor was it the destruction of the elements. It was an act of deliberate mystification. Still, she thought she recognized the patterns, some as concrete as antique sidewalks, some more abstract: accompaniment, betrayal. Some were simple and straightforward, others knotted about themselves, too complicated to be seen, only felt.

When she understood it all, she looked outside. She had expected the old man to be gone, but he was there, watching her. "Can you take me?" He nodded.

Eight fevered days later, they left. The way lay upriver, first through jeweled jungle, then savage savannah. The old man, Joe, led her, but this was not entirely necessary, for once on the proper path, she found that all was as she had been shown. Fearful adolescents accompanied them, young relatives of Joe's, in his command. They were as unfamiliar with the wilderness as she was, and not as driven. She did not rely upon them completely, nor upon the stores they carried. She studied the signs and watched for signals.

Joe still bore his rattan suitcase, keeping it always at hand. Pitying him somewhat, she asked if one of the youths might not carry it for him, but he would not allow it. And in truth, his burden seemed to buoy his steps.

They passed dead villages. Human bones filled huts, spilled out of ceremonial circles, dragged onto the trail by scavengers.

It was the untamed and the unknown that scared her crew; they were not at all put off by these sad, familiar remains. They helped themselves to any ornaments and tools that they came upon, sharing them amongst themselves. Perforce, she accepted an ivory toothpick pressed upon her by one well-muscled youth. It was prettily carved and stained with dark dyes. She decided that this was a signal to her that she must stop abstaining from flesh. Under the shiny leaves of gigantic trees, she joined in a feast of warm, salty stew.

Joe nodded his approval to her across the small, bright fire. There were rules that had to be broken. She had to make them to disregard them. Sometimes it didn't seem worth the trouble she took, prohibiting the pronunciation of different diphthongs, the contact of certain bodily parts. Especially when she had to disobey her own ultimata soon after they were born.

It took so long. There were so many little pieces, so many formalities, so many observations to make. But if she had gone the same way in a hurry, she wouldn't have gotten where she was going. She did not hasten, but neither did she hesitate. There was danger all around, and she had to deal with it, and learn from it. She memorized the patterns woven by snakes, and found how to place her feet to avoid their inevitable strikes.

Incredibly minute insects plagued their path. As she had been instructed to do, she carried a lure before her, sweet-smelling meat that attracted and held the biting flies. Their concentration upon the lure enabled her to pass untaxed.

The savannah was inimical to human life. The river misbehaved itself, winding in fractious turns; to follow it strictly would have meant spending months on the hot, hostile plain. Often nothing appeared on the surface of things but a dry, gravelly bed. The true river ran belowground in these places.

At night, gases emanated by the grass destroyed all extraneous matter with which they came into contact. Fortunately, the fumes clung low to the ground, never rising above knee level. It was possible for the band to clothe themselves in tightly woven sandals fashioned from blades of the grass. In this manner, they were able to shield themselves from the effects of the gases, though the rough edges chafed their skin. During the day they rested, licking their wounds. They had little water.

A woman became ill during the night. She doubled over under her load, grunting, then collapsed to the ground. At first they thought that the gases had dissolved her skin, causing the flow of blood that issued from her thighs. But when they lifted her up it was seen that there had not been time for these to act. The bearer was in the throes of a spontaneous abortion. It was necessary to bathe her with their last bit of water and to carry her on in a grass sling. The sick woman made an awkward burden, tossing and moaning in the darkness. At last the sun rose and a breeze blew, breaking up the deadly vapor.

Joe was gone. The plain extended in all directions, emptily. In the light of the new day the plateau was visible, distant though it was. But of her guide there was no sign. The width of waving grass could not easily hide him yet did not show him. Unperturbed, she settled herself down in the flickering shade. Soon, she slept.

She woke alone. The adolescents had deserted her, taking with them all the equipment except a couple of empty water containers. Undoubtedly, their desire to complete the journey had left with Joe. She remained calm. All would proceed as it was meant to. Heading for the nearest open stretch of river, she made her way among the mounded entrances to deep burrows. Bald, conical, they hunched up warningly in her path. From time to time starlight struck brightness from beady eyes perched on these mounds, waist high and higher. They did not frighten her. Had her followers still accompanied her, they might all have fought together to fend off the creatures, as she had been shown in the bathhouse mosaic. But it was not so, and so to fight would not be necessary. As it was, she kept her distance from the mounds, knowing that the rodents could not attack her through the flesh-melting fog. And when the dawn came and the misty barrier retreated, it seemed they must have other things to attend to, as she had anticipated. She filled her empty water containers from the peaceful river, secure in her belief that the burrowers would not be hungry for some time to come.

Looking for a place to rest for the day, she came upon proof of her conviction: the fugitive crew. The crossing of their path with hers was easily explained by the presence of water. The fact that they remained there when they had been so eager to return to the city was due to their inability to leave. Parts of them protruded from the openings of the burrows. Their limbs and torsos jerked as the carnivorous rodents below struggled to drag in as much meat as they could before the poisonous mists of evening dissolved the bodies. The burrowers were industrious animals, and she was sure that many of the adolescents were already safely buried in chambers far below. Their packs had been rifled, all the sweets pilfered, or spoiled and scattered. She salvaged what she could and continued.

At last she stood at the foot of the waterfall. It towered above her, its heights remotely grand, its base thunderous, overwhelming. All was just as she had thought to find it. Moments passed. Nothing changed. There was something wrong; the dam's spillway remained open, and the white torrent continued to pour down from the head of the falls. She could not enter.

She camped, waiting. Sooner or later, the spillway would have to be closed. The rains were not due yet, not for some time. The flow would have to be cut, or at the very least, slowed. She waited, picturing the Lake of the Clouds receding from its shores, the lotus blossoms sinking lower and lower with each passing day. Surely the giant turtles would be called to their harnesses and instructed to pull shut the great underwater gate? Surely the lake would not be emptied simply to keep her out?

It was not. As she was sitting, watching, nearly tranced by the changeless flood, it thinned to a mere rivulet. Revealed now in the face of the cliff, the entrance to the tunnel yawned wetly before her. Smiling, she rose and took the path within.

There was no light. Dodging dangerous projections, stepping with the precision needed to avoid the numerous chasms, she made her way in and up.

The tunnel debouched upon a natural amphitheater. White sand covered the ground where she stood. She was in the arena. She tensed, looking around with dilated pupils. That shadowy shape, she decided, must be Joe, seated on one of the many curving stone benches that surrounded her.

And there, that was Lilith, dressed in flowers. At first she could not tell, with her dazzled eyes, what was the color of Lilith's hair, what hue her skin. Then her eyes adjusted, and she saw.

Lilith's skin was black, so black it reflected the world, like deep, still water. Her hair was like a nest of petals, white and glowing, shedding its immortal glory on the blossoms she wore. In her shining face, her eyes were wide, drawing secrets into their softness. Her high brow was smooth, clear as volcanic glass. But beneath her proud, arching nostrils, the corners of Lilith's blackberry mouth drooped in a pouting frown.

Panic struck through the supplicant. Why had she come here? Why had she sought this potent female force, a demon, as some said, or a goddess, even? What was her business here, her intention, her own name? It seemed as though she hadn't asked herself these questions for a long, long time, and now there were no answers.

A terrible silence hung around them. Suddenly, she sank to her knees. It was all she could do. She had come, she knew not why. Perhaps the motive for her journey was another's. She could only trust that her persistence would be enough, even without comprehension.

At her action, Lilith relaxed her frown and made a motion with her right hand, the side where Joe was sitting. The movement was vague, yet imperious, and Joe quickly left his seat, lifting the familiar suitcase. With ceremonial precision, he came down the steps. His bare feet slapped on the grey stone, then silenced themselves in the sand. The rattan case rustled. He placed it before her in the ring and resumed his place, all without meeting her eyes.

Helplessly, she stared at the knotted clothesline that held the case shut. She cast her eyes about her. There was no sword, no blade of any sort. She closed her eyes and reached blindly for the knotted mass. The silence was patient, no longer terrible, as she worked the bindings loose. The lines fell free, and she opened her eyes again, blinking in amazement. Hesitantly, she placed her hands on the case's foremost corners, then looked up to Lilith for approval. Lilith nodded.

Taking a deep breath, she lifted the lid of the suitcase. She looked within it. It seemed to be packed with grey and white feathers, gently stirring in the wind. But, no, the feathers stirred of their own accord, lifted, formed themselves into gently beating wings. Geese uncrooked their necks, arched their pinions, and flew out of the suitcase. One, two, three, and then more, faster and faster, clumsily at first, but with gathering grace. An entire flock of geese flew up into the air and circled above the amphitheater. Bright feathers and quiet ones floated down into the arena. Then, the entire flock having organized itself into the proper formation, it flew away to the Lake of the Clouds.

She searched the faces of her audience. They appeared to find the suitcase's contents as marvelous as she herself had.

The feathers lay motionless on the sand. Stooping, she picked them up, placing some of them in her hair and retaining others between her fingers. Then she performed for her guide and goal. She danced the dance she had been taught by the snakes of the jungle, the meandering of the river, the abysses within the tunnel, the knotted cord. As she finished her dance, she realized she had not come for this. She had come to come. She had made the dangerous journey not to reach the end, but to travel to it. She bowed, sweeping her feathers in the sand.

Lilith was alight with approbation. She clapped her hands. "Well done, well done," Lilith said. "I had not been led to expect so much from you." Lilith glanced toward Joe, who only bowed his head. "You will shine as an example to others."

Again Lilith made the vague, imperious gesture. The old man came back down to the arena. This time he faced her squarely. "Did not meant to doubt," he told her, dull eyes apologetic. "You come through. Thank you." He paused a second, putting both hands on her shoulders. "Maybe you come through again."

Then he pushed her down gently, collapsing her and folding her neatly together. Reverently, respectfully, he placed her inside the suitcase and began, once more, to tie the knots.

Vulcanization

*A chemical process for converting natural rubber or
related polymers into more durable materials via the
addition of sulfur or equivalent curatives or accelerators.
These additives modify the polymer by forming cross-
links (bridges) between individual polymer chains.*

Brussels, 1898

Another black. A mere illusion, Leopold knew, but he flinched
out of the half-naked nigger's path anyway.

Of course Marie Henriette noticed when he did so. The
quick little taps of the queen's high-heeled slippers echoed
faster off the polished floor as she hastened to draw even with
him. "My dearest—Sire—"

Leopold stopped, forcing his entire retinue to stop with
him. "What do you wish, my wife?" He refused to turn around.
Once had he done so and had seen then no sign of the savage who'd just the moment before brushed past him—through
him—with a fixed and insolent stare.

Not much longer till he would be rid of his ghosts for
good.

The queen reached for his sleeve but held her hand back
to hover above the gold-embroidered cuff. "Are you quite sure
you need to do this? Are you sufficiently well?"

He had wondered whether to tell her about his appointment with Travert. In the end he hadn't, dreading an increase

in court gossip. "The Museum of the Congo is important to my legacy. We will not be late for the dedication, Marie," he objected, in his usual mild tone. She said nothing further, and he resumed his progress down the passage to the palace's exit.

Outside, the sky's silver overcast was brighter than any light Leopold had experienced in more than a month. Perhaps he ought not to have confined himself so long. It didn't seem to have decreased the apparitions. Nigger visions had plagued him night and day. Sometimes they held up their bleeding, handless arms accusingly, shaking them in his face. Gore fountained and dripped from their wounds, yet the carpets over which they passed remained stainless. Illusion only, but it would be a relief to be done with them.

He settled himself comfortably in the royal steam barouche. Marie Henriette hesitated a moment before climbing in beside him. Her fondness for horses was well known, but Leopold had explained patiently the need to show support for the manufacture of rubber and its essential role in modern mechanization. Absently he patted the reinforced fabric of the seat cushion: water repellent, elastically resilient, warm to the touch as—

Involuntarily he jerked away. He met the eyes of Driessen, his personal physician, taking the opposite seat. Poorly concealed concern peered back at him. Deliberately the king set his hand back on the spot from which he'd removed it. When he could turn his head casually, as if taking in a passing prospect, he saw nothing more than a vague cloudiness roiling the air of the steam barouche's interior. Arriving at the site of the Museum and disembarking from the machine, he left it behind.

The quiet crunch of the gravel walk comforted him. Climbing granite steps to the half-round portico where he would speak, Leopold threw back his shoulders and gave Driessen and Marie Henriette what he hoped was a reassuring smile. Approaching the podium, he pulled his memorandum pad from his military-style jacket's inner pocket and opened it to the relevant page. He looked out at an audience abruptly filled with hundreds of weeping black faces and with a cry let it fall to the ground.

A stifled gasp came from his queen, counterpoint to the sobs only he could hear. Then the pad was set into his nerveless hand, his fingers bent to curl around and hold it. Driessen. The physician was asking him something. Leopold nodded—he hadn't heard the question clearly, but assumed it concerned his welfare. He would go on with his speech. Noblesse oblige.

"Learned and generous contributors to our great enterprise," he began, "the enlightenment of the savage inhabitants of heathen Africa, it is with joy I invite you today to enter with me the magnificent edifice created to shelter the fruits of our noble laboring." Continuation became easier with every word. With his mental faculties fully exercised by the demands of his oratory, Leopold's visions faded till they were virtually invisible. To convince himself those faint specters were truly immaterial, he had only to remind himself that mere minutes remained now till the appointment.

※

Travert was sallow-skinned and pitiably slight—also balding and bespectacled. Perhaps a clandestine Israelite? Quite likely. They were everywhere, and for the most part harmless. This one waited on the king in one of the Museum's private rooms, which Leopold found rather plain. Undistinguished paneling, ugly gas lamps affixed to it such as he would never choose. The smell of some crude cleaning compound troubled his nostrils.

The Jew bowed deeply. "Majesty," he began, "I am mindful of the great favor you do me in granting me permission to share with you my new invention. The Variable Pressure Ethereo-Vibrative Condenser displays the most interesting principles discovered to date in the field to which I've devoted so much study, so much—"

Mary Henriette wrinkled her pretty brow. "But were you not hired to oversee the care of the inhabitants of the museum's model village?" In the confusion following the king's public appearance she had shed her attendants and somehow insinuated herself into the room, taking a seat at Leopold's side. "I'm afraid I see no connection between that and your— Elusively Gyrating—whatever you may say." Her white shoulders shrugged off their covering of lace. "The king is busy. He has been ill, overwrought—"

Driessen coughed meaningfully into his fist.

"My queen," said Leopold, "this very illness is the cause of my curiosity regarding Dr. Travert's investigations. They may perhaps be of help in curing me—" He swept one shapely hand in the little Hebrew's direction. "—by means he was just about to explain."

"Yes, of course." The bald head ducked in acknowledgment. "You see, my Condenser renders palpable the vaporous emanations of the spirit world so that they may be, ah, dealt with in a corporeal manner: jailed, burnt, buried, dissected—"

"It is due to evil spirits you've gone on so poorly? You never told me!" Marie Henriette twisted and leaned toward the king. Her breasts huddled forward, threatening to spill over the loose confines of her satin bodice. "Let me bring my confessor to you—tonight, after supper!"

"Why?" demanded Driessen.

Leopold dragged his eyes to where Driessen rocked heel to toe, toe to heel. His brusqueness was to be expected. The royal physician tolerated this latest attempt at reconciliation with Marie Henriette, but made no secret of his cynicism in regard to her.

"'Why?'" the queen retorted. "To disavow the guilty sorrows such things find attractive. You will feel much better, dearest, once you've relinquished your burden of sin."

But Leopold had done nothing wrong. The casualties in the Congo were necessary to the extraction of its wealth. He looked at Marie Henriette as blandly as possible. With age her fascination was shrinking. "Perhaps," he temporized. "However, first we'll try Travert's method." It seemed more certain, more scientific.

Though there was one point about which he worried. "You have tested the procedure?" he asked.

"Naturally. With the access to your African subjects you have so kindly granted, I was well able. In fact, I have prepared a demonstration for you to view before your own Condensation. It only remains for me to outline for you the particulars of the apparatus's operation and we'll get started."

It required the full force of Driessen's insistence to make the self-aggrandizing Jew realize he could deliver this outline while simultaneously enacting his far more germane demonstration.

Of Leopold's personal guard only Gagnon, its head, had entered the room with him. In the crowded corridor they joined the rest of the detachment, descending thence via unfinished steps to a basement, where the odor of the cleaning compound threatened to overwhelm him, though he couldn't determine if it affected anyone else. After they had negotiated several jogs and branchings, Travert called a halt to the procession and unlocked a large wooden door in the passageway's right hand wall.

The space they entered held charcoal-colored benches, one covered in a jumble of equipment: glass tubes, snakelike hoses, metal fixtures glittering in the scanty light falling from small windows near the room's bare rafters. Its far end was obscured by a brown velvet curtain. Travert drew that aside to reveal a lectern and, looming behind it, a tall, narrow booth. Or a cage—that might be a better word for it, since bars of brass stretched from its raised floor to a height crowned with a barrel-like tank and some geared apparatuses he couldn't quite descry.

Travert swung the cage's barred door open as they approached. A pale face seemed to coalesce behind it, to shiver and deform itself. Then Leopold realized this was but his own reflection. The bars were backed with smooth panes of leaded crystal, as its inventor explained. At length. They helped to hold in certain vibrations that it was desirable to contain in order to concretize the evanescent portion of the targeted phenomenon. Certain chemicals in combination with steam-driven increases in atmospheric pressure wrought bridging chains of causality between the captive spiritual energy's various potential states and resulted in manifestations tangible to all.

Before the fumes of whatever nauseating substance was so prevalent here bested his control completely, a scuffle at the room's entrance ensued. "Ah! Here is my favorite now—" Meeting a couple of men halfway back along the room's length, the Hebrew urged them onward. Between the pair of them the men propelled a struggling nigger woman who slapped and kicked them ineffectually, screeching at them an endless stream of what were doubtless heathen maledictions. Reaching the cage they flung her inside. Like a wild beast she leapt snarling to her feet and charged the door—but Travert speedily shut and secured it.

Her stink fought strenuously against the chemical scent overlaying everything else. Raising to his nose a cologne-soaked handkerchief he hoped would block these disagreeable odors, Leopold leaned forward to scrutinize the lectern to which Travert now advanced. It had been modified by the addition of a peculiar wheel like a gleaming halo, and several switches and levers. Manipulating one of these, the doctor set off a low, heavy-sounding hum. The king looked an inquiry.

"Power from that rank of batteries to your right—" Travert pointed to a row of crates formed of some black, dull-surfaced metal. "—primes the mechanism while the generators build up sufficient steam." The nigger wench had ceased her wailing imprecations and sunk to lie sullenly on the cage's bottom. "Much as when the heat and pressure employed in vulcanization collects prior to..." Ensorcelled by his own arcane activities, Travert allowed the explanation to trail away. Frowning, he slid a yellow-enameled lever down to a position approximating that of a neighboring blue one.

"Go on," Leopold commanded. His stern tone woke Travert from his trance.

"Whatever manifestations Fifine accords us—"

"'Fifine'?"

The doctor's sallow cheeks blushed like a maiden's. "My name for the subject—I must call her *something*, and her African name is far too outlandish."

With the nipples of her flat dugs aimed at the cage floor like dusky arrowheads, the drab resembled no Fifine Leopold had ever known. And he had known a few. But let the man indulge his fancy. "Very well. What would you tell us about the manifestations of this 'Fifine'?"

"The Condenser will render them visible, palpable, subject to study and measurement. From mere ectoplasmic excrescences they will be focused and solidified—"

"Yes, yes." The soft hum stealing out of the rafters had been growing steadily louder. Leopold pitched his invitation above it. "Driessen, if you will do the honors?" The royal physician laid his hand over the Israelite's and gave the lectern's wheel a swift spin. It connected to the apparatus above the cage by a series of looping belts and toothed cogs, all of which now began to turn. They did not cease to do so when the wheel did.

Brushing his hands together as if to remove invisible soil from his fingers, Driessen released his hold, and Travert deserted his lectern for a new post directly before the cage. He addressed its occupant. "Fifine? You are prepared for a demonstration?"

Leopold was taken aback to hear a reply in French. "How can you ask such a stupid question?" He looked to make sure: yes, it was the nigger herself who answered! "The harm you have caused me with your Condenser has no cure. Haven't I told you? Yet you persist in destroying all that remains to me of those I love."

Travert's cheeks reddened again. "Fifine! Must I gag you? I haven't touched a hair upon your head! What will his majesty think?" He turned an embarrassed countenance to the king.

"I think that you had better get on with things."

The doctor returned hurriedly to the lectern, ignoring the nigger woman's yammering—as he ought to have done from the first. A red lever was moved to a position paralleling the blue and yellow. Clouds of fog descended from the cage's ceiling, grey and black. The terrible odor increased, forcing Leopold to retreat to lean upon a bench a few feet back. There was naught to see nearer anyway: coiling smokes filled the cage and obscured its contents.

For long moments nothing more happened. Then the laboring noise of the Condenser's growling motors ground slowly down to silence.

Gradually the clouds within the cage cleared, disclosing the slumped form of the black on its still-murky bottom. And—other forms? Smaller shapes were scattered around the large one. Did they stir? Yes! Leopold drew closer. A quiet chirping rewarded him. Ghostly birds hopped and fluttered through the dissipating mist. Like dusty sparrows on some plebeian roadway they pecked at their fellow prisoner, soon rousing her.

An odd expression came over the woman's face. On a white Leopold would have taken it for a compound of regret and delight. Of course the lower orders were incapable of such complicated mixtures of emotions. If he hadn't known this for a fact, however, he would have been hard pressed not to attribute such feelings to her as she petted the hopping, shadow-tinted birds with the most delicate of touches. Under the machine's noise and the twittering the bird-things emitted, he caught her whispered murmurs and cooed nonsense.

The doctor approached him. "The flock has thinned considerably since our first experiment."

"Indeed?" Leopold imagined the cage busy with the dull-plumed little birds. "What became of them?"

A pursing of his lips made obvious Travert's Oriental ancestry. "They furnished us with material for several informative experiments. But have you comprehended the procedure so far? The carbon and other additives being linked to the interacting surface of the manifestations and showing us thereby their outlines—"

Would the man never cease droning on? Stifling his exasperation Leopold glanced significantly toward Driessen, who stepped forward and placed a silencing finger on the Jew's thick lips. "Enough!"

For a moment Travert's jaw dropped and hung open; for a moment his ungloved hands twitched in the barely breathable air. But then, not being mad, he composed himself and motioned the nigger's escorts to come with him to open up the cage.

Reluctant as she had appeared to enter the brass and crystal enclosure, "Fifine" made yet more difficulty about leaving it. One of the doctor's assistants gripped her wooly head, even bringing himself to insert his fingers in her gaping nostrils; the other secured her kicking feet. But they had to call for a third man to grasp her wildly flailing arms before they managed to eject her from the room.

Leopold's eyes followed the disturbance toward the door, but came to rest on his queen. The sight of her, almost as green and pale as the walls against which she sought refuge, moved him to hold out a welcoming hand. She ran quickly to catch it up. "I'm so sorry you've been put through such an ordeal, Marie," he apologized. "You need not remain longer if it pains you."

"I could *not* desert you!" Her refusal to leave gratified the king. He caressed her plump wrist, intending to raise it to his lips.

WHACK!

Leopold jumped involuntarily. The doctor reacted to his stare with a guilty shift of his eyes, hefting up the meter stick he carried. "My apologies. I missed my mark," said Travert. "For your convenience, it will naturally be best to clear the Condenser's apparatus immediately, and as we've conducted plenty of trials already with this sort of specimen—" He gave a Levantine hunch of his shoulders and returned to clubbing down the dingy birds shut with him inside the cage. Only four remained active, but they gave the Jew an inordinate amount of trouble, their cries loud and frantic as they flew erratically about. The flat crack of the stick meeting bare metal sounded again and again.

Travert's three assistants reappeared and soon dispatched the last of the vermin in a flurry of high-pitched little shrieks. The Jew then had them shovel out the corpse-like refuse.

At last Travert indicated with a bow that the Condenser's cage was ready for Leopold to enter. Driessen walked in before him, examining the situation. "His majesty will require a chair," the royal physician declared.

Seated upon a velvet-covered, spindle-legged stool, Leopold found that the unpleasant odor increased. The cage's door shut, and the heliotrope in which he'd drenched his handkerchief barely compensated for the intensified smell, which filled the surroundings like a half-live thing. After an interval of building noise above his head, he heard a subtle hiss and looked up to see the dark, descending smoke.

Would it affect him, a European, as it had the quasi-animal "Fifine"?

Rotting greyness clogged his eyes, his nose, and when he tried breathing through it, his mouth. Stoic determination fled. The king gagged and fainted.

※

A cool breeze woke him. Refreshed, he opened his stinging eyes to gaze upon a little garden planted with tropical trees, bushes, and flowers—doubtless the produce of his Congolese holdings. He had designed several such gardens to fill the museum's courtyards. One of Gagnon's men must have carried him here so he'd more easily revive. Certainly the fresh air was an improvement, and the scene that met his eyes far more pleasing than that of the stuffy cellar: Fat stems held nodding blooms of cinnabar, violet, and gold, and broad leaves, some veined in white or pink, quivered softly on all sides.

It was proper that the guard, having brought him here, had departed, but where were Driessen and the queen? Was he actually alone? How odd. No—through the foliage Leopold glimpsed a young girl approaching him. Comely enough, though her final steps showed her to be clad in a boy's shirt and trousers.

"Hello. I'm Lily." A frank, open expression sat with habitual ease upon her healthful features.

Meaning to announce his royal status in a charming yet authoritative manner, Leopold was suddenly rendered voiceless: the girl's left leg had that second become a pulpy mess of gore and bone. His throat filled with vomit. He choked it down.

"Ah. My injury disturbs you. You haven't yet had time to get used to it as I have." The girl gazed ruefully down at her shattered limb. "Your soldiers shot me last October, during our rescue of King Mwenda, and I died that very night. Nearly six months now, isn't it?"

Leopold gaped at her. He must have looked exceedingly foolish. Chief Mwenda had led a rebellion against the king's Public Forces. "You are a—a gh-gh-ghost?"

"Isn't it obvious?" She flicked a careless hand at the red ruin on which she stood. Impossibly.

A ghost, then. But she was not black—an English Miss, to judge by her accent. A white girl—though perhaps not of Europe? Of Everfair, then, the Fabians' damned infestation of a colony wreaked on lands they'd bought of him? Yes! Had not Minister Vandelaar told him recently of an attempt by those traitors to aid that black brute's escape? Though temporarily successful, it had, so the Intelligence Minister said, cost the rebels of Everfair an important casualty.

Which would be this Lily. Lily Albin, as he recalled now. Daughter of the rabble's leader, a hoyden suffragette.

Was this to be his sole manifestation?

Where were the sooty multitudes who had haunted him all this while, whose silent groans had pestered him so, bidding fair to drive him mad? As he understood Travert's method, if the nigger ghosts could not be Condensed, they could not be got rid of.

The girl answered as if he'd asked his questions aloud. "Do you think you have any control of who you see?" Her eyes whitened like a blind woman's. "Or how? Or what?"

Rising from beneath the thin scent of the garden's flowers, the mephitic cleaning compound's fumes assaulted him anew. They couldn't have traveled here from the cellar—he must still be inside it! In the Condenser's cage! How could he have forgotten? The stool he sat on was the same. The rest of what he experienced, the vegetation and the building heat, might be nothing more than an hypnotic nightmare induced by that quack Travert.

He swung his head from side to side, peering around the foliage, looking for the Jew or one of his assistants. Shouldn't they be waiting nearby?

The girl Lily laughed. The ivory hollow beneath her neck flexed like the foaming pool below a waterfall. "You thought the Condenser would *cure* you?" She subsided to a low chortle. "Of course you did. Why else submit? But whatever gave you the idea?"

He should humor her. He wiped away a trickle of sweat. His attendants must return soon—or, no, he was asleep and would soon wake. How long had the nigger "Fifine" lain prostrate? Despite his more sensitive and highly evolved nervous system, he surely ought to begin to recover momentarily. He stood up from the stool and thrust aside some obscuring boughs to get a better look around. His entourage remained absent, but a flickering motion just out of sight impelled him forward. A man-like shape, glistening in the patchy sunlight as if made of ebony. He walked swiftly toward it for several meters.

Then he stopped.

This garden was not small. The museum's walls did not enclose it. Nothing did. It was a jungle, not a garden.

Why should this frighten him? Dreams could not hurt or kill him. He would not die.

He reversed his path. Now that he was thinking clearly, he realized how stupid he'd been to leave the spot where he first found himself. But when he returned it was to see his seat occupied by the dead girl. "I hope you don't mind? Easier for me than standing." With smiling casualness she gestured again at her mangled leg.

Ever the gentleman, Leopold refrained from pressing the claim of his superior birth, though the oppressive warmth and the burgeoning smell of the cleaning compound threatened to overwhelm his senses. He put a hand out to halt the world's swaying and flinched back from the pricking thorns of the branch he'd grasped. He stared in pain and surprise at the blood welling quickly out of many little wounds—his sacred essence! Wrapping his handkerchief around the cuts seemed to do no good; if anything they bled more fiercely than before, specks of scarlet growing wider, wetter, joining to make of it one sopping, crimson banner.

His Russian cousins could perish as a result of such small injuries. And he?

"Oh, I don't believe you're done for just yet." The ghost Lily gazed up at him with blank eyes. "Though with so much blood you'll be creating many more _____, of greater power. As you will come to find."

He didn't understand the word she had used. "I beg your pardon? More—more—what do you say?"

"_____!" Again she gave her chilling laugh. "The ones you expected to find here instead of me."

The nigger spirits, she meant. He thought she nodded. "Those spawned so far wait with your retinue for you to waken."

The stink and heat and dizzying sway worsened. He fell to his knees. He felt the hot blood soak through his trousers where they sank into its spreading pool. He must rouse himself out of this trance *now*, then let the Jew doctor's assistants deal with executing whatever this abominable treatment had brought forth. Leopold strove with all his might to wake.

"But no one will be able to do anything to your _____, to even touch them. Except for you."

He was lying on his side. He tried to sit up. What did she mean? "Fifine's" dirty-looking little birds had been easily dispatched.

"Ah, but have you the sort of relationship with your dead she does?" The ghost girl seemed to have lain down next to him, for her face was but centimeters away. "No. You do not."

With those words her white face sprang suddenly nearer— or did it swell with decay? Tightening like a mask, it slipped

242

rapidly to one side and receded on a tide of blackness. Then that tide, too, receded.

※

His eyes were open. Grey clouds parted to reveal the cage's tarnished ceiling. Leopold lay now on his back, looking heavenward. He lifted his wounded hand: no sign of injury remained.

"Your majesty!" The Jew rushed to his side, Gagnon and Marie Henriette right behind him. The dream was over.

Or was it? A haze of darkness formed above them. Gradually it lowered and interposed itself between the king and his attendants, forming at last into the likeness of a group of soot-skinned savages. Which, as before, no one else appeared to see. Which, it seemed obvious now, no one else ever would.

There were three of them: a handless young buck; a withered old granny with her head staved in; a child with only stumps for legs. They closed around him, clumsily lifting him from the cage's floor. Leopold's scalp crept as he felt the soft resilience of their nonexistent flesh. He retched convulsively and shoved away the tiny hands, the yielding arms. These newly palpable horrors.

All his life Leopold had known himself to be as brave and strong as he was good and handsome. All his life till now.

"Sire!" The oily voice of Travert intruded itself into the king's thoughts.

"My dearest!" The queen, too, sought his attention.

Leopold opened eyes he hadn't realized he'd shut. The ghosts were defiantly visible. But still, always, only to him. Ignoring the phantoms' reproachful gazes, he leaned on the arms his supporters offered, letting them lead him out of the Condenser. As if the weeping niggers reaching to interrupt his passage with their weak and truncated limbs weren't present. As if they made no actual contact. As if the king didn't understand himself doomed till death to feel, over and over, the hideous warmth of their touch.

She Tore

Wendy drove fast. She tore through the spring night like the howl of a wolf. Damp, misty air blew in through the Invicta S-Type's open windows, making a mess of her normally tidy crown of braids.

In the passenger seat, Tink scowled and rubbed her bare shoulders. "Are you sure we shouldn't stop and take the top down?" she asked sarcastically. "I can still feel my wings."

"No time." The crossroad loomed ahead. Wendy signaled her turn even though there was no one in sight. She wasn't going to get stopped, ticketed for an avoidable infraction. Fast and legal—that was how she handled motors on or off the racetrack. She slowed as little as possible and spun the steering wheel. Tyres screeched as she sped up again coming around the corner. "Lily's note said dawn."

"Do you even know where we are? How long will it take to get—"

"Shut up." Peter had been always been rude to Tink, and Wendy was, too. Politeness never made any difference in the fairy's own manners.

"Well fuck me with a pry bar. I was only asking. And if you're in such a rush, why poke along on the ground like this when we could fly?"

For answer, Wendy removed one gauntleted hand from the wheel to lift the submachine gun tucked between her and the door, tilting its elegant muzzle to the windscreen. "Weighs something," she said. "Plus we'll want plenty of ammo." She lowered the gun back down, point made.

Never mind that flying terrified her.

At a bend in the road Wendy turned the car's nose northeastward. The fading lights of the British city of Boston disappeared from the rearview. She twisted the knob brightening the Invicta's headlamps. One more jog to navigate. She took it at cruising speed: 40 miles per hour. Then the way ahead stretched flat and straight, a Roman rule dividing black fenlands on either side. Gradually the faint glow of the lights of Skegness climbed up from what must be the horizon. She checked the dash's chronometer. Two hours till sunrise. They were just on time.

Tink had been suspiciously quiet for far too long. Wendy spared a glance from the road and saw by the instrument panel that the fairy's blond head was drooping to the passenger seat's far side. A low snore confirmed that she slept. Effectively immortal, Tink fought off aging with the magic of dreams. When she wasn't busy stirring up trouble, she tended to drowse away like a human-sized cat.

Not Wendy. She looked every bit of her thirty-five years. Wendy was one of those who enjoys growing up.

Now she steered the Invicta through Skegness's streets, avoiding as well as she could the traffic caused by the market at its center. But the car's interior was nonetheless flooded with the cries of vendors, the sweet scent of milk from grass-fed cows, the soft clop of horses hauling wagons filled with the last of the winter's root vegetables, the chatter of ice poured into tubs and barrels, the blood-and-salt-and-iodine smell of the morning's catch. A Londoner born and bred, Wendy found the village market's atmosphere strangely familiar. For how many centuries had these folk gone about their bucolic business, striking bargains in tongues rooted in the ancient shifts of tides and time? Telling stories immemorial—

"What a stench!" Tink had wakened.

"We'll soon be away from it." And indeed they'd come at last to the village's outskirts. Soon the road reduced in size. One lane only. For fear of crashing into a vehicle headed in the opposite direction, Wendy couldn't urge the Invicta on with the quickness she'd anticipated. They were going to be late.

"Throw us a map up, Tink."

The fairy gave an ill-natured sigh. "I *asked* if you knew where we were."

"I do. But there may be better routes to the spot Lily's expecting us to show at."

"May not."

The windscreen stayed stubbornly dark. A greenish glimmer in the corner of Wendy's eye proved to be nothing more than Tink's wings half unfurling, only to settle back again into the semblance of a fashionably spangled wrap.

"There's a thimble in it for you." Wendy said this as carelessly as she could. Her reward spread across the screen's glass like colored dew sparkling in an unseen sun. On one side the map's sea shone a transparent, purplish blue; the road beneath their tyres was represented by a thin stream of crimson slanting right. A miniature mango-yellow Invicta crept upwards along it. A clear brown reminiscent of ginger beer filled the rest of the display.

"Thank you. Any footpaths?" Scrawls of white appeared; several of these tangles ended at an undeviatingly straight section of the red line along which they proceeded, further up. Another remnant of the Romans, that would be: a stretch of road laid out as if drawn on the Earth with a protractor.

Lily's note said that they should meet precisely at that stretch's midpoint.

"We won't be able to drive on any of those," Wendy said.

"Then why'd you ask me to put them on?" The paths began to vanish.

"No! Tink, don't, please—"The road relaxed its kinks and she accelerated a touch. "We'll have to walk at the last anyway—to keep from scaring the kidnappers off with too much noise."

"Walk—not fly? You want me to walk in *these*?"Tink pointed one limber leg toward the Invicta's roof. A delicate slipper dangled from her small pink foot. "Silly girl!" But the promise of a thimble had sweetened her normally acid tone of voice.

"Take them off, then." Wendy focused on matching the map up with what she saw of the road. The straightaway's exact midpoint should be roughly a hundred meters on—but the shortest of the footpaths they needed to take started—*here*. Wendy swung the Invicta to the shoulder, cursing softly as the sandy soil dragged them askew.

An unwelcome beam of newly-risen sun bounced off the chromed radiator cap. Dawn.

Why couldn't it still be dark?

She switched off the ignition, opened her door, grabbed the gun, and climbed free of the car seat. Scraggly, starkly backlit wild plants scratched her shins. Golden light stabbed out of the clouds in the east, dazzling her. She lifted one gloved hand to shade her eyes and could barely see back to where the plants thinned to nothing. She'd overshot her mark—only by a bit, though.

She peered in through the Invicta's open window at the fairy faking that she slept. "Up and at em, Tink."

Black eyes snapped open accusingly. "You were supposed to thimble me awake!"

"Sorry. Other fish to fry."Wendy winced inwardly at confessing her distraction. Tink's jealousy of Lily might easily have kept her from going with Wendy on this rescue mission—if she'd been willing to admit to it. To placate her, Wendy offered the fairy a helping hand out. Which Tink stubbornly ignored, spreading her shining, shawl-like wings and flying ostentatiously through the cranked-down window. A neat trick, Wendy had to admit, unfurling the whole of that yardage inside the car. She smiled, then pursed her lips and leaned forward to plant a thorough thimble with them on the sensitive crown of the fairy's head.

Not that you needed wings to fly. Tiger Lily had no doubt assumed they'd make an aerial entrance. In the darkness. If only—

Heavy grey overcast obscured the rising sun. Too much visibility for flying regardless of whether or not she had the courage. Wendy released her hold on the fairy's naked upper arm to sling on a couple of belts of ammo. Then, hefting her weapon, she trudged resolutely toward Lily's rendezvous.

⌁

Three of them. Blue in the dimness, Lily's captors stood on the edge of a shallow depression in half-grassed sand. Give them credit for facing the right direction at least: the one they'd expect her to come from.

Down in the depression's center, Tiger Lily did their best to lure the three into looking their way. "Heyyyy, you wanna find out how good my pussy feels? My mouth and my ass too? I got a special hole for each and every one of ya." Lily's normally husky voice—the only thing about them that never shifted with their shape or gender—trembled with what probably sounded to the men surrounding them like longing. More like laughter to Wendy's ears. No change in tone or register as Wendy lifted her arm and waved a signal from the surf-wet sands at the thugs' backs.

Didn't these men know Lily wouldn't be here unless they wanted to be? The chains linking the shapeshifter's hands together behind their back were useless. Lily could turn to a snake and slither armlessly out of them. Could be anything, become anyone, including who they appeared to be now: an "exotic" "Red Indian" woman—a favorite manifestation— waiting hopelessly to be ransomed by her rich white friends.

Chilly seawater lapped against Wendy's knees. She rose to a crouch, hoping her silhouette resembled a rock's. Green glittered in the air to her left where Tink flew in circles, speeding faster than the human eye could follow. Motioning with the gun for Lily to flatten theirself on the scrubby sand, Wendy took aim at the furthest man's back and fired.

Her darling SK kicked at her heart once, twice, then settled into an even purr as her bullets ripped into the unsuspecting kidnappers. Waiting only a moment for their screams and groans to subside, Wendy ran to Lily's side.

Already the "Indian" had slipped their bonds. "Ta for coming. I was gettin right bored."

Quick hugs and thimbles to each other's cheeks were all the greeting circumstances allowed. The two headed inland. "Why'd you wait for me then?" Wendy asked.

"Seemed best to get you onsite. These fellows have been thinking they're going to wreck the coastline, build a great big, sewage-spewing holiday camp here."

"And?" Wendy gave the dead bodies a brief glance as they passed between them. "Not much of a threat if you ask me. Not this adventure." Maybe next time they'd have a bit more success.

"Ah. But how'd they know I was spying on em, like? How'd they come to try kidnapping me? Someone smart's behind this one."

"Someone like—" Suddenly Wendy realized there was an important absence in the air.

"Lookit the business card they give me when they thought I was an investor." Lily pulled a white pasteboard rectangle from an obscure pocket and thrust it at Wendy—but Wendy barely noticed it. She whirled on her heels, searching wildly for even the faintest gleam of Tink's green glow.

"What?"

"Where'd she go?" Guilt at robbing Peter of the fairy's fidelity—such as it was—pricked at Wendy's mind like midge bites. "Where's Tink?" A question no sooner asked than answered. A patch of jade-colored light shimmered above the water's edge—which was nearer now than before, with the tide coming in. Wendy reversed course.

Lily followed. Wendy wondered if the shapeshifter's presence would exacerbate Tink's moodiness—if moodiness was the problem. She slowed to consider that. The fairy had a way of becoming scarce when trouble threatened.

"See?" The pasteboard rectangle reappeared. Wendy took it and peered at it, but the early gloom defeated her attempt at reading the card's tiny type on the go. "It's for 'Smee & Assoc.'" Lily explained.

"Hook!"

"Right! And if *he's* involved, no telling what this story is *really* about. Don't you want to know?"

But they'd reached the first curling breakers. Wendy waded out—Tink's shining had drifted further away—or perhaps stayed stationary while the tide rose? So swiftly, though? Sand and salt water dragged at her custom cordovans. She should have shed them. She hesitated, and her feet sank deeper. The swirl of the sea on her calves felt like cold hands.

Because it *was* cold hands. Hands pale as foam emerged from the wine-dark combers to wrap around her legs and tug at her twill skirt; muscular arms embraced her hips and waist and clasped her to broad and pearl-like bosoms. Wendy fought, but the mermaids were too many. Waves filled her mouth when she opened it to cry for Lily's help. The scene was all too reminiscent, though the pain a great deal less. As Wendy was forced beneath the surging surface of the icy April ocean, she pressed her lips tight again but kept her eyes angrily open, glaring into the mermaids' mad grins. She breathed out, then in, choking. Black defeat swallowed her.

～～

Wendy woke puking and shivering. A puddle of bile tilted and ran back and forth as the smooth boards beneath her face rocked. So it wasn't just nausea making everything move about. She must be aboard a ship. The flame in the lantern on the table where her head lay burnt upright, though the candlestick itself heaved about under it mercilessly—

"Ah. Awake enough to vomit, I see. Very good." That rich, dark baritone, like licorice soaked in honey, belonged, she was sure, to only one man: the captain of the Jolly Roger. Wendy attempted to push herself upright so she could see him and verify that. Her arms wouldn't obey her. She shoved with her neck and shoulders.

"Shall I help you?" A velveted steel grip closed on her collarbone and hauled her torso up against a knobbly wooden chair back. "Nicer, don't you think?" A metallic "click" and the grip released her.

Wendy's head swam with that small change in altitude. Her vision blurred, then cleared, and she was looking at the long, once-handsome countenance of Captain James Hook. Olive skin—now sadly etched with time—provided piquant contrast to the delicate cornflower blue of his eyes. Glossy corkscrews of an impossible sootiness spilled from beneath a many-feathered cavalier's hat.

"Do you dye your moustaches as well?"

Hook tittered. "Splendid! I knew I could count on you to recover quickly!" He smiled a sickeningly insincere smile. "Smee! Attend us!"

Wendy heard the rattle and bang of an opening and shutting door. Again she tried to move, attempting to twist toward the sound. Now she saw the problem: thick ropes, dirty with tar, had been wound around her tightly. At least, unlike her clothing, they were dry.

Her bandoliers of ammunition were gone. Her SK likewise.

"Cap'n?" A woman's voice? A child's? The Smee Wendy knew was neither. But there was no way to turn around, no telling who spoke behind her.

"Swab the table clean. Then prepare and serve a light nuncheon: champagne, lobster, asparagus, and creampuffs."

"For how many?"

"Two, of course—can the presence of our guest have escaped your notice?"

"No, Cap'n."

"No. And yet? And still? You hesitate? Go!" Scampering steps sounded, then, once more, the noises of the door's operation. Had Hook left the cabin as well as this new Smee? Was Wendy alone? Alone, she might plot her escape—

The touch of velvet on the back of her neck snuffed out that hope.

"My pretty dear. I apologize for the lack of ebullient warmth in your welcome here. Though you've saved me the trouble of executing my least competent underlings, I neglected to thank you as perhaps I should have. Gossip has informed me of your quarrel with Pan—but I'm hesitant to put credence in mere rumor. Will you forgive me?"

"We've split up. It's true."

The chair was gimballed. Hook spun her around to face him. "You swear so?"

"Solemnly." Pirates put great faith in pledges and oaths, much like the little boys who pretended to be them. "Are you going to untie me, then?"

That slimy smile. The flash of a long sword drawn and lifted to the cabin's low ceiling. "This will be faster."

She shut her eyes. She couldn't help it. A breeze stirred the loosened tendrils of her brown braids. Another. A third.

"There. Raise your arms."

The rope's tight coils fell away—except where they stuck stubbornly to Wendy's wet skirt and tunic. "Thank you."

"Of course. I'd advise you to immediately remove those damp things but for the danger of misconstruction...."

She shuddered or shivered. Or did both. "Yes. That would be bad." Hook was nothing like her type.

"Most distressing," the pirate replied calmly. "Instead, I offer you this nice, warm dressing robe." Reaching to his right with his velvet-covered prosthetic, Hook removed a heavy garment of quilted maroon silk from a wooden peg. Standing creakily, she slipped it on and tied its sash.

"And as we have a while to wait, perhaps, before the refreshments I've ordered arrive—for Smee is new to the crew, and not yet as efficient as one could wish in—perhaps you'll allow me to explain to you a bit of what I'm about?

"Your father is a banker, is he not?"

⌇⌇

Champagne was perhaps not the most sovereign remedy for nausea provoked by near drowning. Sipping from her never-empty glass, however, Wendy allowed its charms. Like angel hair or some ethereal form of excelsior, it cradled her muzzy thoughts, protecting them from damaging each other without crowding them out of her head.

"For a modest sum I can guarantee you'll be recognized in our initial round of construction—and for ages to come. A street name, the name of a building—or for a higher contribution, we'll give you a more substantial form of commemoration, such as a statue," Hook said. "Later, when we get around to hiring strolling entertainers and booking acts into the theater—"

"Theater?"

"Certainly! Some days it will rain—this is England, after all—and our holiday-goers must be amused or they'll leave. We should have a cinema as well—though not, I think, a library. Too bookish. Perhaps some sort of indoor games center..." Dipping a quill pulled out of his hatband into a dish of chocolate sauce, the pirate marked a square on the map pinned to the cabin wall. "...about *there*." He nodded. "Yes.

"But as I was saying, when all that's under weigh, we'll naturally expect you, as one of the principals, to exercise a bit of discretion as to who fills your part. Actually collaborating on the show itself would require further financial involvement, but I'm sure you'll want to take the opportunity. Won't you?"

There was a long pause; the first, really, since Hook's disquisition had begun. Unless Smee's silent interruptions when bearing in trays of food counted.

Evidently it was time in the program for Wendy to assent to helping Hook with his scheme. Instead, she asked, "What's in it for the mermaids?"

"More bathers," Hook answered promptly. "They are particularly partial to adolescent boys. I've promised them plenty."

"But don't they know..." Wendy was at a loss to describe the ruination she felt sure Hook's unnecessary plans would result in. They'd affect not only the seaside, but all the country for miles beyond—the ancient markets would fail for lack of custom. Farmers and goose girls and their ilk would disappear; in their stead thousands of strangers would descend on Skegness's environs, bringing with them their loud motors; their stinking tons of refuse; their demands for fresh water, food, petrol, and who knew what else. All this was to transpire under her aegis? Watched over by her distorted likenesses?

This was nothing like true immortality.

Hook mistook her speechlessness for disbelief. "Mermaids are notoriously bubbleheaded," he said. "Fairies with tails rather than wings."

At this Wendy kept her council, though inwardly she shook her head. Creatures born to magic could be called venal perhaps, but never stupid. Look how Tink disappeared when the action was about to start. And where was she now? And Lily—what had happened to them?

The door opened a crack, then a little wider—wide enough for Smee to squeeze in. Without a word he began gathering their used crockery and the remnants of their feast.

Hook protested the removal of the shell-shaped serving dish of pastries. "Leave that. No—no—I've not finished—and bring us some port. And suitable glasses. No, the champagne stays! Do you understand me? Don't mumble!"

No longer high and piping but hoarse and low, the servant's assent came clear enough to gladden Wendy's quailing heart. It was Lily's voice.

No surprise, then, when on "Smee's" return, the cabin's door remained open behind him. Though the faint green tinting the shadow it threw was another matter.

Tink had returned. A happy ending must be in sight.

"Put the glasses there. You may pour," Hook instructed. With seeming clumsiness, the shapeshifter spilled a gout of deeply crimson wine, creating an enormous stain on the table's white cloth. "Fool! I warrant you'd foul up so simple a task as walking the plank. Shall we discover if tis so?"

"Smee" cowered back toward the doorway, shaking his dirty-looking hair, lips and beardless jaw moving wordlessly in apparent terror.

"Well? Take care of this mess you've made first! Then we shall see!"

The shapeshifter left and returned again—too soon?—carrying a basin of steaming, soapy water. They promptly tripped over absolutely nothing and dropped it. More swearing from Hook. Exeunt Lily. With their next entrance they introduced a wooden pail from which a pair of long rods protruded: a mop handle and a familiar length of gunmetal. Would her captor notice it? Hook's eyes narrowed. "Smee" slipped in the water and fell, spattering suds on the pirate's satin brocade breeches. While rising and fending off Hook's fists, they placed the pail near enough for Wendy to retrieve her lovely SK from it. She raised and aimed it.

Hook froze in the midst of a roundhouse swing. His olive complexion paled to a yellowish ecru. "No! Please!"

Was it possible Peter had neglected to inform the pirate captain of the life cycles natural to Neverland's inhabitants? It would be very like him to forget.

"'To die will be an awfully big adventure,'" sneered a glint of emeralds from the corner by the door. Tink grew to full size and spat a gob of foaming saliva at the pirate's polished boots. It landed accurately.

"You wrong me!" Hook cried. "I'm as brave as any—"

Lily—still being Smee—thrust one grimy hand over Hook's mouth. "Enough yammerin. Crew's sleepin sound and won't be comin to investigate anyways." They puffed up into a semblance of the pirate captain himself—wickedly exaggerating the leanness of his vulpine face, the dramatic slant of his brows. "Break out the rum! Triple rations for every man jack of you!'" The roaring growl of the shapeshifter's delivery served as excuse for their un-Hooklike sound.

"All hands accounted for?" Wendy asked. "We can just leave?" No wonder Tink was back.

"What about them plans? After I brung you all the way here to ruin em—don't you wanna?"

Wendy looked over at Tink. No sign of jealousy. "Was that why? I have a hard time imagining you couldn't have handled this on your own, Lily."

"Whoa there! Stop that squirmin about, you!" Lily clamped their arm around the throat of the original Hook. He continued to struggle. Freeing one befrilled hand, he tugged at its copy.

"Let him talk. No harm in that."

"So you say." But Lily dropped their hand from the pirate's mouth and wiped it on the satin pantaloons he wore—not on their own.

"Papers," Hook gasped. He bent forward as far as Lily's throttling arm let him, gulping for breath. "Before you leave—sign what I've drawn up—I'll not bother you—further. No pursuit—"

"What you've drawn up?" Wendy frowned. "Your notes?"

"Not those—agreements. Dressing gown—lower left pocket—"

Shifting her submachine so it nestled in her crooked right arm, Wendy felt for and found a folded square of stiff foolscap sheets. She opened it one-handed, read the first page, and snorted in derision. "When did you expect to trick me into going along with this?"

"Show me!" Tink demanded, moving to hover at her shoulder. Of course the fairy couldn't read. Wendy pretended not to know that. "Poor penmanship, and it's a very legalistic document. Shall I summarize? Basically this assigns all rights to reproducing my likeness—Ha!—or 'any reminiscent renderings or associated memorabilia'—that's vague enough!—to 'Smee & Assoc.' You, I take it?" She scowled at Hook, who left off his pitiful wheezing.

"For 'a consideration'—the amount's left blank! And I've framed similar contracts for you pair as well. You could each of you name a tidy sum if you chose. And you'd be immortal to boot!"

"Hunh. So you say—a tidy sum of what?" asked Lily. "Tell us why we shouldn't simply slit yer gizzard here and now and have done with you?"

"Two words," simpered the captain with a flirt of his pre-ternaturally long eyelashes. "Peter. And Pan."

The Jolly Roger rocked. The empty bucket slid a small distance on the cabin's floor. The scraping sound it made filled a minute's silence.

"You must understand." Hook stepped away from Lily. Who let him. "I've inquired most minutely into the cause of your disagreement with your former beau, Miss Darling."

"You are going to die."

"The point being, I gather, at whose hands." Strutting over to the table he lifted the black-labeled bottle and poured himself a generous amount of the remaining wine. "Having bargained away the right to kill me yourself in exchange for Pan's acquiescence to the presence at your side of your lovely companions—and they having made like treaties—I believe you have no option left at this point except to join forces with me. Or sign."

"Here." Wendy held the SK out to the shapeshifter.

"What?" But they took the gun.

"Just for a moment." Wendy gripped the unsigned contracts with both hands and tore them in half. Tore the halves again. Again. Opened her fingers and let the pieces flutter down to add to the sad mess of suds and red stains.

"The pleasure of killing you will be Peter's, ultimately, yes. But some lesser sweets we are entitled to claim for ourselves."

"Tink." Wendy undid the dressing gown and removed the sash. "Take this and tie him." Lily gave the SK back to her and helped as well.

Wendy drove fast. She tore through the new night like the screams of the man tied up in the Invicta's rear driver-side seat. Once they passed Skegness, Lily had gotten rid of Hook's gag. Who was there to hear him? At first Tink and Lily added their delighted cries to his wordless yowling.

But now they neared Boston. Too much noise would attract unwanted attention. Nor was Boston to be the only population center on their way to the Peaks. Wendy's companions would have to subdue their prisoner anew. She told them to do what was needed.

A meaty slap resounded behind her, followed by loud snivels. "Will you hush!" Tink scolded. "We've hardly done anything to you yet!" The pirate subsided into low whimpers. "Only a few cuts—no worse than you'd expect from shaving!"

Lily chuckled hoarsely, turning in the passenger seat to comment. "It's his blood. He don't like to see how the stuff's so yellow." The shapeshifter had abandoned their sly parody of Hook's looks for the appearance of his nemesis, Peter. A little taller, a little heavier, a little swarthier about the cheeks— though he wasn't exactly a grown-up, any more than the original. Who would probably laugh heartily when he caught sight of Lily's impersonation.

For that to happen, though, they had to reach him by take-off. No being pulled aside by police officers for investigations of screaming passengers.

And Hook's wails had once again resumed, rising in volume. Reluctantly, Wendy slowed the Invicta to an idling standstill on the A52's bleak emptiness. Setting the brake, she swiveled in her seat to assess the situation by fairy light.

Snot smeared the pirate's bare upper lip, which quivered unbecomingly. But at least he wept more quietly now they'd stopped.

"Mayhap he's grievin for his moustaches," Lily opined. They had been fine, decorative specimens of hirsute masculinity, to be sure.

"Here—give him a hankie," the shapeshifter added, offering their own.

The pirate's hands were bound by the dressing gown's sash. Tink took the used-looking wad of blue cambric with no sign of disgust and swiped it across Hook's face several times, sopping up most of the tears and mucous.

Wendy smiled—encouragingly, she hoped. Perhaps gagging him again would be unnecessary. "That's better, isn't it? Anything else before we get going again to find Peter?"

"Before we—" Hook's red lips hung apart wordlessly. A whine issued between them, building dangerously toward a shriek.

"What's got you so scared? This can't be the first time you've died." Lily's matter-of-fact tone of voice halted the pirate's screeching mid-crescendo.

"You don't like seeing your blood spilled?" Tink asked scornfully. "Ask for a blindfold—Peter won't mind."

"Maybe it *is* his first time." Wendy bit her lip, recalling her fall from the empty sky to the hard surface of the ocean. Her aerial powers had vanished with the fairy dust blown off in the wind of her passage between Neverland and Britain. She well remembered the fear, the bone-breaking pain, the frigid depths opening below, the shrinking circle of her conscious self—all the self she'd ever known. "It's always the hardest."

"I suppose." Lily sounded doubtful. They died whenever they changed.

"Look here, Hook." Wendy took her hands off the steering wheel to grasp his shoulders. "You lost. But you know we're nothing but stories, right? 'Our little life is rounded with a sleep—' and then we wake up to be told again.

"When Peter kills you, you'll die, strictly speaking. You won't stay dead, though. 'As long as children are innocent and heartless,' they'll play at being you. You'll die. But you'll never be dead for long. Trust me.

"Now let's finish up this adventure right. You two take care of him if he gives so much as a peep!" Wendy turned to face forward again, checked the fit of her leather racing gauntlets, and gripped the wheel one-handed. Ignoring Hook's quickly smothered protests, she slipped the Invicta back in gear and headed straight on till morning.

Salt on the Dance Floor

Right away, that first night, I wanted her as much as I wanted him. Of course she was there in the club and he wasn't—only his voice, and on the screen he snapped and dazzled, sparkled and spun. Her moves, so different, wafted, billowed—not completely on the beat. Yet right.

I slipped through the sweating bodies and flashing lights to where she worked it in a white skirt, ruffles falling around her knees. Arms waving and long hair rippling like the scarves she wore around her neck and waist. Hips a little heavy; large, tear-shaped breasts... I fell in, my own moves slowing to match hers. Blue fire flashed along the outlines of her pale arms, then green. Wasn't from the lights. I must have known that then, but she had finally looked at me, and I was trancing on her face, on her eyes, the only dark things about her, and they swallowed me. Whole.

So white. I wasn't sure I was into white girls. If you had asked me in high school, I would have said I wasn't into girls of any kind. But I was at college now, and finding things out.

The music didn't stop, but we did. Washed up in the line to the bathroom, casting harsh shadows in the fluorescents overhead. Walls between us and the main speakers subdued the beat a bit. I asked her name, but she didn't act like she'd heard me. "I'm Draya," I half-shouted, leaning against the hallway's dirty sheet-metal, arcing towards her, aching—for what? For the shell's curve of her ear?

She smiled. Her mouth drew in when she did that instead of spreading out like anyone else's. Were her puckered lips as soft as they—

"Well? You going in or you gonna stand here an piss yer pants?"

I looked around and saw the bathroom's door was open, with no one left in line ahead. "Sorry." I hunched my shoulders apologetically and moved forward.

"Yeah, you are." The smartass's voice followed us in. The bathroom was pink, with black and silver checks. My dancer headed for the sinks and turned the faucets on full, passing her hands back and forth through the water. She cupped them together so they filled and raised them to rinse her face. No make-up?

A stall opened and I went in. When I came out she was leaving. I followed her. Around the edge of the dance floor. Away from it. To the entrance. Through it.

A heavy mist was falling. Or a light rain. Typical Northwest weather. She had no coat. Not that either of us needed one—it was warm, late April. End of the semester. She stopped walking at the first corner, her face turned up to the damp, dark sky. Red traffic lights and neon blinked. Her neck and sleeveless arms were traced in blue and green again.

I reached out and lifted a strand of wet hair curled against her collarbone. I couldn't help it. Even soaked, her hair was so pale, almost translucent. Sheer as glass. "Come to my place." I wanted not to beg. "It's close." Like that was all that mattered. Her eyes widened. They seemed to deepen, too. I took her hand and she let me lead her home.

We made love. Her clothes seemed to melt away. She was incredibly responsive, which was pretty much all I needed to make me come. I cried aloud, but she stayed oddly silent.

Afterwards we lay on our sides on my fold-out futon, facing each other. "What's your name?" A smile. "You're—you

264

can't talk?" I didn't know the civil way to ask. "A mute?" Her head tilted back, sank forward. She was nodding. Like a flower.

"Oh. That's—that's not a problem. Really."

She couldn't write either—at first I wasn't even sure she could read. It didn't matter. I showed her my gallery, the shots and stills of him, TJ, that I'd collected from fan sites and pulled off of my aunt's footage of the concert he gave when he was ten.

She never told me her name. I made one up that very first morning, and she answered to it.

"Victoria." She looked at me. "Here. This is yours." I gave her my old laptop, a 2007 Dell Inspiron. Showed her where the power was and how to horn in on the downstairs coffee shop's wifi, and she went surfing.

Not much social media. I left her alone with the net while I went to my classes and work, checked the cookies when I came home, after a shower. They were always links to images and articles. She was all over Wikipedia and sites like that.

I came back from the library one day and found her deep in an article about TJ's comeback concert series. I read over one soft white shoulder. Twenty-four dates in August had been added. This was June.

"We can't go." The hall where the series would be held was in Japan, Tokyo, too many time zones away. She turned the anemone of her face up to me. Her mouth puckered, opened as if to say "Oh," shut tight again. I had learned to interpret this as a sign of distress. Her fingertips petted the air lying against the laptop's screen, tracing the latest surgical transformation of his face.

"I know. But I'm only working part-time, for minimum wage; I don't have—I can't—"

Hands lowering to the keyboard, she clicked on another tab, and the sweet opening chords of "Ocean Song" rose from the laptop's speakers. Framed by a montage of larger-than-life one-celled animals, he sang and wept and supplicated us to save the sea:

"So much larger than the land;
"So much deeper than we can understand;
"So much wiser, so much more;
"So much richer; without her we're so poor.
"Without her we're nothing; let her live, let her live.
"Without her we are dying; let us live, let us live."

Victoria's tears trembled in the screen's glow. That was the only time I'd ever seen her cry. "All right. All right." I'd get the money for the flight and the tickets and somewhere to stay, borrow it or something.

I knew better than to think Victoria might be able to chip in. She had no money. None. And forget about her finding a job. I understood. Victoria was not like other girls.

Before the first time she disappeared I had figured that much out. Before the first full moon.

~~~

We were so tired of standing up. Terrible this weight. Our amphipods had no way to prepare us. Breathing, yes. For that we were prepared. But walking stabbed us like urchin spines.

We sat on a bench by the water as it rose up, blue and wanting us. We stumbled to the end of the pier and stepped off.

We were in before unshaping. We who worked as ears heard shouting when we sank: humans who feared that we would drown.

We kicked away from the barnacle-covered pilings into our belovely current, loosening ourself from human form to the swirl of us as we are when natural. No feet, no arms, our tentacles drifting and bellyheads pulsing together, in rhythm, together, as the special amphipods of our mother had taught us.

We swam out to the open. As wide as the ocean. As free. Out to where she awaited us. She had emerged from her immemorial trench to make us, and still she stayed up here, up high for her. Deep for us. We went down to find her. All of us in accord, beating our way through the water like hearts traveling through cold blood.

As low.

Oh, languor. Oh, sweet chill. The snow of algae and other foods falling, touching our skins, our skins pressed so tight against the water.

Humans could say what her name was. We could say we touched her, tasted her, smelled her, heard her.

What did she look like? Our amphipods have eyes, but saw only short brightnesses, the flash of her green light, her blue light, her green, her blue. She was our home. Where and who and what we came from. How did your mother look to you when you were a child? Rich as molasses the scent we bathed in; delicate as dreams her tendrils and tentacles, curling about our edges. And she asked us…and she told us…and we answered…

With words the conversation would look like this:

"Have you found the one up there killing us? The one sending down more plastic. More oil. The sicknesses spread fast—our reefs are rotting, our waters losing their oxygen. Have you found the one?" As if, like the oceans, the airs were all responsible to a single entity.

"No." We gave her this reply, in our way. "Not such a one as that. Our enemies are many, too many, and impossible to touch." Those in charge, we had learned, were powerful abstractions: governments, corporations. "However, we have discovered a friend who can help us."

〰〰

She came back. My post about Victoria's disappearance got lots of comments, most of them linked to reports of a suicide with no body found, but I had never believed she would have killed herself. Didn't even go to the cops. Not a week afterwards, there she was on the weedy lawn.

"Hey, where you been?" I had to ask the question, though I knew she'd never answer it out loud.

We went upstairs. I took the cover off the glamp. Its living light glowed below the front room's ceiling, fell yellow and orange over my futon. Which Victoria ignored, heading instead for the kitchen with its big table and both our computers. Booted hers up and logged on, sinking into the seat I shoved behind her.

Had she even missed me? Yes. In a moment her dark glance sought mine. Her so-white fingers clutched my shirt-sleeve, tugging me closer to the screen where TJ sang "Ocean Song" once again.

"I got them. The tickets? I got two. One each." For me, and for the hope of her return. "Want to see?" I started my computer and printed them out.

The designer had done a good job, used thin curving lines layered under thinner ones, like shot silk. She brushed the air above the printouts with the same reverence she'd shown TJ's face. I would have left them on the table, but she brought me my mat knife, insisted I cut them down and put them in my wallet for safekeeping, following me into the front room where my pack hung.

I covered the glamp so it would sleep. I kissed her plump white hands. Her arms were covered in the finest hairs. I breathed against them, flattening them when I turned one way, raising them the other. Left. Right. Up. Down. Down. Further down.

I've heard that lesbian couples eventually tire of sex with each other, fucking less and less frequently. Females have fewer sex hormones than males is how self-appointed experts explain this so-called "bed death." Well it wasn't happening here. Maybe because one of us wasn't really a woman.

Victoria slipped gracefully to the futon's sheets. Her clothes vanished. I went from kneeling to all fours to lying on her full length, moving like a manta ray, rippling, fluttering, then, hell, grinding, humping, thrashing through the gasping deeps of orgasm. And after, the pair of us becalmed again, her touch on my skin still tingled, still thrilled me as much as ever.

After. Ever. Ever after.

Too happy to sleep, I got up. We'd left the kitchen lights on. My computer's stand hummed, the fan a quiet promise of actions seamlessly edited together. Letters on the keyboard kicked back the screensaver's flickering colors in some sort of sequence—a storyline? I sat. I brought my files up, text and stills and clips, opened them, logged on to Sketchit. Wished I'd had a helmet as I reached behind the chair for my earpads. Felt the smile on my face as I sank into my art.

This was what I could do. This was what I could do that would make a difference.

I finished four films before she left the second time. I waited a whole month. She didn't come back.

It was August. I still had our tickets.

～～～

At night. Another pier—this one without any watchers. We went in. Unshaping fast as foam and finding her for whom humans have a name. Praya dubia. She whom we do not need to call.

Her long curtains drew around us. She coiled us tighter, and at her core we posed the problem with our plan. In words:

"Our friend who could help doesn't stay anywhere more than a little while. The land we've been living on is far from the place where we hoped to meet him, on the ocean's other side. Our host has a way there, in the air. A hard way. We have learned it's a way we cannot go." Simpler than saying scanners, passports, proof of identity; simpler, and in effect the same. A hard way, Draya's. A dry way. Impassable. Impossible.

We thought for a long moment our mother had no answer. No solution. Then the cool of movement, the swirl of swimming forward.

Carrying us, she opened and closed, opened and closed, swallowing and spitting out the water and letting it push her through itself, taking us safe across the salty-tasting sea.

〰️

I went without her. I told myself she would have wanted that. I sold her plane ticket and got half what I had paid, so the trip was cheaper by a couple hundred.

I arrived at Narita International eight hours before the hall even opened. The train from the airport took hardly any time to cover thirty miles, and then I was in Tokyo for real and following my cheap shades' glitchy tracking to Kitanomaru Park. They kept trying to get me on the subway, but if I went below street level I lost their link to the cloud. So I walked.

In Seattle it was a few minutes after nine at night, but here the lunch crowds had barely begun to recede. My jean jacket held the heat too close to my body. If I took it off, though, I might lose it—and the mother-of-pearl brooch pinned to it that Victoria had made me buy. Instead I got rid of my shirt. My bra was bright red. It could be mistaken for a halter top. I hoped. Buttoning the jacket partway helped, and I stuck my fingertips in my pants pockets and let my elbows jut out to keep people away.

I reached the park unmolested. Nothing spectacular there: bushes, trees. Foreign fans like me wasting time till we could get into Budokan and sit in our seats and wait some more. Couple of impersonators I watched for a minute, but they'd never be as good as him.

What made me wander off the path and under the trees' warm, limp leaves? Did I only want to escape the dull pounding of sunlight on my head?

Or did I know I'd find her climbing out of the canal?

Victoria. Fully dressed in white skirt and tank top, white scarves. Just as when I'd first met her—or, wait—no shoes.

A ghost? If I touched her would she pop like a bubble? I put out one hand—I was suddenly close enough somehow—and touched her soft skin.

She was dry.

Fresh from the water. Not a drop on her. Clothes lifting gently in the breeze.

But no breeze blew.

I opened my mouth. Only air came out. I gripped her beautiful bare arm tight, too tight. It had to hurt, but I couldn't let it loose, I couldn't let her go. No. She had not come back to me but I had found her, and I would hold on to her always, have her, hold her, wherever she was, whoever. Whatever.

Whatever else she was, Victoria was mine.

She smiled, her lips opening and drawing in. A smile of expectancy. She held out her hand, pale palm up.

I laughed. Her ticket. Of course I had brought it. To sell, I had told myself. I fished it out and gave it to her. She wrapped a couple of her scarves around it and let them toss behind her in the wind.

There was no wind.

We walked back to the path. Her hand settled over mine on her arm, and gradually I relaxed. My grim clutch became a firm clasp, then a caress. Before I knew we were going anywhere we reached the Budokan. She led me around to an unguarded back door. It must have been locked, but the non-existent wind wound Victoria's scarves around the handle and she pulled. The locked door opened and we went inside.

I found our seats. Main floor, unobstructed, as guaranteed. Hidden fans stirred the air. This breeze I felt. Cool at last, I wished I hadn't thrown my shirt away. Wished I'd packed a change of clothes, luggage, something besides my camera, shades, and toothbrush. Wished I had rented a hotel room where Victoria and I could make love after the concert, before our plane.

My plane.

～～～

Better for us than the emptiness of the land's sky, this dark shell in the bottom of which we now rested beside our host. From the seat cushions we looked up into a space large enough our mother might have swum there. If this had been water, not air.

Where was our friend? We knew he would come here to sing, to dance. Thousands would see him. How, though, we wondered, would he see us?

Our host took one who was being a hand to soothe and caress. Above the well-known smell of her sweat we detected something more…the smallest whisper of him! His voice breathed out his scent with his words; he spoke as streaming as the thinnest of currents. As light…

Ribbons of his essence spilled down from high above our head. In water we would rise to find him, separate to navigate whatever secrets barred our way. But we were here. We stood. Not that much nearer. Walked forward hoping this was the way.

Draya, our host, came with us. We turned to her, pleading. Surely she would know what to do now.

～～～

I had an idea what Victoria was up to. Worth a try. I walked coolly, confidently, to where a tall man in a grey suit emerged out of what was obviously a door backstage. "You wanna let us in?"

"Decided to start with filming pre-show after all?" He squinted. "You look way better than the picture. I guess you ain't doin your own publicity shots." We were expected? Not exactly, but somebody like one of us—like me.

The grey suit leaned back against the door and it chunked open just a crack. "Where's your camera?"

Well, I had that. I unfastened my jacket and pulled my Samsung from the inside pocket, flashing more of my bare torso than was really necessary.

But he leered at Victoria, not me. Whitney Houston lookalikes weren't his cup of vodka, evidently—despite my bare midriff and sexy lingerie. "What you gonna be doin while your girlfriend gets her footage?" he asked her.

"She can't talk."

"Hunh. Bet we can find a way to communicate without it. Am I right, sweetie?" The door opened wider. Not wide enough for us to pass through without touching him. "My name's Reggie. Like the comic books."

She turned to me. Her eyes, that's what I miss most. The night we met they took me right inside themselves. A whole new world. That afternoon they were just as wide, and again I felt myself begin to fall.

But then she turned away from me, toward the opening door. Her hair and scarves and hips slid against Reggie's face and hands as she passed him. He nodded to me to join her. I shook my head. "You first," I said, and caught the door as he let it swing to shut me out.

The hallway was floored with old beige linoleum. We went down a flight of stairs, walked past brown doors in white walls. Victoria somehow knew where we were headed; she stayed in front till she stopped at a door like all the rest, and we caught up.

"Been here before, hunh?" Reggie knocked and an even taller man in a red and white jersey let us in.

A long, low-ceilinged room, lined with mirrors—big, but only a fraction of the size of the actual concert hall upstairs. A tiny stage at the far end, and him on it.

He wasn't doing anything but giggling with a bearded man holding a keyboard on his lap, but he had everybody's attention. He shone. His thin body was the wick and desire the flame. I wanted him as much as I wanted her, and there they were, in the same room. I wanted both of them, each more than the other.

Reggie introduced us. Me, anyway. My name was supposed to be Pauline Wilson. Of course I'd heard of her work.

I shook TJ's hand. I touched his glove. I pulled Victoria forward and told him the name I'd made up for her. Her hand now felt damp, the way it should have been coming out of the canal—all her softness gleamed, wet and glinting oh so faintly blue and green. My dear, sweet monster.

No one else seemed to notice. Maybe they thought the moisture was some sort of cosmetic? Reggie got her away from me for a minute by dragging her over to a refreshment table.

"Your girlfriend's very beautiful, Pauline," TJ said, and suddenly I felt bad, lying to him like everyone else in his life.

"Actually, my name is Draya. Draya Hudson. I'm a film-maker, too—not the one you invited, but—"

"Draya? Aren't you—You posted a few shorts to my site, didn't you?" He had seen them—my silly tributes, remixes of music videos and nature docs and his long-ago appearances on TV game shows. How many stars bothered visiting their fan sites? He smiled over the tops of his shades. "Girl, you got somethin good you doin."

Victoria headed back toward us holding a paper plate piled with something dark green. Reggie trailed after her. TJ put an arm around me and leaned to whisper in my ear. "Let's fool him, okay? Make believe you're who he thinks you are—Victoria—that's still her name?" I nodded, my ear burning from his breath. "Victoria doesn't talk, right? She won't tell on us—" He stopped talking as his bodyguard approached.

I knew TJ loved practical jokes. What harm would it do to humor him?

﹏

Him. Our friend, here where he could see and touch us, where we could see and touch him. Our host had brought us to the place just right. When the music made itself we wanted so much to loosen—as clear, as close—but managed to stay human. Barely. Because that way we could dance.

Oh, blending. Warm as sun and straight and sudden, strong and fast and laughs and breaths to take. Oh, yes and yes and yes. The power of his quick hands. The speed of his hips revolving, rocking free of heavy gravity.

Then he went away from us. Not far. In back of black velvet, in a hidden pool of shadows, with our host beside us, we could wait. While he, in front, poured upon with gold, with rich and changing sounds, showed everyone, if they would only see, his love.

﹏

Nobody else thought Victoria was scary. After all, all she did was dance. It was me they worried about, ironically. Stupidly.

Had she always eaten without chewing? Without swallowing? Why was I only now noticing? Why wasn't anybody else?

Me, I was surprised I paid attention to anything except how fucking sexy she was. And TJ. But I was mostly able to keep my focus on the viewfinder. Slight problem: some of the people present didn't want me filming them. Reggie and the other bodyguard on duty—Frank—moved out of frame whenever they noticed me shooting. Frowned if it looked like I might be about to aim the camera in their direction. And another suit—blue—who appeared briefly before the show, he didn't like me one little bit, either. They called him Dr. Cunningham. At the time things were too busy for introductions.

I watched the show from the wings with Victoria and Reggie. Got some nice sequences.

Good thing.

They'd taken over a low-rise apartment building in Meguro. Victoria and I got a room together on the top floor. Connection was fine, so I uploaded my footage to the cloud. Seeing as it'd had all eight bars even on ground level, I set the Samsung's link for continuous. Every inch I shot from then on uploaded automatically. Immediately.

Another good thing.

Victoria's skin was dry again. I didn't know what that meant. Something different for her than for other girls. I kissed her fingertips a long time, but she got up from the bed before I did anything more, and I let her. She headed out the door and I followed. I thought I'd better go along with her and see what was going on in the rest of the building, see what I could record. I thought we'd come back up and make love after that the rest of the night.

Our apartment was on the street side. Not till we got off the elevator did we hear the noise of the party. The lobby's lights blazed across empty stonework floors and shone through long, low windows into the building's courtyard. I saw a blue swimming pool with dark shapes gliding in it, and a crowded teakwood deck. So crowded, in fact, that finding TJ took me a while.

I should have trusted Victoria to home in on him. A conference between Reggie, Frank, Dr. Cunningham, and a man I'd never seen before distracted me, though—the more they obviously didn't want me to take their pictures, the more I was determined to immortalize them for TJ's fans. When I finally lowered the Samsung, I saw my stars right away. They knelt together next to the deck's fence. A fat-bristled pine sheltered them.

From a few feet away I could tell they were gazing raptly at something small. I had to kneel down with them myself to see it, though: a turtle maybe two inches wide. A striped head with bead-bright eyes poked hesitantly from its shell.

"Shhh! It's a baby." TJ's whisper was weirdly easy to pick out. "We're just getting it to not worry enough so—"

"Time for your milk, TJ. Long day tomorrow." Dr. Cunningham had joined us under the pine. "What's that?"

"Someone else who needs to sleep."

"'Someone?' Nobody there. Now come on." He couldn't see the turtle; too tall. But the turtle saw him, or probably heard him, and his head vanished back inside his shell.

"Wish I could do like that." Like a child, TJ let himself be hustled off to bed.

The party showed no sign of quitting after he left, but I quickly persuaded Victoria we should follow suit.

I switched off the overheads, and our apartment was still so white. Modern floating ceilings, deep pile carpets, muted table lamps—all were white or not far from it. On a bed so big they probably hadn't come up with a name for the size, Victoria lay like a line drawing by Picasso, inky definition where her shoulder pressed into the pillow, where her lips met in a dark, essential crease, where her eyes drowned me....

I woke up.

I woke alone.

〰

We would not often dream. Why need to? Up in the air, sometimes we would, yes, to remember our mother. Not now, not since we had found him. We only wanted a way to describe to him how he could help us. We would find it soon enough; for now it made us happy that our friend slept so nearby we could sip his breath.

But should it be so shallow? Should it be so slow?

We rose. We put on the shapes of clothes. We went to the rooms where we had marked his presence. Even worse than earlier—hardly moving, his heart, the sponges of his lungs. Wearing down the lock, we went in, only we had nothing we could do. Where should we go? Who would know how to make him breathe as much again? Humans had to have air, fresh air, all the time.

We thought the one with the name of Reggie might make this better. We smelled him behind the next door. We pounded on it and pulled him out when he opened it and shoved him ahead of us, and then he stopped asking us what we wanted.

"Oh god! Oh no!" and other words he shouted. He called a number on his phone and pushed on our friend's body, on a place outside his heart. Which no longer beat. No longer beat.

Others arrived. They didn't matter. He was dead. Last night our friend was alive. This morning he was not.

This morning our mother had no one to defend her. We had failed. We had failed. How would we make amends?

Who caused this? No way to be sure. Traces of too many humans filled the dying room.

They took what was left of our friend away, somewhere he could fall apart in peace. We drifted down to the waterside. We had not felt this way before. Too hot, and not with his kind heat. Shame and hurting boiled in us, churning us, eating us apart. So we slipped in the pool. Cooler, easier. We loosened but we did not lose our form.

Who caused his death? Who would we kill?

We would kill who we could.

A short while. Then the first one came. Dr. Cunningham. We reached out one who was an arm. Touched him. Tasted. Loosening a little further, we let him feel our sting. Till he could feel no more. Set him to float with his face to the dawn. Listened to his slowing heart and waited for another.

<hr />

The pool was full of corpses and plastic bags. That's what I thought. That was what it looked like from TJ's balcony.

He wasn't there. I didn't know it then, but he wasn't anywhere. He was dead, and his body on its way to the morgue.

There were lots of other bodies, though—not in the apartment itself, but visible from it, from where I stood. I couldn't tell whose. Not mine. Not—wait, no, please not—Victoria's?

I ran down the fire stairs. I knew I ought to call the police, an ambulance, somebody, but first I had to see.

Five dead men. Two dead women. Neither her.

Seven corpses—plenty, though not enough to literally fill the pool. The plastic bags weren't actually plastic, either. Nor were they bags. Jellyfish. Transparent, with traces of blue and green bioluminescence showing in the shrinking shadows thrown by the courtyard's pines.

Seven corpses. Yes, I'd have to call, and be questioned, and put my budding career as filmmaker in jeopardy. I'd have to explain TJ's joke—his last joke, as I later learned. What was I doing there? Why had I missed my plane? Where was my mysterious girlfriend?

The jellyfish seemed fine. For jellyfish. The pool was probably that new saline kind. Lower maintenance. No chlorine. I put on my shades, but stooped down to confirm my theory before hitting their panic button. Dipped one finger in, pulled it out, touched my tongue. Tasted tears.

Beyond the Lighthouse

Life was not a dream. At times its shallows had abraded her, rubbed rocks against her, polishing what wouldn't wear away. Now life's currents moved deep and strong beneath a smooth, deceptive surface. You might mistake that surface for a dream.

The first white men to come here had refused to see the river they were looking at. So broad, seeming so still. And yet, it flowed. Easy to hear that happening, if you knew how to listen: lapping wetness slapping against concrete, drops sliding down, slipping away.

Leelah let the river leave her, let it move westward, into the last of the night's darkness. This pier was for tourists, for earlier in the year. Nothing to see now, in autumn. She turned back toward the town lights sparkling anxiously along the shore. Walked deliberately, as if on a tightrope, the one hundred yards to the Sunset Empire Transportation stop. Her palms pricked, her soles ached, every step another increment of nearness. She would catch this bus, and he was sure to get on at the next stop.

How she hated hoping again.

She paid her fare and took her seat, a bench near the front to which her grey hair entitled her. Schooled herself to expect nothing, no one, but felt relief when the bus driver slowed, pulled to the curb, and opened the doors. He boarded, mounting the stairs upright as a warrior. Which she had learned he was.

He sat opposite her and smiled. Only about as tall as her now: his height was all in his legs. He kept his short brown hair combed back above a face conventionally handsome: jutting chin, cheekbones wide and high. His appearance was why she'd paid him no attention at first. He was so handsome, and he seemed to be decades younger than her.

That sort of man never noticed her anymore. This one, though…he was kind. She saw him offering his seat to other riders. They'd started talking. He had a fine mind, one with room enough inside to move around, levels to climb, spirals to turn. When he brought up Karel Capek's plays, she fell in love.

The way she acted, no one would guess. "I have something to show you," she told him, and bent to open her rolling backpack.

"Should I come closer, then?"

Oh, yes. "Sure."

Leelah handed him a bakery box. He raised the lid and his face grew still. Inside lay the silk scarf Rutha's wife had crocheted: fine lace, the green of new leaves, with five hundred gold beads in tassels along the edges. "That's so beautiful."

"Isn't it?"

He touched her arm several times. Just to emphasize what he was saying, she explained to herself at the transfer point where they parted till next Thursday. The sky was overcast, smeared with clouds the color of unfulfillment.

He waved goodbye and got on the West Waldorf circulator, headed for the community college—he taught there. Leelah walked to the theater, four short blocks. On Thursdays and one other weekday she went in for office hours: meeting with potential donors and advertisers, interviewing volunteers, making herself available. Most rehearsals happened evenings and weekends, which meant extra trips downtown—especially if she had to direct. She'd only ever seen him on morning rides.

His name was Felix. Felix Andersen, with one "ess," two "e"s. Leelah tried to concentrate. The woman in the uneasy chair on her desk's far side would make a great usher. What else? She could paint, saw, sew, hammer, glue, screw, iron, cook, clean—and keep accounts. A good bookkeeper was hard to find. Doubtless Genevyve Hartman expected to fill a more glamorous role with the Little Moon Theater Company—just look how she spelled her name—but Leelah could handle that.

"Auditions for the next production won't be till after Christmas. Meanwhile…" Leelah checked boxes matching Genevyve's actual skill set and signed her up for the difficult-to-staff Thanksgiving weekend matinees. The idea of bookkeeping could be introduced after she experienced that madness, when any other task would sound inviting.

Leelah gave Genevyve a post-interview tour of the Little Moon's facilities; she made every effort to slow down and allow Genevyve time to ooh and ahh over the vintage elevator and reinstalled flashpots. Watching her climb the spidery staircase to the catwalk where the lights hung, Leelah wondered if this was the kind of build Felix felt attracted to: pear-bottomed, slim-bellied, breasts two sugar lumps entirely within the average spectrum of cup sizes. Nothing like her own body had ever been, not even in her youth. And certainly not now.

At the door to the street, blinking in the unexpected brightness, noon sunshine a November bonus, Leelah shook the woman's hand. That was when Genevyve made her unfortunate series of remarks. Most whites did, sooner or later.

"Good thing my skin's so dark—you can cast me as black with practically no make-up. And my hair's curly, too." She laughed nervously, pulling a lock loose from one brunette ponytail and flipping it back and forth. It was indeed very curly. Not kinky. Leelah wished everyone understood the difference.

"Of course you'd never know from my hair how my great-grandmother was an Indian Princess." Leelah heard the capital letters clearly, but hurrying back to her office, she gave only a passing thought to how she would manage to educate this one, too. Later.

Leelah's search engines had nothing new to show her about Felix, though. She'd found all the available photos back in mid-October and downloaded her favorites to a file with the innocuous designation "Pretty." She'd read précis of six papers he'd written on topics ranging from the third chapter of Moby Dick to John Malkovich's most recent comedy.

Leelah knew more than the Internet ever would about Felix Andersen. Because of what she did at home, at night. Alone.

She didn't call it dreaming.

The last half hour before leaving she spent with Rutha, the company's Artistic Director, reviewing possible locations for "The Round," Little Moon's outreach program. She'd come up with some fairly interesting venues: the trolley car would maybe be a bit crowded, but for a monologue or dialogue, ideal, and sure to draw publicity; the lightship, great—and she knew who to ask for a grant for that one. The Column? Leelah glanced at her AD. "You're not thinking of using the top?" 160 stairs up to the platform, which was only eleven feet across.

"No," Rutha said. "Or just for tech—have people fly down the sides, hang a banner, that sort of thing. Our actual performance will be around the base—I know," she added at Leelah's wince. "But in July we should be safe from rain, and the view of the river's spectacular!"

"Which might prove a distraction from the show—" Leelah noticed a penned-in line of dots running between listings for the Column and another location, Cracker Isle. The last land before the river joined the sea. Frequent site of Leelah's nocturnal visitations. She traced the broken line with one gold fingernail. "What's this?"

"Oh." Rutha's olive cheeks grew red. "I had this concept— put someone with a mirror on the island to flash signals, Morse code or something to the Column's top, and we'd beam them down to the ground there. We could get the audience in on it, have them think up messages to send back…" She trailed off uncertainly.

Cracker Isle was uninhabited. And with good reason: the winds and currents made it almost impossible to reach, and its lack of fresh water, the fogs and tides and storms, made living there too much of a chore. Which was mainly why she'd chosen it.

She doubted anyone who actually managed to get to the island by day would notice anything out of the ordinary. Nonetheless. "No," Leelah proclaimed. "Too many liabilities."

After that she was free to go home. And on from there.

⁂

Leelah lived alone. Her apartment occupied the top floor of an old farmhouse built on what had been Waldorf's outskirts a hundred and fifty years ago. Now a dozen newer structures lined the winding street climbing Coxcomb Hill. From her gable window Leelah could see the entrance to the park where the Column rose. In winter, soon, she'd be able to glimpse its rounded sides through bare branches: shell-colored, fluted, carved with scenes of conquest.

She ate a sandwich, drank a mug of ordinary green tea. Wrote the requisite ninety minutes on her novel, which was shaping up to be a semi-memoir. She'd set it in the seventies, in a sleepy college town modeled on her birthplace, Boiling Pot. This chapter, heavily influenced by the sweetness washing through her like waves of honey, had a decidedly erotic tone. It dealt with David, her first love, the one she'd ever after tried to replace, source of her fascination with white men. She dwelt on David's hands, long and warm and comforting, on the soft sweep of his smooth hair against the nape of her neck, the hours they spent talking without saying a single word…the springs of her affection.

Her affection for this new man.

Dark came early. Fast. She turned off her computer. Night time. Time to fly.

That was what she called it: flying.

The basic technique came from a book David gave her back in high school, and which she'd lost track of in the wake of his death. The exact title escaped her. But what the book taught her to do stayed with her, became easier and easier.

With practice, Leelah had learned how to prepare. A light meal an hour or so beforehand. Clothing loose. She formed a nest of pillows on the floor—once, eighteen years ago, she'd rolled off the bed, fallen thirty-six inches to the carpet—unhurt—but she'd had a hard time coming back inside herself afterwards because she was so much lower than her bird remembered. So the nest, where she lay relaxing, letting go of muscle tension, fluffing out her mind.

Felix Andersen. No profit in ignoring him. How was he so beautiful? Not much to do with his looks—it was what he saw, what he said, and how…. She let her thoughts of Felix turn to feathers, airy light, bearing her upwards, out of the carefully cracked window. Which kind was she tonight? Dun-backed and buff-bellied, the size of a small robin—a nightingale. Not a natural inhabitant of the Northwest. But Leelah understood the symbolism.

She stretched her wings. Before, she had found traces of him, scents strong and faint like streams and rivers in the sky. She had moved upwards along those tributaries, against their flow, wanting to discover his sources. Which was when she found out his true age. Not that much younger; he was forty-seven.

And a fighter—the first scene she'd flown to, the earliest she'd found him, he was seventeen and entering a dojo. Perched on a high windowsill she'd watched him kick and punch, sparring wildly against a middle-aged man who brought him to the mat over and over without even seeming to notice his opponent. But Felix had persevered. Finding her way to later moments, she saw him improve, focus in, become calm. Disciplined.

Like acting. Like directing. Like Leelah.

She wheeled higher, lights below spinning white and gold, emerald and ruby, sapphire, amethyst, opal pale as memories, flashing and fading like words said and gone.

He never talked about his training. The college had a gym. Was that where he was now?

Tired of the past, she sought his present. His scent, his sound—her circles widened. And there. Him. Guarded, fierce, clear, deep, dear, joys growing like crystals, coalescing out of the saturated medium of his sorrows, wishes, regrets, desires… She heard him. Felt him. Smelt him. Followed.

Color fell behind her. Leelah left the shore, the glittering piers, the wavering reflections of lights. He had gone north, out over the river. Then west.

Skimming low above the black water, Leelah flew in his wake. Only a little ways, she told herself.

Her bird dipped and swooped like a swallow chasing insects, an acrobat swimming in the moist air. The river was her life, the only life she'd ever known, flowing, filling up the low spots, brimming over, moving ever onwards. After the river, the sea. After life? Death.

Leelah didn't want to die. And when she flew, the figurative became literal. That was how the power she used worked: it made imaginary changes real.

Deciding to come to Waldorf had been hard, though the Little Moon Theater's offer was amazing. Positions like Leelah's were vanishingly rare in the arts: complete control, a decent salary. But being so near the open ocean scared her.

Up ahead stood all the protection she'd been able to devise. Leelah swerved from bank to mile-distant bank, making sure she didn't miss Cracker Isle.

She had planted a beacon on the last land before the wide, cold ocean. Invisible to others, the signal gleamed brightly in the eyes of Leelah's bird, giving her clear notice: this far. No further.

Unlike everyday lighthouses, her Cracker Isle beacon's beam stayed steady, unwinking. Also unlike other lighthouses, it warned of water, not rocks or sandbars or navigational hazards. It warned of dissolution, boundarilessness.

Often Leelah felt the urge to pass the island, to go on and keep going, arriving at last at the sea—like the river, mixing freshwater with salt, sweetness with tears, till no hint of its might remained. Till it had utterly disappeared.

Tonight her bird came to rest in a bower of gold, fragrant with roses. Flying here brought Leelah into the flowerings of realities she had seeded earlier, poems she had whispered into the island's soil in anticipation of her needs. Attractions, tender traps. On nights when her bird was an owl she hunted timid balls of fur pulsing with blood. Once, a heron, Leelah stalked a pond filled with silver-scaled fish, stabbing her prey with her sharp beak, ripping apart the moon's mirror.

Now, a nightingale, she sang. She felt him near. Would he come closer, be drawn to drown in the sound of her? She trilled and lilted, linked note to note, a chain of delight, climbing higher, higher, calling him to her side.

When she reached the end of her song, with the chain stretched to its full length, her bird sat still alone upon the golden bough where she'd begun it. Perhaps Felix had gone beyond the beacon, past the island, over the world's edge? Straining, she caught a glimpse of him, a whiff, a lingering echo of his laughter ringing faintly out to sea.

She fluttered aloft, unsure. Should she try to join him? His pull gripped her. Rain began falling—pearl drops illuminating the river water, giving its inkiness a sheen by which she could see—what? Movement? Him? There, in the distance, something, someone—She flew on.

The jaws of the river's mouth opened, and she passed out between them. Now there lay only grey emptiness before her, above and below her. Soaring higher she seemed to see, impossibly, a far shore, a smudge of lavender pricked with apricot. Heaven? Japan? But merciless winds came roaring at her, knocked her back and forth, twisting her feathers. She dropped below them, then fell through a thinness more insubstantial than air, reaching with her bird's wings to clutch at nothing there, tumbling tail up, beak down, no control, and was there a bottom? And would she hit it?

Not a dream. No way to wake up.

Without transition she found herself underwater, freezing cold and moving fast with the last of the river's current. She was not lost. Eyes stinging with salt, throat choking, she struggled to break free and breathe, beat with her battered bones against the torrents dragging her out, away from everything familiar. Something hard bumped her, and she scrabbled up its side, lay panting and exhausted on its top. The South Jetty.

An indeterminate time later, she deemed herself dry enough. She spread aching wings and took limply to the air. Without thinking she found Felix's trail, crossed it twice to be sure where it went, but no. Not in that direction. Leelah was never flying out over the ocean again. Not even for him.

Disconsolate, she flapped her way homeward, toward the dawn.

⚊

Friday. She rested in bed all morning and all afternoon. Not since her first experimental flights had she chanced approaching the sea. Was it was worse now, when most would consider her nearer the end of her life?

By evening she felt well enough to attend the read-through with blocking of "Miracle on 34th Street." This was Rutha's pet project, a musical version featuring pseudo-Tin Pan Alley tunes penned by a Portland math teacher. It wasn't as bad as it could have been.

Saturday. Volunteers showed up at one as scheduled to clean the chandelier. Leelah rode the bus in hours early, but this was the weekend. No Felix.

Sunday. She called Aunt Floyd and Cousin Ray. They lived in Saint Louis, so noon for her was two for them: after church but before they hit the Old Country Buffet.

Cousin Ray hung up first; he was younger than Aunt Floyd but had never had her stamina. "All right, Miss Leelah Ferrell," the eighty-year-old said when they were alone on the phone. "You can tell me now. What's goin on in the love department?"

Leelah confessed her crush on Felix Andersen and told her Aunt Floyd a few facts. His age. His job. His race, which was no surprise, given her history. Her aunt let that pass without comment. "So where'd you find him? You meet in person yet, or is this one a them cybernet connections?"

"On the bus."

"That's good. That's real." Aunt Floyd didn't approve of online dating sites. Full of losers, she said. Leelah's last two relationships had started online. And ended IRL. "So you been talkin how long now?"

"A month."

"Shoot girl, you better ask him out. What you waitin for? Only forty more shoppin days till Christmas!"

Ask Felix out? On a date? Leelah felt panic tighten her skin. She couldn't. Like some sort of cougar. "You don't understand."

"And I ain't gotta. He the one need to understand. So tell him."

"But he's gorgeous, he's—"

"You gorgeous too, girl."

Thirty years ago. Maybe.

She hated hoping again. At fifty-five, what was there left to expect? Love had slammed her face repeatedly to the pavement; life's currents had rubbed her hard against the rocks. She did her best to believe something good had come of all that: a polish, a shininess.

For which no man gave half a fuck that she'd ever heard of.

But Aunt Floyd pointed out that if Leelah asked Felix out and he refused her, it was over. No more imagining romantic motives for his politeness. End of nonstory.

So she rode the bus in Monday morning.

⚋⚋

"Nice to see you today." He smiled. Politely.

Leelah spent most of the trip not looking at him. This final time—she should engage, savor one last conversation. He sat opposite her as usual, but facing forward. Though there was that moment she caught him watching her from the corner of one eye. Which could mean anything.

She waited till they disembarked together at the transfer point. Less embarrassing. "So, Felix, would you ever want to talk to me some time when we're not on the bus?"

He gave his briefcase a little swing. "Sure."

What now? "Umm, when?" They settled on Friday, 5:30 p.m. at the Finnish Café. For tea.

Leelah marked time at the theater till she wouldn't look ridiculous if he saw her going home. Restless, she stopped in her apartment only for a minute, dropping off her backpack, then headed to the park.

The Column so reminded her of David. She ran her hand along the base's smooth white concrete, wishing she could touch and stroke the plaster that began curving gently higher just out of reach. The eternal spiral upward; she remembered holding him in her hands, the luxury of skin on skin, the promise of more, forever, ever after.

She climbed carefully, setting her left foot precisely to avoid that pain in her knee. 160 stairs. Maybe David had had the right idea after all, killing himself young. Fewer indignities.

At last she came to the top, walked out onto the windy platform. Mackerel clouds barely masked the lowering sun.

She went to the Column's opposite side. East, where David's grave lay. These days they had drugs to heal people who suffered depression. David hadn't been able to wait till they figured those out. He'd used a gun. But thoughtfully—he'd wrapped a towel around his head first, to minimize the mess.

She'd only been at college a semester. Her parents waited till after final exams to tell her, worried for her grades.

She looked a long time at the river. The sun sank below the clouds, its rays slanting over her left shoulder, gilding the waters.

Leelah had dropped out anyhow. Been married once since, lived with another man three years. Never loved anyone so much again till now.

Why Felix? There was no reason. Love didn't need one.

Tuesday Leelah bought new clothes. Which was stupid. Nothing was going to happen. Talking. Nothing else.

A soft, clinging, tartan-print skirt. And tops: scarlet, mustard yellow, and forest green, matched to the skirt's stripes. She could tell the clerk who waited on her believed they were too small. She didn't care. What wouldn't be, in any store? She paid and took them home.

At dark, she flew again. This night she headed her bird resolutely inland. Felix filled her thoughts, but Leelah resisted their tugging. Tomorrow. She would be with him tomorrow. Best not to become obsessed.

Inland, up the gorge, then over deserts dry and cold, haunted by missing rains. From there via gradually moister air to the valley of her first river, her home. As she passed over the intervening lands faster than the starling she appeared to be, Leelah wondered. Would she find what she was looking for? As she landed in the juniper outside the cemetery, her wondering grew harder, more pointed. Where was David, really? She swooped over the iron fence to land on his headstone. Not here.

With her bird's eyes she sought her way back to when he lived and watched her younger self walk with him to the soft grass behind the stadium. Watched Leelah-then lie down with him, staining the right hip of her jeans and one sharp elbow. Watched him furrow his forehead over the difficult questions she posed. Saw how delicately he sniffed her hair, like a cat. And now he would lift her shirt, and sweep his fingers across her back…. She had seen it all before. Every moment always happened the same. This was the past. The past was over. Done.

Dead.

Which left her with what?

⟞⟝

Genevyve pulled espresso at the Finnish Café. Of course. In a town of ten thousand, bit actors played several roles. Ensemble theater. Leelah ordered a pot of white tea and sat to drink it and await her humiliation with stoic patience, because Felix would fail to show. Then she saw him through the window. Walking toward the door. He opened it and came in.

"Sorry I'm late," he said.

"You're not. Not very."

"No, something came up, and I had to take care of it— administrative, it wasn't even real teaching. I hope you haven't been waiting long." He ordered tea, too, and sat holding his steaming cup in both hands.

They talked for an hour and a half. About books and whales and unicorns, robots and Ray Bradbury. About pie and nail polish. About Holland and the Philippines. About polar bears and PCBs. About caring. About happiness: what it was, where it came from, how to get it.

Seven o'clock came. The Café was closing. Genevyve collected their cups.

"What's next for you?"

She had no idea. "Home?"

"Want a ride?"

He owned a car? "Sure."

As they drove up the hill it finally sank in. He wanted to be with her. He wanted to breathe her breath and have her breathe his. To hear her, see her. He hadn't touched her, yet, except to help her on with her coat. He didn't have to: he touched the air. The air came inside of her. The air entered her blood. His touch with it. It was much, much better than a dream.

He parked a block past her apartment. He walked her to her door.

"Come up," she said. "Please. I have something to show you."

She climbed the stairs with him behind her. She built the nest. Together, they flew west. Into an ocean of stars.

To the Moment

We are not extinct. There are sixteen of us, and I'm pregnant. I only just found out.

I like to travel. Not by plane, because on long flights I get restless, and the changes in air pressure hurt. My cavities ache terribly with every ascent and landing, unless I've managed to fill them just before boarding. This is difficult to do at almost any airport.

So I am on a ship, a big white cruiser headed south through the Atlantic. The sun is bright, but winter thin. I'm wearing a coat of ivory wool and large, hexagonal sunglasses with honey-colored frames. They make me think of bees. The wind does what it wants with my long, dark hair; nothing pretty or symmetrical. I don't care. I've been told I resemble Jackie Onassis since 1971. Monkeys always assume I'm beautiful, no matter how I look.

There's one sitting next to me where I stand on deck. I've been considering him since we started out from Lisbon two days ago. Balding—lots of testosterone. From England—skin that lovely rose-flooded milkiness they get in these Northern latitudes. Wife weak with sea-sickness before we left the harbor.

Now I'm afraid. I'm pregnant, and this monkey alone simply will not do. He reaches up with a long, possessive arm and pulls me down beside him. He doesn't care who sees. He wants them to see. In his mind I belong to him. I doubt that, even using great discretion, I will be able to supplement what I can get from him. Which will not be enough.

He leans over to nuzzle my ear, masking the sound of the wind and the waves with his noisy breath and blood. Canvas snaps, flapping loose from the frame of a nearby chair. The gulls come and make their cries, high, wheedling, fearful. Strollers on the deck below have brought table scraps to feed them. Little beggars. They snatch what is offered from the air: a crust of someone's sandwich, a crisp, a bit of pink tomato. They feed flying in the light, which reveals the beautiful separateness of all things. While I must go below.

I take him to my cabin. He has his own, since his wife, even on dry land, is a semi-invalid, and they can well afford it. But the two adjoin, so I take him to mine, because there might be noise. I even say that's why I want to go there, and he smiles. He's so sure it will be me.

We take off our clothes in the dark, stuffy room. I could have a better one, if I wanted. But this cabin, so low down, is more isolated. Insulated by emptiness on either side.

I have removed my glasses. My eyes are adjusted now, and I can see how self-conscious he is without his clothes. He bumps against the bed and sits down, then fumbles for the light switch. I kneel on the floor in front of him and make him stop. It's easy. I let my tongues relax and wrap around his penis, which is a good size, not too big. Things are going well, considering. I'm sure I'll be able to restrain myself and use only my mouth. I won't get as much at a time, but the monkey will last longer.

Then, amazingly, he resists. He pushes me away by my shoulders, slides his hands into my armpits and lifts. He's trying to get me to sit on him, he mumbles how he's always wanted to do it this way. The soft hairs covering his legs brush the backs of my thighs, my calves, as I obediently slide my knees up beside his hips. He rolls his penis against my pubic bone in a practiced move, which might excite me if I had a clitoris there. He makes me taste his antiseptic, minty lips, the breath between them laden with the odors of coffee, sugar, flour, eggs. Breakfast. Then he pushes me up again, grappling me into position. He is strong, but I could fight him. I don't want to. I want this, now, this way. I need it. I take it.

He does scream. I do too, and shout Oh God, I'm coming, I'm coming, so if anyone hears us they'll stay away. It lasts a little long for an orgasm, but after a couple of minutes he stops thrashing on the bed and lies still, deflating. I pump and pump. The rosy goodness suffuses me, warming my womb. When I'm done I fall into a dream, sliding slowly off the monkey and curling up next to him on the soiled sheets.

———

D. is with me and we're on a mountain in Costa Rica, in the seven-sided house he had them build. He tries to tell my why it's better, how the design dissipates the energy of earthquakes, which are common, but I am looking at the green, a green so very green I think my eyes will turn to emeralds before the sun has set. Behind a distant peak it goes, but the green does not go with it. Instead the valleys brim with green darkness, leaf-filled shadows expanding and thickening, clotting up the night with a truer, deeper green.

I realize my companion has been silent for some time. "D.," I say, "it's good to be here, really *here*. Do you know what I mean?" He nods and touches the back of my neck. His sensitivity to the moment must be, in large part, responsible for the lengthiness of his life. Nine hundred years without even a half-hearted attempt at suicide. That's good, for a male.

Just as though it hadn't happened hundreds of times before, I find myself kissing him. Our tongues separate, then twine, like lashing vines.

No force is applied on either side, but slowly we grow closer, closer. I am penetrated by the breeze coming through the open window, sharp as citrus, by the fine, probing mouths of flying insects, frustrated in their search for food. By D.'s mouth, too, delicately drawn along my skin, in an empty, reflexive action. Or I assume its emptiness, in the moment and as I return to it, dreaming.

Knowing this is wrong disturbs my sleep.

I wake. The monkey's corpse reeks of feces and the barest beginnings of decay. No blood—that's all mine now, mine and my offspring's.

D.'s offspring, too. Precocious D., sexually mature a good century before it might have been expected. When my jelly didn't come, I should have known. But it's so unusual. Not until I noticed other signs did I fathom the truth of my condition. Anxiously I examine myself once again, to be sure. Nipples dark and hardening. Waist thickening. Sudden cravings. Vaginal dentata pronounced and multiplying—the normally flat triangular flaps are distended with hunger, even so soon after my recent, reckless meal. Reassured, I try to come to some conclusion as to how to dispose of the remains.

I'm no longer used to having to plan things. Although I concentrate, my head is filled with aimless, rootless thoughts. Perfume ads. Nursery rhymes. *Three, six, nine, the goose drank wine. The monkey chewed tobacco on the street car line.* I remember watching one of them, a small one, a female, jumping rope. The glass of shattered bottles glittered in the sun and she sang fiercely, breathlessly as she leapt and fell, leapt and fell. *The line broke, the monkey got choked.* This is really very bad. *And they all went to heaven in a little row-boat.*

The sad thing is, I have no choice in the matter. Even if I manage to escape suspicion, the next stop is an island. Madeira. Entirely as problematic as a cruise ship. So I spend an hour being charming, a few minutes being devious, and everything works out all right.

It's not that I don't care about the monkeys. I'm genuinely sorry that they have to die, especially when it's such a waste. I manage to salvage a handful of the crew, the ones in my lifeboat. Not the boilermaster, nor his mate, so no one knows I have any idea about the cause of the explosion. Even in memory it's tremendous, the most profound sound; much more ringing and metallic than any volcano.

A stiff breeze keeps most of the smoke to our south. Rainbows of oil and bobbing detritus surround us, carried here on contrary currents. Each is unique: each pattern, each odd, useless object. Removed from context, these fragments of enameled metal, plastic, and wood, charred and reshaped by the forces I have unleashed, are new and sweetly wonderful.

I wish I could show D. I know how deeply he understands these sorts of things. It is this that makes me sure he will live long, unlike so many others I have loved. As the coast of Africa comes into view, shorebirds soaring over white-capped waves, I am buoyed by confidence. He will live many, many more years. Centuries. Long enough to witness the birth of each and every child I am carrying within my womb.

Just Between Us

Dolores opened the closet door. Here was the problem. A dead woman hung by her neck, suspended from the cross bar by a man's tie. Violet in color, probably silk from the look of the knot. She shut the door quickly and called up her landlady.

Mrs. Pawkes was dressed for golf. Her clothing glowed a golden green in Dolores' vision. Her sharp-chinned, line-seamed face managed to project warm but distracted concern as she assured Dolores that the dead women were nothing to worry about.

"Women? You mean this isn't the only one?"

"Well, I've had to take care of one a week now for—seems like maybe the last couple of months. But it's just like the refugees, isn't it?"

"No, Mrs. Pawkes, it is not." The last time she came in, Dolores had opened the closet door to find a huddled group of thin, brown, anxious people, clutching fearfully at blankets, newspapers, cooking pots. The detritus of displacement. "Corpses smell. Worse," she amended. "And I had to come back before I wanted to. I think they scared Little Girl. She's gone out."

"Oh, I'm so sorry. The poor thing." The image of Mrs. Pawkes switched from head-and-shoulders to full length as she removed her bag of clubs and leaned it against something—a wall or a doorway, it wasn't quite clear. "I wish I'd known. She didn't say anything…"

"Well, what did you expect?" Little Girl was barely verbal. She knew Mrs. Pawkes existed, but there was very little contact between the two.

"I just didn't have anywhere else to put them, Dolores. They keep—popping up. I wish I could tell you where from."

"I'll look into it. Meanwhile, what am I supposed to do about Little Girl?"

"Send someone after her, I guess…unless you'd rather go yourself?"

"You know there isn't room enough for both of us out there."

"Well, I'm sure you'll think of something, dear. You're so resourceful." Mrs. Pawkes glanced longingly over her shoulder at her golf clubs. The vision began to fade. Dolores could have held it together, but what would be the point? As usual, everything was up to her.

She opened her eyes, which she had squeezed shut during the conversation, massaging the wrinkles where her eyebrows furrowed together. She looked around the place. Not bad, except for the smell. She was in the upper story of a white-painted frame house. Old. Interesting. Lots of windows with tiny panes shaped like diamonds, crescents, tears. Hardwood floors, oriental rugs. Little Girl had left her playthings strewn around the apartment: a rocking horse, cardboard boxes painted to look like bricks. A pink tutu and a cone-shaped hat, white-spangled chiffon streaming from its peak. On the enamel-topped kitchen table a bubble pipe and a tub full of sudsy water waited next to a bowl of soggy cereal.

How could Mrs. Pawkes have been so insensitive? This was supposed to be a safe place. Not a morgue. And Little Girl wasn't really equipped to handle most of what went on outside. How to get her back?

She sat down to think on a love-seat that hadn't been there when she came in. It was hers. She recognized the blue wool upholstery from her last time in. The longer she stayed, the more the place would bear her mark.

Send someone after her. Sure, but who? Dolores and Little Girl were the main tenants, the oldest and biggest ones. There were others, though. Neighbors. Guests. Dolores struggled to classify those she knew.

Patcheddy. She was like Little Girl, only thin and weak and poor. That big, red, roaring—Dolores had never given that a name. Call it Red. Red was too scary to help with this. And Patcheddy wasn't much good for anything, except to whine. It had to be someone small enough so they could both fit outside, but strong enough to bring Little Girl back in.

There was a tapping at one of the windows. A big black bird with blue and white wings was pecking at the glass. Dolores got up to let it in, then hesitated with the window open only a crack. "Who is it?"

It was Hermie.

"Oh, yes." Little Girl's imaginary playmate. She swung the casement wide and he flew in. Hermie had come to Little Girl along with the mumps and an interminable stay in bed. Usually, though, he looked more like light reflecting from a glass of water—or nothing at all. "What brings you here? And why so—so—"

So visible. The bird cocked his head knowingly. He was practicing. He wanted to go outside, to find Little Girl, and he needed to practice pretending to be real.

"Perfect!" she exclaimed. She sat back down on the love seat, and Hermie hopped onto the far arm. "Thank you, thank you, thank you."

Actually, the going out part would be easy. For him. Finding her, too. But he would need help bringing her back.

"But I'm too big to get outside while she's still there."

But she could help inside. She had to. She had to get rid of the dead women. She had to stop them coming. Otherwise he could find Little Girl, but what good would that do? She'd never come back in.

"Okay, Hermie. Okay. I'll see what I can do." He flew back to the windows. They were French, now, with crystal doorknobs. He flapped back and forth noisily while she walked over, turned a knob and pushed. There was a balcony on the other side, weeping black wrought iron. Hermie flew out over it and became one with the powder blue mist beyond.

※

Am I all right they keep asking, asking. I always tell them no. My favorite word. It's the best. Nonononono. I use it all the time.

I'm hungry. I want a candy bar, or an icecream. I ask the waiter for one I remember that is orange. A Dreamsicle is the name. But when it comes it is all melted in a glass. No stick. And it tastes like medicine. Nasty. I drink it anyway.

I try again. A Heathbar, too, is all melted. Everything in this place is nasty and served in a cup. I'm going to leave. It's closing anyway. They want to know if I need them to call me a cab. I use my word and go.

It's pretty out in the dark. There aren't too many things to see. The wind kisses me with long, dry kisses, brushing down my cheeks. I think the wind is like a pretty young lady aunt. She runs around doing interesting things, so she doesn't have to tell you how big you're getting. And she kisses you, but then she moves away, not holds you tight so you can't go and it's scary and your word won't even work.

There is a park, but I'm not supposed to go in there. Bad men are waiting to hurt a Little Girl. But if they saw me they would think I was big, like Dolores is. Only still they might want to hurt me. Anyways, I don't have to want to go there, because out of the park flies a bird I like. Dark and dry and friendly, the way the wind is in this night. I hold out my finger and he grabs it with his feet. It hurts, but not too much, and also it feels good. The bird's feet are strong. It is holding on to me and I am holding it up.

Come on, says the bird. Let's go.

Dolores cut the woman down. She stunk like old rotten stew. Her face was blotched and flaccid. She collapsed in an ugly heap on the closet floor.

Dolores thought that was strange. Shouldn't you be stiff if you were dead long enough to smell? But it made the woman a lot easier to handle. All she had to figure out now was what to do with her.

She took her into the bathroom. While hot water ran into the big white tub she removed the woman's clothing. It was basically nondescript: grey sweater, beige and grey and cream plaid skirt. Underwear from Penney's, with comfortable, band-sewn legs. Little balls of rolled up lint on the bra. Support pantyhose. Loafers.

Everything from the waist down was soiled. What wasn't smelled like spoiled meat from long, close contact with the corpse. She sat the body on the edge of the tub and guided it gently into the water. It slid so the head was under. She didn't see how that could matter.

While the corpse was soaking she rinsed out the skirt and things in the toilet bowl, thinking how she was going to do this seven more times, if she could find the rest. It was worse than having kids. With them you could use disposables.

She rinsed the dirty clothes out again in the sink, then had to go down to the laundry room to get a basket. She didn't like the basement. It never seemed very clean. Too many things were the same there as outside.

The furnace had long twisting ducts coming out of it, like fat metallic tentacles. Over in the far corner there was a freezer. Nobody used it anymore, not since her mother disappeared. It was chained shut and locked.

When she came back upstairs the body was gone. The water in the tub was clean. She pulled out the stopper by its chain, took the clothes down and loaded them in the machine. Delicate fabrics, short cycle. She left the machine whirring and sloshing away, went to the kitchen and made herself a cup of tea. Then she called up Mrs. Pawkes again, to see if she had any possible clue as to what the hell was going on.

"Well, dear," said Mrs. Pawkes, "I really don't know where I put them all." She raised a be-ringed finger in protest of Dolores' anger. "In my defense—don't frown, you'll make lines, you don't want to end up looking like me, do you?—In my defense, I have to say it's mostly because you two *change* the place around so *much*. I mean, I'm sure I could find them, but they're probably not where I put them because where I put them is undoubtedly *gone*, you see…. She waited for Dolores to do or say something to show she understood. Dolores nodded tiredly.

"And as far as where they're coming from, Dolores, I really couldn't say."

"You don't have even the slightest idea?"

"Well, it's not the sort of thing…" She trailed off again. "It's a delicate subject, I'm afraid. I don't think your father would approve." Dolores thought maybe she should just give up. There were subjects Mrs. Pawkes refused to talk about at all. Sex. Bodily functions. Violence of any sort. That fight two months back, right before her mother had run off—Mrs. Pawkes referred to it as, "That discussion between your parents." Sometimes Dolores wondered how she ever wound up being their landlady.

"Thanks," she said, hoping she didn't sound too sarcastic. "I'll let you know how it all works out."

❧

His name is Hermie. I know him. I like him, but I don't want to go back. I say no.

He says o.k., but it's going to get cold later. Maybe we can find a donut shop. We do. It has a roof like an orange skirt swirling out dancing. The walls are all glass. I wonder if they'll let me in carrying a crow.

Magpie, says Hermie. I am a magpie, not a crow. Anyway, they probably won't even see me.

Why? I ask. I open the door. Hermie is on my shoulder now.

Because I'm a figment of your imagination.

Oh, I say. I thought you were a magpie. It's a joke. I know you can be more than one thing at a time.

Quiet, says Hermie. You don't want them to think you're crazy, do you?

There were dead women all over, once she started looking. Stuffed under the kitchen sink. In the laundry hamper. The pantry. One was wedged into the little space between the fridge and the wall. One was in the spare room, neatly tucked in bed. She had to wash the sheets and mattress pad as well when she did that one's clothes.

They all dissolved in the tub. Their clothes stayed. She had a whole wardrobe of shapeless, baggy, colorless garments on hangers in the laundry room. No two outfits were identical, but they might as well have been. Mix-and-match.

All except the things this one wore. The one she held in her hands. This corpse was only eight or nine inches tall. It still smelled awful. She had found it in the sugar bin.

Washing them got rid of the dead women, but it didn't bring her any closer to the problem's cause. This one was obviously special. Maybe if she did something different this time she could revive it enough to ask it some questions. She thought.

The cookie sheets were in a tall, narrow cupboard made just for them. She rinsed off the heaviest, the best one, while waiting for the oven to preheat. Stuck it in for a moment to dry. Took it out and coated it with butter, deciding against a dusting of flour on top of that.

She removed the doll-like clothes and sponged off the small, naked corpse, nervously expecting it to dissolve and disappear. It didn't. She laid the body on the cookie sheet and brushed it with lemon juice. What else? She got some raisins, put two over the dead woman's eyes, one between her slack lips. Was that it? Almost. With a paring knife she cut another raisin in two, then stuck the resulting halves over the nipples. That looked right. The oven was ready. She slid the woman in, set the timer, and put everything away.

❧

I get two fried cakes and a jelly donut. And hot chocolate. It's really good. I hand up crumbs to Hermie where he's still sitting on my shoulder. I giggle and wonder if everybody else just sees pieces of donut disappear into the air. Or maybe they are floating inside Hermie's invisible, imaginary crow-belly.

Magpie, he says, and I laugh out loud.

Am I all right? No.

❧

Nothin says lovin like somethin from the oven. Dolores didn't really need the timer to know when the dead woman was done. The aroma said it all. She smelled kind of good, actually. Kind of—juicy. Delicious, really. Like baked apples. The odor spoke to her invitingly as she pulled out the cookie sheet. She spatulaed up the corpse and transferred it to a cooling rack. Now she'd get some answers.

The dead woman, however, was obstinately silent.

All right, thought Dolores. She reached out and broke off an arm. It tasted sweet and gingery. She closed her eyes to analyze the flavor. Sugar and spice and everything nice. She opened them and saw that the pan was empty.

The dead woman must have shinnied down a table leg. She was running across the kitchen floor, headed for the basement steps.

"Oh, no," said Dolores. "Don't go down there." She hurried but she was too late. The little woman fell headlong down the stairs and broke into pieces at the bottom.

Dolores walked down to her carefully, holding on to the rail. Why was she so sad? The other corpses were gone, too, but she'd never cared one way or another about them. She started crying. She picked up the pieces, brushed off some bits of lint. She took a bite of one big fragment; she thought maybe it was the head. In the far corner the padlocked freezer clicked and hummed to life. Then she remembered.

Two policemen come in. I don't know if I like that. But they just sit down at the other counter, which is this really ugly color like moldy bread. That's why me and Hermie picked the pretty bright orange one on this side.

The man brings them coffee and long, twisty rolls before they even ask for anything. Then he comes back to me again. And I tell him no. No and no and no and no and no. I keep saying no, even after he walks away. Maybe he will get it.

He goes and bothers the police instead. They are talking real quiet, and I can't hear the words, but Hermie says uh-oh. I shut up.

One of the police gets off his stool and comes over to me. He calls me ma'am. Do I need help?

I think I better go. It's time to be inside.

Dolores came out. Dolores answered. She said yes. She could use some help. Dolores said there was a problem at her house. She said the policemen should come with her and see. It had to do with the way her mother disappeared a couple of months ago, and how her father had acted ever since. She gave them her name and address, and said she'd be glad to accept their offer of a lift. Yes, it was kind of dangerous being out alone this late.

She wanted to know if they had anything in the squad car that would be good at breaking chains or busting a lock. If not, maybe they ought to stop by the station on the way. She assured them that would be okay. What she wanted to show them was in the freezer. It wasn't going anywhere. It would be all right.

✎

I'm glad Hermie brought me back inside. The policemen were scaring me, and it's good to be home again. He says there won't be any more ghosts to come, either. Dolores made it better.

Dolores is nice. But she always puts away all my toys, and then I have a hard time finding them again. What's left now is my goldfish. I sit down and watch them swimming around and around and around. I wonder if they think they're going anywhere, or if they know what they are in.

About the Author

Nisi Shawl is best known for fiction dealing with gender, race, and colonialism, including the 2016 Nebula finalist novel *Everfair*, an alternate history of the Congo. They're also the coauthor of the Aqueduct Press Conversation Piece *Writing the Other: A Practical Approach* and a cofounder of the Carl Brandon Society, a nonprofit organization dedicated to improving the presence of people of color in the fantastic genres. They have served on Clarion West's board of directors for two decades.

Filter House, Shawl's first Aqueduct Press story collection, co-won the 2008 Otherwise/James Tiptree, Jr. Award. They edited the World Fantasy, Locus, and Ignyte award-winning anthology *New Suns: Speculative Fiction by People of Color*, published in 2019; a sequel, *New Suns 2*, is forthcoming in 2023. Additional awards include the Kate Wilhelm Solstice Award and the British Fantasy Award. Shawl co-edited *Strange Matings: Science Fiction, Feminism, African American Voices, and Octavia E. Butler* with Dr. Rebecca Holden. A Middle Grade historical fantasy novel, *Speculation*, is forthcoming in January 2023 from Lee & Low. Shawl lives in Seattle, one block away from a beautiful, dangerous lake full of currents and millionaires.

Books Written or Edited by Nisi Shawl

Writing the Other: A Practical Approach (co-author Cynthia Ward), Aqueduct Press, December 2005

Filter House, Aqueduct Press, June, 2008

Something More and More, Aqueduct Press, May 2011

The WisCon Chronicles 5: Writing and Racial Identity (editor), May 2011, Aqueduct Press

Strange Matings: Science Fiction, Feminism, African American Voices, and Octavia E. Butler (co-editor with Rebecca J. Holden), Aqueduct Press, May 2013.

Bloodchildren, (editor) Carl Brandon Society, 2013

Stories for Chip: A Tribute to Samuel R. Delany (co-editor with Bill Campbell), Rosarium, 2015

Everfair, Tor Books, September 2017.

People of Color Take Over Fantastic Stories of the Imagination, (editor) Positronic, 2017

Exploring Dark Short Fiction: A Primer to Nisi Shawl, Dark Moon, 2018

New Suns: Original Speculative Fiction by People of Color (editor), Solaris, March 2019

Talk Like a Man, PM Press, November 2019

Black Stars (co-editor with Latoya Peterson and Diana Pho), Amazon Originals, 2021

Speculation, Lee & Low, forthcoming in January 2023